Also by Sharon Kendrick

A Royal Vow of Convenience
Secrets of a Billionaire's Mistress
The Sheikh's Bought Wife
The Pregnant Kavakos Bride
The Italian's Christmas Secret
Bound to the Sicilian's Bed
Crowned for the Sheikh's Baby

Also by Chantelle Shaw

Trapped by Vialli's Vows
Acquired by Her Greek Boss
Hired for Romano's Pleasure

The Saunderson Legacy miniseries

The Secret He Must Claim
The Throne He Must Take

Discover more at millsandboon.co.uk.

Sharon Kendrick once won a story-writing competition by describing her ideal date: being flown to an exotic island by a gorgeous and powerful man. Little did she realise that she'd just wandered into her dream job! Today she writes for Mills & Boon, featuring often stubborn but always *to die for* heroes and the women who bring them to their knees. She believes that the best books are those you never want to end. Just like life…

Chantelle Shaw lives on the Kent coast and thinks up her stories while walking on the beach. She has been married for over thirty years and has six children. Her love affair with reading and writing Mills & Boon stories began as a teenager, and her first book was published in 2006. She likes strong-willed, slightly unusual characters. Chantelle also loves gardening, walking and wine!

THE GREEK'S BOUGHT BRIDE

SHARON KENDRICK

WED FOR HIS SECRET HEIR

CHANTELLE SHAW

MILLS & BOON

First Published in Great Britain 2018
by Mills & Boon, an imprint of HarperCollins*Publishers*
1 London Bridge Street, London, SE1 9GF

The Greek's Bought Bride © 2018 by Sharon Kendrick

Wed for His Secret Heir © 2018 by Chantelle Shaw

ISBN: 978-0-263-93542-4

MIX
Paper from
responsible sources
FSC™ C007454

Printed and bound in Spain
by CPI, Barcelona

THE GREEK'S BOUGHT BRIDE

SHARON KENDRICK

This book is dedicated to the greatly loved
Sara Craven (Annie Ashurst),
whose talent, humour and sharp wit are much missed.
And if you want a masterclass in writing romance,
read *Comparative Strangers* (and prepare to tingle…).

CHAPTER ONE

HE RECOGNISED HER straight away, though it took him a
moment to remember why. Xan Constantinides gazed
at the tiny redhead whose thick curls were tumbling
over her shoulders and a flicker of something between
desire and anger whispered across his skin. But he welcomed the distraction—however temporary—which
allowed him to forget the promise he had made so long
ago. Was it the wedding of one of his oldest friends
which had pushed the unavoidable into prominence,
or just the march of time itself? Because it was easy to
believe that nothing would change. You acted as if the
fast days weren't spinning into years. And then suddenly there it was—the future—and with it all those
expectations...

A marriage he had agreed to.

A destiny he had always been determined to honour.

But there was no point in thinking about it now, not
with a packed weekend lying ahead of him. Friendship and a valuable business partnership dictated he
must attend the wedding of his friend the Sheikh, even
though he usually avoided such events like the plague.

Xan returned his attention to the redhead. She was
sitting on her own in the small terminal of the private

airfield, waiting to board the luxury flight, the fiery disarray of her hair marking her out from the other women. Her clothes marked her out too and not simply because they were a far cry from the skimpy little cocktail dress she'd been wearing last time he'd seen her—an outfit which had sent his imagination soaring into overdrive, as it had obviously been intended to do.

Xan slanted her an assessing glance. Today there was no tight black satin Basque or skyscraper heels, nor fishnet stockings which had encased the most delicious pair of legs he had ever seen. No. She had taken the word *casual* and elevated it to a whole new level. Along with a pair of tennis shoes, she was wearing cut-off jeans which displayed her pale, freckled ankles and a plain green T-shirt which echoed the cat-like magnificence of her emerald eyes.

It was the eyes he remembered most. And the slender figure which had failed to fill out the curved dimensions of her skimpy uniform, unlike her over-endowed waitress colleagues who had been bursting out of theirs. And the way she had spilt the Old-Fashioned cocktail all over the table as she bent to serve him. The dripping concoction had caught his trouser leg—icy liquid spreading slowly over his thigh. He remembered flinching and the woman he'd been with snatching up her napkin to blot at it with attentive concern, even though he'd been in the middle of telling her that their relationship was over.

Xan's lips flattened. The redheaded waitress had straightened up and mouthed an apology but the defiant glint in her green eyes had suggested the sentiment wasn't genuine. For a moment he had found himself wondering if it had been a gesture of deliberate clumsiness on her part—but surely nobody would be that stupid?

Would they?

And now here she was in the most unexpected of places—waiting to board a luxury flight to the wedding of Sheikh Kulal Al Diya to the unknown Englishwoman, Hannah Wilson. Idly, Xan switched his cellphone to airplane mode as the redhead began to scrabble around inside an oversized bag which looked as if it had seen better days. Was she also a guest at the glittering royal marriage? His lips curved with something like contempt. Hardly. She was much more likely to have been hired to work at what was being described as the most glitzy wedding the desert region had seen for a decade. And in a country which demanded the most modest of dress codes, it was unlikely that she would be showing as much of her body as last time.

Pity.

Sliding the phone into his pocket, he allowed himself the faintest smile as she glanced up to notice him staring at her and a spark of something powerful passed between them. A full-blooded spark of sexual desire which fizzled almost tangibly in the air. Her magnificent eyes widened with disbelief. He saw the automatic thrust of her nipples against the thin T-shirt and his groin tightened in response.

Sometimes, Xan thought, with a frisson of anticipation, sometimes fate handed you something you hadn't even realised you wanted.

It was him.

It was definitely him.

What were the *chances*?

Somehow Tamsyn managed to stop her jaw from dropping—but only just. She'd been expecting the great and the good to be gathered together here at this small airport, ready to board the royal flight which would whisk them to Zahristan, but she hadn't really been paying attention to the other guests as they were all being guided into the small departure lounge. She'd only just got her head around the incredible fact that her sister Hannah was about to marry a desert king and would soon become a real-life queen. And even though Hannah was pregnant with the Sheikh's baby and such an unlikely union made sense on so many levels, Tamsyn hadn't quite managed to contain her disgust at the proposed nuptials. Because in her opinion, the man her sister was marrying was arrogant and domineering—and it seemed he chose his friends on the same basis.

She stole another sneaky look at the Greek billionaire who was lolling against a sofa on the other side of the small terminal, his exquisitely cut suit doing nothing to disguise the magnificence of his muscular body. Xan Constantinides. An unforgettable name for an unforgettable man. But would he remember her?

Tamsyn offered up a silent prayer. *Please don't let him remember her.*

After all, it was months and months ago and only the briefest of encounters. She bit the inside of her lip. Oh, *why* had she decided to send out a message of sisterly solitude to the woman the tycoon had been in the process of dumping in the swish bar where she'd been working? At least until her employment had come to a swift but wholly predictable termination...

She'd noticed Xan Constantinides from the moment

he'd walked into the twinkly cocktail bar. To be fair, everyone had noticed him—he was that kind of man. Charismatic and radiating power, he seemed oblivious to the stir of interest his appearance had created. Ellie, one of the other waitresses and Tamsyn's best friend, had confided that he was a mega-rich property tycoon who had recently been voted Greece's most eligible bachelor.

But Tamsyn hadn't really been listening to the breathless account of his bank balance or his record of bedding beautiful women before callously disposing of them. His physical presence made his wealth seem almost insignificant and she surprised herself by staring at him for longer than was strictly professional, because she wasn't usually the sort of cocktail waitress who ogled the better-looking male customers. And there had never been a customer quite as good looking as *this* one. She remembered blinking as she registered a physique which suggested he could easily go several rounds in the boxing ring and emerge looking as if he'd done nothing more strenuous than get out of bed. When you teamed a body like that with sinfully dark hair, dark-fringed eyes the colour of cobalt and a pair of lips which were both sensual and cruel—you ended up with a man who exuded a particular type of danger. And Tamsyn had always been very sensitive to danger. It was a quality which had hovered in the background during her troubled childhood like an invisible cosh—just waiting to bang you over the head if you weren't careful. Which was why she avoided it like the plague.

She remembered feeling slightly wobbly on her high-heeled shoes as she'd walked over to where the

Greek tycoon had been sitting with the most beautiful blonde Tamsyn had ever seen, when she heard the woman give an unmistakable sniff.

'*Please*, Xan,' she was saying softly, her voice trembling. 'Don't do this. You must know how much I love you.'

'But I don't *do* love. I told you that right from the start,' he'd drawled unequivocally. 'I explained what my terms were. I said I wouldn't change my mind and I haven't. Why do women refuse to accept what is staring them in the face?'

Tamsyn found the interchange infuriating. *Terms*? He was talking as if he was discussing some kind of business deal, rather than a relationship—as if his lovely companion was an object rather than a person. All she could think was that a woman didn't just come out and tell a man they loved them, not without a certain degree of encouragement. Her irritation had intensified while she'd waited for the barman to mix two Old-fashioned cocktails and when she'd returned she had noticed Xan Constantinides watching her. She wasn't sure which had annoyed her more—the fact that he was regarding her with the lazy assessment of someone who'd just been shown a shiny car and was deciding whether or not he'd like to give it a spin—or the fact that her body had responded to that arrogant scrutiny in ways which she didn't like.

She remembered the peculiar melting sensation low in her belly and the distracting tingle of her breasts pushing against the too-skimpy top of her uniform. She remembered being acutely aware of those cobalt eyes being trained on her, uncaring of the woman beside him who was trying very hard not to cry. And

Tamsyn had felt a kick of anger. Men. They were all the same. They took and they took and they never gave back—not unless they were forced into a corner. Even then they usually found some way of getting out of it. No wonder she deliberately kept them at arm's length. With an encouraging smile she'd handed the woman her drink, but as she lifted the Greek's cocktail from the tray, Tamsyn had met a gaze full of sensual mockery.

She told herself afterwards that she hadn't deliberately angled the glass so that it sloshed all over the table and started to seep onto one taut thigh, but she couldn't deny her satisfaction when he recoiled slightly, before the blonde leapt into action with her napkin.

She was sacked soon afterwards. The bar manager told her it was a culmination of things, and spilling a drink over one of their most valued customers had been the final straw. Apparently she wasn't suited to work which required a level of sustained calm, and she reacted in a way which was inappropriate. Secretly she'd wondered whether Xan Constantinides had got her fired. Whether he was yet another powerful man throwing his weight around and getting the world to jump when he ordered it to. Just like she wondered if he would remember her now.

Please don't let him remember her now.

'Would all passengers please begin boarding? The royal aircraft will be departing for Zahristan in approximately thirty minutes.'

Obeying the honeyed instruction sounding over the Tannoy, Tamsyn bent to pick up her rucksack as she rose to her feet. Didn't matter if he remembered her because he was nothing to her. She was on this trip for one reason and that was to support Hannah on her wedding day, no matter how big her misgivings about her choice of groom. Because, despite having tried to persuade her big sister not to go through with such a fundamentally unsuitable marriage—her words had fallen on deaf ears. Either Hannah hadn't wanted to listen, or she hadn't dared—probably because she was carrying the desert King's baby and there was all that stuff about him needing a legitimate heir. Tamsyn sighed as she rose to her feet. She had done everything she could to influence her sister but now she must accept the inevitable. She would pick up the pieces if necessary and be there for her—just as Hannah had always been there for her.

Hooking her bag over her shoulder, she trooped behind the other passengers—many of whom seemed to know each other—thinking this was like no journey she'd ever been on, with none of that pre-flight tension which usually made everyone so uptight. But then she'd always flown budget before—with that feeling of being herded onto the aircraft like wildebeest on the Serengeti, followed by a futile attempt to claim a few inches of space in the overhead locker. Not so on this flight. The glossy attendants looked like models and were unfailingly polite to all the passengers, as they gestured them forward.

And suddenly Tamsyn heard the sound of a deeply accented voice behind her. Rich and resonant, it sounded like grit being stirred into a bowlful of molasses. She felt her throat dry. She'd heard it once when it had cursed aloud in Greek before asking her what the hell she was playing at. It had made her spine tingle then and it was making it tingle now as the powerful Greek tycoon moved to stand beside her.

Tamsyn stared up into a pair of cold blue eyes and wished her heart would stop crashing against her ribcage. Just like she wished her nipples would cease from hardening so conspicuously against her cheap T-shirt. But her senses were refusing to obey her as Xan Constantinides dominated her field of vision, his presence imprinting itself on her consciousness in a way she could have done without.

She noticed how softly his olive skin gleamed beneath the pristine cuffs of his snowy shirt. And that he carried with him a faint scent of sandalwood, underpinned with the much more potent scent of raw masculinity. Somehow he seemed to suck in all the available oxygen around them, leaving her feeling distinctly short of breath. He was the epitome of vibrancy and life, and yet there was a darkness about him too. Something unsettling and strangely *perceptive* in the depths of those amazing cobalt eyes. Suddenly Tamsyn felt vulnerable as she looked up at him and that scared her. Because she didn't do vulnerability. Just like she didn't react to men—especially men like this. It was her trademark. Her USP. Beneath her fiery exterior beat a heart of pure ice, and that was the way she intended to stay.

She told herself not to panic. People were slowly filing forward and in a few minutes she'd be safely on the plane and hopefully sitting as far away from him as possible. If it had been a commercial flight she would have been perfectly entitled to ignore him, but this was not a commercial flight. They were all guests at the same exclusive royal wedding and even

Tamsyn's shaky grasp on protocol warned her that she mustn't be rude.

But she could certainly be cool. She didn't have to gush or be super-friendly. She didn't owe him anything. She was no longer in the subservient role of waitress and could say exactly what she wanted.

'Well, well, well,' he murmured, his English faultless as he pulled his passport from the inside pocket of his suit jacket. 'Fancy seeing you here.'

Tamsyn fixed her face into a mildly questioning expression. 'I'm sorry? Have we met?'

Cobalt eyes narrowed. 'Well, unless you have a doppelganger,' he drawled. 'You're the waitress who hurled a drink into my lap last summer. Surely you can't have forgotten?'

For a moment Tamsyn was tempted to tell him that yes, she had forgotten. She thought about pretending she'd never seen him before, but suspected he would see through her. Because nobody would ever forget crossing paths with a man like Xan Constantinides, would they? Not unless they were devoid of all their senses. She gave him a steady look. 'No,' she said. 'I haven't forgotten.'

His eyes narrowed. 'I was thinking about it afterwards and wondering if you made a habit of throwing drinks all over your customers.'

She shook her head. 'Actually, no. It's never happened before.'

'Just with me?'

'Just with you,' she agreed.

There was a pause. 'So was it deliberate?'

She considered his silky question and answered it as honestly as she could. 'I don't think so.'

'You don't *think* so?' he exploded. 'What kind of an answer is that?'

She heard his incredulity and as Tamsyn met his piercing gaze she suddenly wanted him to know. Because maybe nobody had ever told him before. Maybe nobody had ever pointed out that the opposite sex were not something you could just dispose of, as if you were throwing an unwanted item of clothing into the recycling bin. 'I'm not going to deny that I felt sorry for the woman you were dumping.'

He frowned, as if he couldn't work out which particular woman she was talking about. As if he were running over a whole host of candidates who might have fitted the bill. And then his face cleared. 'Ah, *neh*,' he murmured in his native tongue, before the frown reappeared. 'What do you mean, you felt sorry for her?'

Tamsyn shrugged. 'She was clearly very upset. Anyone could see that. I thought you could have done it in a kinder way. Somewhere more private, perhaps.'

He gave a short and disbelievingly laugh. 'You're saying you made a negative judgement of me based on a few overheard words of conversation?'

'I know what I saw,' said Tamsyn doggedly. 'She seemed very upset.'

'She was.' His eyes narrowed. 'Our relationship was over but she refused to believe it, and this time she needed to believe it. We hadn't seen each other for weeks when she asked to meet me for a drink and I agreed. And I left her in no doubt that I couldn't give her what she wanted.'

Slowly Tamsyn digested all this, her curiosity aroused in spite of herself. 'What was it she wanted that you were unable to give her?'

He smiled at her then—a brief, glittering smile which momentarily made one of the female ground staff turn and look at him in dazed adoration.

'Why marriage, of course,' he said softly. 'I'm afraid it's an inevitable side-effect of dating women—they always seem to want to push things on to the next level.'

It was several seconds before Tamsyn could bring herself to answer. 'Wow,' she breathed. 'That is the most arrogant thing I've ever heard.'

'It may be arrogant, but it's true.'

'Has nobody ever dumped *you*?'

'Nobody,' he echoed sardonically. 'How about you?'

Tamsyn wondered why she was having a conversation like this while waiting in line to get on a plane but, having started it, it would be pathetic to call time on it just because he'd touched on a subject she found difficult. No, she had never been dumped, but then she'd only ever had one relationship which she'd ended as soon as she realised that her body was as frozen as her heart. But she wasn't going to tell Xan Constantinides that. She didn't have to tell him anything, she reminded herself, replacing his question with one of her own.

'Did you complain about me to the management?'

He dragged his gaze away from the pert stewardess, who was ticking off passenger names on her clipboard. 'No. Why?'

'I got the sack soon after.'

'And you think I orchestrated it?'

She shrugged. 'Why not? It happened to my sister. The man she's marrying actually got her fired from her job.'

'Well, for your information, no—I didn't. I have

enough staff of my own to look after without keeping tabs on those employed by other people, no matter how incompetent they are.' There was a pause. 'What happened to your sister?'

It occurred to Tamsyn he didn't have a clue who she was. That he had no idea it was the Sheikh himself who'd got her sister fired, or that after Saturday's glittering ceremony he would be her new brother-in-law. To Xan Constantinides, she was just a judgmental cocktail waitress who couldn't hold a job down and he probably thought it ran in the family. 'Oh, you wouldn't know her,' she said truthfully, because Hannah had confided that she hadn't yet met any of her Sheikh fiancé's friends and was absolutely *terrified*, because they were all so high-powered.

Their conversation was halted by a smiling stewardess with a clipboard and as she was given her seat number, Tamsyn turned back to Xan Constantinides with a forced smile.

'Nice talking to you,' she said sarcastically and saw his navy eyes darken. 'Enjoy the flight.'

Her heart was still pounding as she took her seat on the aircraft and picked up the book she'd so been so looking forward to—a crime thriller set in the Australian outback—which she'd hope would pass away the hours during the long journey to Zahristan's capital city of Ashkhazar. But it was difficult to concentrate on the rather lurid plot, when all she could think about was the powerful Greek who'd managed to have such a potent effect on her. She tried to sleep, and failed. She stared out of the window at the passing clouds which looked like thick fields of cotton wool. She attempted to tuck into the variety of delicious foodstuffs which were placed before her, but her appetite seemed to have deserted her. She was just thinking gloomily about the days of celebration ahead of her, when that gravelled molasses voice broke into her thoughts.

'I suppose you'll be working as soon as we get there?'

Tamsyn looked up to see that Xan Constantinides had stopped in the aisle right beside her seat and was deigning to speak to her. She looked up to meet that distracting cobalt stare. 'Working?' she echoed in confusion.

'I'm assuming that's why you're here,' he murmured.

Suddenly Tamsyn understood. He thought she was here to act as a waitress at the royal wedding!

Well, why wouldn't he think that? She certainly wasn't dressed like the other women on the flight, with their discreet flashes of gold jewellery which probably cost a fortune and their studiedly casual designer outfits. Her sister had tried to insist on buying her some new clothes before the wedding, but Tamsyn had stubbornly refused. Because hadn't Hannah helped her out too many times in the past—and hadn't she vowed she was going to go it alone from now on?

'Just because you're going to marry a rich man, doesn't mean *I* have to accept his charity,' she remembered responding proudly. 'Thanks all the same, but I'll wear what's already in my wardrobe.'

Was that why Xan Constantinides was so certain she was a member of staff rather than a wedding guest? Because she was wearing old sneakers rather than those fancy shoes with the red soles which everyone else seemed to be sporting? Suddenly, Tamsyn thought she could have a bit of fun with this and liven up a wedding she was dreading. Wouldn't it be priceless to have the Greek tycoon patronise her—before he discovered her connection to the royal house of Al Diya?

She met his scrutiny with a bashful shrug. 'Yes,' she said. 'An event like this pays very well and they wanted to have some British serving staff among the Zahirstanians. You know, to make sure the English-speaking guests felt at home.'

He nodded. 'Good of them to fly you out in style.'

Tamsyn bit back an indignant laugh. Any minute now and he would start asking her if she'd ever been on an airplane before! She reached out and gave the plush leather of the armrest a quick squeeze, as if it was the chubby cheek of a particularly attractive little baby. 'I know,' she sighed. 'Let's hope I don't get too used to all this luxury before I go back to my poverty-stricken existence.'

'Let's hope not.' His smile was brief and dismissive—the smiling equivalent of a yawn—as if he had already grown bored with her. His gaze drifted towards the curvy bottom of one of the stewardesses, as if already he was miles away. 'And now, if you don't mind—I have work to do.'

Tamsyn opened her mouth to say that *he* was the one who had started the conversation, but something made her shut it again, as he continued his journey up the aisle of the plane. And she wasn't the only person looking at him—every female on the plane seemed to be following his sexy progress towards the front of the aircraft. Resentfully, Tamsyn found herself noting the powerful set of his shoulders and the way thick, dark tendrils of hair curled around the back of his neck.

She thought she'd never seen a man who was quite so sure of himself. He seemed to inject the air around him with a strange and potent energy and she resented the effect he seemed to have on her without even trying.

An unfamiliar shiver whispered its way down her spine and she clenched her hands into tense little fists as the plane soared through the sky on its way to the desert kingdom.

CHAPTER TWO

TAMSYN STOOD IN the centre of the huge room, her head spinning as she gazed around her in amazement. She'd known that her sister's fiancé owned an actual palace which she was going to be staying for the forthcoming wedding celebrations, but the reality of being here was so far outside her experience that for a moment she felt as if she were dreaming.

Drinking in her surroundings, she craned her neck to look up at the high ceiling which was vaulted and gilded with gold. She didn't think she'd ever seen so much gold! Soft drapes fell from the floor-to-ceiling windows which overlooked surprisingly green and lush gardens—surprising, because this was, after all, a desert country. Her bed was huge and closer to the ground than she was used to and it was covered with rich brocade and velvet cushions. And everywhere she looked she could see flowers. Big, claret-coloured and sunset-hued roses crammed into what looked like solid gold vases. Their heavy scent vied with the incense which was burning softly in one corner, in a container which seemed to be studded with genuine rubies and emeralds. As for the bathroom, Tamsyn swallowed. The bathroom was something else—exceeding the standards of every upmarket hotel she'd ever worked in—and she'd worked in quite a few. She spent several minutes running her fingertips over the fluffy bathrobe and eying up the gleaming glass bottles of bath oil and perfume, wondering if she'd be able to take some of them home with her.

She had sent away the servant who had hovered around after her arrival, because just the thought of *having* a servant had made her feel uncomfortable, since that felt like *her* natural role. She'd thought she would be alone until she was summoned to the pre-wedding dinner, but a knock at the door interrupted her reverie and Tamsyn went to answer it, her eyes narrowing as she stared at the woman who was standing there. She was wearing beautiful silk robes of sapphire blue, which flowed to the ground like a waterfall. Her shiny hair was covered in some gauzy veil of silver and the sparkling earrings which dangled from her earlobes echoed the aquamarine brilliance of her eyes. Tamsyn stood in shocked silence, realising that for a few seconds she hadn't recognised *her own sister!*

'Hannah,' she breathed. 'Is that really you?'

Hannah came in and closed the door behind her, before enveloping Tamsyn in a crushing bear hug. 'Of course it's me—who did you think it was?'

Tamsyn gave a mystified shake of her head. 'I can't believe it. You look so different. Like…like a real-life queen.'

A wry smile touched her sister's lips. 'Well, that's kind of appropriate, seeing as of Saturday that's exactly what I'm going to be.'

Tamsyn stilled. Was she imagining the strained quality in Hannah's voice or the faint shadows around her eyes? 'You don't have to go through with it, you know,' she said instantly, but her sister shook her head.

'I'm afraid I do. I can't back out of it now and I don't want to. I have to do this—for the sake of the baby.'

At the mention of the baby, Tamsyn's gaze swivelled to her sister's belly. She supposed that most people might not even have guessed Hannah was pregnant— she looked more like someone who'd just come back from holiday having been a bit too liberal with the hotel buffet. But she knew Hannah better than anyone. Hannah who had acted more like a mother than a big sister when they were growing up. They had shared a mother who had given them up when they'd been very young—but they each had different fathers.

Just the thought of *fathers* made an acrid taste rise up in Tamsyn's throat because her own had been a waster in every which way. She tried her best not to judge all men by his miserable standards, but sometimes it was difficult. But then, life was difficult, wasn't it? Everyone knew that. These days she understood why Hannah had kept her in the dark about her parentage for so long, though she had been bitter and angry about it for a long time. But now was not the time to rake up the perceived sins of the past. She was here, not because she wanted to be—but because she was determined to support her beloved sister—the only family she had left in the world.

'So what's it like living with a sheikh? Is Kulal treating you properly?' she demanded.

Hannah shot a nervous glance in the direction of the door as if she was afraid someone might be standing outside, listening.

'He is.' The Princess-in-waiting forced a smile. 'How was your flight?'

Tamsyn hesitated, thinking it would probably be un- wise to offload onto her pregnant sister on the eve of her wedding. No need to mention that she'd met Xan Constantinides once before and certainly no need to mention that she'd tipped a drink over him. 'Very com- fortable,' she said. She saw Hannah frown—as if she hadn't been expecting such polite diplomacy so she injected her next remark with just the right amount of carelessness. 'I bumped into some Greek tycoon in the queue.'

'Xan Constantinides?'

'That's him.' Tamsyn paused and then, despite her best intentions, she couldn't resist her next comment. 'He's pretty full of himself, isn't he?'

Hannah shrugged. 'Why wouldn't he be? He made billions at an early age and is built like a Greek god. Apparently women fall at his feet like ninepins and I guess those kind of things can go to a man's head. And of course, he's never been married—which makes him a bit of a target for predatory women. Never even got close, so Kulal tells me.' She frowned. 'You didn't… you didn't fall for him did you, Tamsyn?'

'Oh, please!' Tamsyn manufactured a disbelieving snort. 'I don't go for men with egos the size of Mars.'

'And you didn't fall *out* with him, I hope?' contin- ued Hannah nervously.

'Oh, come on, Han. As if I could be bothered!' Tam- syn gave an airy shrug. 'Why, I barely exchanged two words with the man.'

'Good. Because Kulal is very fond of him and they're in the middle of some hugely important business deal together.' Hannah smoothed down her silky robes, the movement drawing attention to her massive diamond engagement ring which glittered on her finger like a constellation of stars. 'But that's enough about Xan. I thought we could discuss your wardrobe.'

'My wardrobe?' Tamsyn's eyes narrowed with suspicion. 'What about it?'

There was a pause, during which Hannah seemed to be choosing her words with care. 'Tammy, what are you planning to wear to the rehearsal dinner tonight?'

Tamsyn had been waiting for this. Bad enough that Hannah seemed to have morphed into someone completely different—ever since the arrogant Sheikh had swept into her life and carried her off to his desert kingdom. Why, she barely recognised the elegant creature who stood before her as the same person who had once made beds for a living as a chambermaid at the Granchester Hotel. But that didn't mean *she* had to do the same, did it?

'I've got a very nice dress I bought down the market,' she said. 'I'm going to wear that. And how many times do I have to tell you not to call me Tammy?'

'Tamsyn, you *can't*. You can't wear some dress you've bought down the market to a royal wedding!'

'Why not?'

'Because…because….' Distractedly Hannah began to pace around the vast suite, her silken robes swishing against the floor as she moved. 'Well, the guest list is pretty daunting, if you want the truth. Even to me. Especially to me,' she added, on a whisper.

'I'm not daunted by other people's wealth,' said Tamsyn proudly.

'I know you're not—and there's no reason you should be. It's just…'

'Just what? Come on, Hannah—spit it out.'

Hannah drew to a halt beside Tamsyn's open suitcase, shooting a quick glance inside before sucking in a big breath which failed to hide her instinctive grimace. 'You can't wear any old thing,' she said gently, as she turned to look at her sister. 'Not to a function as important as this. It's my wedding and you're my sister. I'm the bride and the groom just happens to be a desert king. People are going to be looking at you, you know—especially as you're the only family I've got.'

Tamsyn's first instinct was to say she didn't care what other people thought. And if she fancied wearing her canvas sneakers beneath the dress she'd picked up for a bargain price—then that's exactly what she would do. But something about Hannah's anxious face tugged at a conscience she would prefer not to have. Suddenly she recognised that any defiance in the clothes department might reflect badly, not necessarily on her—but on her sister. And hadn't Hannah always done so much for her? Cared for and protected her during those deprived days of their fractured childhood…didn't she owe her for that?

'I don't have any fancy clothes,' she mumbled, feeling once again like the little girl who'd been mocked in the school playground because there was nothing in her lunchbox but a few scraps of bread and jam. *You're poor*, the other children used to taunt—and Tamsyn had been too ashamed to admit that her foster father had spent all his money on gambling and womanising and her foster mother had been too weak to object. Her education had suffered as a consequence and she'd left school without qualifications, which didn't exactly make her a big player in the job stakes. Money remained tight for Tamsyn and what little money she *did* have she certainly wasn't going to waste on an expensive dress she'd only get to wear once. 'I'm not stupid, Hannah,' she said huffily. 'I'm not planning to let you down. I'll make the best of what I have, just like I've always done.'

'I know you will. And when you bother to pull out all the stops you can look amazing. But this is different. I don't want you and I to stick out any more than we already are. So let me give you something to wear, Tamsyn. Something beautiful—the like of which you will never have worn before.' There was a pause. 'Please.'

Tamsyn had vowed she wasn't going to accept any more of Hannah's charity, no matter how scared she was about the future. Her latest job in a café paid only peanuts and in the meantime her overdraft was getting steadily bigger. The latest blow had been the recent rent raise on her crummy little apartment, leaving her wondering how on earth she was going to pay it.

She thought about the glamourous women she had travelled over with on the Sheikh's private plane and wondered what glorious surprises they would be pulling out of their suitcases for the glittering dinner tonight. And then she thought about a pair of cobalt eyes and the way they had trained themselves on her. She'd seen the way the Greek's gaze had focussed in on her scruffy tennis shoes and the disdainful curve of his lips in response. Was it that which made her suddenly decide to take up her sister's offer? To dress up for the party so that she might fit in, for once in her life?

'Okay. You can find me something to wear, if you like,' she said, casting a doubtful glance at Hannah's covered head. 'But I'm definitely not wearing a veil.'

Peering into the silvered surface of the antique mirror, Xan gave his tie a final unwanted tug. Raking his fingers back through the raven disarray of his hair he did his best to stifle a yawn as he deliberated on how he was going to get through the long evening ahead.

He *hated* these affairs with a passion and part of him felt deeply sorry for his royal friend, for being forced to marry some gold-digging little chambermaid from England. Contemptuously, his lips curved into their habitual line of disapproval. How could Kulal—a desert king renowned for an extensive list of sophisticated lovers—have fallen for the oldest trick in the book? There had been no official announcement but you wouldn't need to be a mathematician to work out that a hasty wedding arranged between one of the region's most exalted sheikhs and an unknown commoner—was bound to end up with a baby a few months down the line. Had the chambermaid deliberately trapped him, he mused? And if so, how could his friend bear the thought of that deception for all those long years which lay ahead?

He thought of his own marital destiny and not for the first time, began to see that it could have much to commend it, because Sofia was sweet and undemanding. He couldn't imagine her ever trying to trap him by falling pregnant—probably because he doubted she would ever consent to sex before marriage. His mouth hardened for it was many months since he had seen his unofficial fiancée and he knew he couldn't keep putting it off their arranged marriage indefinitely. Up until now it had been a private and completely confidential agreement between two families, but the longer he stalled, the more likely that the press would get hold of it and have a field day with it. His jaw clenched. He would set in motion the formal courtship when he flew out of here after the weekend, with a wedding pencilled in for the middle of next year.

But for now he was still technically a free man and unwillingly his thoughts turned to lust, for it had been a while since he had enjoyed a woman in his bed.

He was discreet about his relationships—for obvious reasons—and nobody outside their immediate families knew he had been promised to a beautiful young Greek girl. His recent sexual abstinence had certainly not been caused by a lack of opportunity— but because he had become jaded and bored by the attentions of predatory women on the make.

He scowled at his reflection before turning away. The press didn't help his endeavours to maintain a low profile and he cursed the obsession which made certain newspapers speculate about when he intended to tie the knot. Wasn't it such careless speculation which caused women to pursue him, as if they were hunting down some particularly elusive quarry? Didn't they realise that the chase was the thing which fired up a man's blood? Xan's mouth flattened. At least, that was what he had been told—for he had never had to pursue a woman. They came after him in their droves, like dedicated ants flocking to a spoonful of spilled honey. Some he enjoyed and others he discarded—but he made it plain to each and every one that there was no point in wishing for any kind of future with him, though he never explained why. And wasn't the truth that he enjoyed the protective barriers which his long-term engagement placed around him? It kept women at a safe distance and that was the way he liked it.

A servant came to fetch him to take him to the pre-wedding dinner and Xan quickly became aware of the excitement in the air as the wedding grew closer. Tall, burning flames lit the courtyard and in the distance he could hear the low beat of unfamiliar music which only added to the febrile build of atmosphere. Through wide corridors scented with jasmine and gardenia and lit with gold and silver candles, he followed the silent servant—taking his place at last in some inordinately grand ballroom, which he hadn't seen on his last visit.

He had visited Zahristan once before, when Kulal had taken him out to the desert to see the state-of-the-art solar panels which the country's scientists had designed, and in whose manufacture Xan had invested a great deal of money. He had combined the work trip with some serious riding on the most magnificent stallion he'd ever mounted and then he and the Sheikh had camped beneath the blinding brilliance of the stars in an opulent Bedouin tent. Xan remembered thinking that his powerful royal friend had the world at his fingertips—yet now he was being forced into a corner, trapped into a relationship he did not really want.

And wasn't exactly the same thing happening to *him*? Briefly Xan thought about the Greek girl with dark eyes who was everything a man could possibly desire. No. He was walking into his future with his eyes open. Not for him the lottery of chance or ignorance. There would be no skeletons emerging from the closet of Sofia, for she was someone he had known all her life. She was pure and beautiful and… His mouth hardened as he allowed the unwanted thought to flit into his mind.

The chemistry would come later.

Most of the other guests were already assembled in the huge gilded ballroom, which led into a banqueting hall almost as vast. Beneath chandeliers which glittered like shoals of priceless diamonds, women paraded in their finery, the men beside them wearing dark suits, desert robes or uniform. For some reason Xan found himself looking round for the redheaded waitress but couldn't see her anywhere and he wondered if she was somewhere deep in the palace kitchens, loading up her tray. Instead, he accepted a drink from someone else—a sharp-sweet cocktail containing fire-berry juice and drank it silently as they awaited the arrival of the royal couple.

At last, a single musician stepped forward to play a fanfare on the traditional *mizmar*, heralding the arrival of the Sheikh and his bride-to-be and there was a murmur of expectation as the couple paused in the open doorway of the ballroom and all heads turned in their direction.

And then he saw her.

Xan's fingers tightened around his drink so tightly that for a moment he was afraid that the delicate glass might shatter. He expelled a long, low breath as his disbelieving gaze settled on the feisty redhead who was following behind the royal couple as if it was her every right to do so.

His eyes narrowed. No sawn-off jeans and canvas shoes tonight. She was wearing an exquisite dress of

emerald silk which matched the brilliance of her eyes
and looked as if had been made just for her. The design
was simple and in many ways modest, but it accentu-
ated her body in a way which her sexy cocktail waitress uniform had failed to do. In that rather *obvious*
black satin ensemble she had looked more like a little
girl playing dress-up, while tonight she looked like a
woman. Xan swallowed. A very sensual woman. Her
lustrous red curls had been caught back, displaying
dazzling diamond and emerald earrings which brushed
the sides of her long neck. He felt the pooling of blood
at his groin and suddenly she turned her head to look
directly at him—as if some sixth sense had told her
he was staring. A faint flicker of triumph illuminated
her extraordinary eyes before, very deliberately, she
turned her back on him and began chatting to a tall
man in some sort of military uniform who seemed to
be devouring her with his hungry gaze.

Xan felt the hard beat of a pulse at his temple. He
had imagined her gliding around between the guests
with a tray of drinks in her hand and this sudden
unexpected elevation of status left him feeling confused. If she wasn't a waitress, then who the hell *was*
she? He found himself dipping his head to speak to
the blonde woman beside him who had been slowly
edging herself closer in a way which was boringly
predictable.

'Who is that woman in green?' he questioned silkily.
'The one who entered with the Sheikh and his fiancée.'

The blonde gave a discernible pout of disappointment followed by a slight shrug. 'Her? Her name is
Tamsyn,' she said reluctantly. 'Tamsyn Wilson. She's
the sister of the bride.'

Xan nodded as suddenly it all made sense. The reason why she had been dressed down and out of place on the flight over. The reason why a cocktail waitress was hobnobbing with one of the most powerful royal families in the world. Wilson. Of course. The bride's sister. The bride who had trapped his friend into marriage by getting pregnant. Xan gave a short laugh. How the redhead must have been laughing to herself when he'd made the—very understandable—assumption that she was here on a working trip. Was she enjoying the fact that he'd made such a fundamental mistake? He watched as she walked straight past him, ignoring him completely, her glorious fiery head held high in the air. And he felt the corresponding roar of his blood in response.

It was a long time since Xan could remember the minutes passing so slowly and never had he been so comprehensively ignored by the person he most wanted to speak to. He'd never had to work to get a woman to join him—usually the briefest of glances would send them scuttling over with an eagerness which was sometimes enough to kill his desire stone-dead. But Tamsyn Wilson wasn't playing ball. He watched her dip her glorious red head to the side as the Sheikh introduced her to a group of people and he saw the automatic light of interest in the men's eyes. He thought about infiltrating the group and commandeering her for himself, but instinct told him such a plan would be foolish. Only a quick glance at the seating plan yielded up the satisfying information that once again, they were seated next to each other. Xan's lips curved into a smile of anticipation. Far better to have her captive at his side and then...

Then what?

He hadn't yet gone that far in his imagination, but the increased pound of blood at his groin gave him a very good idea of how he intended the evening to end. And why not? His formal courtship of Sofia had not yet started. Was it not better to indulge his desires and rid himself of them? To eradicate all restlessness before finally settling down?

The distinctive sound of the trumpet-like *mizmar* broke into the chatter as servants began guiding the guests towards the galleried dining room, where the gleam of the dazzling long table and the perfume of countless roses awaited them. Xan stood beside the vacant chair next to his, watching the redhead approach without any kind of smile on her face, the defiant spark of her eyes the only acknowledgement she had seen him.

In stony silence she came to stand beside him.

'So,' he said softly as the faint drift of her scent washed over his skin and it became clear she wasn't planning to greet him with any kind of rapturous joy. 'We meet again.'

Her expression was cool. 'It would seem so.'

'Would you care to sit down?'

She gave a sarcastic elevation of her eyebrows. 'Since the alternative is eating on the hoof, I suppose the answer must be yes.'

Her insolence was turning him on almost as much as the slender curve of her breasts beneath her exquisite green silk dress. Xan pulled out her chair, her mulish look indicating that such display of chivalry was unnecessary but as she lowered her bottom onto the carved golden seat his blood pressure rocketed once more. As he guided the chair back in, his fingers briefly brushed against her narrow shoulders and he had to resist the urge to let them rest there and to massage away the undeniable tension he could feel.

'You didn't tell me you were the bride's sister,' he said, as he sat down beside her.

'You didn't ask.' She turned to him, her eyes full of an emerald light which tonight seemed almost unworldly. 'You just *assumed* I was here to work, didn't you? To ferry drinks around and wait at table. That someone like me couldn't possibly be one of the guests.'

'Was that such a crazy assumption to make, given the circumstances?' he mused. 'Last time I saw you that's exactly what you were doing. You made no mention of your connection with the bride and you have to admit, you didn't exactly blend in with the other guests on the plane. At least,' he amended softly. 'Not until now.'

'Now that my sister has given me the dress she secretly had made for me?' she demanded hotly. 'Or forced me to wear a necklace I'm terrified is going to fall off and deplete the royal coffers by several million quid, is that what you mean?'

Xan found himself having to bite back a smile. 'You cannot deny that you look very different tonight.'

Tamsyn picked up a jewel-encrusted goblet and sipped at the cold fizzy water it contained. No, she wasn't going to deny she looked different but beneath her fine new trappings—she felt exactly the same. Like someone who never fitted in—not anywhere. And tonight the sensation of being out of place was even more acute than usual. It wasn't just that everyone here was richer than her and seemed happy in their own skins, her disorientation was compounded by the unfamiliar feelings which were ripping through her like a spring tide. Feelings which were hard to define and even harder to understand. She wondered why she was feeling such a powerful *desire* for the man beside her, even though he was the most arrogant person she'd ever met. She wondered why her skin had felt as if it were on fire when his fingertips had brushed against her shoulder blades. Or why, beneath this fancy dress which Hannah had foisted on her—the tips of her breasts were as raw as if someone had been rubbing them with sandpaper.

Remember how he looked down his nose at you when you were boarding the flight. Remember how upset that ravishing blonde had been when he'd been cold-heartedly dumping her in the cocktail bar.

Yet right now it was difficult to think about anything other than the smile which was softening the edges of his lips and making her wonder what it would be like to be kissed by Xan Constantinides. Her gaze twitched to his long olive fingers and once again her throat constricted with an unfamiliar surge of lust. Because she didn't *do* desire. It was yet another side of her character which made it hard for her to fit in. It was her own private and horrible little secret—or rather, it was *one* of them—that despite all the fiery promise of her looks, she was about as responsive as a piece of wood. Hadn't she been told that by men deeply unhappy that she wouldn't 'put out', until she'd stopped going out with men altogether because life was easier that way?

'No, I'm not going to deny I look different tonight,'

she said. 'Which is why I assume you're talking to me, which you clearly didn't want to do when you thought I was nothing but a lowly waitress. Or was it the sight of my canvas tennis shoes which made you decide I wasn't worthy of your time?'

He looked as if he was about to contest the point before seeming to change his mind and subjecting her to a smile of such intensity that Tamsyn's heart felt as if it was going to burst right out of her chest.

'Look, why don't we wipe the slate clean and start again?' he suggested smoothly, extending his hand with practised ease. 'I'm Xan Constantinides. Short for Alexandros, in case you were wondering.'

'I wasn't,' she said moodily.

And you're Tamsyn, aren't you?' he continued, undaunted. 'Tamsyn Wilson.'

Behind her unsmiling lips, Tamsyn gritted her teeth. He hadn't bothered finding out her name before, had he? But now he'd discovered she was related to Hannah, he was behaving *very* differently She glanced up at where the prospective bride and groom were sitting next to one another on some amazing dais. Hannah was smiling but Tamsyn knew her well enough to see the strain of the occasion on her face—*and* she was pregnant. And since Hannah had stressed that Xan was engaged in some important business with the Sheikh, then shouldn't she at least *try* to be polite to him, at least for the duration of the meal itself?

'Yes,' she said, as a delicate mango and walnut salad was placed in front of her. 'That's my name.'

'So why don't you tell me something about yourself, Tamsyn Wilson?'

Picking up a golden fork to half-heartedly push

her food around the plate, Tamsyn wondered what the Greek tycoon would say if she told him the truth. That if her parents had been married, her *real* surname would have been one of the most memorable in the world. But she had never used it. She'd never had the right to use it—not then and certainly not now. She looked into his cobalt eyes and tried to suppress the insane flutter of her heart. 'What would you like to know?'

He gave a shrug of his broad shoulders. 'Why don't we start with the obvious. You say you're no longer working at the Bluebird Club?'

'I told you—I was sacked.'

'So what are you doing instead?'

Perhaps if she hadn't been feeling so out of place then Tamsyn might have engaged in small-talk. She might have skated over her nomadic existence and pretended she was just like every other woman there. But somehow those words wouldn't come. Maybe Xan Constantinides was too unsettling a presence and those cobalt eyes too deeply penetrating. Because the idea of putting a positive spin on a life which had felt like it was spiralling out of control lately, suddenly seemed too big an ask. Why bother trying to impress someone who was only deigning to speak to her because she was soon to be related to the Sheikh?

'Oh, I have a terribly glamorous life—you wouldn't believe,' she said airily. 'I work in a coffee bar by day and stack supermarket shelves by night.'

He frowned. 'Those sound like very long hours.'

'Go straight to the top of the class, Mr Constantinides—they are.'

His eyes narrowed. 'Aren't you qualified to do anything other than waitress work?'

She put the golden fork back down on the plate with a clatter, her starter untasted. 'Actually, no, I'm not. Exams were never really my number one concern when I was at school.'

'So why not retrain to do something else?' he questioned as he lifted up his own goblet, his steady cobalt gaze surveying her over its jewelled rim. 'You seem bright enough.'

Tamsyn nearly laughed out loud and not just because the remark was deeply patronising. That was the trouble with rich people. They had no idea how the world really worked. They'd been cushioned by their wealth and privilege for so long, that they couldn't put themselves in someone else's shoes. 'And who's going to fund me while I do that?' she questioned, trying to keep her voice from shaking. 'When I've just had a rent raise from my landlord? And before you tell me to move to somewhere cheaper, I've lived in London all my life and can't imagine going anywhere else. Some problems don't have easy solutions, I'm afraid. Not unless you're prepared to throw wads of cash at them, which isn't an option for most people. Welcome to the real world, Mr Constantinides.'

Xan wondered if she was aware that her defiant words were causing her chest to heave, making it difficult for him not to stare openly at the silk-covered perfection of her breasts. With an effort he focussed his gaze on his wine glass, twirling the stem between his fingers and watching as the different jewels sparkled in the light from the overhead chandeliers. 'It's true I have made a sizeable amount of money,' he conceded. 'But that certainly doesn't guarantee a trouble-free life.'

'You mean like someone forgetting to peel your grapes for you, or your private jet failing to take off on time?'

'That's a rather predictable response, Tamsyn,' he mused softly. 'You know, I'm almost disappointed. I was hoping for something a little more original.'

'Oh, dear,' she said, pushing out her bottom lip in an exaggerated pout. 'The billionaire is disappointed. We can't have that, can we?'

He met the hectic glitter of her green gaze and the pooling at his groin increased. Xan shifted in his seat. He had tried to be polite but she was having none of it and he suspected he knew why. Because something was flowing between them. Something powerful. The kind of physical attraction he'd been encountering from women ever since he'd reached puberty though it had never felt like this before. Women didn't usually glare at him as if he was the devil incarnate, or try to rub him up the wrong way. He suspected that Tamsyn's supposed dislike of him was masking a much deeper response and that her darkened eyes were telling the real story. A flicker of a smile curved his lips. She wanted him just as much as he wanted her. And why not? Why not enjoy one final taste of freedom before destiny beckoned?

But he didn't intend spending the entire meal fighting with her and not simply because fighting was a bore. Because he understood the psychology of women only too well. They always wanted what they thought they couldn't have. She needed to understand that she was in danger of missing out if she continued to be insolent towards him. He would make her wait and make her squirm, so that by the time she came to him she would be so aroused that...

The pressure at his groin was almost unbearable as, very deliberately, he turned his back on her and began to speak to the Italian heiress to his right.

CHAPTER THREE

IT WAS JUST a wedding. That was all. Just a few more hours to get through before she could go home. That's what Tamsyn kept telling herself as she made her way towards the grand throne room, in yet another outfit which Hannah had insisted she wear. She supposed her sister must have secretly had all these clothes made for her before she arrived, but she couldn't deny that the long, floaty dress suited her. Unlike the dramatic emerald gown she'd worn to the rehearsal dinner last night, this one was a much gentler hue. The soft grey colour of a pigeon's wing, the bodice and silk-chiffon skirt were sprinkled with tiny crystals which sparkled like stars as she moved.

Tonight, the jewels she'd been loaned were diamonds—some more chandelier drop earrings, along with a priceless choker which blazed like ice fire around her neck. And just like last night, when Tamsyn glanced in the mirror before leaving her suite, she didn't recognise the image reflected back at her. To the outside world she looked sleek, expensive and polished but inside she felt....disgruntled. And although she hated the reason for her discontentment, she wasn't deluded enough to deny it. Because wasn't the truth that her irritation had been caused by Xan Constantinides ignoring her throughout most of the pre-wedding dinner? He'd been laughing and joking *in Italian* with that stunning woman on his other side and making out like *she* was invisible. And yes, she *had* been behaving in a particularly waspish manner beforehand, but even so...

She'd made her escape as soon as the food part of the evening was over. She'd gone back to her suite of rooms and run herself a deep and perfumed bath—then spent most of the night tossing and turning as the image of a man with black hair and cobalt eyes kept haunting her thoughts. More than once she'd awoken to find the tips of her breasts all pointy and aching and a molten heat throbbing between her thighs, causing her to writhe frustratedly between the fine cotton sheets. She'd told herself she needed to pull herself together and put the infuriating Greek right out of her mind, but somehow it wasn't turning out to be that easy.

The moment she entered the throne room, Xan Constantinides was the first person she saw, despite the fact that the Sheikh was already at the front of the gilded throne room, waiting for his bride. Tamsyn's heart gave a powerful lurch as she willed her face not to register any emotion.

He looked...

She swallowed against the sudden rawness in her throat. He looked delectable. In a charcoal suit which suited his colouring, he stood taller than any other man there else. Even more disturbing was the fact that he seemed to sense when she entered, because he turned his head and she was caught in that cobalt stare, making her feel as if she was imprisoned there. As if she *wanted* to be imprisoned there. She willed him not to come up and talk to her and then of course, she wished he would, but Tamsyn told herself to concentrate on the ceremony itself and to fix her eyes on the bride, who was just arriving.

Hannah looked gorgeous, her pregnancy bump a subtle swell and well disguised by her unusual wedding gown of beaten gold. She'd apologised for not making Tamsyn her bridesmaid, explaining that it wasn't Zahristanian custom to do so. Not that Tamsyn had minded. Marriage had always seemed such an outdated institution to her and one which rarely lasted. More than once she'd wondered why it couldn't be replaced by something more modern.

Yet she sensed the historical significance of the vows being made, though Hannah's voice was so low she could barely hear them and the Sheikh looked so stern that Tamsyn was certain he felt as trapped as her sister did. But she clapped and cheered along with the other guests once the couple had been pronounced King and Queen, and she toasted their health in spiced fire-berry juice, as was traditional.

The meal which followed was far more formal than the one they'd eaten last night and Tamsyn told herself she was pleased to sit between the Sultan of Marazad and a representative from the desert kingdom of Maraban. Glad to be miles away from Xan Constantinides and relieved she didn't have to endure his unsettling presence.

But that was a lie.

All she could think about was the Greek tycoon, and her body seemed determined to reflect her increasingly distracted thoughts. She felt as if her skin had become too tight for her body. As if her senses had suddenly become sensitised. The sound of her heart seemed amplified, its beat a million times more powerful than usual. And there was no respite from these unsettling feelings which made her feel as if she was fighting something deep inside herself. Nowhere she could escape to, because she couldn't just get up and leave in the middle of a royal wedding. She tried to chat politely to the men on either side and not glance further down the long table to where a Hollywood actress and a female member of the British royal family were giggling like schoolgirls at something Xan was saying.

She wondered how early she could decently leave, especially when a troupe of musicians started playing in the galleried ballroom next door. She knew there would be dancing after dinner because Hannah had told her so, but Tamsyn had no intention of watching couples circling the dance floor and pretending she was fine on her own. Usually, she was—mainly because she had made self-sufficiency into an art form. She never yearned for a partner because that was the only way she knew how to function. If you didn't yearn for something, you wouldn't be disappointed—and anyway, relationships were a waste of time. Experience had taught her that.

Yet tonight she keenly felt the absence of something in her life. Or rather, someone. Maybe it was the inevitable sentimentality conjured up by the wedding vows, or the realisation that Hannah was now married which was making her feel so shockingly alone. Or perhaps it was the just the realisation that there was nothing waiting for her back in England other than a pile of mounting debts.

Dabbing at her lips with a napkin, she decided to slip away, just like last night. Who would notice *her* when there were so many important guests present? She rose from her seat and was just bending to retrieve the Dior bag Hannah had insisted on lending her, when she heard a rich voice from behind.

'You're not leaving?' came the silky question.

She didn't need to turn around to know who was speaking, but prior knowledge offered no protection against her feelings and Tamsyn's heart was hammering as she straightened up to meet that mocking cobalt stare. He didn't want to talk to you last night, she reminded herself—so why not continue with that state of affairs and everyone will be happy. She gave him a tight smile. 'Oh, dear. Nobody was supposed to notice.'

'Where are you going?'

Tamsyn shrugged. *Where did he think she was going?* 'Back to my room. Or should I say—to my vast suite of rooms.'

'But the night is young.'

She opened her eyes very wide. 'I didn't think people actually said that kind of thing any more.'

He raised his brows. 'You're implying it's clichéd?'

'I suspect you're clever enough to work that one out for yourself, Mr Constantinides.'

Their gazes clashed in look which made Tamsyn feel almost *playful* and the desire to flirt was overwhelming. Yet she never flirted—she wasn't sure she even knew how. She'd always been closed up and defensive because she didn't particularly like men and she certainly didn't trust them. So how come she was suddenly playing a game she'd never played before and finding she was comfortable with it? How come she wanted to tease this darkly impressive individual and for him to tease her back? She found herself wanting to stroke her finger over the curving lines of his sensual mouth, and…and…

And she had to stop this.

Because this was dangerous. More than dangerous. Tamsyn's heart clenched with something which felt uncomfortably close to vulnerability, and that scared the hell out of her. 'I have to go,' she said.

'Not yet.' He laid his hand on her arm. 'I get the distinct feeling that I really need to change your impression of me.'

Chin lifting, she offered him a belligerent gaze. 'And why would you want to do that?'

'Call it a peace-making move in honour of your sister's wedding, if you like. Just a little light-hearted fun, that's all. And the dancing has only just started,' he observed. 'You can't possibly leave until you've had at least one dance.'

'I didn't think it was obligatory. I wasn't planning on dancing with anyone.'

An arrogant smile touched the edges of his lips. 'Not even with me?'

'Especially not with you.'

'Oh? And why not, *agape mou*? Don't you like dancing?'

His voice had deepened and the throwaway endearment in his native tongue made him even more irresistible. Tamsyn stared into his dark blue eyes. When she was younger she had thrown herself around a dance floor with the rest of them, swaying beneath the flash of lights, to the DJ's heavy beat. She had shaken her arms in the air and tossed her curls while her skin had glowed and grown hot. But she'd never been asked to dance by a devastatingly handsome man in a fancy ballroom, while wearing a silken dress which pooled around her ankles.

'Because it's a bad idea,' she prevaricated.

'Stop fighting it, Tamsyn. You know you want to dance with me,' he said with silky perception, his hand moving to the small of her back as he propelled her gently towards the dance floor.

Even then she might have stopped him had Tamsyn not glanced up at the dais and seen the newly married Sheikh looking down on them, with what looked like bemusement in his eyes. Was he surprised she was planning to dance with such an honoured guest as his rich pal? She knew Kulal didn't like her, just as she didn't like him. In fact, they'd had an almighty row before the wedding when he'd turned up on her sister's doorstep. But you had to let bygones be bygones, especially now that he was her new brother-in-law.

So why not show the Sheikh she could behave with dignity—and prove to herself that she wasn't a total social misfit? Why *shouldn't* she dance with the best-looking man in the room? With a resolute nod of her head, she allowed Xan to lead her onto the ballroom, pleased there were enough people to ensure they could just blend into the crowd. Just one dance, she told herself. One dance to fulfil her obligations and she could be off.

But life never quite conformed the way you wanted it to. One dance became two, which then somehow morphed into three, and each dance seemed to propel them closer, so that their bodies felt as if they were glued together. And Xan wasn't saying anything. Well, neither was she, come to think of it. Tamsyn blamed the loudness of the lilting music but the truth was that she couldn't think of anything she wanted to say other than something wholly inappropriate.

Like: *I love the way you make me feel when you tighten your arms around my waist like that.* Or, *could you possibly press yourself a little closer?*

Did he realise that, or did she somehow silently communicate her wishes to him? Because surely there must have been a reason—some defining moment—when Xan Constantinides thought it was perfectly acceptable for him to run his fingertips down her back in a way which even to her inexperienced self, spoke of careless intimacy. For several minutes, she let him do just that and she couldn't deny how good it felt. She began to shiver each time he made the tantalisingly slow journey from the top of her neck to the base of her spine. Her heart was hammering and the rush of heat to her face echoed the molten heat which was clenching at her sex. Yet far from being disturbed by the sultry desire she was experiencing Tamsyn was aware of an intense feeling of *relief.* Briefly she closed her eyes as she dipped her forehead to rest on his shoulder as she felt the squirm of excitement. So she wasn't frigid, after all. She could feel the things other women felt. Sweet heaven—could she feel them! It was as if someone had just flicked a switch and brought her body to life, so that every sinew and fibre was thrilling with the potent power of his proximity.

She heard him murmur something in her ear, it's meaning a mystery because it was said in Greek. But then he pushed one thigh hard against hers, as if urging her legs apart and she found her super-susceptible body obeying his silent command. Her knees widened and a sudden thrill of pleasure shot through her as she felt the pressure of his hard thigh pushing against the softness of hers. Her breasts were thrusting insistently at his chest and her knees had become all wobbly and weak. She could feel the rub of her panties over a sudden honeyed slickness and felt an insistent yearning to have him touch her there...to whisper his finger over her most intimate place. To ease that escalating ache which was making her want to squirm with frustration. She swallowed, trying to ignore the heat which was flaring in her cheek—and that was when alarm bells started ringing. What was she *doing*? After years of being purer than the driven snow, was she really planning to make a slutty spectacle of herself on the dance floor—just because some super-smooth man was pressing all the right buttons?

Removing her hands from his shoulders she flattened her palms against his chest, trying not to be distracted by the hard wall of muscle as she stared up into his face. 'What the hell do you think you're doing?' she demanded.

He didn't look the slightest bit bothered by her furious accusation as he lifted his broad shoulders in a careless shrug. 'I should have thought that was perfectly obvious.'

'So suddenly you're all over me, having ignored me all the way through dinner last night?' she accused.

'You were so combative that you deserved to be ignored,' he said softly. 'But I thought we'd agreed on a truce tonight?'

'Does...?' She swallowed, willing the erratic hammering of her pulse to subside. 'Does a truce involve you coming on to me like that, in such a public way?'

'Oh, come on, Tamsyn. Let's not be hypocritical about what just happened. I thought you were enjoying yourself.' He flickered her a slow smile. 'I know I certainly was. And most people are too busy dancing to notice how close we were getting.'

Tamsyn shook her head, aware of the swing of heavy diamond earrings against her neck and nervously she touched the sleepers to check the precious jewels were secure. Which they were—unlike her. She was one seething mass of insecurity. And fear. She mustn't discount the dominant emotion which was making her feel so scared. She felt as if she'd just stepped onto a sturdy wooden floor and it was about to give way beneath her. As if Xan Constantinides had the ability to waken something inside her—something which had been sleeping all these years. Suddenly the defiant persona she had perfected to protect herself from the kind of life her mother had lived, was in danger of crumbling before her eyes. Suddenly she was terrified of just how *exposed* he was making her feel. As if she was nothing but a bunch of sensitised nerve-endings which were jangling with hungry need. She shook her head again.

'Look, I can't do this,' she whispered. 'I'm sorry. Enjoy the rest of the party but I'm going to bed. It's going to be a long flight tomorrow and I have a double shift on Monday. Nice meeting you, Xan,' she said, and without another word she began to walk off the dance floor, aware of people turning to look at her as she hurriedly brushed past them.

Xan watched her go, caught in a rare moment of indecision, his eyes drawn to the bright shimmer of curls which cascaded like flames down her back. The voice of reason was urging him to let her go, because she was trouble. Anyone could see that. All mixed up and not his type. But the hunger of his body was more powerful than reason and he'd never had a woman walk away from him before—not like this. Was this how Hannah had snared the Sheikh—the two very ordinary Wilson sisters possessing a simple but effective strategy which would make powerful men lust after them?

Like a man hypnotised he found himself following her, mesmerised by the slender curve of her glittering bottom as she left the dance floor, surprised when she didn't look back. Not once. There was no furtive side glance to check whether he was on her tail. And *that* was exciting, too. Her steps were determined—as if she really *wanted* to get away from him. This was the chase, he realised—the chase which other men spoke of but which he'd never encountered before. He could feel the tightening of his groin and hear the wild thunder of his heart, when suddenly she disappeared from sight and he was unprepared for the disappointment which flared through him. Purposefully increasing his pace, he rounded the corner and saw her—and perhaps the sound of his footsteps was enough to make her stop and turn around—a look of bewilderment on her face, as if she was genuinely surprised to see him. As if she doubted her ability to make a man follow her.

'Xan?' she said, creasing her forehead in a frown.

'Tamsyn,' he answered, and began to walk towards her, aware of her nipples pushing hard against the crystalline bodice of her dress. As he approached, he could feel the warm rush of blood pumping through his body and in that moment he felt as if he would die if he couldn't have her.

He had reached her now and could see her darkened pupils making her green eyes appear almost black— just as the moist tremble of her lips indicated an unspoken desire to have him to crush them with his own. And he would, he thought hungrily. He would take the wildcat Tamsyn Wilson to his bed and subdue her in the most satisfactory way possible.

CHAPTER FOUR

BENEATH THE FRETWORK of lanterns lighting the palace corridor, Tamsyn's heart was thundering as she watched Xan approach, his powerful body outlined by the dark fabric of his formal suit. His face was dark too and his eyes glittered out a message of intent which started a tug of longing deep inside her. It scared and excited her and she wanted to carry on running, but something was keeping her feet fixed to the spot.

'Nobody has ever walked off and left me standing alone on the dance floor like that,' he observed huskily.

From somewhere she found a remnant of her usual flippancy. 'Oh, dear. Poor Xan. Is your ego suffering?'

'It's not my ego I'm thinking about right now,' he ground out.

Some of her composure began to slip away as Tamsyn became aware of how big and strong he looked and how it had felt to be in his arms. *Hadn't it been the most incredible sensation she'd ever experienced?*

She cleared her throat, trying to dispel her euphoric recall. 'Look, I thought I'd made my feelings clear. I'm tired and on my way to bed. I don't know why you're chasing me through the corridors as if we're a pair of kids playing cops and robbers.'

'Yes, you do. You know exactly why,' he said softly. 'Because I want you and you want me. We've wanted each other from the moment we met, Tamsyn and unless we do something about it, it's going to drive us both crazy.'

It was one of those slow motion moments and Tamsyn felt her heart leap in her chest. Like when you heard something life-changing on the news. Only this wasn't something which was happening to somebody else—it was happening to *her*. She was being propositioned by Xan Constantinides—the arrogant Greek billionaire!

Her throat grew dry as she looked at him, trying not to drink in all his dark beauty, knowing she had plenty of options available. She could call for a servant. Or carrying on walking and even if he followed, she could slam the door in his face, because instinct told her he wouldn't charge at it with a battering ram, even if he looked physically capable of doing so. But even as these thoughts flickered through her mind, she realised none of them were an option. Xan Constantinides might not like her very much—nor she him— but she couldn't deny that something had happened when he'd touched her on the dance floor.

He'd cast a spell on her. Woven some sensual kind of magic which was snaring her with invisible threads. She stared into the rugged beauty of his face, aware that this was a chance to shake off the real Tamsyn—the one who'd become brittle and defiant in order to survive. This was her opportunity to become someone else for a change. Somebody soft and dreamy and different.

'You want to kiss me,' he persisted softly. 'You want that very badly, don't you, Tamsyn?'

She wanted to deny it. To tell him that he was talking rubbish and to take his ego somewhere else. But she couldn't. She found herself lifting her eyes to his, her heart filled with foreboding and longing as she attempted a shrug which didn't quite come off. 'I suppose so,' she mumbled.

He seemed to find this amusing for his lips curved into a mocking smile. 'You suppose so?' he echoed, stepping forward to tilt her chin upwards with his finger. 'I don't think I've ever been damned with so much faint praise.'

This was Tamsyn's cue for a clever retort but right now she didn't have one because he was slowly lowering his mouth on to hers. His lips were brushing over her trembling lips and she was finding it impossible not to respond. Her hands fluttered to his shoulders for support and suddenly he was pulling her closer with effortless mastery as he deepened the kiss.

And Tamsyn just lost it.

She'd been kissed before—of course she had—but never like this. She'd only ever known the thrust of a tongue and the unwanted slick of saliva. She hadn't realised that a kiss could feel like a one-way ticket to heaven. Did her dreamy gasp startle him? Was that why he drew back, before glancing both ways down the corridor and lacing her fingers with his. 'Come with me,' he said, his voice curiously uneven.

'Come where? Where are we going?'

'Where do you think we're going?' His eyes glittered with unmistakable promise. 'I'm taking you to bed.'

His masterful and slightly callous statement should have shocked her, but it didn't. Instead it thrilled her and Tamsyn could feel her cheeks glowing as he led her through endless corridors, the click-clacking of her high heels against the marble floor the only sound she could hear above the deafening thunder of her heart. Afterwards she would try to justify her behaviour by telling herself she'd been disorientated at finding herself in a desert palace, which was only adding to the fantasy-like feel of what was happening. As if the real Tamsyn Wilson was looking down and seeing a breathlessly excited woman who couldn't wait for the powerful Greek tycoon to take her to his bed.

Lit by soft lamps, his suite was just as fancy as hers—only with a much more masculine feel. Strong scarlets and deep golds dominated the high-ceilinged room and on an inlaid desk she noticed a golden pen, studded with diamonds. A collection of horse paintings took up an entire wall and one in particular caught her eye—a black stallion with yellow flowers looped around its glistening neck, as it stood against a sunset backdrop of the stark desert. Xan didn't say anything until the heavy door had closed behind them and as he drew her into the powerful warmth of his body, Tamsyn felt her heart thunder.

'Now,' he said softly, tilting her face upwards. 'Where were we?

For once in her life she had no smart answer. All her usual flippancy drained away from her as Tamsyn stared into the Greek's rugged features and her heart gave a great punch of delight. Yet she didn't have a clue how best to respond to him. Would he be horrified if he knew what a novice she was and should she tell him?

Did it matter?

She swallowed.

Why should it matter—and why *should* she tell

him? She couldn't be the only virgin in the history of the world and there was no shame to it—even though sometimes you were made to feel like a freak just because you'd reached the grand old age of twenty-two without ever having had sex. But then, she'd never responded to a man like this before, because no man had ever made her feel like this. And was it such a crime to want to capitalise on it? To feel like a normal woman for once, instead of someone who was made of ice from the neck down?

She tried to remember what he'd just asked her. Some flirty question about what they had just been doing and that certainly wasn't something she would be forgetting in a hurry. 'You were kissing me,' she reminded him softly.

He gave a slow smile. 'So I was,' he agreed, framing her face between his palms and looking at her for a long moment before lowering his mouth to hers, exploring her lips with a thoroughness which left her reeling.

Against the jewelled bodice of her gown Tamsyn could feel her breasts growing heavy as he reached down to whisper his thumb over her peaking nipple, lazily circling it in a way which made her moan with pleasure. She pressed her lips against his neck, feeling the rapid beat of a pulse there. As his hand began to sweep luxuriously down over her satin-covered belly, she felt another great clench of her sex and she shivered. Did he sense that already she wanted to explode with pleasure? Was that why he moved his head back to survey the rapid rise and fall of her chest.

'I think we need to get on the bed,' he said unevenly. Tamsyn wasn't known for her compliancy and when people 'suggested' something, her natural instinct was to rebel. But she found herself nodding at him like some eager little puppy. 'Okay,' she whispered, tightening her grip around his neck like the clinging tendrils of a vine. 'Let's.'

Xan felt his erection pushing almost violently against his trousers and silently he cursed, because the effect she was having on him was undeniably... *urgent*. She made him feel about fifteen years old instead of thirty-three, and while he was in such a high state of arousal it made more sense to keep movement to a minimum. So why not push her to the floor and do it to her right there, on the silken rug? It would be fast and a little bit dirty but he could rid himself of this fierce hunger which was running through his veins like a fever. His mouth hardened because that might be the perfect solution—a quick coupling to alleviate their mutual frustration and allow them to discreetly go their separate ways soon afterwards?

But something about the way she was responding to him was making such an action seem almost unsavoury. She was holding onto him as trustingly as a tiny kitten—leaving him with little choice other than to carry her across the room in a macho display which wasn't really his style. He was taken aback by how shockingly *primitive* the gesture made him feel as another spear of lust shafted through him.

Bemusement filled him as he set her down beside the brocade-covered divan, because Tamsyn Wilson wasn't turning out to be what he'd expected. In fact, none of this was what he'd expected. She was confounding him with mixed messages. The street-wise minx was behaving in a way which was almost *naïve*.

He'd imagined that someone so sassy and sexy would by now be unzipping him, before taking him boldly in her hand, or her mouth—because that seemed to be the current trend for first time sex. The cynic in him often wondered if this was the moment when women attempted to showcase their sexual skills in as short a time as possible—rather like a job applicant deftly running through their entire resume on a first interview. But not Tamsyn. She seemed more concerned with removing those ostentatious diamond earrings and finding a low table beside the bed on which to safely put them, quickly followed by the glittering diamond choker. And while she was turning round to do that, he moved behind her, lifting the thick curtain of her curls to drift his lips over her neck. He felt her tremble then slump against him and she wondered if she could feel his hardness pressing into her bottom.

'I want you,' he said, very deliberately, as he turned her round to face him.

'D-do you?' she said, her voice barely a whisper.

How did she manage to sound so convincingly *shy*, he wondered? Pulling a couple of clips from her hair, he unzipped her gown so that it slithered to the ground in a pool of glittering silk and net and she was left standing in nothing but her bra and panties. He felt another kick of desire. Her legs were bare and he bent before her to remove one silver shoe, quickly followed by another, but when he stood up again he was taken aback by how tiny she seemed without the towering heels.

Shrugging off his jacket and yanking off his tie, he let them fall to join her discarded dress. 'Unbutton my shirt,' he growled.

Tamsyn's fingers were trembling as she lifted them to Xan's chest, because for all her bravado she'd never seen a man naked and she'd certainly never undressed anyone before. Yet her instinctive fear was banished by that first sweet touch of the skin which sheathed his hard muscle and she heard him groan as the buttons flew open. Now what, she wondered, as she gazed at his bare chest—too daunted to think about attacking the zip of his trousers.

Did he sense her sudden nervousness? Was that why he gave another slow smile and unclipped her front-fastening bra so that her breasts spilled into his waiting palms and suddenly her nerves were all but forgotten? She writhed as his thumbs circled her nipples and her excitement grew as he moved his hand down between her thighs. Pushing aside the damp, stretched panel at her crotch, he found her slick heat, sliding his finger against the engorged bud with practised ease. And this was *heaven*. Her hips were circling of their own accord and she was moaning now and the part of her brain which was urging her to be careful, was abruptly silenced by the most powerful desire she could ever have imagined.

'Xan…' she breathed, looking up to meet the smoky lust which had narrowed his eyes.

'You are just as hot as I thought you'd be,' he declared unevenly.

She should have said something then, but she couldn't even think of the words—let alone form a sentence with them—not when he was laying her down on the bed and pulling off the rest of his clothes with unsteady hands. And then he was naked—his body warm and strong as he lay down beside her. His hungry kiss was fuelling this wild new hunger which was spiralling up inside her and suddenly Tamsyn was on fire. His lips were on her breasts and her belly—tantalising her until she thought she would go out of her mind. And when he guided her hand to his groin, there was no shyness as she encountered the hard ridge of his erection. Instead, she felt nothing but joy as she began to whisper her fingertips against it. But he shook his head as he reached for something on the nightstand and she heard the little tear of foil and realised he must be sheathing himself.

This was it. The moment she'd never thought she'd reach because she had always been unresponsive and afraid. But she wasn't afraid now as he moved over her and spread her legs apart. Not even when she felt that brief burst of pain and momentarily, he stilled. Instinct told her to angle her hips and to propel them forward so that he slid inside her completely—and once her body had grown accustomed to his width—those incredible sensations of pleasure were back. And how. She cried out with it so that he stilled once again and his words came out clipped, like bullets.

'I am hurting you?'

'No. No. Not at all. It's…*oh!* Oh, Xan. It's heaven.'

'Is it now? Then I had just better…. *Do. It. Some. More.*'

With each emphasised word, he thrust deeper and deeper, until her nails were digging into his back. Tamsyn could feel the build-up of something. Something so delicious she didn't believe it could get any better, except that it did. And then better still. It was like being whizzed to the top of a high tower block and being told to jump off, and willingly she did, gasping out his name in an expression of disbelief as she went flying over some sunlight ledge.

As he heard the helpless sound of her cries, Xan knew he couldn't hold back. Not a second longer. And when his orgasm came it left him shaken. His head fell back and it took several breathless minutes before he could distance himself by rolling away from her. Because he needed to do that. He needed to make sense of what had just happened—even though all he could think about was the folly of what he'd just done.

He had seduced the Sheikh's sister-in-law!

And against all the odds, she had been a *virgin*.

He stared down at her, at where her magnificent hair tumbled like fire against the muddled pile of pillows. Her eyes were closed though experience told him she was not asleep, though he suspected she wanted him to think she was. But she was in his room and he wanted answers.

Now.

'That was some...surprise,' he drawled.

She opened her eyes and he steeled himself against their beauty, but somehow they had lost their luminous quality. They looked as flat as pieces of jade as she returned his stare and he could see her dreamy expression being replaced with her more usual look of rebellion.

'What, that the woman you'd clearly slotted into the category of "she'll be up for anything", turned out to be less experienced than you imagined?' she challenged.

He made a growling little sound at the back of his throat. 'Didn't you think it was a big enough deal to tell me I was your first lover?' he demanded. 'Or that it might be the *polite* thing to have done?'

At this, Tamsyn nearly burst out laughing. 'Polite? We haven't exactly been polite to each other up until now, have we?' she retorted. 'At what point *exactly* was I supposed to tell you? You'll forgive me if I don't know the protocol for this kind occasion.'

'Well, neither do I!'

'Are you saying that I'm the first virgin you've ever had sex with?'

'*Neh*… Yes,' he translated.

There was a moment of silence. '*Why*?'

'Why do you think?' he questioned sarcastically. 'If someone your age has waited all this time to have sex, it's usually an indication of her having unrealistic expectations.'

'Such as?'

He shrugged. 'Holding out for a wedding ring is the first thing which springs to mind.'

'You really are the most arrogant man I've ever met.'

'I don't deny it,' he said, unabashed. 'But at least you can't accuse me of being dishonest.'

But wasn't there a part of Tamsyn which wished he had been? A previously unknown side of herself which longed for him to tell her that it had been wonderful and she was wonderful, and from now on she was going to be his girlfriend.

Had she taken *complete* leave of her senses?

She needed to face the facts, like she'd always done. She'd just had sex, that was all. It might not have been the smartest move to chose Xan Constantinides as her first lover but she wasn't going to deny how superb he'd been. And what she was *not* going to do was to regret it. Didn't she have enough regrets already, without adding one more to the list? Couldn't she take pleasure from the most amazing thing which had ever happened to her, without carrying around a whole she-dload of guilt?

She shifted her weight again and the slippery golden sheet slithered away to her breast and suddenly he was saying something in thick and urgent Greek before pulling her hungrily into his arms. Maybe Tamsyn should have been daunted by the newly massive erection she felt pressing against her belly but she wasn't—mainly because she was remembering what had just happened. And she wanted it to happen all over again.

Eagerly she raised her face to search for his kiss, feeling a shiver of excitement rippling uncontrollably through her body as the Greek billionaire reached blindly for a second condom.

CHAPTER FIVE

TAMSYN HAD HEARD plenty about the 'walk of shame' but she'd never experienced it before. The furtive walk from a man's bedroom back to your own, wearing last night's clothes and praying that nobody would notice you. But how on earth was she going to manage that when she was wearing *full evening dress*?

Tamsyn quickly realised it was a naïve and futile hope. Not only did she pass countless servants silently scurrying through the sunlit corridors—she even had the misfortune to encounter a large group of wedding guests who were clearly being given an early-morning guided tour by one of the Sheikh's assistants. It would have been almost comical to see their reaction to her sudden appearance, if it had been happening to anyone other than her.

The guide's voice faded away and everyone's mouths fell open as a barefooted Tamsyn rounded the corner, wearing a now crumpled grey evening dress and dangling her silver high-heeled shoes from one hand, while her other tightly grasped a pair of priceless diamond earrings and a matching choker. The guide seemed to recover himself—maybe he recognised her as the Sheikh's new sister-in-law—because he cleared his throat and gave a strangled kind of smile.

'You are lost, mistress?'

Tamsyn gave a thin smile. Yes, she was lost—but only in the emotional sense of the word, and once again wondered what on earth had possessed her to indulge in a long night of sex with a man she instinctively sensed was dangerous.

You know why. Because you couldn't stop yourself. Because the moment he touched you, you went up in flames.

Ignoring the knowing side glances of the men and the hostile glare of the women in the group, Tamsyn gave a determined shake of her head, making her unbrushed curls fly around her shoulders like angry red corkscrews. 'I'm just on my way back to my room,' she said cheerily. 'It seemed a pity not to get up early and watch the sun rise over the desert.'

They obviously didn't believe a word she was saying, but since she would never see them again after today—who cared?

She made it back to her room at last, tearing off her dress, throwing aside the shoes and carefully putting the jewellery down, before escaping into the sanctuary of the luxurious bathroom. At least the steam of the hot shower and the rich lather of perfumed soap made her feel marginally better, but not for long, because flashback images kept coming back to haunt her. Imagines of a hard, muscular body driving down on hers and warm arms enfolding her and holding her tight. *Just concentrate on what you're supposed to be doing*, she told herself fiercely as she dragged a brush through her unruly curls. She had just slithered into her old denim cut-offs and a clean T-shirt, when there was a rap at the door.

She wasn't going to deny the leap of her heart in response, or the determined pep talk she gave herself as she walked across the palatial suite. She told herself to play it cool. If Xan Constantinides wanted her phone number then she would give it to him, but she wasn't going to act like it was a big deal. She might never have had sex before but over the years she'd listened to how friends and colleagues dealt with the thorny issue of The Morning After. And apparently the most stupid thing a woman could ever do, was to come over all eager.

Composing her face into what she hoped wasn't an over-the-top smile, it faded immediately when she opened the door to discover it wasn't Xan standing there but the newly crowned Queen of Zahristan—her sister Hannah! A sister whose face was filled with anger as she walked in without waiting to be invited, pushing the door shut behind her, before assuming a grim expression of accusation which Tamsyn recognised all too well.

'Would you like to tell me what's going on?' she demanded.

'I could ask the same thing of you!' retorted Tamsyn, reframing the accusation and turning it on its head since attack was always the best form of defence. 'It's the first day of your honeymoon—so what are you doing barging into my bedroom at this time in the morning? Won't your new husband be wondering where you are?'

Hannah bit her lip and Tamsyn was shocked to see the despair which briefly darkened her sister's eyes because she was usually cheerful, no matter what life threw at her. And despite her own predicament, Tamsyn felt her heart plummet as her worst fears began to materialise. Was Hannah's marriage already starting to go off the rails, even though she had only been crowned Queen the previous day? She had warned her sister that it was a mistake to marry such a man as arrogant as Kulal. She'd begged her not to go through with the marriage just because she was pregnant, but Hannah hadn't listened. What if the powerful Sheikh was being cruel to his pregnant wife—what then?

'So where's Kulal, Hannah?' Tamsyn probed, as suspicion continued to stab at her heart like a dagger. 'Doesn't he mind you being here, quizzing me, on the first morning of his honeymoon?'

'I'm not here to talk about my relationship!' declared Hannah, but Tamsyn could hear the sorrow in her voice. 'I'm here to ask whether you spent the night with Xan Constantinides.'

And despite all her bravado, Tamsyn felt a shiver whisper over her skin. Was it hearing someone else say the words out loud which drove home the true nature of what she had done? After years of fiercely guarding her innocence she had let the Greek tycoon lead her back to his suite and take her virginity with barely an arrogant snap of his fingers. A man she barely knew. A man she would probably never see again.

And it had been the most amazing thing which had ever happened to her.

They had spent the night having passionate sex— over and over again. He'd said things to her in Greek she hadn't understood and things to her in English which she had, and which made her blush just remembering them.

'You drive me crazy. Your breasts are small but the most perfect I have ever seen,' he had growled at one point, lifting his head from her nipple, where the lick of his tongue and the graze of his teeth had been enough to have her writhing on the bed in ecstasy. 'And do you want to know what else about you is perfect?'

She remembered thinking how delectable he looked with his cheekbones all flushed and his black hair wild as a lion's mane from where she'd been running her fingers through it. She remembered an instinctive feeling of sexual power flooding through her as she met his hectic cobalt gaze. 'Yes,' she whispered. 'Yes, I do.'

But he had answered with the urgent thrust of his seemingly ever-present erection, and Tamsyn had almost passed with pleasure as he brought her hurtling over the edge of fulfilment, again and again and again.

She must have fallen asleep eventually, because when she opened her eyes it had been to discover herself alone in the rumpled bed with bright sunlight on her face and only a scrawled note occupying the space where Xan had lain. She had picked it up with trembling fingers and read it.

> *Gone riding in the desert. That was the most perfect night.*
> *Thank you.*
> *Xan.*

Tamsyn's heart had sunk for it had read like the farewell it was obviously intended to be. There had been no line of kisses. No phone number or email address, or invitation to have dinner with him back in London.

Well, what had she been expecting—everlasting love?

Of course she hadn't, but even facing up to the folly of her actions didn't make it any easier. She'd done some pretty stupid things in her time, but sleeping with Xan Constantinides must rank right up there with some of the worst decisions she'd ever made. Easy come, easy go—that was probably how he saw it. If you slept with a man without even going out on a formal date, then why would he treat you with respect? Tamsyn swallowed. Was she doomed to follow the path laid down by her own mother, despite her determination to live her life in a very different way?

Now she stared into Hannah's aquamarine eyes which were so unlike her own. She guessed they each carried a legacy from their different fathers—both useless in their different ways—and fleetingly she wondered whether that was why they'd both made such bad choices when choosing men. Except that she hadn't chosen Xan—he had chosen her.

And he had done a runner as soon as possible.

She shrugged her shoulders with a familiar gesture of defiance. 'Yes, I spent the night with Xan Constantinides.'

'But Tamsyn, *why*?'

For the first time Tamsyn felt like smiling as she looked at her sister. Her pale-faced sister with dark shadows under her eyes. 'You're honestly asking me that? You might be a married woman now—but surely you're not completely immune to the charms of a man like Xan Constantinides.'

At the mention of marriage, Hannah flinched. 'No, of course I'm not,' she said quietly. 'And that's precisely why he's the wrong kind of man for you, Tamsyn. He might be obscenely good-looking and have the kind of sex appeal which should carry a public health warning, but he's known for his…his…'

'His *what*?' prompted Tamsyn, though her heart was smashing against her rib cage because she guessed what was coming.

'Let's just say he *enjoys* women! He enjoys them very much.'

'I wasn't expecting him to be celibate!'

Hannah sucked in a long breath, her face growing serious. 'It's more than that. He usually dates actresses. Or models. Or heiresses.'

'Not waitresses on short-term contracts who are always getting fired for insubordination, you mean?' offered Tamsyn drily.

'And you…'

Tamsyn watched as Hannah unconsciously rubbed her enormous gold and ruby wedding band, as if reaffirming to herself that she really *was* married. And once again she wondered why her sister was standing *here* on the first morning of her honeymoon, looking like the very opposite of what a glowing newlywed should be. Why wasn't she romping in bed with her husband? 'I what, Hannah?'

The new Queen chewed on her lip. 'I know you were inexperienced with men, Tamsyn,' she breathed. 'And by associating with someone like Xan, you're operating right out of your league.

'Oh, don't worry,' Tamsyn assured her airily. 'I'm

not anticipating any kind of future with him. I'm not *that* stupid.'

'But what…' Hannah sucked in a deep breath. 'What if you're pregnant?'

Tamsyn knew she didn't have to have this conversation, no matter how close the two sisters had been when they were growing up. But in a way she *did* need to have it, because wouldn't voicing her inner fears help put them into perspective? Like when you had a terrible nightmare and the shadows in the room seemed to symbolise all kinds of terrible things—yet when you put a lamp on you soon saw that the imagined monster was a chair, or a dressing table.

'We used protection,' she said quietly.

Hannah's eyes were very big. 'So did we,' she whispered. 'And look what happened.'

And suddenly Tamsyn was made very aware of how easily a woman could be trapped by her own passion. Hannah had accidently become pregnant by the Sheikh which was why she had married him. Who was to say the same thing wouldn't happen to her? She found herself uttering a small, silent prayer. 'We'll just have to hope it doesn't happen to me,' she said quietly.

'And what if it does?'

'Then I'll deal with it. But I'm not going to project like that. I'm just going to carry on as before.'

'Doing what?'

Tamsyn patted the back pocket of her cut-offs to check she had her cellphone. 'Doing what I always do. Adapting. Moving on.'

Distractedly, Hannah began to pace up and down the room, the silken shimmer of her flowing robes seeming to emphasise the growing differences between them. Stopping in front of one of the tall windows which overlooked the palace gardens, the streaming sunlight had turned her pale blonde hair into liquid gold and Tamsyn thought how scarily royal she looked. 'Kulal says we might be able to find a role for you in the London Embassy.'

'As what? The new attaché?' enquired Tamsyn, deadpan.

'I'm serious, Tamsyn. There are always cleaning jobs available—or we thought you might like to help the chef in the Ambassador's private kitchen.' Hannah gave a somewhat helpless shrug. 'Something like that.'

'Well, thanks but no thanks,' said Tamsyn firmly. 'I don't want to be beholden to your husband and I'd prefer to make my own way in life, just like I've always done.'

At this, Hannah walked forward to place her hand on Tamsyn's arm. 'But if anything *happens*,' she said fervently. 'If you find out you *are* pregnant—then you will come to me for help, won't you, Tamsyn?'

'If I were you, I think I'd be concentrating on your life rather than mine,' said Tamsyn sharply. 'I've never seen you looking so pale. What's the matter, Hannah— have you suddenly discovered there are serpents in paradise?'

Was her remark too close to the bone? Was that why Hannah's face crumpled and she looked as if she was about to cry? Tamsyn felt a sudden pang of guilt as her sister turned towards the arched doorway, but any remorse was quickly cancelled out by the enormity of what her sister had just said to her. Because that was something she hadn't even considered. Her stomach performed a sickly somersault as Hannah left the room and Tamsyn stared unseeingly at one of the priceless silken rugs. What if Hannah's fears were true? What if she *was* pregnant?

She tried to put it—and him—out of her mind, though it wasn't easy on the flight back to England. Especially when the stewardess had answered her studiedly casual query about Xan by informing her that Mr Constantinides had summoned his own jet and left Zahristan earlier that morning.

But the anxious wait to discover if she was carrying his baby was even harder when she was back in London and the whole thing seemed like a dream. Tamsyn tried all kinds of coping mechanisms. Just like she'd promised Hannah, she threw herself into her latest job—working in a steam-filled café in one of the tiny back roads near Covent Garden, which was mainly frequented by taxi drivers. It wasn't the best-paid work she'd ever done and it certainly wasn't the most exciting. She suspected it had been called The Greasy Spoon in an ironic sense, though it certainly lived up to is name since no meal was served unless it was swimming in its own pool of oil. But she wasn't going to waste hours hunting for some rewarding position which was never going to materialise. She needed to be *busy*—doing something other than neurotically ticking off the endlessly long days as she waited for her period. She needed to focus on something other than the fact that her first and only lover had not bothered to seek her out—not even to enquire whether she had arrived home safely.

She hated the way she kept glancing at her phone. Even though she hadn't given him her number, hadn't part of her thought—*hoped*—that the Greek tycoon might have somehow tracked her down? It wasn't outside the realms of possibility that he could have asked the Sheikh, was it? But deep down Tamsyn knew she was clutching at straws and it was never going to happen. For a man to go to the trouble of finding you, he had to like you enough to want to see you again. And you certainly didn't have to *like* a woman in order to have sex with her.

But she wasn't going to beat herself up about it. She hadn't planned on being intimate with Xan, but she hadn't planned to be a virgin for ever either. She had been waiting—not for a wedding band, because marriage was something she simply wasn't interested in. No. She had been waiting for someone to make her feel desire—real, bone-melting desire—even though she'd secretly thought it would never happen. Yet it had. Xan Constantinides might not be a keeper, but she wasn't deluded enough to deny that he'd had a profound effect on her.

So she tried to be practical rather than wistful. She would probably see him again at the naming ceremony of Kulal and Hannah's baby, sometime in the not too distant future. And before that happened, she would need to school herself in the art of pretending not to care. If she worked on it hard enough, she might actually have achieved that blissful state by then. Her heart pounded. And if she *was* pregnant, what then? Then the world would look like a very different place.

But then her period arrived and for some inexplicable reason, she cried and cried. But not for long, because she knew tears were a waste of energy. She just carried on getting up every morning and going to work. It was dark when she started and dark when she finished and although spring was just around the corner, the bitter wind was harsh and unremitting.

And then she had one of those days when everything seemed to go wrong. A customer queried his change, causing the sharp-eyed manageress to watch her like a hawk, which made Tamsyn clumsier than usual. Outside, heavy rain was bashing against the window, making the steamed-up café resemble a sauna, and some inane pop quiz was blaring from the radio, the words incomprehensible above the laddish shouts of conversation. She had just muddled up two egg orders and was anticipating the kind of stern lecture which usually preceded being asked to leave a job, when the doorbell tinged and unusually, the whole place became silent.

Tamsyn looked up as a reverential hush fell over the boisterous customers and she had another of those slow motion moments. Because it was Xan. Xan Constantinides was walking into the crowded café and every single eye in the place was fixed on him.

She wasn't surprised. Not just because his costly clothes proclaimed his billionaire status, it was more the sense that he was a super-being—somehow larger than life and more good-looking than anyone had a right to be. His rain-spattered dark overcoat was made of fine cashmere and she doubted whether any other Greasy Spoon customer had ever worn handmade shoes, or moved with such a powerful sense of purpose.

She hated the instinctive ripple of recognition which shivered through her body. Hated the sudden clench of her nipples beneath the manmade fabric of her uniform. He was walking towards her, those cobalt eyes fixed firmly on hers and Tamsyn was doing her best to look at him with the kind of politely questioning smile she would give to any other customer, even though she wanted to spit venom at him. But the manageress was literally elbowing her out of the way, surreptitiously patting the bright red perm which the steam had turned to frizz, her fifty-year-old face filled with the gushing excitement of a schoolgirl as she stepped forward.

'Can I 'elp you, sir?'

Was Xan clued-up enough to realise the power structure which was being acted out in front of him? Was that why he turned the full wattage of his incredible smile on the manageress? Or maybe that's just what came naturally, thought Tamsyn disgustedly. Maybe he used his remarkable charisma as a means to an end, no matter where he was.

'You certainly can,' said Xan, his honeyed Greek accent sounding almost obscenely erotic. 'I was wondering if I might borrow Tamsyn for a little while?'

The woman's smile instantly turned into a grimace. 'She doesn't finish her shift until seven,' she answered unhelpfully.

And that was when Tamsyn piped up—and to hell with the consequences. She stared at Xan, determined not to be affected by the gleam of his gaze as she tried desperately to forget the last time she'd seen that powerful body. Yet how could she forget all that olive-skinned splendour as he'd held her tightly in his arms? Or discount the temporary sanctuary he'd provided as he rocked in and out of her body all night.

And then he had left her. Had walked away as if she didn't exist. Left her open to pain and self-doubt. Was she going to keep coming back for more?

'You can't *borrow* me,' she snapped. 'I'm not a book you take from the library.'

'Tamsyn! I will not have you speaking to a customer like that!' the manageress cut in, revelling in the opportunity to administer a public telling-off.

'Please.' Xan's intervention was smooth. 'It's no problem. I can see you're very busy here and unable to spare her. I'll come back at seven, if that's okay.'

Tamsyn wanted to scream at them to stop talking about her as if she wasn't in the room, because hadn't that been what all those case-workers used to do when they held those interminable meetings to discover why she kept bunking off school? And she wanted her stupid, betraying body to stop reacting to the Greek. She didn't *want* to look at the sensual curve of his lips and be reminded of how it had felt to have him kiss her. 'I'm busy at seven,' she said.

The cobalt eyes narrowed. 'Really?'

'Really.' It was a lie, but Tamsyn didn't care—because surely a small white lie was preferable to doing or saying something you might later regret. And she didn't owe him *anything*.

'Then when are you free?' he persisted.

'I'm not,' Tamsyn answered. 'There's absolutely nothing I want to say to you, Xan. It's over. You made that perfectly clear. So if you'll excuse me—the kitchen has just rung the bell with another order.'

And with that, she marched over to the aluminium serving hatch to pick up the bacon butty which was already growing cold.

CHAPTER SIX

STANDING HUDDLED IN a shop doorway opposite the now dark café, Xan waited for Tamsyn to emerge but it was already ten after seven and still she hadn't shown.

The shop doorway remained defiantly closed and he wondered if perhaps she'd slipped away unseen from the back of the building. He wondered what lengths she would go to in order to avoid him.

He'd imagined…

What?

That she would be deliriously happy to see him, despite him having failed to contact her after their passionate night at the palace? Despite the fact that he'd hired a private jet to get away from Zahristan as quickly as possible the next morning, after leaving her only the briefest of notes, and then had disappeared for the best part of three months?

Yes. That's exactly what he'd imagined because it had happened so often before. Women took whatever crumbs he was prepared to offer them. They were grateful for anything they got and even when they complained it wasn't enough, they still came back for more. He'd meant it when he'd told Tamsyn he wasn't deliberately cruel—despite the tearful accusations sometimes hurled at him in the past. He was just genuinely detached. He'd learnt detachment from the moment he'd left the womb—that was one of the inevitable legacies of having a mother who was so bogged down with self-pity that she barely deigned to notice her child. He never raised hopes unnecessarily, or proceeded with a relationship if the odds were stacked against it. And breaking the heart of his friend's new sister-in-law was never going to be on the cards.

He shouldn't have bedded her in the first place which was why he hadn't hung around the day after the wedding. Why he'd deliberately avoided seeing her and instead gone riding with the Sheikh, who had seemed to have enough problems of his own without Xan adding to them.

He had waited for the dust to settle and his libido to cool and for a short period of time to elapse. Then he had flown out to his beautiful waterfront estate in Argolida on the Peloponnese Peninsula, to begin the future which had been mapped out for him so long ago. There had been several meetings with the young woman he'd once agreed to marry and he had gone through the motions of what was expected of him. It should have been simple, but it had turned out to be anything but. He had stumbled at the first hurdle—he who never stumbled. Failure wasn't a word which featured in his vocabulary and for weeks he had attempted to cajole then scold himself into a state of acceptance—an acceptance which had stubbornly refused to materialise. He'd witnessed Sofia's bewilderment as he struggled to find the right things to say. He had pictured his father's distress when he explained that the marriage was a no-go he should never have agreed to. For the first time in his life he hadn't known which way to turn. If he married Sofia he could not make her happy, but if he walked away—what then? Her pride would be wounded and his family's reputation tarnished.

It had been at the beginning of a conference call with the Sheikh last week that a solution had suddenly occurred to Xan. It wasn't perfect—but then, what in life could be regarded as perfect? But it would suffice. It would have to. And surely it was better than the alternative.

His throat dried as the café door swung open and Tamsyn stepped out into the rainy night and suddenly every thought drained from his mind. Yet why should his heart race like a train when she was dressed so unbecomingly? In her faded jeans and ugly padded jacket, she shouldn't have merited a second glance. But something seemed to happen to his vision whenever Tamsyn Wilson was around and he found himself unable to tear his eyes away from her. It had happened the first time he'd laid eyes on her but it was a whole lot worse now. Was it because, despite her sassiness and outspokenness, she had been an innocent virgin— thus defying all his jaded expectations? He kept replaying that moment when he'd first penetrated her sweet tightness and she'd made that choking little cry, her mouth open and moist as it had sucked helplessly against his shoulder.

Her hair was tied back, her ponytail flowing behind her like a curly red banner, but her face was pale. So pale. From here you couldn't see the freckles which spattered her skin like gold. He found himself remembering the ones which reposed in the soft flesh of her inner thighs. How he had whispered his tongue over them…tantalising and teasing her, before bringing her to yet another jerking orgasm, which had left her shuddering against his mouth.

He began to walk towards her, aided by the red gleam of the traffic lights which was reflecting off the wet road like spilled blood. And then she saw him, her eyes first widening and then narrowing as she put her head down and increased her speed and Xan felt a flicker of excitement as he realised she was trying to get away from him, just like she'd done at the palace. Did she really think she would outpace him? Didn't she realise he'd seen the yearning look of hunger in her eyes when he'd walked into that steamy café, and it had echoed the hunger in him?

'Tamsyn!'

'Can't you take a hint?' she shouted back over her shoulder. 'Just go *away,* Xan!'

She didn't slow down as he followed her along the wet pavement but he caught her up easily enough, his long strides easily outperforming her small, rapid steps. 'We need to talk,' he said, as he caught up with her.

She stopped then. Lifted up her chin to glare at him and the raindrops glistened like diamonds on her freckled skin as she stood beneath the golden flare of the streetlamp.

'But that's where you're wrong!' she contradicted fervently. 'We don't *need* to do anything. Why would we when there's nothing between us? Didn't you make it plain that's what you wanted when you slipped out of bed that morning, taking great care not to wake me?'

'Why?' he parried softly. 'Did you want there to be something between us?'

'In your dreams!' she declared. 'Even if I did want to get involved with a man—which I don't—you're the last person on the planet I'd ever choose! I already told you that.'

A low sigh of relief escaped from his lips and some of the tension left him. 'That's probably the best news I've heard all week,' he said. 'And yet another reason why we need to have a conversation.'

Tamsyn steeled herself against the sexy dip in his voice, brushing the rain away from her cheeks with an impatient fist. 'You just don't get it, do you?' she hissed. 'I'm not interested in what you've got to say, Xan. I've just been sacked and it's all your fault.'

His eyebrows shot up. '*My* fault?'

'Yes! If you hadn't come into the cafe—swaggering around the place as if you owned it and demanding I take a break I wasn't entitled to—then I'd still have a job. Your attitude made me so angry so that I answered you back, giving that witch of a manageress the ideal opportunity to tell me not to bother coming back tomorrow.'

'So that's the only reason you were fired?' he questioned slowly.

Tamsyn told herself she didn't have to answer. That she owed him nothing—and certainly not an explanation. Yet it was difficult to withstand the perceptive gleam in his eyes or not to be affected by the sudden understanding that since Hannah had gone away to live in the desert, she really *was* on her own. That once again she was jobless, with nobody to turn to—with outstanding rent to pay on her overpriced bedsit. Giving a suddenly deflated sigh, she shrugged, all the energy needed to maintain the fiction of her life suddenly draining away. 'Not the only reason, no,' she agreed reluctantly. 'I guess I'm fundamentally unsuited to being a waitress.'

Beneath the streetlight, his eyes gleamed. 'All the more reason for you to have dinner with me, since I have a proposition to put to you which you might find interesting.'

The suggestion was so unexpected that Tamsyn blinked. 'What sort of proposition?'

Tiny droplets of rain flew like diamonds from the tangle of his ebony hair as he shook his head. 'This isn't a conversation to have in the rain. Let's find a restaurant where we can talk.'

Her stomach chose that moment to make an angry little rumble and Tamsyn realised she hadn't eaten since breakfast. She told herself it was hunger which made her consider his suggestion—it definitely wasn't because she was reluctant to see him walk out of her life for a second time. But then she looked at her damp jeans and realised what a mess she looked. 'I can't possibly go out looking like this.'

'You could go home first and get changed.' He gave a small inclination of his head. 'I have a car here.'

Tamsyn stiffened as a black limousine began to drive slowly towards them. Was he out of his mind? Did he really think she'd let someone like him within a mile of her scrubby little bedsit? She could just imagine the shock on his over-privileged face if he caught sight of the damp walls and the electric kettle which was covered in lime-scale. 'I live miles away.'

'Then let's just go to the Granchester.'

Tamsyn nearly choked as he casually mentioned the exclusive hotel where her sister used to work before being fired for sleeping with one of the guests. 'The Granchester is just about the most expensive hotel in London,' she objected. 'We'll never be able to get a table at this short notice, and even if we could there's no way I could go somewhere like that for dinner, wearing this.'

'Oh, we'll a get a table,' he said smoothly, as the limousine drew up beside them. 'And my cousin's wife Emma is staying there at the moment. You look about the same size as her. She'll lend you something to wear.'

Tamsyn shook her head. 'Don't be so ridiculous. I can't possibly borrow a dress from a complete stranger!'

'Of course you can.' He spoke with the confidence of someone unused to being thwarted, as he opened the door of the car and gently pushed her inside. 'Don't worry. I'll fix it.'

Afterwards Tamsyn would put her uncharacteristic compliance down to his distracting presence, or maybe it was just his sheer *certainty*. She'd never experienced the sensation of a man taking control of a situation in such an unflappable way. She wasn't used to someone offering to *fix* things. She was used to drama and chaos. She wondered if there was some biological chink in her armour which made her yield to his superior strength, or whether she'd just had the stuffing knocked out of her by the loss of yet another job? Either way, she found herself climbing into the back of the taxi with Xan sliding next to her as they began to drive at speed through the rain, towards the Granchester.

The rain-blurred lights of the city passed in a streak while Xan made a phone call. She heard him say her name as he began speaking in rapid Greek, before laughing at something the person on the end of the line must have said. And it was the laugh which made Tamsyn's heart clench with unexpected wistfulness. Imagine living the kind of life where you could just jump into the back of a limousine without worrying about the cost, and laugh so uninhibitedly as you chatted on the phone—as if you didn't have a care in the world.

Like a glittering citadel, the Granchester Hotel rose up before them and as the car slid to a halt, a doorman sprang forward to greet Xan like an old friend. The flower-filled foyer was busy as expensively dressed guests milled around, looking as if they had somewhere important to go. A woman was walking purposefully towards them, one of the most beautiful women Tamsyn had ever seen. Slim and smiling, her hair was as pale as moonlight and she was wearing a short blue dress which hugged her hips and a tiny cardigan just a shade darker.

'Xan!' she said fondly, rising up on the toes of her ballet pumps to kiss the Greek tycoon on both cheeks, before turning to Tamsyn with a wide smile. 'And you must be Tamsyn,' she said. 'I'm Emma and I'm married to Xan's cousin. I gather you need something to wear for dinner tonight and time is tight—so why don't you come with me and I can sort you something out?'

It was weird—maybe because Emma was so polite and so...*gracious*—that Tamsyn didn't find herself frozen by her usual air of suspicion. Instead, she smiled back and the three of them walked over to an elevator which nobody else seemed to be using. And of course, the presence of Emma in the enclosed space meant that Tamsyn's conversation with Xan was temporarily interrupted, although she couldn't help but be acutely aware of his presence and the mocking light in his eyes. What on earth have I got myself into? she wondered as the elevator slid to a silent halt and they stepped directly into an enormous room whose wall to ceiling windows gave a stunning view over the glittering skyscrapers of London.

'Xan, why don't you help yourself to a drink?' Emma gave another soft smile. 'Tamsyn, come with me.'

In a dream-like state, Tamsyn followed the elegant blonde down a long corridor and into a dressing room which led off from an huge bedroom. Maybe if she hadn't just lost her job for the umpteenth time and maybe if the image of her tiny bedsit hadn't just flashed into her mind, then she might have told Emma she'd changed her mind, thanked her for her kind offer and just left. Xan might be keen to put some mysterious 'proposition' to her, but despite what she suspected was his tendency to always get his own way—she doubted whether he would actually try to keep her here by force.

But she didn't do any of those things. Perhaps it was the blonde's serene presence or just the fact that Tamsyn was tired. Bone tired. As if she could sleep for a hundred years and then maybe a hundred more. So she nodded politely as Emma ran her perfectly manicured fingernails—a deep shade of blue which matched her cardigan—along a line of colour-co-ordinated clothes hanging in the biggest closet Tamsyn had ever seen.

'I'm not going to stand over you and influence your choice,' she told Tamsyn softly. 'Just wear whatever takes your fancy—and that includes shoes, if they fit. I'll go and entertain your man and see you back in the sitting room.'

Mutely, Tamsyn nodded. She wanted to tell Emma that Xan wasn't her anything but surely that was an over-complicating factor and things were complicated enough already. Her heart was racing as she quickly washed in the en-suite bathroom before slithering into a long-sleeved dress in green cashmere which she cinched in at the waist with a belt. Her tiny feet swam like boats in tall Emma's sleek footwear so she packed the toes of some green suede shoes with wads of tissue paper. Liberating her curls from their elastic band, she raked a comb through them in a vain attempt to tame them and, tucking her own damp clothes under her arm, walked back towards the sitting room.

She was surprised to hear Emma speaking in Greek to Xan, but the conversation died away as she walked into the massive room. She couldn't deny the inordinate amount of pleasure she took from the look of disbelief on Xan's face as slowly he looked her up and down. It reminded her that she really *could* scrub up well—even if she had to rely on the charity of other people in order to do so.

The tycoon was rising to his feet, dominating the room with his powerful presence, a faint smile curving his lips. 'I've told Emma we have a table booked downstairs.'

It seemed almost rude to just *use* the kind blonde's

apartment like some kind of upmarket changing room, but Emma was also getting to her feet, giving Tamsyn another genuine smile which made her feel momentarily disconcerted.

'And Zac is just flying in from Zurich,' she said, her cheeks growing pink with pleasure. 'Where it appears that my husband has bought yet another hotel.'

It was only then that Tamsyn made the connection and she wondered how she could have been so dense. Emma was married to Zac Constantinides—the billionaire owner of the Granchester group of luxury hotels and Zac was Xan's *cousin*? Why hadn't Hannah reminded her of that? As the lift zoomed them back down to the hotel foyer, she wondered why she hadn't made the link herself, when it wasn't exactly the most common surname in the world. Probably because her mind and her body had been so full of new and conflicting emotions. And they still were. Surreptitiously, she touched her tongue to lips which were as dry as washing hung out in the sun, achingly aware that she was far from immune to the statuesque man who walked beside her.

They were shown into Garden Room, which overlooked an outdoor space which was surprisingly big, given its central London location. A discreet notice on the wall informed customers that the gardens had recently won a top horticultural award and although it was dark outside, cleverly placed lighting illuminated the tall shrubs and rare trees. As the maître d' showed them to what was obviously the best table—tucked away in a corner but with a birds-eye view of the floodlit gardens—Tamsyn became aware of people watching them. Or rather, they were watching Xan.

Did he realise that, or was his sense of self-worth so strong that he didn't notice?

'So why have you brought me here?' she questioned as she sat down to face a gleam of silver and crystal, tightening her hands as she laid them down on the snowy linen tablecloth. 'And more importantly, why have I *let* you?'

He paused for a moment while the waiter handed them menus, a wry smile touching the edges of his lips. 'Because we have been lovers and because you're curious.'

She gave a defiant tilt of her chin. 'I don't usually let people move me around like I'm a chip on the gaming table.'

'I get that. Just as I don't usually rush in and mastermind a transformation scene for my dinner dates,' he added drily, flicking her a cool cobalt gaze. 'You look absolutely sensational in that dress, by the way.'

Stupidly, the compliment made her want to squirm with pleasure until Tamsyn reminded herself that she still didn't know why she was here. But he was right. She *was* curious.

'So what do you want to talk about?'

'Why don't we choose what we want to eat first, otherwise the waiter will keep hovering over us.' He glanced at the menu before fixing her with his dark blue gaze. 'Would you like me to order for you?'

Tamsyn glared. Did he think she was so poor and humble that she'd couldn't interpret the French menu? Didn't he realise she'd worked in more fancy restaurants than he'd probably had hot dinners? She was sorely tempted to tell him she'd changed her mind, when she spotted something being lit with blue flames on a nearby table. Something delicious enough to make her mouth water and once again she was reminded that it was ages since she'd eaten.

'I'll have the lobster thermidor and the green salad with vinaigrette on the side,' she said carelessly. 'And no wine—just sparkling water.'

She enjoyed his faint look of surprise as he slapped his own menu shut and handed it to the waiter. 'I'll have the same,' he said, leaning back in his chair to study her.

'So,' she said, when he appeared in no hurry to break the silence. 'I'm still waiting for some sort of explanation. I mean, you've been content to ignore me for weeks and then you just turn up out of the blue and bring me here with the offer of some mystery proposition. What is it, Xan? Do you happen to own a café with an opening for a waitress who urgently needs a job?'

Xan realised that he was going to have to exercise great care in his choice of words because Tamsyn Wilson was both volatile and unpredictable. In a way she was the worst possible candidate for what he had in mind, but ironically it was her very unsuitability which made her the ideal candidate.

'You're in a bit of a fix right now aren't you, Tamsyn?' he questioned softly.

Her emerald eyes narrowed suspiciously. 'How do you know that?'

He shrugged. 'Call it intuition or call it observation. You seem to switch jobs quite frequently and being fired doesn't seem to freak you out as much as it would some people.' His gaze stayed fixed on her face. 'And I noticed you had a hole in your coat.'

She blushed and seemed to hesitate. As if wondering whether or not to brazen things out and keep pretending that, apart from urgently needing a job—everything else was okay. But the strain around her eyes told him that her plight was chronic and maybe she realised that, because some of her defiance seemed to ebb away as she lifted her shoulders in a shrug which didn't quite come off.

'I've known better times,' she admitted.

'But your sister has just married one of the wealthiest men in the world,' he probed. 'Surely she can come to your rescue if you're in need of money.'

For the first time he saw emotion on her face. Real emotion. Was it pride or distress which made her lips tremble like that? 'I'm not going to ask Hannah for help,' she said fiercely. 'She's helped me too often in the past and it's about time I stood on my own two feet.'

Xan nodded, realising that her misplaced pride was playing right into his hands. 'Then I think I can help you,' he said quietly. 'Or rather, I think we can help each other.'

She had recovered from her brief spell of vulnerability and that familiar challenge was back in her eyes. 'Me, help the powerful Xan Constantinides? Gosh. I can't imagine how I would do that.'

Xan paused for a moment because even though they meant nothing, the words he was about to say still had the power to make him tense. He'd had a blueprint for his life and up until now it had all gone according to plan, for he had micro-managed and controlled every part of it. It was how he had won a straight scholarship to Harvard from a humble village school and made a fortune in the property market, soon after graduating. He'd thought of matrimony to Sofia as just another stage in his game plan, but suddenly all that had changed. Suddenly he could understand why they called it wed*lock*. His eyes didn't leave Tamsyn's face.

'By marrying me,' he said.

CHAPTER SEVEN

XAN HAD NEVER seen anyone look so startled. Across the restaurant table, he watched Tamsyn's lips open and the pink tip of her tongue reminded him of the erotic pathways it had traced over his sweat-sheened skin. He shifted his weight a little and swallowed, because Tamsyn Wilson had given him more orgasms in a few short hours than any other woman—so many he'd lost count, and a man never forgot something like that.

The hardness in his groin increased, because didn't his current dilemma provide him with the perfect opportunity to feast on her delectable body once more? He hadn't pursued the affair not just because she was Kulal's new sister-in-law but because she had an inner wildness which made him uneasy—a wildness he had responded to in a way he didn't quite trust. Because something about her fire and her spirit had made him ignore his instinct to take her to bed in the first place. And ignoring his instincts had made him feel as if control was slipping away from him, which he didn't like. He didn't like it at all.

'Did you really just ask me to marry you?' she was saying, her green eyes unnaturally bright in the flicker of the candlelight.

'You want me to repeat it for you?' he drawled.

He was curious to see what her reaction would be, because that would colour his future behaviour towards her. If she looked as if he was about to present her with the moon on a platter and make her every dream come true, then he would have to be wary. But if, as he suspected—she cared as little for him as he did for her—there was no reason why they couldn't both enjoy what he had in mind.

But there was no sign of longing or triumph on her freckled face. Her green eyes were as suspicious as they'd been before. And Xan couldn't deny a brief kick of incredulity, for he was used to women making no secret of their adoration for him.

'Is this some kind of bad joke?' she was demanding. 'Have you had a bet with someone to see how much of a sucker I can be?'

He shook his head. 'I have often been described as difficult, but I am never knowingly cruel.'

There was a trace of uncertainty in her demeanour now. He could see her computing his words and failing to make sense of them.

She waited until the waiter had deposited their food in front of them before raising her eyebrows. 'So, why? I mean, why do you want to marry *me*? Did it take you all this time to realise that you can't possibly live without me and the only way to guarantee having me for the rest of your life is to slip a wedding ring on my finger?'

He stiffened before detecting sarcasm. 'Hardly,' he said.

She picked up her fork and hungrily began to eat. 'So why?'

Xan sucked in a long breath. Explanations he found

difficult. Almost as difficult as intimacy. It was in his nature to keep his thoughts and feelings to himself— or maybe that was just the way he'd been raised. His mother had been indifferent towards him and his father had been too busy trying to claw back his land and his heritage, to have any time for his only son. Either way, Xan had never let anyone close enough to worry about whether or not he trusted them. Yet to some extent he was going to *have* to trust Tamsyn Wilson if she agreed to his plan. And wouldn't that give her power over him? He swallowed, recognising that if he didn't want her abusing that power, he was going to have to reward her very handsomely.

'How much do you know about me?' he demanded.

She dabbed at her lips but the large linen napkin failed to hide her smile. 'You think I was so obsessed after our night in Zahristan that I hunted around to find out everything I could?'

'I don't know.' He sent her a look of challenge. 'Did you?'

'Funnily enough, no. I've had enough experience of lost causes to know when to quit. I certainly didn't waste any time mooning over someone who couldn't wait to get away from me. What do I know about you? Let me see.' She began to tap each finger, as if counting off the facts. 'Basically, you're loaded—my friend Ellie told me you were born mega-rich, though I think I could have worked that out for myself judging by your fancy suits and your swagger. My sister mentioned you were a hugely successful business-man—oh, and you're arrogant. I didn't need anyone to tell me that since that's a quality you seem to have in abundance.'

An unexpected smile touched the edges of Xan's lips. Clearly he wasn't going to have to worry about Tamsyn Wilson putting him on a pedestal!

'Anything else?' he questioned sardonically.

She shrugged. 'You don't seem as if you like me very much and yet now you're asking me to marry you?' She shook her red curls and scooped up another forkful of lobster. 'Forgive me if I sound confused—it's because I am.'

Discreetly, Xan gestured to the Sommelier, who returned moments later bearing a dusty bottle. A dark red liquid was dispensed into his glass and when Tamsyn shook her head in reply to the silent question in his eyes, he took a sip of the wine before continuing.

'There are only two things you need to know about me, Tamsyn,' he said. 'The first is that I believe there is no problem on this earth you can't buy your way out of, and the second is that there is a woman in Greece to whom I have been unofficially betrothed for many years.' He paused. 'Except I've realised that I cannot go through with it. I cannot marry her.'

He saw her eyes darken in distress. Saw the brief stabbing of her teeth into her lower lip before she displayed her more habitual air of nonchalance. 'Then don't. Just tell her. Dump her as comprehensively as you dumped me. She might be a bit upset but I should think one day she'll be grateful she isn't stuck with a misogynist like you for a lifetime. What's the problem, Xan? Has she found out you were sleeping with me—and maybe others—behind her back? Has she gone on the warpath in the way that only a jealous woman can?'

Angrily, Xan slammed his glass down on the table.

'Just for the record, I haven't had sex with anyone since the night I spent with you and I certainly haven't had sex with Sofia,' he growled. 'It's not that kind of relationship.'

At this, she put her fork down and the look she gave him was cynical. 'Let me guess,' she said tiredly. 'You play around and have your fun with women like me, is that right? And in the meantime there's a pure young virgin back home in Greece, just waiting for you? The age-old double standard of which so many men are guilty?'

Once again her perception startled him and she must have read the confirmation in his face because he could see her pushing her chair back as if preparing to walk out.

'You're disgusting!' she flared.

'Don't go,' he said urgently as he leant across the table towards her. 'Hear me out first. Please, Tamsyn.'

His words seemed to startle her but not nearly as much as they startled him because making pleas wasn't something he did very often. Had he thought she would be instantly malleable? So impressed by this introduction to a very different and glamorous kind of world, that she would leap at whatever he asked of her? Yes, he probably had thought exactly that. His lips flattened. How wrong he had been.

'What's there to hear?' she demanded.

'You said I was born wealthy but that certainly wasn't the case.'

'You mean you were born poor?' she questioned disbelievingly.

'Not poor but something in between. What is it they say? Asset rich, cash poor.' He met the question in her eyes and shrugged. 'My father inherited an island, a very beautiful island, called Prassakri. He was born there. Grew up there. Generations of his family lived and died there.' His voice tailed off as he recalled the story of how fortunes could wax, then wane without warning. 'Once many people inhabited that place, with enough work for all but gradually the work dried up and the young men began to leave, my father among them. Fortunately he had enough money to buy agricultural land on the mainland in Thessaly and for a while he was successful. But then came the drought, the worst drought the region had ever seen...'

His paused for a moment and she sat forward, genuine interest lighting up her freckled face. 'Go on,' she urged.

He grimaced. 'My father lost everything. And more. What the drought and resultant fires didn't take, bad investments soon took care of the rest. From being affluent, suddenly there wasn't enough food on the table. My mother took it badly.'

'How badly?' she questioned, her eyes narrowing.

'Badly enough.' He shut down her question sharply. Because he'd never talked about this with anyone. There hadn't really been the need to resurrect the pain and the discontent. Until now. 'The atmosphere of blame and recrimination in the house was unbearable,' he remembered suddenly, as he recalled walking into the house and seeing his mother's cold face and icy demeanour. 'My father was forced to sell the island to a neighbour and although it broke his heart to do so, he vowed that one day he would buy it back, because the bones of his ancestors are buried on that island and that means a great deal to a Greek.'

He took another mouthful of wine. 'Soon after that, land prices began rocketing and the purchase of Greek islands became beyond of the reach of most people. I could see my father's increasing powerlessness as he sensed the opportunity to buy back Prassakri slipping away from him. But his neighbour had a daughter—an only daughter—who just happened to be very beautiful. And I had just won a scholarship to an American college. It was a pretty big deal at the time and I was seen as someone who would one day make good. And that was when the neighbour made my father the offer.'

'What offer?' she breathed, her green eyes huge, her expression rapt.

'That if I were to marry Sofia, then he would allow my father to buy back the island at the original price.'

'And you agreed?' she breathed.

The facts when recounted now sounded like an extreme reaction but Xan recalled vividly that the offer had made perfect sense at the time. Hadn't he agreed in an attempt to bring about some sort of peace to his damaged family? To stop his mother haranguing his father with her bitter lament? *I didn't marry you in order to end up a pauper.*

'I was nineteen,' he said harshly. 'And it didn't seem real at the time. Sofia was a sweet young girl who would make any man a good wife, and if it meant the end to my father's heartache, then why wouldn't I agree? With one stroke I could restore the pride which was so important to him and maybe stop my mother from withdrawing more and more.'

'Yes, I know—but even so.' Sitting back in her chair with her hair looking like living flame in the candlelight, she threw him a perplexed look. 'It seems very extreme.'

'To be honest, I thought that Sofia would back out of the offer before I did,' he said, he said with a shrug. 'That she would fall in love and want to marry someone else.'

'But that didn't happen?'

'No.' He shook his head. 'It didn't happen. I tried to convince myself that arranged marriages work in many countries. That we share a common language and upbringing. And as time went on I found it a useful deterrent to the ambitions of other women, knowing I had an arranged marriage bubbling quietly away in the background and therefore was not in a position to offer them anything.'

'But you're a modern Greek! This sounds positively archaic.'

'I am not so modern as I might appear on the surface, Tamsyn.' His voice grew silky as he corrected her. 'At heart I have many values which some might consider old-fashioned.'

At this she screwed up her face, but not before he had seen the brief shiver rippling over her skin. Was she remembering how it had been between them in bed that night? When he'd experienced an almost *primitive* pleasure as he had broken through the tight barrier of her hymen and given an exultant shout of joy? No, he had been anything but modern that night.

'And what about love?' she challenged. 'Isn't that supposed to lie at the foundation of every marriage?'

His laugh was bitter but at least now he was on familiar territory. 'Not for me, Tamsyn. Only fools buy into romantic love.'

For the first time since they'd started this extraordinary conversation Tamsyn experienced a moment of real connection as she recognised a sentiment which was all too familiar. She thought about her feckless mother and the way she'd hocked up with all those different men. Hadn't that been why she and Hannah had been left abandoned and taken in by a pair of dysfunctional foster parents—because their mother had fallen *in love* for the umpteenth time? 'Well, that's one thing we do have in common,' she said. 'Since I feel exactly the same.'

He gave a cynical laugh. 'You actually say that like you mean it.'

'Why, do people normally say things just to please you?''

'Something like that,' he agreed.

Tamsyn wondered what it must be like if everyone was tiptoeing around you all the time. Was that what made him so sure of himself? 'So what's the problem?' she questioned. 'It sounds like the perfect solution. You've played the field and now you're settling down. A practical union between two people who know exactly where the boundaries lie.'

'And that's exactly what I thought—until the theory became reality and I realised there was no way I could marry Sofia.' He met the question in her green eyes. ' Oh, she's still a nice enough woman, but she is not my type Most of all, I do not desire her.' His voice hardened. 'And there can be no marriage without desire.' There was a long pause. 'Which is where you come in,' he added, breaking into her unsettled contemplation.

She narrowed her eyes. 'How?'

'I don't want to hurt Sofia or tarnish her reputation by telling her I don't want her. If I do that there's no way her father will sell back the island, even if I offer him double what it's worth by today's values.' Cobalt eyes bored into her. 'But an acceptable way of breaking off the engagement is to explain that I've fallen in love with someone else and am planning to marry her instead. Which will allow Sofia the chance to walk away with her pride intact.'

'You mean a fake marriage?' Tamsyn frowned. 'Like fake news?'

'A temporary marriage,' he amended drily. 'With a very generous divorce settlement at the end of it. Sofia gets a dignified let-out clause. I get to buy the island and you end up with a hefty pay-out. This could make you a very wealthy woman, Tamsyn. You could have the kind of lifestyle most people only dream of.'

Tamsyn stared at him, trying not to be swayed by the thought of all that money—but for someone who'd always lived hand-to-mouth, that was easier said than done. She thought about not having to watch every single penny. About being able to buy clothes which didn't come from the local market, or thrift store. She thought about having food in the fridge which wasn't past its sell-by date. Being able to take buses instead of walking all the time. Yes, it was tempting—but not tempting enough. Didn't Xan's arrogant certainty that there was no problem money couldn't solve make her want to reject his offer? Because she wasn't some *commodity*. She shook her curls. 'Go and ask someone else,' she said coldly. 'There must be loads more suitable candidates who would happily masquerade as your wife.'

'Oh, there are,' he agreed benignly. 'But that's the whole point. You are so eminently *unsuitable* that everyone will believe it's true love.'

His words hurt. Of course they did. Tamsyn might have always thought of herself as someone who didn't conform. Who swam against the tide. But considering yourself a bit of a rebel was very different to the man who'd been your first lover, saying you were the most unsuitable person he could think of to marry. Her heart clenched with pain and this time she really *did* want to get up from that pristine white table. In a parallel universe—she might have upended it, letting the crystal and the silver cutlery cascade to the floor in a satisfying cacophony of sound. But she'd tried that kind of approach with him once before and all it had done was made her look stupid.

And something was keeping her rooted to her seat. She tried telling herself she should wait to see how much he was offering in return for accepting his extraordinary proposal, but deep down Tamsyn knew it was more than that. He was right. She *was* curious.

'So why didn't you fancy her?' she questioned, like someone determined to rub salt into an already raw wound. As if by hurting herself, it meant nobody else would be able to. 'If she's so beautiful?''

Xan stared at his lobster which had already congealed on his plate. There was no need to explain that somehow, Tamsyn Wilson made every other woman look almost *tame* in comparison. That he hadn't been able to shift the stubborn memory of how her skin had tasted or how it had felt to have her legs wrapped around his thrusting hips. Why flatter her with the knowledge that she was the fire which made every other woman seem like a mere flicker? He swallowed. That kind of information was irrelevant.

'Chemistry is intangible,' he said roughly. 'It's not like a shopping list you just tick off as you go along.'

For the first time during the entire conversation, she smiled. 'You do a lot of shopping do you Xan?' she questioned. 'Somehow I can't really imagine you pushing a trolley round the supermarket,. I've certainly never see anyone like you when I'm stacking the shelves.'

Xan was unable to stop the brief curving of his lips in response. 'I buy cars and planes and works of art. The purchase of food I leave to my housekeeper. But you're trying to change the subject, Tamsyn. Is that because you find my suggestion unpalatable?' he said softly.

Tamsyn shrugged. She wasn't sure *how* she felt. About anything. Something told her to walk away while she still could, but she couldn't deny that the delicious food had lulled her into a state of sluggishness. And wasn't Xan's powerful presence only adding to her languor? Wasn't she stupidly reluctant to turn her back and never see him again? 'It's a crazy idea,' she said weakly.

He leaned forward as if sensing a window of opportunity and suddenly she could see why he was such a successful businessman.

'Imagine no longer having to work unless you wanted to. You could go back to school—you are an intelligent woman,' he said, his Greek accent dipping into a sultry caress. 'Imagine being able to live somewhere which isn't a...

Tamsyn's shoulders stiffened as tactfully, his words faded away. 'Isn't a *what*?'

'It doesn't matter,' he said.

Somehow his careful diplomacy was more insulting than if he'd come right out and told her she lived in a slum. 'Of course it does! It matters to me. How the hell do you know where I live anyway?'

He gave her an odd kind of look. 'I had you checked out, of course.'

'You had me checked out,' she repeated slowly. 'By who?'

'There are people on my payroll who can find out almost anything. How else do you think I knew where you worked, Tamsyn?'

'I just assumed... I thought you might have asked the Sheikh.'

'No.' He shook his dark head. 'Kulal and Hannah know nothing about this.'

It was the mention of her sister's name which startled Tamsyn out of her lazy stupor. She had been about to tell Xan exactly what he could do with his offer—without letting him know how much he'd managed to hurt her. She would have told him that she mightn't have a job right now, but she would find one soon enough. She always did. Because one of the advantages of casual labour meant there were always vacancies for women like her. Women who had slipped through the net at school and at home. Who'd never had the comfort of regular meals or someone gently nagging at them to do their homework. She would get by because although she might not have any formal qualifications to her name, she was a graduate from the School of Survival. You didn't sleep in a room with winter frost inside the windows listening to sounds of arguments bouncing off the thin walls next door, without developing a tough exterior.

But what about Hannah? Her sister was in an entirely different situation. She might now be the wife of the world's richest men but that didn't necessarily mean she was safe. When she'd been in Zahristan for the wedding, Tamsyn had sensed all was not well in the new marriage. How could it be—when it had taken place between a powerful sheikh and someone as humble as Hannah? They had married because Hannah had been pregnant with the Sheikh's baby—but what if Kulal had only married her sister to get some kind of legal hold over his offspring? The Sheikh had all the power now that he had married her, didn't he? While Hannah had none. Not really. She might be the new Queen of a powerful desert region but she couldn't even speak the language of her adopted home.

Tamsyn folded up her napkin and placed it neatly on the table beside her empty plate. What if she agreed to Xan's crazy proposal, but on *her* terms? What if she demanded a whole load of money—more even than he'd probably contemplated giving her? Enough to bail out her sister, should the need ever arise. Wouldn't it be beyond fabulous to have enough cash to buy Hannah and her baby airline tickets out of Zahristan, if marriage to Kulal should prove intolerable? To give her a wad of that same cash to purchase a bolthole somewhere? Wouldn't it *mean* something to be able to do that—especially after everything her sister had done for her when they'd been growing up? To redress the balance a little. Even though…

Tamsyn swallowed down the suddenly acrid taste in her mouth.

Even though Hannah had been the reason Tamsyn had never met her father and it had taken her a long time to forgive her for that...

She looked up to find Xan watching her closely, the way she imagined a policeman might scrutinise a suspect from behind a piece of two-way glass. Well, he certainly wouldn't be able to read very much from *her* expression! Hadn't she spent all her formative years hiding her emotions behind the blasé mask she presented to the world?

'How long would this marriage last?'

'Not long. Three months should suffice. Any less than that and it will look like a stunt.'

She nodded. 'And how much money are you prepared to offer me?'

She saw him flinch—but that didn't surprise her either. Rich people never wanted to talk about money. They thought it was vulgar. Beneath them. Had Xan forgotten was it like to be poor, she wondered? Was that something else he'd blocked from his mind—like an agreement made by a teenage boy to marry a woman so his father could claw back an important piece of land?

'How much did you have in mind?' he questioned.

Her birth father had taught her everything she needed to know about desertion and rejection while her foster father's life lessons had been about infidelity and gambling. No wonder she distrusted men so much. But some of those lessons had been useful. She'd overheard enough bluster around card games to realise that you had to start high and be prepared to be knocked down whenever you were bargaining for something. So she mentioned an outrageous sum of money, prepared for yet slightly shamed by the brief look of contempt which hardened Xan's cobalt eyes. But it was gone almost immediately, because he nodded his head.

'Okay,' he said.

She blinked in disbelief. 'Just like that?'

He shrugged. 'You clearly want it. I can afford it. And obviously, the more I am prepared to pay—the more I get out of our brief union.'

The silky inference behind his drawled words made Tamsyn's stomach clench with anger. And something else. Something far more potent than anger. Because at times during his story she had wanted to reach out to him. To comfort him? Or to kiss him? Or both. Maybe both. Especially when his face had grown hard and hurt when he'd mentioned his mother. She could feel her breasts pushing against the fine wool of the cashmere dress as she directed him a heated look, forcing herself to be bold enough to ask the question. 'You think I'm going to have *sex* with you?'

'That's a pretty naive question, Tamsyn,' he answered softly. 'Why wouldn't I? We've had sex before and it was good. Very, very good.' He raised his eyebrows. 'And isn't it a very necessary part of the marriage contract?

There was a pause during which Tamsyn steeled herself against the shocking beauty of his face and her own even more shocking reaction to him…the heat of excitement in her blood and the soft throb of hunger between her legs. But somehow, using the kind of resilience which every abandoned child needed in order to survive, she managed to present to him a face devoid of expression. 'Not in this case, because it's only make-believe,' she said coolly. 'I'll marry you because I want your money. But it's nothing but a business arrangement and there's no way I'm being intimate with you again, Xan. Because it wouldn't be right. Not after everything that's happened.'

CHAPTER EIGHT

SOMEHOW THE FLOWERS woven into her hair stayed in place, even though the sea breeze was whipping wildly all around her. Tamsyn guessed that was one of the benefits of marrying a billionaire—that he could afford to pay a top hairdresser to tame his prospective wife's unruly curls into an elaborate style which had miraculously stayed put all day. She clutched the railings of Xan's luxury yacht as it skimmed through the sapphire waters, trying to get her head around the fact that she was now the Greek tycoon's wife, and that the shiny golden ring which glinted on her finger was for real.

Well, as real as a fake wedding would allow.

Determined not to let herself be led like a lamb to the slaughter on her wedding day, she'd stated her terms before the ceremony, insisting she didn't want a big fuss—opting instead for something low-key and pared down. She thought it would have felt *cheap* to put on a big public show which meant nothing, and there was no way she could have made hollow vows in a place of worship. Most important of all, she didn't want Hannah hearing about the marriage until it was over, just in case she decided to do something dramatic like arriving in a flurry of royal pomp to try and talk her out of it.

But keeping their nuptials quiet seemed to have appealed to Xan as well and in a quiet moment he'd admitted that he had no stomach for weddings in general and his own in particular.

'The details will be posted in the local town hall which is a requirement by law,' he said. 'But since the mayor is a friend, our privacy will be respected and there's no way word will get out to the press. At least, not until I am ready to issue a statement.' A hard glimmer of a smile had followed. 'And it adds a little passionate *authenticity* to our whirlwind romance if we keep it all very hush-hush don't you think, *agape mou*?

What Tamsyn thought wasn't really here nor there. It bothered her that Xan seemed to be almost *relishing* the clandestine nature of the wedding, until she forced herself to remember that most men enjoyed secrecy. This was nothing but an elaborate game to Xan, she reminded herself, and since they weren't planning to be married for very long, what was the point in objecting?

'We will have a big party straight after the honeymoon,' Xan had informed her the day after she'd accepted his proposal, when he had turned up unexpectedly at her tiny bedsit, his lips curving with distaste as he looked around, before announcing that from then on she would be staying at the Granchester until the wedding. 'A big, lavish party to which we will invite family and close friends, and announce that we are man and wife.'

'And Sofia?' Tamsyn's voice had asked, wondering how the Greek woman who had been Xan's bride intended would take the sudden news. 'When are you planning to tell her?'

'I will phone her after the ceremony, once I've spoken to my father.'

Something about the obvious omission made her tentatively ask the question. 'And what about...your mother?'

She had never seen his face so expressionless. As if it had been wiped clean of all feeling—his features looking as if they had been hewn from some dark and impenetrable marble. 'My mother died a decade ago.'

'Oh, Xan, I'm sorry.'

It had been an instinctive condolence on her part but he hadn't wanted it, cutting short the conversation with a cool determination she had come to recognise as Xan's way of doing things. And in a way she could understand his reluctance to talk. She didn't want to him delving into *her* past, did she? Didn't want him probing her own areas of painful memory. Why rake all that up, when this was a relationship which was never intended to last?

'But do you think Sofia will be upset?' she had persisted. 'The last thing I want is to cause another woman pain.'

His mouth had hardened. 'Let's hope not. Maybe she will have realised that she's better off without a man like me,' he'd added, his voice growing harsh. 'A man who cannot give her the love she deserves.'

Recalling those words, it was difficult for Tamsyn not to conclude that he considered her somehow unworthy of those things. In Xan's mind she was greedy and acquisitive. He thought of her as a gold-digger, just like her sister—she knew that. And although it wasn't necessary for him to have a high opinion of her, she couldn't deny it hurt that he thought so little of her.

They had married in a tiny ceremony outside Athens earlier that day—without fuss or fanfare, just two anonymous witnesses plucked from the street and a single photographer, who had captured the event for posterity. It was the first time she'd seen Xan smile all day.

'It will be no hardship to lose the obnoxious tag of "Greece's most eligible bachelor",' he had drawled, those thick, dark lashes shuttering the cobalt brilliance of his eyes. 'At least in future I might just be left alone to get on with my life and to live it as I please.'

His words had been arrogant enough to make Tamsyn bristle, but she'd bitten back her sarcastic response, deciding that having a stand-up fight right before the ceremony might not be the best way of portraying marital harmony. Instead, she'd concentrated on her appearance, determined to play her own part with aplomb. She'd chosen an extremely short white wedding dress in diaphanous layers of silk-chiffon which came to mid-thigh and defined the shape of her legs beneath. It was pretty and delicate as well as being slightly daring, but that was exactly what she wanted. She wanted people to look at her and tut. To remark that she really *was* an outrageous choice of bride for the Greek tycoon because that would pave the way for their speedy divorce.

What she hadn't banked on was Xan's reaction when he saw her walking towards him clutching a scented bunch of white flowers. He had looked her up and down as if he couldn't quite believe what he was seeing, his gaze lingering on her bare legs and a little muscle flickering at his temple. And when she'd enquired—a little anxiously—if the short dress was emphasising the freckles on her thighs, he had given her an odd kind of smile before shaking his head and guiding her towards the car waiting to take them to Piraeus.

'Not at all, *agape mou*.' His denial had been husky and the little muscle had still been flickering at his temple. 'Not at all.'

And now she and her new husband were skimming over the sapphire sea towards the Peloponnese peninsula, because Xan had told her the best way to see his home for the first time was from the water. Almost as if was a *real* honeymoon and he was trying to impress her!

She'd never been on a yacht before—just ferries—most memorably a day-trip to Calais when she'd been just seventeen. But Xan's sleek craft was worlds away from the lumbering ferry which had moved through the water with all the grace of a giant tractor. This boat gleamed silvery-white in the spring sunshine. It drew the eye of every passing yacht—especially with Xan at the helm. He had swapped his dark wedding suit for a pair of faded denims and a white T-shirt which emphasised the contrasting gleam of his olive skin. The muscles in his arms bunched as he did impressive-looking things to the billowing sails and his raven-dark hair rippled in the Aegean breeze. With an effort, Tamsyn tried to concentrate on the horizon, trying to prevent her gaze from sliding to his powerful body as he tugged on a rope—as she wondered how difficult it was going to be to resist him during the fortnight's honeymoon which lay ahead.

'Tamsyn! Look over there.'

Over the white noise whoosh of the sea, Xan's voice broke into her thoughts and Tamsyn glanced up to follow the direction of his gaze. She hadn't really thought about what she might find at the end of her journey but now her heart contracted with something like yearning as suddenly she understood the meaning of the word paradise.

Xan's home was situated on a strip of land surrounded on three sides by the sea, like a green finger dipping into pot of blue water. A large, elevated modern house glinted in the bright sunshine of the spring morning but there were other buildings occupying the sprawling estate too, which made her realise just how vast it was. Outside seating areas with wicker chairs and tables and a long veranda, festooned with bright flowers and green climbers. In the distance was the seductive glitter of a sapphire swimming pool which blended into the ocean beyond, and impossibly smooth, emerald lawns sloping down a private beach, where a curve of sugar-white sand tempted the eye. Tamsyn watched as Xan expertly brought the yacht skimming into the small harbour where two fishermen were waiting, greeting him affectionately as they helped him anchor the boat.

Still in her wedding heels, Tamsyn consented to being lifted onto the sand by her new husband, which she supposed only added to the supposed romance of their arrival. And despite trying to convince herself that the gesture was functional rather than emotional, that didn't stop her skin from shivering in response when he briefly held her in his powerful arms. Did her eyes darken or some other barely visible response communicate itself to him? Was that why there was a speculative narrowing of his eyes? Tamsyn stiffened. Just because she *felt* desire, didn't mean she was going to act on it, did it? Even if it *was* difficult to shake the memories of just how good it had been between them...

'Let's go up to the house,' he said, indicating a steep flight of stone steps, before casting a doubtful look at her towering white heels. 'Think you can manage to walk in those, or would you like me to carry you?'

'I think I can manage,' she said, seeing the answering smile which curved his lips.

'I thought you might say that,' he commented drily.

But by the time they reached the top of the steps with Tamsyn panting slightly, Xan caught hold of her hand, lacing his fingers in hers as they began to walk towards the lawn.

She shot him a questioning glance, hating the sudden thrill of her hand as it was enclosed in the warmth of his. 'Xan?' she said breathlessly.

'My housekeeper is watching from the house,' he said. 'And I know how disappointed she would be if she thought we were anything other than a pair of deliriously happy newlyweds.'

His housekeeper was watching.

Well, what had she expected? That he had been suddenly overcome with emotion? Tamsyn tried to pull away but he stayed her with the feather-light circling of his thumb and instead she found herself shivering in response. What was the *matter* with her? Was she so starved of physical affection that even a tiny stroke could reduce her to such a state of longing? Maybe she was. Or maybe gestures like that mimicked *real* closeness and made her realise with a sudden shock just what she'd never had. No mother to cuddle her. No father to bounce her on his knee. Nobody except Hannah who back then had only ever given her the occasional half-hearted hug, because it was kind of embarrassing to cuddle your kid sister.

So remember why you're here, she told herself fiercely. Remember why you're doing this. Not for love, or scraps of affection, but for *money*. Money for Hannah—the only person who'd ever really been there for her.

But it was easy to forget reality when the housekeeper was standing in the doorway watching them approach, her face creased with pleasure as she clapped her gnarled hands together in delight. The greeting she gave Xan was a surprise—Tamsyn hadn't expected the tycoon to consent to being embraced so fervently by his elderly housekeeper. But neither was she prepared for the crushing embrace to which *she* was subjected afterwards and for a moment she stood, stiff as a board before gradually relaxing into the woman's cushioned flesh. And wasn't she secretly glad of that brief opportunity to compose herself and the chance to blink away the tears which had inexplicably sprung to her eyes.

'Tamsyn, this is Manalena,' Xan was saying as the woman relinquished her hold at last. 'Who has been with the family for a very long time.'

'*Kalispera!*' beamed Manalena, mimicking a rocking movement with her arms. 'I have known Kyrios Xan since he was a baby.'

It was difficult to imagine this towering man as a baby, thought Tamsyn. To picture him small and helpless and vulnerable. 'And was he a good baby?' she asked, with a smile.

Manalena gave a shake of her greying head. 'He never sleep and when he was a little boy, he never sit still. He is still like that now, and I am very happy he find a wife at last.'

Tamsyn remembered Xan telling her that his engagement to Sofia had been a private matter and for that she was grateful. Imagine if his staff regarded her as some kind of usurper and resented her, making her sense of isolation even more pronounced. She wondered how the housekeeper would feel if she knew the truth behind their whirlwind wedding and that Tamsyn was not the genuine and loving bride she must have hoped for. A flicker of discomfort washed over her as she glanced up at Xan while Manalena spoke to him in a torrent of rapid and babbled Greek.

'Manalena has just been explaining that a special wedding breakfast has been prepared for us,' he translated. 'She is also complaining that this morning a member of my staff arrived from Athens and is getting under her feet.'

As if on cue, a sleek brunette emerged from the house, talking excitedly into a cellphone, before quickly terminating the call. Slim and sophisticated, it was impossible to know exactly how old she was, though Tamsyn would have guessed mid to late thirties. Shiny shoulder-length hair swung in a raven arc around her chin and her linen trousers and pristine cream blouse made her appear the very definition of cool. In her too-short wedding dress with the flowers beginning to wilt in her windswept curls, Tamsyn felt inferior in comparison, even though the woman was smiling at her in a friendly manner.

'Hello! You must be Tamsyn,' she said, her perfect English tinged with a fetching Greek accent. 'I'm Elena and I'm very pleased to meet you and to offer my congratulations.'

'Elena is my personal assistant from the Athens office,' explained Xan. 'She's been overseeing all the wedding party preparations.'

'I hope everything will be to your satisfaction,' said Elena quickly. 'Xan gave me *carte blanche* to make decisions about food and drink and decorations, so I did. I would have communicated with you directly except—'

'I told Elena you were busy winding up your life in England,' said Xan, meeting Tamsyn's eyes with a bland look.

Tamsyn forced a smile because what could she say? That packing up her few miserable possessions had taken about five minutes and she might have welcomed having a little input into her own wedding party, rather than sitting around in the unfamiliar luxury of the Granchester Hotel, wondering what on earth she had let herself in for. Xan had given her a credit card and told her to buy an entire new wardrobe, one befitting the wife of a Greek tycoon. And although Tamsyn had half-heartedly done as he'd asked, she'd bought only what was strictly necessary, obsessively keeping all the receipts so that they could be included in a final tally when the divorce settlement came through.

Perhaps Xan had drafted Elena because he was afraid his new wife might prove incapable of choosing a sophisticated menu for their wedding party, despite holding her own that night they'd dined together at the Granchester. Or maybe he was worried she might let slip the true nature of their whirlwind romance—although he didn't seem to be doing anything to bolster the false fairytale himself. He wasn't exactly acting like a man who'd been swept away by passion, was he? She doubted whether that brief hand-holding exhibition would have convinced his housekeeper—or anyone else—that this marriage was for real.

'I'm very grateful for your help,' she told Elena brightly. 'For a start, I don't speak any Greek.'

'Well no, not *yet*,' said Elena with a friendly grin. 'But you will. Like your new husband, it isn't easy—but it's certainly possible to master.'

'I think you should kiss goodbye to your bonus, Elena,' said Xan mildly, propelling Tamsyn forward with the brief caress of his fingers. 'Come and meet the rest of the staff.'

The *rest* of the staff? Exactly how many people did he have working for him? Suddenly Tamsyn felt daunted by the line of workers who were waiting to meet her. Silently, she repeated their names before saying them out loud, terrified she would forget them before wondering why she was so anxious to please. There was Rhea the cook and pretty young Gia, who was in charge of the cleaning. A part-time driver named Panos, and Orestes the gardener, whose wife Karme helped Gia in the house when the need arose.

Tamsyn said hello to them all, using the few words of Greek she'd managed to learn before leaving England, but once again she felt faintly uneasy about deceiving these people who obviously adored her Greek husband and wanted the best for him.

Once again Manalena said something in Greek and Xan nodded, before glancing briefly at his watch.

'The meal is almost ready, but there are a couple of phone calls I need to make first,' he said. 'Manalena will show you where to freshen up and I'll meet you downstairs in the dining room in ten minutes.'

Feeling as if she'd been dismissed, Tamsyn followed the housekeeper up a sweeping staircase to the first floor, wondering how Xan was expecting to maintain the image of doting bridegroom if he couldn't even be bother to show her to the bathroom himself! Yet she couldn't deny a feeling of relief, that she would be spared the intimate reality of their shared marital space for at least a little while longer.

She walked down a wide and airy corridor, past walls covered with dramatic seascapes, until at last Manalena halted in front of a set of double doors. 'This is your room,' said Manalena, a note of pride creeping into her voice as she pushed open one of the doors.

Tamsyn walked into a room of breathtaking splendour with views right over the water, so that sunlight danced in an ever-moving lightshow over the pale walls. On the dressing table she could see the a pair of gold cufflinks set with sapphires which perfectly matched her new husband's eyes. Xan's room, she thought. And now hers, too. Her throat constricted. If it had belonged to anyone else she would have walked straight over to the window and feasted her eyes on the dark swell of the sea, but her attention was caught by something else. By the vast bed, on whose snowy covers someone had scattered pink rose petals—dozens of them—their scented splendour seeming to mock her.

Another reminder of a romance which wasn't real, she reminded herself, trying to erase the stupid sense of wistfulness which was clenching at her heart. Yet what could she do other than smile at the faithful housekeeper who stood anxiously in front of her, obviously awaiting her verdict on the honeymoon suite.

'It looks very beautiful, Manalena,' she said softly. '*Efkaristo.*'

Looking gratified, Manalena beamed and nodded. 'I wait for you outside.'

Alone at last, Tamsyn kicked off her high-heeled shoes and wiggled her newly liberated toes. And even though she could have happily thrown herself onto the bed and tried to blot out what was coming next, she freshened up in the lavish bathroom, helping herself from a selection of costly bath products which had obviously been acquired for the new bride. Pulling the wilting flowers from her hair, she raked a brush through her hair, gradually removing the tangles until it fell in a thick and vibrant curtain all the way down to her waist. She eyed the spindly wedding shoes doubtfully and decided against putting them back on. With a final tug at her short dress, she went back downstairs with Manalena, where Xan was waiting for her in the dining room.

And Tamsyn could do nothing about the overwhelming rush of desire which pulsed over her. It seemed incongruous to see the Greek tycoon standing there, still in his sailing clothes, his cobalt eyes darkening with unmistakable appreciation as he surveyed her. Her heart began to thunder as she realised that this powerful man was now her husband.

And she needed to keep it together. Not let desire

weaken her. To remember that this was nothing but an elaborate ruse. A business transaction, that was all.

'You don't look much like a bridegroom,' she commented lightly, in a vain attempt to defuse the sudden tension which seemed to have accompanied her into the room.

His gaze raked over her, lingering on the filmy white dress and focussing last on her bare feet whose toenails were painted a shimmering iridescent silver. 'Whereas you look exactly like a bride, *agape mou*,' he said unevenly. 'If a somewhat unconventional one.'

'Wasn't that the whole idea?' she questioned acidly.

Xan couldn't quite bring himself to answer, because he wasn't sure *where* his head had been when he'd asked Tamsyn Wilson to marry him. Had he thought she would be easily manipulated? That her humble status and the knowledge he was paying her a great deal of money, would give him the upper hand? Yes, he had. Guilty on all counts.

Pulling out a chair for her, he felt the silkiness of her loose curls brushing tantalisingly against his hand and his groin hardened. He hadn't believed her when she'd told him there was to be no sex, but her distant behaviour since they'd made their deal, had convinced him that she'd meant every word she said. He'd tried convincing himself that he wouldn't find it too much of a problem—and that three months enforced celibacy was easily doable. What he had failed to take into account was just how entrancing he would continue to find her, or that her stubbornness would act as an aching kind of aphrodisiac. His mouth hardened. He should have picked a bride from the type of woman with which he was familiar. The type who would jump when he snapped his fingers. Who would do whatever he asked of them, and do it with gratitude and pleasure. Not some feisty woman who seemed determined to oppose him every step of the way.

He poured two glasses of vintage champagne and handed her one, his throat drying with lust as their eyes met over the rims of the fine crystal. Suddenly he wished he'd told Manalena that they would eat something light on the balcony of his bedroom, so that he could have had Tamsyn all to himself. To test just how strong her resolve was. Too late, he thought grimly, knowing how much trouble his cook would have gone to.

But his expression betrayed none of his disquiet as he raised his glass to hers. 'So. What shall we drink to, Tamsyn?' he questioned.

For a moment she looked uncertain—like a small creature who'd strayed too far from her natural habitat. She stared down at the fizzing wine before lifting her gaze and chinking her crystal glass against his.

'To money, of course,' she said defiantly. 'That's what this is all about, isn't it? Money and land.'

And all that flippancy was back—the defiant tilt of her chin just daring him to challenge her, when ironically—all it made him want to do was kiss her.

CHAPTER NINE

IT WAS THE longest meal she'd ever endured but Tamsyn was determined to spin out her wedding breakfast as long as she could. Because eating and drinking would delay the inevitable—and she was terrified of accompanying Xan upstairs, to that vast bed scattered with pink rose petals. Terrified that she would give into the demands of her traitorous body and fall hungrily into his arms. Because that was the last thing she needed.

Dutifully she picked at course after delicious course, trying to give every impression of enjoying the food which had been so carefully prepared by Rhea, the cook. The Greek salad topped with fragrant basil, still warm from the herb garden. The fish with delicious sauce, followed by *giovetsi*—a dish of lamb baked in a clay pot, served with green beans stewed with tomatoes. Rhea's final flourish was a traditional wedding dessert called *diples*, a sweet fried concoction covered in a great deal of honey and crushed walnuts. The honey kept sticking to the roof of her mouth and she really didn't need another morsel, but Tamsyn was determined to eat it.

And each course had an accompanying wine—fine wines in different colours. Tamsyn rarely drank but today she sipped a little, so that by the time the sweet wine was served with dessert, she felt better than she had in days. It was as if a tight knot at the base of her stomach had slowly begun to unfurl, allowing her to relax at last.

Staring across the table at Xan, she tried not be affected by his rugged masculine beauty, but that was easier said than done. His skin gleamed like gold in the sunlight and the close-fitting jeans and T-shirt gave him a deceptively laid-back air. At times she was in danger of forgetting that he was a billionaire control freak who was calling all the shots, because right now he looked like some rippling-fleshed fisherman who'd just wandered up to the house for a bit of lunch.

'So,' she said, finally admitting defeat and putting her dessert spoon down. 'Here we are. Mr and Mrs Constantinides. How weird is that?'

A glint of amusement entered the cobalt eyes. 'Pretty weird,' he admitted.

'Have you issued your statement to the press yet? Is that what the phone call was all about?'

'I have no intention of speaking to the press today, Tamsyn. I will respond to questions if and when necessary. I was speaking to my father.' There was a pause. 'And Sofia.'

Tamsyn felt her heart lurch. 'And?'

'Sofia took it better than I expected. She seemed more resigned than upset. Which is a good thing.'

'Like I said,' Tamsyn observed. 'She's probably secretly pleased not to have to spend a lifetime with you.'

'Thanks for the vote of confidence, sweetheart,' he said drily.

She wanted to tell him not to tease her like that,

just like she wanted to tell him not to look at her with that sexy glint of amusement in his eyes. Mainly because she liked it. She liked it way too much. It made her want to do what she had vowed she wasn't going to do—mainly to rush upstairs and get up close and personal with him. She cleared her throat. 'And your father?'

For the first time, his face showed a flicker of darkness. 'My father took the news less well. He was angry, which didn't surprise me, but his concerns were focussed more on his island inheritance than on the people involved. No change there.' His laugh was tinged with bitterness. 'He seems to think that Sofia's father might refuse to sell me the island now that I've jilted his daughter. I think it will depend on Sofia's reaction, but better that than breaking her heart,' he added harshly.

'And if he's right? If Sofia's father won't sell?'

'Oh, if Sofia is okay, he'll sell—don't you worry about that.'

'How can you be so sure?'

'Because Tamsyn, everyone has their price' He gave a cynical smile. 'Even you.'

It was a timely reminder of her new husband's cold-heartedness but Tamsyn forced herself not to react, instead fixing him with a look of interest. 'Is your father coming to the wedding party?'

'He said not, but I know his bluster of old and he'll be there—if only because the cream of Athenian and international society will be attending and he'd hate to miss out.'

'And in the meantime, we have a whole two week honeymoon to get through.' Tamsyn resisted the temptation to chew on her fingernails which had been varnished silver to match her toes. 'Wasn't that a rather unnecessary addition to this sham marriage?'

'I told you. We don't want to make it look like a stunt.' He leaned back in his chair to study her. 'And we can make this as easy or as difficult as we like.'

Tamsyn wondered if he was out of his mind. Didn't he realise that there was a constant battle raging inside her? That while her head was telling her not to have sex with her new husband—her body was urging her in the opposite direction. Did Xan know that every time she looked at him she wanted to touch him, even though to do so would be madness. Or that at night she was haunted by the memories of his hard body thrusting into hers and giving her pleasure, over and over again? Running her trembling fingertip round the edge of her crystal glass, she struggled to find a neutral topic. 'Manalena seems very sweet,' she said at last.

'She is.' He took a mouthful of wine, his expression mocking her.

'Why did she used to look after you? Did your mother go out to work?'

'No. But motherhood appealed to her about as much as being poor, and she didn't care who knew it. Including me, just for the record. She went to great pains to assure me that some women simply weren't maternal, and she was one of them.'

His words were terse and he spoke them as if they didn't matter but they told her a lot, mainly that his mother had been emotionally distant. Tamsyn nodded, wondering just how far she could push him—without stopping to ask herself why she wanted to. 'Do you think that's what made you so...'

'So what, Tamsyn?' he questioned sardonically as her words tailed off.

'So… I don't know.' She straightened her napkin so that it lay at a ninety-degree angle next to her place-setting, just as she would have done if she'd been at work. 'So anti-love and marriage…'

He shrugged. 'That's what the psychologists would say, I guess.'

'And was it bad?' she questioned suddenly, her heart going out to him despite telling herself that he didn't need her sympathy. 'Your childhood, I mean?'

'Bad enough. But I happened to like the independence which came about as a result of having a mother who was never there for me. The thought of having to answer to someone every hour of every day filled me with horror and still does.' His eyes were like dark blue ice. 'In future all my bios will say, *he was briefly married*. And you, *agape mou*, will have liberated me from the expectation which society heaps on every wealthy man, that he is not complete until he finds himself a suitable wife. You will have done me a big favour, Tamsyn.' His lips curved into a reflective smile. 'And that in itself is worth the money I'm paying you to wear my ring.'

His mocking words effectively terminated the conversation, but it left Tamsyn thinking that maybe they were more similar than she'd imagined, despite the great difference in their lifestyles.

'So what now?' she questioned, aware that they couldn't sit amid the debris of their wedding breakfast all day.

His eyes gleamed. 'Now that you've made lunch last as long as you possibly could?'

'I was hungry.'

'Of course you were, *agape mou*,' he agreed, silkily. 'Hungry enough to pick at your food with marked indifference and then to push it around your plate? But your face is pale and your eyes strained, so I suggest you retire to the bedroom and take an afternoon nap. It's been a long day.'

His words made sense because Tamsyn *was* tired. But the memory of that petal-strewn bed kept flickering into her mind and she knew she couldn't keep skirting round the issue. In London she'd told him there was to be no sex and he needed to realise she meant it. But she couldn't discuss the subject here—not with Manalena poking her beaming head around the door and asking if they'd like coffee.

Her husband declined the offer, his drawled response bringing an instant smile to Manalena's face as she remained in the doorway, watching them. And when Xan walked around the table and held out his hand towards Tamsyn, she found herself taking it. She told herself she was doing this for the housekeeper's benefit and maybe she was. But she couldn't deny that she was enjoying the sensation of Xan's strong fingers encircling hers, as he led her upstairs towards the master bedroom. Of course she was. Because in those few moments she felt safe. As if nothing could ever harm her so long as she was with this powerful and charismatic man.

And that was nothing but an illusion. She was nothing but a bought bride, to be disposed of as soon as possible.

She was shivering as he closed the bedroom door behind them, acutely aware of the intimacy of the enclosed space. She ran her fingertips over the wilting bouquet she'd placed on a nearby table and then, when there was no room left for prevarication, looked into his face. 'Where am I sleeping?'

He raised his eyebrows. 'Judging by the amount of petals which seem to have been offloaded onto the bed, I'd say right here.'

She shook her head, hating the sudden hot prickle of her breasts. 'I told you I didn't want any intimacy, Xan, so therefore it makes more sense for me to have my own bedroom.'

'And if I were to grant you your wish, that would bring into question the validity of our marriage,' he answered coolly. 'Which kind of defeats the whole purpose of you being here.'

'So we've got to share a bed?'

'It's a very large bed.'

'I can see that for myself. But it doesn't matter how big it is,' she snapped. 'I don't want…'

'What don't you want, Tamsyn?'

She stiffened as she heard the soft mockery in his voice. Was he going to make her spell it out? And if he was, so what? She was no longer the shrinking little virgin who had given herself to him one starry desert night, even if right now she felt like it. This man knew her like no other. He had kissed her lips and suckled her breasts. He had shown her how he liked to be touched and stroked and had then thrust deep inside her hungry body. He had seen her vulnerable in the midst of her orgasm. Had heard her stumble out his name in a choking cry as she tumbled over the edge. Surely that gave her the right to say what was on her mind. 'Sex,' she managed, her cheeks growing hot.

'It isn't obligatory to have sex with me.' He shrugged. 'I'm not planning to demand my conjugal rights, if that's what you're worried about. Like I said, it's a big bed.'

'And you think it's possible for us to lie side by side and, and…' Her voice tailed off, unable to articulate the confusion of her feelings which were compounded by the sheer depth of her inexperience. Did he guess that? Was that why the look he slanted her seemed almost *compassionate*?

'I think it's possible,' he said slowly. 'It won't be easy and it certainly won't be enjoyable, but in the end the decision is yours, Tamsyn. Yet all you have to do is say the word and we could have one hell of a honeymoon.'

Her cheeks grew even hotter. 'I don't know how you can be…so…*callous*.'

'And I don't know why you're making such a big deal out of it. You think every time a couple have sex, there has to be some great big emotion underlying it?' His cobalt gaze seared into her. 'Didn't it ever occur to you that sexual gratification is just one of life's fundamental pleasures, Tamsyn?'

Tamsyn was aware of a sudden emptiness. A disappointment. As if he'd just burst some invisible bubble. As if the stories women told themselves about happy-ever-after really *were* a myth. 'And that's all there is to it?' she asked, in a small flat voice.

He shrugged. 'It exists for the procreation of children, but that's not going to be an issue for us, is it?'

'No,' she agreed, unprepared for another unexpectedly painful clench of her heart. 'It's not going to be an issue.'

'Don't take it so personally,' he advised softly. 'Sex doesn't have to be about love.'

'I realise that. I may be relatively inexperienced, but I'm not stupid!' she declared. 'I'm not looking for love but if I was, you'd be right at the bottom of my wish-list, Xan Constantinides!'

Her words sounded genuine and Xan gave the ghost of a smile because she really was surprising. Up-close contact with his enormous wealth didn't seem to have blunted her determination to do things *her* way, nor to subdue her feisty nature. She was behaving like his equal and that was doing dangerous things to his libido. He was used to female subjugation and was finding the lack of it a powerful aphrodisiac. Lust pulsed through him, hot and potent. She was such a contradiction in so many ways. Tough and outspoken—and yet at times he was certain he'd detected a glimpse of frailty beneath her waspish exterior. And didn't that intrigue him? Make him wonder what had put it there?

He stared out of one of the windows where he could see Orestes tending to the violet blooms of an exotic flower and he thought about the fortnight ahead, realising that this fabricated honeymoon would drag like hell unless he could find something pleasurable to fill the time. And sex with his fiery new bride would certainly while away the hours in the most delicious way.

She hadn't moved from where she'd been standing and he reached out to touch his fingertip against her mouth, instantly feeling it tremble. He could see her throat constricting and her eyes briefly closing as if she was trying to fight her own desire. And that turned him on even more, because he wasn't used to women fighting their attraction to him. 'You still want me, Tamsyn,' he observed thickly. 'And it's the same for me. I want you so much that I'm aching just thinking about it.'

He could see the uncertainty flickering in the depths of her green eyes. 'Nobody's denying the desire, Xan. Doesn't mean we're going to do anything about it though.'

'Why not?'

'Because….' She moved away from him then, wriggling her shoulders restlessly as the little white wedding dress shimmied provocatively over her bare thighs. 'It seems wrong to have sex just for the sake of it.'

'Says who? Why does it bother you so much?'

She stared at him and suddenly her eyes were very bright. 'It doesn't matter.'

'Oh, but it does. I'm interested in why you're such a fundamentally old-fashioned young woman at heart.'

Tamsyn gave a careless shrug which didn't quite come off, because it was difficult to remain indifferent to her past when he was looking at her so piercingly.

'I didn't realise I was.'

'Psychologists usually say it something to do with your parents and your upbringing,' he said wryly. 'So let's start with that.'

This is what she'd been trying to avoid telling him. But what difference did it make if she told him about her mother? This part of her life wasn't the part she had buried in a deep, dark place which she never ventured near.

'I don't remember my birth mother, because I was just a baby when she gave me and Hannah up for adoption,' she said baldly. 'But nobody wanted to adopt us because we were too much of a handful. Or rather, I was. Apparently it's quite common for abandoned babies to grow into troublesome children.' She shrugged. 'That's why we put up with so much from our foster parents, despite all their failings.' She shrugged as she met the question in his eyes. 'There was a terrible atmosphere in the house, mainly because my foster father used the grocery money to fund his card games, or to buy dinner for one of his many mistresses. We were terrified that if we complained we'd get split up. And neither Hannah or I could bear the thought of that.'

There was a silence during which she thought he was about to let it go. And didn't she *want* him to let it go?

'So what do you know about your birth mother, Tamsyn,' he prompted softly.

Tamsyn swallowed. If she told him he would judge her and she didn't want to be judged. Because that's what the girls at school had done, once they found out about her mum. They'd picked on her and bullied her and the strong skin she'd grown had been as a direct result of that. But talking about it would reinforce the certainty that there could never be any kind of future between her and Xan. And it might stop him from probing further—keeping him away from the stuff which was *really* unpalatable.

She shrugged. 'From what I understand, she was pretty liberal with her body. She liked men. A lot. And she wasn't that careful about contraception. Hannah and I have different fathers and apparently there's a younger brother out there, who we've never met.'

'And your father?'

'I never met him.' She moved away. 'And if you don't mind, I'd rather not discuss it any more.'

'Of course not.' He nodded slowly, his eyes gleaming with perception. 'It's no wonder you hung onto your virginity for so long. No wonder that behind that spiky exterior beats the heart of someone who only ever wanted to be a good girl. But you don't have to spend your whole life paying for the perceived sins of your mother, you know, Tamsyn. It won't make the slightest difference if you deny yourself pleasure, just for the sake of it.'

'You mean, now I've actually lost my innocence, I might as well capitalise on it?'

'That's one way of looking at it. If you could stop being so damned stubborn and think about the possibilities open to you, you might be able to see some of the benefits.'

'What kind of *benefits*?'

He gave a slow smile. 'Well, for a start I could teach you how to enjoy your body. I could show you just how sublime sex can be. Wouldn't you like that, Tamsyn? Wouldn't you like to walk away from this marriage knowing how to please a man, and how best *you* like to be pleased?'

Tamsyn shook her head because she hated his logic. For making it sound as if sex was just another new skill to learn—a bit like when she'd studied to be a silver-service waitress. His words reminded her that she was only here for a short while and soon she would be on her own again—back to her nomadic existence. It made sense to tell him no and to stick to her self-imposed celibacy.

So why couldn't she silence the memory of what it

had been like to be naked in his arms…how he'd made her glow and shout with pleasure and then tremble helplessly in his arms? Why not concentrate on how empty she'd felt afterwards, when he'd left her and gone away? 'It seems so…cold-blooded,' she breathed.

'Does it?' he said softly, as he walked towards her.

'Yes,' she whispered.

'On the contrary,' he husked, pulling her roughly into his arms. 'I would describe this as nothing but hot-blooded.'

The first kiss knocked some of the fight out of her and the second had her hungry for more. And when he cupped his trembling hand over her thrusting breast, Tamsyn moaned with pleasure.

Because it felt good. Way too good to resist. She knew she should tell him no. That being physically close again would put her in danger of something she couldn't understand. But how could she refuse something which felt like this? When he was sliding his hand up the filmy skirt of her dress and caressing the shivering skin of her inner thigh?

'Xan,' she moaned, as his finger edged inside her panties and she writhed with pleasure as he found her wet heat.

'You like that,' he observed thickly.

She was too het-up to reply, but maybe she communicated her need to him. Maybe that was why he halted his intimate caress and picked her up, carrying her effortlessly over to the bed. He unzipped her dress and dropped it to the floor, before laying her on top of the petal-strewn cover.

'I see you wore white lingerie for your wedding day,' he observed thickly, tracing a slow finger over the snowy lace edge of her balcony bra. 'How very traditional.'

'It was the only underwear which didn't show beneath my wedding dress,' she said defiantly.

Xan understood a little now of what had made her so defensive, but the thought left his mind the moment he brushed against the taut wetness of her panties, hearing her gasp as he encountered her sweet spot. He slid the zip of his jeans over his aching hardness and pulled off his own clothes before removing her underwear with hands which were inexplicably shaking, something which had never happened to him before. Yet as he climbed onto the bed beside her, he was forced to admit that this *did* feel different—and this time he couldn't blame it on her innocence. Had all the fuss made by his staff about their mock wedding somehow got to him? As if some of their thankful celebration had seeped into his system, kicking his habitual cynicism into touch, making what was happening between him and the little redhead seem especially intense.

Never had a woman seemed so responsive to his touch. She shivered as he reacquainted himself with every inch of her skin, his lips hungrily kissing her neck and breasts and belly as he began to finger her. He played with her until she was writhing and gasping his name, her fingernails clawing frantically at his shoulders. He remembered thinking that she was going to mark him and make him bleed—and that he didn't care.

His gasps became urgent as he entered her and she cried out with each deep thrust, soft thighs wrapped tightly around his back. And nothing had ever felt this good, thought Xan with delirious pleasure. Nothing.

He wanted it to last and last but she was too close, and so was he. He splayed his fingers over her peaking nipples as she began to spasm around him, and his own orgasm hit him like a speed train.

On and on it went, until at last he collapsed against her shoulder with his lips pressed against her damp and tumbled curls. It was a while before he could bring himself to withdraw from her, but just as soon as he did, her tiny fingers curled intimately around him and he could feel himself hardening again beneath her light touch. He slid inside her for a second time and before too long she was bucking wildly beneath him and crying out his name. Soon after his third orgasm, he lay stroking her head and realising that for the next two weeks of his honeymoon, it was just going to be him and Tamsyn.

He stared down at the satisfied slant of her lips. At the lazy flutter of her eyelashes as she gave a sleepy little sigh of contentment. She snuggled deeper into the crook of his arm and Xan felt the automatic stir of overpowering lust and something else. Something he couldn't seem to define....

Maybe it was panic.

CHAPTER TEN

THE MORNING SUN drifted in through the open windows of the bedroom but Tamsyn kept her eyes tightly shut, listening to the even sound of Xan's breathing. She needed to get her thoughts straight before he awoke. She needed to get her mask firmly in place, knowing he would baulk if he ever realised the truth. That their marriage of convenience was about to get a whole lot more complicated.

How the hell had it happened? At what point during this crazy honeymoon, had she started to care for her husband in a way which suddenly seemed unstoppable? She risked turning her head, to see his ruffled black hair lying against the pillow. Was she such a sucker for affection, that she'd fallen for a man just because he clearly enjoyed having sex with her and they spent long hours romping in bed together?

She swallowed. No. It was more than that. Xan could be *kind*, she had discovered. She'd seen that in the way he was with his staff, but he was also kind to her—and interested. In fact, he'd surprised her by wanting to know her views on all kinds of things. Things which nobody had ever bothered asking her about before—like politics and space travel and global warming. And Tamsyn had discovered how flattering it was when a powerful and successful man elicited the opinion of someone who didn't have a formal exam qualification to her name.

Nearly two weeks into her marriage and she had turned from being a reluctant bride to somebody who found joy in pretty much every moment she spent with her husband. But at least Xan didn't have a clue how she was feeling, because concealment was something she excelled at, when she put her mind to it. She'd had a lifetime's practice in emotional subterfuge. She might now want him, but he certainly didn't want her. That had never been part of the deal. No man had ever wanted her, she reminded herself grimly. Not even her own father.

This marriage couldn't last. It was never intended to last. *And the deeper she fell for him, the more painful their split was going to be…*

Dark lashes fluttered open and Tamsyn saw the cobalt gleam from between Xan's shuttered eyes. He gave a lazy stretch and yawned, before pulling her against his warm nakedness and kissing the top of her ruffled curls.

'And what would you like to do today, *sizighos mou*?' His voice deepened as his hand slipped beneath the sheet and he began to massage one erect nipple. 'Since it's the last day of our honeymoon.'

Tamsyn bit her lip, wishing he hadn't reminded her, especially since tomorrow was the day of their post-wedding party and one which his father had now announced he would definitely be attending. She wasn't looking forward to all his friends giving her the once-over and finding her wanting. Her thick skin seemed to have thinned these last few days and suddenly the thought of having to play the unsuitable wife was filling her with dread.

'We could spend the day on the beach,' Xan was saying, stroking the flat of his hand over her belly.

'Beach sounds good,' she agreed.

'Picnic or restaurant lunch?'

She tried to summon up some enthusiasm. 'Picnic, I think.'

'*Relios.*' He gave a slow flicker of a smile and bent his mouth to her nipple. 'My thoughts exactly.'

Reluctantly, she pulled away. 'I'll go and get showered—'

'Hey,' he protested, his hand reaching out to capture her waist. 'What's the hurry?'

Tamsyn's answering smile was tight as she wriggled free, because the last thing she needed was another example of an easy compatibility which meant nothing. 'I need to speak to Rhea about lunch,' she insisted, jumping out of bed before he could distract her again. 'If we're not careful, we'll end up spending the day in bed without actually having our picnic.'

'And would that be such a crime?' he grumbled. 'Isn't that what honeymoons are supposed to be about.'

'Today it would,' she said briskly. 'I need to speak to Elena about flowers for the party and to Rhea about all sorts of boring things, including canapés.'

There was a moment of silence. 'How quickly you have adapted,' he observed silkily, with a note of something she didn't recognise in his voice. 'You are beginning to sound like a real wife, Tamsyn.'

'And we wouldn't want that, would we?' she questioned brightly. 'Don't worry, Xan. I'll have re-adopted my wild-child persona by tomorrow..The shortest dress, the biggest hair and the most make-up. That should do the trick, don't you think? I can't wait to see the reaction of your friends and colleagues.' She forced a smile. 'And now I really *must* go and shower.'

Moodily Xan leaned back against the pillows and watched his wife sashay across the bedroom towards the bathroom, the globes of her buttocks paler than the tanned perfection of her shapely legs. Frustration heated his blood and his erection throbbed uncomfortably between his legs. Why hadn't he overridden her desire to help with the party and encouraged her to give into a far more satisfying kind of desire instead?

He was still engaged in silent contemplation when she returned, dabbing drops of moisture from her dewy body with a towel before slipping on a tiny yellow bikini, which she covered up with a green cotton dress.

His groin ached as he watched her. He had scheduled this honeymoon to give credibility to their whirlwind union, with the party tacked onto the end to indicate a return to normal life. He had planned to use this opportunity to slake himself of his seemingly inexhaustible appetite for his new wife, before she departed from his life for ever with her divorce settlement clutched tightly in her hand.

But his anticipation of all the sex he wanted had been tempered by caution, because he wasn't used to having a woman around full-time. Even during his longer relationships, he rarely stayed with a lover longer than twenty-four hours at a stretch, because by then he'd usually reached his boredom threshold. The thought of fourteen whole days and nights with one person had filled him with panic and he'd imagined he would be climbing the walls by day three. He'd planned to make an urgent visit to his office in Athens on some hastily constructed urgent business if necessary, using the trip as a badly disguised means of escape.

Only it hadn't turned out like that. He hadn't gone near his computer—not once—and the feeling of being trapped simply hadn't materialised. It turned out that Tamsyn liked her own space just as much as he did.

'Of course,' she had informed him carelessly when one day, frustrated at finding her curled up in the garden reading some lurid crime novel, he had enquired rather acidly whether she'd always been *quite* so independent. 'It's the way I was raised.'

Xan frowned. Was it contrary of him to find himself resenting the fact that she seemed intent on racing through the pile of novels she'd brought with her from England? Or excitedly informing him that his infinity pool gave her the ideal opportunity to perfect her breaststroke? And what about the afternoon when he'd fallen asleep beneath a pine tree and she had slipped away. He'd awoken up and gone looking for her and found her in the kitchen with Rhea, who was showing her how to make baklava which Tamsyn seemed to be alternating with colouring in a picture with Gia's young daughter Maria. This scene of domestic bliss should have spooked him but it hadn't, mainly because she had looked up at him with those big green eyes, and smiled and at that moment he had felt completely enslaved by her.

Xan scowled as he pushed away the rumpled sheet and got out of bed. The sooner he got back to work the better, he thought grimly. Work and distance would allow him to put this whole crazy marriage in perspective and to see it for what it really was.

Out on the sun-washed terrace, they breakfasted on fruit and honeyed yoghurt, served with strong black coffee. Afterwards Xan sailed his yacht to a sheltered cove—a favourite place whose inaccessibility always guaranteed privacy. Beneath the deep blue sky they spent the morning swimming and snorkelling in the crystal-clear waters and afterwards drank homemade iced lemonade. But although the food Rhea had stowed away in a cool box was carefully unpacked and looked delicious, he noticed Tamsyn seemed as disinterested in their picnic lunch as he was.

'Not hungry?' he murmured as he lay back on the soft sand.

She sat, ramrod-straight, looking out to sea. 'Not really.'

'Not for food?'

She cleared her throat. 'Something like that,' she agreed reluctantly, as if she resented his perception.

He smiled as a whispered fingertip down the entire length of her spine soon had the tension leaching from her shoulders and the touch of his lips which followed made her give an impatient little wriggle. He brushed his hand against her breasts and saw her lips open with hunger, clamping shut afterwards when he teased her by moving his fingers away from the thrusting nipple. He waited until he sensed complete readiness and then pulled her down next to him.

'Is there anything you want which I can give you?' he drawled lazily.

'Xan,' she said shakily.

'*Neh?*' he replied, as he stripped the tiny yellow bikini from her body and the sight of her naked in the sunshine made his blood roar. Tearing off his trunks with impatient hands, he parted her thighs and pushed deep inside her and she gasped as her hips lifted up to meet the hard slam of his. Never had she felt so hot or wet or deep and Xan could do nothing to stop the thoughts which flooded into his head as he drove into her. In a couple of days time he would be in his office in Athens, with back-to-back meetings and conference calls. He wouldn't see Tamsyn until he got home in the evening—probably not before eight at the earliest—because he always worked late. Was it that which made this seem so *poignant*? The sense of something ending which somehow increased the intensity, making his climax explode at exactly the same time as hers, which had never happened to them before.

They lay there afterwards, resting in the shade of rocky outcrop and for a moment he thought she was asleep. But no. He heard her sigh as, her eyes concealed by her shades, she stared up at the sky above.

'Was that good?' he questioned, with sleepy satisfaction.

'It's always good.'

'I don't know how you do it.' He gave another yawn. 'But every time I have you, I just want you all over again.'

'It's because you know it's only temporary,' she said lightly.

'Maybe.'

Tamsyn heard the sound of his breathing deepening and a quick glance at his supine form told her he'd fallen asleep. Reluctantly she dragged her gaze away from all the unleashed power of his magnificent body and stared out to sea. Out on the horizon was nothing but a deep slash of dark sapphire water and in front of it, the sugar-white grains of sand. The air was still and warm and fragrant and her body felt utterly satiated by Xan's sublime lovemaking. She wished she could capture that moment and keep it in a bottle.

But she couldn't.

She couldn't hold onto any of this. It was slipping through her fingers just like the fine sand on which she lay. She'd agreed to a three-month marriage but now she could see that her decision to put a time limit on their union might have been too hasty. Even reckless. How could she possibly endure another ten weeks of pretending that her feelings for Xan hadn't changed—when she was putty in his hands after a mere fortnight together?

Behind her dark glasses, Tamsyn blinked away the incipient threat of tears. She'd been told by men in the past that she was cold and frigid. That behind her vibrant exterior was nothing but ice—and she had believed it, because nobody before Xan had ever made her melt. But Xan had. How could she not grow closer to a man when he was inside her and they were staring deep into each other's eyes? When she became unsure where he began and she ended—as if they were both parts of the same body. That was when wishful thinking found an opportunity to creep into her mind and take root there. Started making her long for things which were never going to happen.

Because none of this was real, she reminded herself. They were just playing make-believe. Her Greek husband had embraced the physical, but his emotional barriers remained firmly in place. And so did hers, if she was being honest. Because otherwise, why hadn't she just come out and told him about her dad?

She swallowed. She'd never discussed her father, not even with Hannah. Especially not with Hannah— not after what had happened. Perhaps if she'd fallen in love with someone kind and approachable, she might have opened up her heart to him. But Xan wasn't that man. His lovemaking might be completely fulfilling— but that didn't detract from his hard and critical side.

He'd married her to get himself out of a tight corner.

An unsuitable wild-child bride he just happened to be sexually compatible with.

And the longer she stayed with him, the more vulnerable she made her already damaged heart.

CHAPTER ELEVEN

'So WHAT'S ALL this about?' questioned Xan softly.

Tamsyn didn't immediately look up from the mirror. She was going to need her best smile to get through the next few hours, so maybe she'd better practice composing her face accordingly. Straightening up, she slowly turned to face her husband, stupidly gratified by the instant desire she could read in his eyes. And she wasn't supposed to be feeling *gratified*. She was supposed to be distancing herself from the charismatic Greek billionaire, not revelling in the physical power she could still—unbelievably—wield over him.

'What's what all about?' she murmured absently.

'Don't act like you don't know what I'm talking about, Tamsyn,' he said, treating her to another assessing look. 'I'm just wondering why the sudden dramatic change of image for tonight's party.'

'Could you be a little more specific, Xan? What exactly are your objections?'

Objections? Xan's throat dried to dust. Who said anything about objections? It just wasn't what he'd been expecting, that was all. His wife was wearing a white dress—as befitting a new bride just freshly back from honeymoon—but the outfit was a world away from the flirty mini which had barely covered her bottom on the day they'd wed. This concoction was made from a rich, heavy silk which moulded every curve of her delicious body yet fell decorously to the knee. Her hair had been coiled into an elaborate style, the lustrous curls tamed and gleaming like silken flames, with only a few strands left dangling, drawing attention to the swan-like length of her neck. The strappy silver sandals which gleamed against her bare feet were the only frivolous thing about her tonight, but even they exuded a certain class and style. This was a Tamsyn he'd never seen before. Sophisticated. Elegant—and the very opposite of unsuitable.

'It doesn't look like you,' he observed unevenly. 'This isn't the edgy little redhead I know.'

A flash of colour flared into her cheeks. 'So you don't like it?'

He gave a short laugh. 'Tamsyn, you could wear sackcloth and I'd still want to rip it from your body. I'm just not sure what has prompted this sudden transformation.'

She wound a strand of hair around her forefinger, so that when she let it go, it sprang into a perfect little ringlet which brushed against her neck. He suddenly thought how slim she looked—and how breakable.

'I'm a chameleon,' she said flippantly. 'Didn't you know? I can be whatever people want me to be and tonight I've gone for the sleek and understated look.'

His mouth twitched. 'Any particular reason why?'

She shrugged. 'I've seen the guest list.'

He raised his brows. 'And?'

'And it was exactly as I could have predicted.' She tilted her chin defensively, her eyes momentarily uncertain, as if deciding whether or not to tell him. 'Rich people. Well-connected people. The current darling of the Greek cinema who just happens to be bringing two hulking great bodyguards with her. An international politician or two—including a man they're describing as the frontrunner candidate for the next-but-one US Presidential election.'

'What do you want me to say? I've known Brett since I was at college and to me he's just someone I learnt to play tennis with at Harvard.' He raised his brows. 'I offered to fly your friends over and put them up in a local hotel, but you refused.'

Tamsyn bit her lip. It was true, she *had* refused. Was that because she'd been terrified one of them might see past all the trappings and pick up on the heartache which was building inside her, minute by minute? Or because she was determined to keep her old enemy—pity—at arm's length? She wanted to remember this night as you might remember a particularly beautiful rainbow, or sunset—something amazing but short-lived.

Her sister wasn't coming either, citing a busy royal diary which was planned weeks in advance and didn't allow for last-minute invitations to rushed weddings. But Tamsyn had detected a strong sense of disapproval in Hannah's reply as well as disbelief that she'd actually tied the knot with Xan Constantinides. Tamsyn had wanted to write and tell her she was doing this mainly for her, but her sister suddenly seemed a very long way away.

'Those are the kind of people I associate with, Tamsyn,' continued Xan quietly. 'You knew that.'

'Yes. But it's one thing knowing something and another thing facing them all for the first and probably only time—and that includes meeting your father. I've realised I don't want to turn myself into some sort of spectacle—some caricature of a tart, who people can poke fun at and laugh about behind their back. I've realised I don't want to be *unsuitable*. Not tonight. If I do that it's going to make this evening even more of an ordeal.' She expelled a sigh. 'If you want to know the truth, I'm beginning to wish I'd never agreed to throw the wretched party in the first place.'

He gave an odd kind of laugh. 'Well, just for the record, so do I and if people weren't already on their way from halfway across the globe, I'd consider cancelling it. But we can't. Which means we just have to get through it and make the best of it.' An unwilling kind of admiration sparked in the depths of his dark blue eyes. 'And just for the record, it's a very beautiful dress. You look every inch the suitable bride.'

Trying not to be swayed by his soft praise, Tamsyn smoothed down the silk-satin bodice of the outfit she'd ordered online from a store in Athens and which Elena had smuggled in yesterday. It had given her a ridiculous amount of pleasure to see herself looking like the kind of bride she'd never thought she could be, but in the end—her clothes were irrelevant. All she wanted was for tonight to be over, so she could start thinking about her future.

She watched him walk over to the open windows of their terrace, thinking how much she was going to miss this. And him. She could hear the chink of glasses from out on the lawn as waiters began loading up their trays and in the distance, could see a long line of approaching headlights travelling along the coastal road.

Her eyes ran over Xan's powerful physique, trying to commit it to memory. The snowy white dinner jacket which contrasted vividly with the close-fitting dark trousers. She loved the way those coal-black tendrils of hair brushed against the collar of his shirt, reminding her that he looked as much at home on a sailing boat as he did a boardroom. But as he turned around she quickly wiped her face clear of emotion—eradicating all the yearning, so she was able to meet his cobalt gaze with nothing more telling than a look of cool enquiry.

'Let's go,' he said abruptly.

Xan felt the adrenalin pumping through his body as he took Tamsyn's hand and led her out into the garden, where burning flames lined the paths and fairy-lights were strung from the trees. The huge swimming pool had been illuminated with floating lights, which gleamed in the turquoise water like surreal water lilies and the front of the house had been floodlit in soft colours of rose and blue. He told himself it was pride in his beautiful home which was making him feel so pumped-up tonight, but it was more than that. He looked at the woman by his side, thinking that Tamsyn had never looked lovelier. The most beautiful woman he had ever seen.

Easily visible in her white gown, he watched men turning to stare at her, just as they had once done at Kulal's palace. Back then he remembered feeling nothing but a destabilising lust but now that had been over-ridden by a primitive satisfaction that she belonged to *him* and only him. His mouth hardened. But she didn't, did she? Not really. She was his only for a little while longer and he needed to accept that soon she would be free, because that was what the plan had always been.

Free for other men to pursue and to benefit from all that shining sexual promise which he had awoken. A powerful surge of jealousy coursed through him, even though jealousy had never been his thing. He told himself that the feeling would soon pass. That he'd never relied on a woman before and didn't intend to start now. His life had been fine before Tamsyn Wilson had fallen into it like some wayward star, and that state of affairs would resume once they'd split.

Slightly mollified by his own reasoning, he introduced her to a number of guests and she responded with a charm which was contagious. Everyone wanted to talk to her and she instantly hit it off with a European princess, herself a former wild-child, and he could hear the two of them giggling together. Soon she was deep in conversation with a sultan she'd met at her sister's wedding, and several other desert princes moved to join in with the conversation, so that very quickly she was at the centre of a significant power hub. At one point she looked up at him and he raised his glass in mocking salute, as if to silently remind her that her fears of blending in had been groundless. But something in the gesture made her eyes grow dark. He saw her bite her lip and a few moments later she murmured to him that she needed to speak to Elena, and slipped away.

Xan accepted a glass of champagne and looked around. A group of musicians were playing traditional Greek music and out of the corner of his eye, he noticed that Salvatore di Luca had arrived, with the requisite glamorous blonde hanging from his arm like a glittering accessory. But there was still no sign of his father.

He took a sip of his drink. Was the old man wor-

ried that Sofia's father would refuse to sell him the island after all—and would that be enough to make him
cut Xan from his life for ever? His lips hardened into
a humourless smile. What exquisite irony that would
be—if an island coveted because of its precious links
with his ancestors, should be the cause of alienating
his father from his only son.

He looked around again, his eyes scanning the
crowded lawn with dissatisfaction as he realised he
was looking in vain for his wife. Xan scowled as he
handed his half-drunk glass of champagne to a passing
waiter, the memory of emerald eyes and fiery curls an
image he couldn't seem to shift from his mind.

It was all about sex, he reassured himself heatedly.
Nothing but sex.

Tamsyn melted into the shadows, trying to gather her
thoughts together. Yes, the party was loads easier than
she'd imagined—but it was still stressful, which was
why she had sought a moment of quiet refuge at the
darkened side of the house, at the top of a gentle sloping incline, which gave a fabulous view of the glittering estate. Carefully smoothing down the rich silk of
her dress, she sat down on a bench—tempted to kick
off her silver sandals but knowing if she did so, she
would be reluctant to put them on again. And tonight
there would be no barefoot bride, looking like she'd
wandered in from a nearby rock festival.

She sat back against the wooden bench and sighed.
It had been strangely gratifying that Xan's friends had
seemed genuinely happy to meet her. Was that because
she had taken charge of her own destiny, so that for
once she actually *felt* as if she fitted in—in a way she'd

never done before? Even at Hannah's wedding she'd worn her fancy gowns with a distinct air of resentment—probably because she'd been forced to wear them. But tonight she was revelling in the fact that she looked like a bride her husband could be proud of. She'd felt like a grown up and sophisticated version of the newest member of the Constantinides family. And weren't those thoughts dangerous?

A few times she'd found herself beguiled by the elusive possibility of something which could never happen, not in a million years. Of a life here, with Xan. A proper married life together—with a brood of babies and a golden future. And a shared love? Yes. Oh, yes. That was the ultimate dream. But Xan didn't want that. He'd told her so enough times. He didn't *do* love and he was okay with that. So she needed to be okay with it, too.

A sudden lump constricted her throat as she found herself thinking about her mother. About the paperwork which had been discovered after her death. Her mother had been a foolish dreamer, too—and where had it got her? All those stupid poems she'd written. And the letter addressed to her—the daughter she had abandoned. She mustn't forget that. The letter which Hannah had only shown Tamsyn a long while afterwards, which had told her something it might have been better not to have known. Something which for a long time had made her feel rotten to the core—and still could, if she wasn't careful.

She could see the powerful beam of headlights tracking along the road towards the house and from her secluded vantage point, could sense the excited bustle of the guests as a huge car drew to a halt and a man got out. Even from this distance, from the few photographs she'd seen of him, Tamsyn recognised the distinctive curved features of Andreas, Xan's father. She watched as Xan moved purposefully towards the car, but you didn't need to be a body language expert to notice the coolness between the two men. After a brief and business-like handshake, they began to walk towards the house, making no attempt to join the party.

Tamsyn sat on the bench, filled with indecision. She ought to go and meet him. Hadn't that been part of the deal? Her heart was pounding as she moved through the shadows towards the back of the vast house, away from the main party which was mostly happening poolside. For a moment she stood in silence, until she located the sound of voices which were coming from behind the closed doors of Xan's study. Tamsyn frowned. Xan and presumably Andreas were angrily talking over each other, the volume of their discussion getting louder and louder until she heard someone rasp out a curse. She meant to take a deep breath. To knock politely and walk in, but then she heard her own name and it halted her right in her tracks. Tamsyn froze. She almost wished they were speaking in Greek so she wouldn't understand what they were saying, but Xan had told her that after winning his American scholarship, English had been the language he and his father had conversed in, the older man refusing to be outdone by his fluent son.

'You know what kind of a woman she is?' came the ragged accusation. 'When you rang to tell me you'd married her, I had her investigated and discovered she's a nobody who can't even hold a job down. And she looks like a slut in every photo I've seen of her!'

Tamsyn flinched as she waited for Xan to reply and his next words came as such a shock that she had to put her hand against the wall to steady herself.

'She's no slut,' Xan said. 'She's honest and decent and true. And I will not have you speaking about her that way. Do you understand?'

'And you know her mother was no better than a whore?' continued the older man. 'That she has children by many different men?'

'Yes, I know that,' replied Xan slowly. 'But that isn't Tamsyn. She's never really had a chance, but now she's been given one, she's come into her own. She'd uneducated but she's bright. She reads. She plays with Gia's little girl—and that child thinks she's an angel. She's funny. You should meet her. I think you'll be surprised.'

'Oh, I'm not denying she's beautiful.' His father gave an ugly kind of laugh. 'But that's the main reason she's here, isn't it? You turned down the chance to marry a woman like Sofia, for her? I've heard she's hot, but so what? Whores usually are. You get what you pay for.'

There was a loud bang, which sounded like a fist being smashed against a desk and Tamsyn was vaguely aware of Xan's furious response, but by then she had started to run. To run and run until she had left the house and been swallowed up by the dense shadow of a fragrant pine tree.

Her brow felt hot and sticky by the time she came to a halt and it took a long while before she had calmed down enough to be able to think straight. Time for her breathing to slow and her heart to stop feeling as if it were going to burst out of her chest. Something made her tidy up the strands of hair which must have escaped during her run and to extract a slim tube of lipstick from the concealed pocket of her dress, before applying it to her trembling lips with shaky fingers. Her dress was smooth and she needed her features to mimic that smoothness, so that to the other guests it would appear as if nothing had happened.

Because nothing had.

Xan's father had simply told the truth—and he didn't know the half of it. And although Xan had sprung to her defence and her heart had melted slightly at his defence of her—it had still been lacking in emotion. He had still somehow managed to make her sound like piece of rock which had been carved into a rough approximation of a human being.

And suddenly she knew she couldn't endure any more. There was no way she could stay here, pretending to be someone she wasn't. If she did that, then these crazy feelings would keep building and building until she was ready to explode. She needed to walk away with Xan never guessing what had happened. To escape, and quickly—but not tonight. Tonight she would continue to play the role expected of her. The shining and loyal wife, basking in her newly-wed golden glow. The woman lucky enough to have finally snared the elusive Greek billionaire.

She drank a glass of champagne before going back to the illuminated swimming pool to join the other guests, chatting brightly and forcing herself to smile as she accepted congratulations. But her stupid heart turned over with sorrow when Xan reappeared and began to walk towards her.

Did he read something untoward in her expression?

Was that why a frown had creased his brow beneath the delicious tumble of his black hair?

'You okay?' he questioned.

She could tell him, of course. She could say she'd gone into the house to meet his father and heard him calling her a whore. But if she did that, the evening would be ruined—and for what purpose? The fact that Xan's father didn't like her should be regarded as a positive, surely? It meant he would be delighted when his son announced they were splitting up. Maybe their own relationship would even improve as a result. What was it they said? Every cloud has a silver lining.

You can do this, Tamsyn, she told herself fiercely. *You've had a lifetime of pretending everything's okay. Of acting like it doesn't matter when other people judge you, or look down their noses at you.*

'Yes, I'm fine,' she said, then cleared her throat. 'Did I see your father arrive?'

'You did.' An odd expression darkened his face. 'But he couldn't stay.'

'Oh? Was he—?'

'I don't want to talk about my father, Tamsyn,' he interrupted, and suddenly his voice sounded urgent. 'I just want to be alone with you.'

Her heart felt like it wanted to break when she heard the note of hunger she heard in his voice, but she couldn't stop herself from responding to it. 'Xan,' she said, mock-sternly. 'We have guests.'

'I don't care about the guests.' His voice dipped. 'There's only one thing I care about right now.'

His smile was hard and his eyes gleamed with an unspoken message. It reminded her that Xan remained a man who always got what he wanted, and right now he wanted sex. Tamsyn shivered as he traced a finger down her arm, knowing she should refuse to go along with it, especially in view of what his father had said earlier.

You get what you pay for.

But her mind was made up. She wasn't going to ruin the night by dwelling on the negative and besides, she wanted him just as much as he wanted her. Maybe even more. Xan had no idea this was going to be the last time, but she did—and wasn't it crazy not to want to make the most of every precious second with him?

'Then what are we waiting for?' she questioned huskily, as she went into his warm and waiting arms.

CHAPTER TWELVE

'WHAT ARE YOU talking about?' Xan stared at his housekeeper in disbelief. 'What do you mean, she's *gone*?'

But he barely listened to Manalena's distressed explanation as he stormed up to the bedroom because the evidence was there for him to see. He shook his head with disbelief as he pulled open one of the closet doors. Only the most basic of Tamsyn's clothes were missing—all the fancy ones remained. His throat dried as he reached out to touch the white gown she'd worn at their wedding party, which he'd almost torn in his eagerness to remove it from her body last night. Her unread books were no longer in a pile beside the bedside table and that wide-toothed comb thing she used to rake through her unruly curls in the mornings was nowhere to be seen.

He dismissed the housekeeper as he saw a note she must have left lying on the pillow, striding across the room to pick it up and resisting the desire to crush it to a pulp within the palm of his hand. It was short and to the point. Was that deliberate? Was she mocking him for that terse note he'd once left *her* in a faraway desert palace?

Xan,
I've decided to go sooner rather than later and I
didn't want the bore of saying goodbye, I'm sure
you'll understand.
  Below you'll find all my bank details and I
look forward to hearing from your lawyer.
Yours, Tamsyn.

He stared at it, his eyes scanning the words in disbelief, as if there had to be some kind of mistake. But there was no mistake. There it was, in black and white. A stark farewell, which seemed mainly concerned with getting her payment for their short-lived marriage.

His mouth twisted. He'd gone back to the office this morning, strangely reluctant to leave the seductive warmth of his wife's body and the lazy caress of her arms after their surprisingly satisfactory honeymoon. The day had seemed to drag in a way he wasn't used to and several times he'd found himself picking up the phone to ring her, just to say hello, before reminding himself that wasn't his style and putting it down again. He'd told himself it was normal to be physically aching for her, because they'd been having so much amazing sex since the day of their marriage and they'd been together exclusively for fourteen days and nights. Elena had looked startled when he'd suddenly announced he was leaving early and his heart had been beating like a drum as his car had been driven at high speed to the estate, only to discover that his wife had gone. And to discover just how she had spent *her* day...

A bitter taste coated his throat. She must have

been silently planning her get-away. How long had she been plotting that, he wondered? While his own driver had been busy ferrying him around the city, she had persuaded Manalena to call her a cab to take her into Athens, supposedly on a shopping trip—before slipping away to the airport to catch a regular flight to London. Had she been laughing quietly as her lips had locked against his that morning, knowing what a surprise she was about to spring on him? Was that why her hand had slid between his legs to find his hardness—he was always hard for her—and guided him inside her slick, waiting heat for one last, bone-melting time?

He paced over to the window but the bright beauty of the Aegean failed to stir his heart, for his rage and incomprehension were all-consuming. Didn't she owe him the common courtesy of telling him she was breaking their agreement by leaving early, or at least explaining why?

He told himself not to do anything. To give himself time to calm down. But even as he thought it, he found himself lifting his phone and barking out instructions to Elena to have his private jet made ready. He didn't know what he was going to say to his runaway bride, all he knew was that he had to say *something*.

Tamsyn stared at the photograph, as if doing so could help. It was that old trick of voluntarily subjecting herself to pain before anyone else got the chance to do it. As if that could somehow make her immune to it.

Some hope. The photograph was from a gossip column and had obviously been taken at the wedding party. She didn't imagine Xan's friends were the type who sneaked photos at exclusive social events, but there had been a lot of outside caterers there that night and maybe one of them had captured the moment. And, oh, what a moment to have captured.

Beneath a headline which proclaimed *Greek Tycoon Weds at Last!* was a photo of her and Xan. She thought how dreamy she looked and how *happy* she seemed as she stared up into his face. And Xan? Tamsyn sighed. His darkly contoured features gave little away, but maybe it was good to recognise that. To reinforce that she'd done the right thing in running away from his luxury estate, because if she'd stayed around, growing fonder and fonder of him—then her heart would have been truly broken.

Yet didn't it feel a little bit broken now?

From a long way downstairs she heard the doorbell ring, but she didn't move. It wasn't her house—she was just lucky that her friend Ellie from the Bluebird Club had an attic room going free and had told Tamsyn she was welcome to stay there until she'd found her feet again. Funny expression, really. As if someone could lose their own feet. She couldn't imagine going back to waitressing, yet neither could she summon up the enthusiasm to enrol in college to get herself a late-in-the-day education, despite Xan's faith in her. And the craziest thing of all was that, having married just to get her hands on his money, she now found herself reluctant to take any of it. The deliberately cold note she'd left for him had been nothing but bravado—done to ensure that he would ultimately despise her and leave her in peace.

'Tamsyn!'

It was Ellie. With a sigh Tamsyn got up off the single bed, walked across the tiny room and stuck her head outside the door. 'Yep?' she yelled down.

'There's somebody here to see you.'

Tamsyn blinked. Nobody other than Ellie knew she was back, because that was how she wanted it. Time to lick her wounds and recover—even if right now that seemed like an impossibility. She'd told Hannah she was here, in a rushed phone call to the palace in Zahristan when she'd tried her very best—and somehow succeeded—in not sobbing her heart out as she explained that her brief marriage was over. Surely her heavily pregnant sister hadn't impulsively flown over to see her?

'Who is it?' she called back.

'Me,' said a dark, accented voice which carried up the stairs. 'Your husband.'

Tamsyn clutched onto the door handle, trying not to react as she saw a glimpse of the top of Xan's dark head as he walked up the stairs. A lurch of joy and fear made her feel almost dizzy, but most of all she could feel an overwhelming sense of yearning as his broad shoulders came into view. But she wasn't going to let him know that, because one thing she knew was that there could be no going back. She could be strong, yes—she'd spent her life trying to be strong in the face of adversity. Just not strong enough to stay with a man who was never going to care for her.

'Xan,' she croaked, as he drew closer. 'What…what are you doing here?'

'Not now,' he said grimly as he reached the top of the stairs. 'In private.'

'Everything okay?' called Ellie's anxiously from the bottom of the stairs.

'Everything's just fine,' said Xan, in the kind of tone which broached no argument.

Tamsyn felt even more dizzy as he reached the top of the stairs and gestured for her to proceed him into the room, still with that same grim expression on his face. She told herself she didn't have to let him in. After all, it was *her* room, not his—and technically he could even be described as trespassing. She could tell him to leave and only to contact her through her lawyers, but deep down she knew that wasn't an option—and not just because she didn't actually *have* any lawyers. It was more because she wanted to feast her eyes on him one last time. To file away the memory of those cold blue eyes, that hot body, and the sensual mouth which had brought her so much pleasure.

'So, Tamsyn,' he said, once he was inside the miniscule room and completely dominating it, having flicked a dismissive glance at the tiny bed and the view out over an alley which was lined with overflowing dustbins. 'Are you going to explain why you decided to run off without telling me?'

Her heart was beating very fast as she sucked in a deep breath. No, she wasn't. Because she didn't owe him anything. Nothing.

But the defensiveness which had always been second nature to her wasn't coming as easily as usual and she wondered how convincing her nonchalant shrug was. 'We both knew it had to end sometime,' she said carelessly. 'I just made an executive decision to end it early. It was a fake marriage, Xan. It was conceived to get you out of a tight spot and as far as I'm concerned, I've performed my part of the bargain.'

'Why, Tamsyn?' he said simply.

Once again, she shrugged, even though when he said her name like that it made her want to cry. 'I heard… I heard you talking with your father.'

His eyes narrowed in comprehension and then he nodded. 'Did you now? So you will have heard me defending you.'

'Yes, I heard you. Thanks.'

He looked at her. 'And that's it?'

She nodded. 'Yep, that's it. There's nothing more to say. I don't even know why you're here.'

'Because I don't understand. And I need to understand.'

She shook her head so that her unruly curls flew all around her shoulders and impatiently she pushed them away. 'No,' she negated heatedly. 'You don't *need* to understand, Xan. You *want* to understand—and there's a difference. I know you're rich and powerful, but even you have got to realise that you can't always get what you want. So will you please go?'

He shook his head. 'There's something you're not telling me, Tamsyn.'

'And? What if there is? You're not privy to my innermost thoughts—even if we were a real married couple, which we're not! You have no right to expect explanations.'

'I disagree,' he said coolly. 'I think I do, and I'm not going anywhere until you start talking to me. I want the truth, Tamsyn. I think you owe me that, at least.'

Did she? Did she owe him *anything*? For the sexual awakening, or for making her realise that she was as capable of love as anyone else? As she stared into his resolute face, Tamsyn recognised she was in real danger here. She wanted her heart to stop hurting but the only way that was going to happen was if Xan went away and left her alone, and he wasn't showing any sign of doing that. She could see the look of determination on his face and realised he meant it when he'd said he wouldn't be satisfied with anything but the truth.

So should she tell him and witness his disgust when he realised what kind of person he'd really married? Watch his gorgeous face freeze with fastidious horror when he learned the truth about her gene pool? And that might that be the best outcome of all, because then he really *would* say goodbye and she could begin the long process of getting over him. If she pushed him away first—at least he wouldn't be able to turn round and do it to her. She sucked in an unsteady breath. 'You described me as honest and decent and true,' she said quietly. 'But I'm not. At least, I'm not honest.'

'What are you talking about?'

Don't let your voice shake. And, above all, don't cry.

'You only know half the truth. That my mother was a groupie—'

'Yes, yes. That's old news,' he said impatiently.

She shook her head, but her determination not to cry was failing her. She felt her eyes brimming with tears and saw Xan flinch, as if he found such a spectacle distasteful. He probably did. He didn't like emotion. It was messy and he wasn't used to it. Well, neither was she if it came to that, but for once in her life Tamsyn was finding it impossible to hold back the shuddering sob which seemed to erupt from the very bottom of her lungs.

'Well, here's some hot-off-the-press news!' she snarled. 'My father was a rock star. A very famous rock star. His name was Jonny Trafford.'

'Jonny Trafford? Wow.' He frowned. 'But he—'

'I'm not interested in how many albums you had of his. You want to know what happened?' she rushed on, waving her hand impatiently to silence him in her determination to tell him the facts. The unvarnished facts—not the version which everyone knew. It was the only thing she had left of Jonny Trafford—her few brief and bitter memories. 'He had a one-night stand with my mother.' Her voice shook with something like shame. 'According to his official biography, he had similar nights with lots of women. Sometimes with more than one at the same time...'

'Tamsyn—'

'Shut *up*!' she declared as the tears now began to stream down her cheeks and the words came choking out. 'You know my mother had us fostered because we got in the way of her latest love interest? I know. Shocking, isn't it? And after she died Hannah came into possession of her paperwork, including a letter addressed to me which contained the bombshell discovery that Jonny Trafford was my father. But Hannah didn't tell me that. At least, not straight away.'

He narrowed his eyes. 'Why not?'

'She was trying to protect me, just like she'd always done.' Tamsyn stabbed at her wet cheeks with a balled-up fist. 'She thought I'd been through enough hurt and wanted to make sure I wasn't going to endure any more. So she went to see him.' Her voice tailed off but his face was intent as he leaned forward.

'Tell me, Tamsyn.'

She shook her head as she looked at him, knowing this was it. The words tasted sour as she began to speak them but she forced herself to keep looking at the man she had married, no matter how much it hurt. No matter how much disgust he showed when he heard the truth. 'He was a full-blown junkie by then, of course. She said she'd never seen anyone look so pathetic, in his huge mansion with all those great big mirrors and shaggy rugs, and the dusty platinum discs on the walls. But when she told him about me, she said she thought she saw a light in his eyes. He told her straight off he was going to go into rehab, like his manager had been nagging at him to do for years, and he did. And that was when she told me about him.'

'Well, that was good, wasn't it?' Xan questioned.

Tamsyn shrugged. 'Yeah, I suppose so. He wasn't allowed any contact with the outside world for six weeks, not until he was properly clean, but he was allowed to write letters. He wrote to me and said he was looking forward to seeing me and I can remember how excited I felt. I had no real memories of my mother, but here was the chance to connect with my roots at last. I know it sounds stupid but I wanted to see if I had the same nose, or eyes, or if we walked in a similar way. I wanted to feel *connected*.'

'It doesn't sound stupid.' There was a pause and his eyes were very steady as he looked at her. 'What happened?'

'We arranged to meet in a famous London hotel, for tea, but…' She swallowed, then shook her head and it took a couple of moments before she could compose herself enough to continue. 'He couldn't face it—or maybe the lure of heroin was stronger than the thought of meeting his daughter for the first time. I sat in that fancy hotel for ages with barely enough money to pay the inflated price of the pot of tea I'd had to order.

I remember getting lots of pitying looks—probably because of the way I was dressed. Or maybe people thought I'd been stood up. Which I had, I g-guess.' She swallowed again, but now the tears were like hot rivers coursing down her cheeks and the pain in her heart was fierce and intense as she relived a scenario she hadn't allowed herself to think about for years. 'When I came out it was dark and the evening news bulletins were flashing up on TV screens in a nearby department store—and the lead story was that Jonny Trafford had been found dead in a hotel room with a needle hanging out of his arm.'

'Tamsyn—'

'No!' she interrupted, her voice trembling as she fished a tissue out of the back of her jeans and loudly blew her nose. 'Don't say all the things you think you're supposed to say. Because words won't change anything, Xan. I know it was terrible but I've come to terms with the fact that neither my father nor my mother wanted me, and that's why I'm so screwed up. Whichever way you look at it, I'm not the right type of wife for you. My unsuitability runs deeper than you thought and it's far better we split now, rather than later. So just go, will you? Go now and leave me in peace.'

He shook his head. 'But I don't want to go.'

'When will you get it into your thick skull that I don't care what *you* want?' she flared back. 'I'm telling you my wishes and since this is my home, for now at least, you will have to listen to them!'

But Xan didn't move. There was silence for a moment as he glanced over his shoulder to survey the bleak view outside the window and then looked back at her, the woman he had married. He saw the way her lips quivered with belligerence and pride and shame. Her cheeks were wet and streaky and fiery strands of hair were matted with tears. Her expression was defiant but wary as she returned his gaze—like a dog which had spent its life being kicked but had just enough spirit left to fight back. And that was Tamsyn all right. He admired her spirit and always had done.

He hadn't been expecting yet another layer to her tragic life story. He hadn't realised just how deeply she'd been damaged. He'd imagined coming here today and after some token resistance, the two of them having some pretty urgent sex up against the wall, since that bed looked way too small to accommodate two people. Unwilling to let her go just yet, he'd planned to take her back to Greece, thinking that a few months more of his feisty spouse would be enough to get her out of his system.

But now he recognised that he couldn't do that. He couldn't pick her up and put her down, using her like his own sexy little toy. To do that would be to dishonour and disrespect her—and damage her further. Didn't she deserve every bit of his respect after what she'd been through? His heart clenched, knowing that if he wanted this to work—he was going to have to give more than he'd ever given before. He was going to have to have the courage to open up and confront his feelings—just as she had done with him.

'You know that with you, it's like it's never been for me before,' he said softly.

Her emerald eyes clouded with suspicion. 'What are you talking about?'

'I'm talking about you. How different it is with you.

It's been different from the start, Tamsyn—in every way. You're fresh and feisty and original—and more fun than any other woman I've ever known. And we're alike. I see that now. We both grew up rejected by our mothers. We didn't know how to express love because nobody had ever shown us how.' He sucked in a deep and unsteady breath. 'The thing is that I think we could be good together. Not for three months, or a year—but for ever.'

'For ever?' she echoed, as if this was a concept beyond her comprehension.

He nodded. 'It won't always be easy and it won't always be fun. There'll be bad times as well as good, because my married friends tell me that's what life is like. But I think we can be strong for each other and supportive of each other, if the will is there.'

He saw the brief hope which flared in her face before it was banished by that determined little expression of mutiny once more. 'No. It won't work. It can't work,' she husked. 'It'll all end in tears, I know it will. So do yourself a favour, Xan—and get away from me.'

'Sorry.' He shook his head again. 'No I can't do that. You aren't going to sabotage this, Tamsyn—no matter how hard you try. And even if you continue to glare at me and send me away—I'll just keep coming back until you give me the answer that both of us really want. Which is that you will be my wife for real.'

She chewed on her bottom lip as her eyes swam with green tears and it took a full minute before she could form the words. 'You...you really mean it?' she whispered.

He slammed his palm against the left side of his sternum. 'From the bottom of my heart.'

At this she started crying again but this time the tears were different and her mouth was trying to smile instead of wobbling with pain and Xan pulled her into his arms and kissed her with a tenderness he hadn't known he possessed. For a long while they just stood there, locked in each other's arms as their mouths connected in kiss after kiss, and not long after that, Xan made the discovery that the bed was plenty big enough for what he had in mind.

Efficiently, he stripped off all their clothes and it wasn't until he had filled her with his seed and heard her choke out her own cry of fulfilment, that he finally felt as if he was exactly where he needed to be in the world. That everything he'd ever wanted was right here, right now. They lay there, quiet and contented and Xan was stroking Tamsyn's tumbled curls when he tilted her chin to look at him.

'One thing interests me,' he said.

Dreamily, she looked up into his face. 'Mmm?'

'Why didn't you make a claim on Jonny's estate, which presumably you didn't? You could have been a very wealthy woman.'

Tamsyn shook her head. Even Hannah had told her she should try to get something from Jonny Trafford's property portfolio and his back catalogue of songs,, but Tamsyn hadn't wanted to know. 'It all just seemed too sordid,' she said slowly. 'I knew there would be publicity and DNA tests and inevitable opposition to my claim and I couldn't…'

'You couldn't face them?'

'That's right. It wasn't worth it. All the money in the world wouldn't have tempted me to put myself through an ordeal like that.'

He flinched. 'Yet you were willing to marry me for a price.'

She met the question in his eyes and shrugged. 'To be honest, it wasn't for me. I was worried about my sister.'

'Hannah?' He looked at her in bemusement. 'Who's married to one of the wealthiest men on the planet?'

She nodded. 'At the time I wasn't sure if her marriage to the Sheikh was going to last and realised I needed funds to help her if she needed to get away from him. That's why I did it.'

He pulled her closer and his eyes were darkly blue. 'Oh, I love you, Tamsyn Constantinides. I love you because you're strong and brave and loyal. You are the bright fire in my life, my love—and the world would be a very dark and cold place without you.'

Tamsyn swallowed, knowing that there was one thing more which needed to be addressed. 'It doesn't matter what my reasons were, Xan,' she said quietly. 'I still married you for money, didn't I? All your life you've been pursued by women who know how wealthy you are and maybe at heart, you think we're all gold-diggers. I can't blame you for that, Xan. If I were you, I might even think the same!'

He traced his finger thoughtfully over the trembling outline of her mouth. 'Okay. Let's sort this out once and for all. Will you answer me just one question, Tamsyn, with all the honesty you have already demonstrated today?'

She hooded her eyes suspiciously. 'Just one?'

'Just one.' He looked her straight in the eyes. 'If I didn't have a cent in the world, would you be lying with me now, like this?'

It wasn't a fair question because there could be no equivocation about her answer and more stupid tears sprang to Tamsyn's eyes as she nodded. 'Of course I would,' she whispered. 'Because I love you for you, Xan—you and only you. All the other stuff simply doesn't matter.'

His face was serious as he kissed away her tears and only when her cheeks were dry did he turn his attention to her mouth. And the kiss which followed was like no other. It wasn't about sex, or ownership or possession. It was seeking and tender. It spoke of compassion and true intimacy. It spoke of the powerful trust which existed between them now. It spoke of sanctuary and a golden future.

And for the first time in her life, Tamsyn felt safe.

EPILOGUE

'It's so *BEAUTIFUL*,' breathed Tamsyn as the sun sank slowly into the sea, turning the surrounding water into contrasting shades of deep purple and gold.

'I know,' said Xan softly. 'Utterly beautiful.'

Tamsyn looked up to find her husband's gaze fixed not on the magnificent spectacle taking place over the Aegean but on her. 'Xan,' she said, in mock-reprimand. 'I was talking about the view.'

'So was I. But in my mind there's no contest. The sunset on this island is always magnificent—but its blaze is nothing compared to the colour of your hair, *agape mou.*'

Tamsyn gave a shiver of delight as his silken words washed over her. 'If only I'd realised I was marrying a poet.'

'There were a lot of things we didn't know about each other back then.'

Their eyes met. 'But we do now,' she said.

'Yes.'

He walked over to where she stood, on the strip of land not far from the beach. Behind her was the small stone house where their son lay sleeping and in front of her was the endless potential of the night ahead. This was their fourth day on Prassakri, where the bones of Xan's ancestors lay. They'd spent lazy hours walking and talking and teaching their son how to swim. They'd built sandcastles and eaten picnics as they explored the stunning island, where little had changed over the centuries.

But it had been a rollercoaster three years since their wedding.

After initially refusing to sell Xan the island, Sofia's father had eventually agreed on a deal. A deal prompted by the discovery that his daughter was in love with one of his farm labourers, and had been for years—and they needed an injection of cash to start up on their own. Sofia had met Tamsyn and Xan for lunch in Athens and told them everything.

'I knew Papa would never allow me to marry Georgiou because he was so poor,' she'd explained, looking down at her plain gold wedding band with an expression of delight. 'Which was why my long-term engagement to Xan worked so well. It's why I was so happy to go along with it. As a kind of smokescreen, I guess.'

Xan had smiled and so had Tamsyn, glad that no hearts had been broken during the fictitious understanding.

The reconciliation with Xan's father had happened slowly—bolstered by the knowledge that his ancestral island was back under the ownership of the Constantinides family. But the real rapprochement had come after the birth of Tamsyn and Xan's child. Andreas had unexpectedly turned up on the doorstep with a jar of honey—which apparently was a Greek tradition—his eyes filling with tears as he had gazed down at his newborn grandson. These days he came to their house on the Peloponnese peninsula often, enjoying the kind of warm family life he'd never really experienced before.

Tamsyn glanced up at the sky. The sun had almost disappeared and in the darkening indigo sky was the first faint sprinkle of stars.

'I think it's time for us to go to bed, *agape mou*,' observed Xan throatily. 'Don't you?'

Leaning back against his broad chest, Tamsyn nodded. 'Mmm,' she agreed. 'Let's.'

It was still early but they liked to retire early for they enjoyed nothing better than the endless discovery of each other's bodies. The ancient stone steps absorbed the sound of their footsteps as they went upstairs and peeped in on their toddler son who lay contentedly sleeping and sucking his thumb.

'He's worn out,' said Xan approvingly.

'Are you surprised?' She wrinkled her nose. 'He seems a bit young to start playing tennis.'

'That's not what his godfather says.'

'No.' There was a pause while Tamsyn considered the very real chance that her son's godfather would one day be president of the United States of America. She looked down and smiled as she studied the unruly black curls which looked so dark against the sheet. Andreas Alexandros Iohannis. She'd known that another tradition was to call the first born son after his paternal grandfather, but it had been Xan who had suggested including the Greek version of John among his names. At first Tamsyn hadn't known how she felt about that, until a sudden rush of emotion had reminded her that nobody could deny their roots, even if those roots had been allowed to wither, and die. Nobody knew that Jonny Trafford was her father, but echoes of him would live on in her child. She hoped that Andreas inherited some of his undoubted talent, and prayed that they could nurture him with enough love to defeat his demons.

She drew in a deep breath as she stared up at Xan, her heart suddenly beating very fast. 'We won't make the mistakes our own parents did,' she said unsteadily.

'No,' he agreed, his watchful gaze understanding. 'We'll make our own. But we'll try to limit them.'

'Yes,' she agreed as he pulled her into his arms.

'And we'll be honest enough to say if we think either of us is stepping out of line.' He tilted her chin to look directly into her eyes. 'Because we love each other and we're completely honest with each other, Tamsyn—and nothing is ever going to change that. Do you understand?'

Clamping her lips together, she nodded. 'Oh, Xan,' she said eventually, as she touched her fingertips to the roughened shadow at his jaw. 'I must have done something very good in a previous life, to have ended up with you.'

His eyes glinted as he led her from the nursery. 'I like the thought of you being good,' he murmured, as he began to undo the sarong which was knotted around her hips. 'But I like the thought of you being bad much better.'

'Do you really?' she said, tugging eagerly at the zip of his jeans. 'Then I'd better do as my husband desires.'

And she could hear nothing but his growl of contentment as she climbed on top of him in the silver moonlight, and day gave way to night.

* * * * *

WED FOR HIS
SECRET HEIR

CHANTELLE SHAW

For my gorgeous grandson Casey James

CHAPTER ONE

THE PRE-DINNER DRINKS seemed to be lasting for ever. Giannis Gekas glanced at his watch as his stomach rumbled. He had been in meetings all day and the tired-looking sandwich his PA had brought him at lunchtime had lived up to its appearance.

He sipped his Virgin Mary cocktail and considered eating the celery stalk that garnished the drink. The voices of the other guests in the banqueting hall merged into a jangle of white noise, and he edged behind a pillar to avoid having to make small talk with people he did not know and had no interest in.

It was then that he spotted a woman rearranging the place name cards on one of the circular dining tables. He supposed she might be a member of the events management team responsible for organising the charity fundraising dinner and auction. But she was wearing an evening gown, which suggested that she was a guest, and she cast a furtive glance over her shoulder as she switched the name cards.

When Giannis had taken the private lift from his penthouse suite in the exclusive London hotel, down to the foyer, he had checked the seating plan in the banqueting hall to find out where he would be sitting for the dinner. He wondered why the woman had put herself next to him.

It was not the first time such a thing had happened, he acknowledged with weary cynicism. The phenomenal success of his cruise line company had propelled him to the top of the list of Europe's richest businessmen.

He had been blessed with good looks and even before he had accrued his wealth women had pursued him, since he was a teenager taking tourists on sailing trips around the Greek islands on his family's boat. At eighteen, he had relished the attention of the countless nubile blondes who had flocked around him, but at thirty-five he was more selective.

The woman was blonde, admittedly, but she was not his type. He thought briefly of his last mistress Lise—a tall, toned Swedish swimwear model. He had dated her for a few months until she had started dropping hints about marriage. The dreaded 'm' word spelled the end of Giannis's interest, and he had ended the affair and arranged for Lise to be sent a diamond bracelet from an exclusive London jewellers, where he had an account.

Dinner would be served at seven-thirty and guests were beginning to take their places at the various tables. Giannis strolled over to where the woman was holding on tightly to the back of a chair as if she expected to be challenged for the seat. Her hair was the colour of honey and fell in silky waves to halfway down her back. As he drew closer to her, he noted that her eyes were the soft grey of rain clouds. She was attractive rather than beautiful, with defined cheekbones and a wide, pretty mouth that captured his attention. The full lips were frankly sensual, and as he watched her bite her lower lip he felt a frisson of desire to soothe the place with his tongue.

Surprised by his body's response, after he had decided that the woman did not warrant a second look, Giannis roamed his eyes over her. She was average height, with a slim waist and unfashionably curvaceous breasts and hips. Once again he felt a tightening in his groin as he allowed his gaze to linger on the creamy mounds displayed to perfection by the low-cut neckline of her black silk jersey dress.

She wore no jewellery—which was unusual at a high society event. Most of the other female guests were bedecked with gold and diamonds, and her lack of sparkling adornments focused his attention on the lustrous creaminess of her shoulders and décolleté.

He halted beside the table. 'Allow me,' he said smoothly as he drew out her chair and waited for her to sit down, before he lowered his tall frame onto the seat next to her. 'It appears that we will be companions for the evening…' he paused and glanced down at the table '… Miss Ava Sheridan.'

Wary grey eyes flew to his face. 'How do you know my name?'

'It is written on the card in front of you,' he said drily, wondering if she would explain why she had swapped the place cards.

A pink stain swept along her cheekbones but she quickly composed herself and gave him a hesitant smile. 'Oh, yes. Of course.' She caught her lower lip between her even white teeth and a flame flickered into life inside him. 'I'm pleased to meet you, Mr Gekas.'

'Giannis,' he said softly. He leaned back in his chair, turning his upper body so that he could focus his full attention on her, and smiled. With a sense of predictability, he watched her eyes darken, the pupils dilating. Charm came effortlessly to him. He had discovered when he was a youth that he had something: charisma, magnetism—whatever it was called, Giannis had it in bucketfuls. People were drawn to him. Men respected him and wanted his friendship—often only discovering after he had beaten them in a business deal that his laid-back air hid a ruthless determination to succeed. Women were fascinated by him and wanted him to take them to bed. Always.

Ava Sheridan was no different. Giannis offered her his hand and after an infinitesimal hesitation she placed her fingers in his. He lifted her hand to his mouth and she caught her breath when he brushed his lips across her knuckles.

Yes, she was attracted to him. What surprised him more was the shaft of white-hot desire that swept through him and made him uncomfortably hard. Thankfully, the lower half of his body was hidden beneath the folds of the tablecloth. He was relieved when more guests took their seats at the table and while introductions were made and waiters arrived to pour the wine and serve the first course Giannis regained control of his libido. He even felt amused by his reaction to Ava Sheridan, who was simply not in the same league as the sophisticated models and socialites he usually dated. He hadn't had sex for over a month, since he'd broken up with Lise, and celibacy did not suit him, he acknowledged wryly.

He finished his conversation with the hedge fund manager sitting on the other side of him and turned his head towards Ava, hiding a smile when she quickly jerked her gaze away. He had been aware of the numerous glances she had darted at him while he had been chatting to the other guests around the table.

As he studied the curve of her cheek and the elegant line of her neck, he realised that he had been wrong to dismiss her as merely attractive. She was beautiful, but her beauty was understated and entirely natural. Giannis suspected that she used minimal make-up to enhance her English rose complexion, and her round-as-peaches breasts did not owe their firmness to implants or a cosmetic surgeon's skill. In a room full of primped and pampered women adorned in extravagant jewellery, Ava Sheridan was like a rare and precious pearl found in the deepest depths of the ocean.

She was also as stubbornly resistant as an oyster shell, he thought, frustrated by her refusal to turn her head in his direction even though she must be aware of his scrutiny.

'Can I pour you some more wine?' He took his cue when she placed her half-empty glass down on the table. Now she could not avoid looking at him and, as their eyes met, Giannis felt the sizzle, the intangible spark of sexual attraction shoot between them.

'Just a little, thank you.' Her voice was low and melodious and made him think of cool water. A tiny frown creased her brow as she watched him top up her glass before he replaced the wine bottle in the ice bucket. 'Don't you want any wine?'

'No.' He gave her another easy smile and did not explain that he never drank alcohol.

She darted him a glance from beneath the sweep of her lashes. 'I have heard that you regularly make generous donations to charities... Giannis. And you are especially supportive of organisations which help families affected by alcohol misuse. Is there a particular reason for your interest?'

Giannis tensed and a suspicion slid into his mind as he remembered how she had contrived to sit next to him at dinner. The media were fascinated with him, and it would not be the first time that a member of the press had managed to inveigle their way onto the guest list of a social function in order to meet him. Mostly they wanted the latest gossip about his love life, but a few years ago a reporter had dug up the story from his past that he did not want to be reminded of.

Not that he could ever forget the mistake he'd made when he was nineteen, which had resulted in his father's death. The memories of that night would haunt Giannis for ever, and guilt cast a long shadow over him.

His expression hardened. 'Are you a journalist, Miss Sheridan?'

Her eyebrows rose. Either she was an accomplished actress or her surprise was genuine. 'No. Why do you think I might be?'

'You changed the seating arrangement so that we could sit together. I watched you switch the place cards.'

Colour blazed on her cheeks and if Giannis had been a different man he might have felt some sympathy for her obvious embarrassment. But he was who he was, and he felt nothing.

'I…yes, I admit I did swap the name cards,' she muttered. 'But I still don't understand why you think I am a journalist.'

'I have had experience of reporters, especially those working for the gutter press, using underhand methods to try to gain an interview with me.'

'I promise you I'm not a journalist.'

'Then why did you ensure that we would sit together?'

She bit her lip again and Giannis was irritated with himself for staring at her mouth. 'I… I was hoping to have a chance to talk to you.'

Her pretty face was flushed rose-pink but her intelligent grey eyes were honest—Giannis did not know why he was so convinced of that. The faint desperation in her unguarded expression sparked his curiosity.

'So, talk,' he said curtly.

* * *

'Not here.' Ava tore her gaze from Giannis Gekas and took a deep breath, hoping to steady the frantic thud of her pulse. She had recognised him instantly when he had walked over to the dining table where Becky, bless her, had allocated her a place. But her seat had been on the other side of the table—too far away from Giannis to be able to have a private conversation with him.

She had taken a gamble that no one would notice her swapping the name cards around. But she *had* to talk to Giannis about her brother. She'd forked out a fortune for a ticket to the charity dinner and bought an expensive evening dress that she'd probably never have the chance to wear again. The only way she could keep Sam from being sent to a young offender institution was if she could persuade Giannis Gekas to drop the charges against him.

Ava took a sip of her wine. It was important that she kept a clear head and she hadn't intended to drink any alcohol tonight, but she had not expected Giannis to be so *devastatingly* attractive. The photos she'd seen of him on the Internet when she'd researched the man dubbed Greece's most eligible bachelor had not prepared her for the way her heart had crashed into her ribs when he'd smiled. Handsome did not come close to describing his lethal good looks. His face was a work of art— the sculpted cheekbones and chiselled jaw softened by a blatantly sensual mouth that frequently curved into a lazy smile.

Dark, almost black eyes gleamed beneath heavy brows, and he constantly shoved a hand through his thick, dark brown hair that fell forwards onto his brow. But even more enticing than his model-perfect features and tall, muscle-packed body was Giannis's rampant sexuality.

He oozed charisma and he promised danger and excitement—the very things that Ava avoided. She gave herself a mental shake. It did not matter that Giannis was a bronzed Greek god. All she cared about was saving her idiot of a kid brother from prison and the very real possibility that Sam would be drawn into a life of crime like their father.

Sam wasn't bad; he had just gone off the rails because he lacked guidance. Ava knew that her mother had struggled to cope when Sam had hit puberty and he'd got in with a rough crowd of teenagers who hung around on the streets near the family home in East London. Even worse, Sam had become fascinated with their father and had even reverted to using the name McKay rather than their mother's maiden name, Sheridan. Ava had been glad to move away from the East End and all its associations with her father, but she felt guilty that she had not been around to keep her brother out of trouble.

She took another sip of wine and her eyes were drawn once more to the man sitting next to her. Sam's future rested in Giannis Gekas's hands. A waiter appeared and removed her goat's cheese salad starter that she had barely touched and replaced it with the Dover sole that she had chosen for the main course. Across the table, one of the other guests was trying to catch Giannis's attention. The chance to have a meaningful conversation with him during dinner seemed hopeless.

'I can't talk to you here.' She caught her bottom lip between her teeth and a quiver ran through her when his eyes focused on her mouth. She wondered why he suddenly seemed tense. 'Would it be possible for me to speak to you in private after dinner?'

His dark eyes trapped her gaze but his expression was unreadable. Afraid that he was about to refuse her request, she acted instinctively and placed her hand over his where it rested on the tablecloth. '*Please.*'

The warmth of his olive-gold skin beneath her fingertips sent heat racing up her arm. She attempted to snatch her hand away but Giannis captured her fingers in his.

'That depends on whether you are an entertaining dinner companion,' he murmured. He smiled at her confused expression and stroked his thumb lightly over the pulse in her wrist that was going crazy. 'Relax, *glykiá mou.* I think there is every possibility that we can have a private discussion later.'

'Thank you.' Relief flooded through her. But she could not relax as concern for her brother changed to a different kind of tension that had everything to do with the glitter in Giannis's eyes. She couldn't look away from his sensual mouth. His jaw was shadowed with black stubble and she wondered if it would feel abrasive against her cheek if he kissed her. If she kissed him back.

She took another sip of wine before she remembered that she hadn't had any lunch. Alcohol had a more potent effect on an empty stomach, she reminded herself. Her appetite had disappeared but she forced herself to eat a couple of forkfuls of Dover sole.

'So tell me, Ava—you have a beautiful name, by the way.' Giannis's husky accent felt like rough velvet stroking across Ava's skin, and the way he said her name in his lazy, sexy drawl, elongating the vowels—*Aaavaaa*—sent a quiver of reaction through her. 'You said that you are not a journalist, so what do you do for a living?'

Explaining about her work as a victim care officer might be awkward when Giannis was himself the victim of a crime which had been committed by her brother, Ava thought ruefully. Sam deeply regretted the extensive damage that he and his so-called 'friends' had caused to

Giannis's luxurious yacht. She needed to convince Giannis that her brother had made a mistake and deserved another chance.

She reached for her wine glass, but then changed her mind. Her head felt swimmy—although that might be because she had inhaled the spicy, explicitly sensual scent of Giannis's aftershave.

'Actually I'm between jobs at the moment.' She was pleased that her voice was steady, unlike her see-sawing emotions. 'I recently moved from Scotland back to London to be closer to my mother…and brother.'

Giannis ate some of his beef Wellington before he spoke. 'I have travelled widely, but Scotland is one place that I have never visited. I've heard that it is very beautiful.'

Ava thought of the deprived areas of Glasgow where she had been involved with a victim support charity, first as a volunteer, and after graduating from university she had been offered a job with the victim support team. In the past few years some of the city's grim, grey tower blocks had been knocked down and replaced with new houses, but high levels of unemployment still remained, as did the incidence of drug-taking, violence and crime.

She had felt that her job as a VCO—helping people who were victims or witnesses of crime—made amends in some small way for the terrible crimes her father had committed. But living far away in Scotland meant she had missed the signs that her brother had been drawn into the gang culture in East London. Her father's old haunts.

'Why do you care what I get up to?' Sam had demanded when she had tried to talk to him about his behaviour. 'You moved away and you don't care about me.' Ava felt a familiar stab of guilt that she hadn't been around for Sam or her mother when they had both needed her.

She dragged her thoughts back to the present and realised that Giannis was waiting for her to reply. 'The Highlands have some spectacular scenery,' she told him. 'If you are thinking of making a trip to Scotland I can recommend a few places for you to visit.'

'It would be better if you came with me and gave me a guided tour of the places you think would interest me.'

Ava's heart gave a jolt. *Was he being serious?* She stared into his dark-as-night eyes and saw amusement and something else that evoked a coiling sensation low in her belly. 'We…we don't know each other.'

'Not yet, but the night is still young and full of endless possibilities,' he murmured in his husky Mediterranean accent that made her toes curl. He gave a faint shrug of his shoulders, drawing her attention to his powerful physique beneath the elegant lines of his dinner jacket. 'I have little leisure time and it makes sense when I visit somewhere new to take a companion who has local knowledge.'

Ava was saved from having to reply when one of the event organisers arrived at the table to hand out catalogues which listed the items that were being offered in the fundraising auction.

Giannis flicked through the pages of the catalogue. 'Is there anything in the listings that you intend to bid for?'

'Unfortunately I can't afford the kind of money that a platinum watch or a luxury African safari holiday are likely to fetch in the auction,' she said drily. 'I imagine that art collectors will be keen to bid for the Mark Derring painting. His work is stunning, and art tends to be a good investment. There are also some interesting wines being auctioned. The Chateau Latour 1962 is bound to create a lot of interest.'

Giannis gave her a thoughtful look. 'So, I have already discovered that you are an expert in art and wine. I confess that I am intrigued by you, Ava.'

She gave a self-conscious laugh. 'I'm not an expert in either subject, but I went to a finishing school in Switzerland where I learned how to talk confidently about art, recognise fine wines and understand the finer points of international etiquette.'

'I did not realise that girls—I presume only girls—still went to finishing schools,' Giannis said. 'What made you decide to go to one?'

'My father thought it would be a good experience for me.' Ava felt a familiar tension in her shoulders as she thought of her father. The truth was that she tried not to think about Terry McKay. That part of her life when she had been Ava McKay was over. She had lost touch with the friends she had made at the Institut Maison Cécile in St Moritz when her father had been sent to prison. But the few months that she had spent at the exclusive finishing school, which had numbered two European princesses among its students, had given her the social skills and exquisite manners which allowed her to feel comfortable at high society events.

It was a pity that the finishing school had not given advice on how to behave when a gorgeous Greek god looked at her as if he was imagining her naked, Ava thought as her eyes locked with Giannis's smouldering gaze. Panic and an inexplicable sense of excitement pumped through her veins. She was here at the charity dinner for her brother's sake, she reminded herself. Giannis had said he would give her an opportunity to speak to him in private on the condition that she entertained him during dinner.

She did not know if he had been serious, but she could not risk losing the chance to plead with him to show leniency to Sam.

'It's not fair,' she murmured. She had to lean towards Giannis so that he could hear her above the hum of chatter in the banqueting hall, and the scent of him—spicy cologne mixed with an elusive scent of male pheromones—made her head spin. 'I have told you things about me but you haven't told me anything about yourself.'

'That's not true. I've told you that I have never visited Scotland. Although I have a feeling that I will take a trip there very soon,' he drawled. His voice was indulgent like rich cream and the gleam in his eyes was wickedly suggestive.

A sensuous shiver ran down Ava's spine. Common sense dictated that she should respond to Giannis's outrageous flirting with cool amusement and make a witty remark to put him in his place and let him know she wasn't interested in him. Except that he fascinated her, and she felt like a teenager on a first date rather than an experienced woman of twenty-seven.

She wasn't all that experienced, a little voice in her head reminded her. At university she'd dated a few guys but the relationships had fizzled out fairly quickly. It had been her fault—she'd been wary of allowing anyone too close in case they discovered that she was leading a double life. Two years ago, she had met Craig at a party given by a work colleague. She had been attracted to his open and friendly nature and when they had become lovers she'd believed that they might have a future together. A year into their relationship, she had plucked up the courage and revealed her real identity. But Craig had reacted with horror to the news that she was the daughter of the infamous London gangland boss Terry McKay.

'How could we have a family when there is a risk that our children might inherit your father's criminal genes?' Craig had said, with no trace of warmth in his voice and a look of distaste on his face that had filled Ava with shame.

'Criminality isn't an inherited condition,' she had argued. But she continued to be haunted by Craig's words. Perhaps there *was* a 'criminal gene' that could be passed down through generations and she would not be able to save Sam from a life of crime.

Ava forced her mind away from the past. She refused to believe that her kind, funny younger brother could become a violent criminal like their father. But the statistics of youths reoffending after being sent to prison were high. She needed to keep her nerve and seize the right moment to throw herself on Giannis's mercy.

In normal circumstances Ava would have found the bidding process at the charity auction fascinating. The sums of money that some of the items fetched were staggering—and far beyond anything her finances could stretch to. Giannis offered the highest bid of a six-figure sum for a luxury spa break at an exclusive resort in the Maldives for two people. Ava wondered who he planned to take with him. No doubt he had several mistresses to choose from. But if he wanted more variety, she was sure that any one of the women in the banqueting hall who she had noticed sending him covetous glances would jump at the chance to spend four days—and nights—with a gorgeous, wealthy Greek god. Giannis was reputed to have become a billionaire from his successful luxury cruise line company, The Gekas Experience.

'Congratulations on your winning bid for the spa

break. I don't blame you for deciding that a visit to the Maldives would be more enjoyable than a trip to Scotland,' she said, unable to prevent the faint waspishness in her voice as she pictured him cavorting in a tropical paradise with a supermodel.

'I bought the spa break for my mother and sister. My mother has often said that she would like to visit the Maldives, and at least my sister will be pleased.' There was an odd nuance in Giannis's tone. 'Perhaps the trip will make my mother happy, but I doubt it,' he said heavily.

Ava looked at him curiously, wanting to know more about his family. He had seemed tense when he spoke about his mother, but she was heartened to know that he had a sister and perhaps he would understand why she was so anxious to save her brother from a prison sentence.

The auction continued, but she was barely aware of what was going on around her and her senses were finely attuned to the man seated beside her. While she sipped her coffee and pretended to study the auction catalogue she tried not to stare at Giannis's strong, tanned hands as he picked up his coffee cup. But her traitorous imagination visualised his hands sliding over her naked body, cupping her breasts in his palms as he bent his head to take each of her nipples into his mouth.

Sweet heaven! What had got into her? Hot-faced, she tensed when he moved his leg beneath the table and she felt his thigh brush against hers. He turned his head towards her, amusement gleaming in his eyes when he saw the hectic flush on her cheeks.

'It is rather warm in here, isn't it?' he murmured.

She was on fire and desperate to escape to the restroom so that she could hold her wrists under the cold tap to try to bring her temperature down. Perhaps spending a few minutes away from Giannis would allow her to regain her composure. 'Please excuse me,' she muttered as she shoved her chair back and stood up abruptly.

'*Ow!*' For a few seconds she could not understand why scalding liquid was soaking into the front of her dress. The reason became clear when she saw a waiter hovering close by. He was holding a cafetière, and she guessed that he had leaned over her shoulder in order to refill her coffee cup at the same time that she had jumped up and knocked into him.

'I am so sorry, madam.'

'It's all right—it was my fault,' Ava choked, wanting to die of embarrassment. She hated being the centre of attention but everyone at the table, everyone in the banqueting room, it seemed, was looking at her. The head waiter hurried over and added his profuse apologies to those of the waiter who had spilled the coffee.

Giannis had risen from his seat. 'Were you burned by the hot coffee?' His deep voice was calm in the midst of the chaos.

'I think I'm all right. My dress took the brunt of it.' The coffee was cooling as it soaked through the material, but her dress was drenched and her attempts to blot the liquid with her napkin were ineffective. At least it was a black dress and the coffee stain might wash out, Ava thought. But she couldn't spend the rest of the evening in her wet dress and she would have to go home without having had an opportunity to speak to Giannis about her brother.

The hotel manager had been called and he arrived at the table to add his apologies and reprimand the hapless waiter. 'Really, it's my fault,' Ava tried to explain. She just wanted to get out of the banqueting hall, away from the curious stares of the other diners.

'Come with me.' Giannis slipped his hand under her elbow, and she was relieved when he escorted her out of the room. She knew she would have to call for a taxi to take her home, but while she was searching in her bag for her phone she barely noticed that they had stepped into a lift until the doors slid smoothly shut.

'We will go to my hotel suite so that you can use the bathroom to freshen up, and meanwhile I'll arrange for your dress to be laundered,' Giannis answered her unspoken question.

Ava was about to say that there was no need for him to go to all that trouble. But it occurred to her that while she waited for her dress to be cleaned she would have the perfect opportunity to ask him to drop the charges against her brother. Was it sensible to go to a hotel room with a man she had never met before? questioned her common sense. This might be her only chance to save Sam, she reminded herself.

The doors opened and she discovered that the lift had brought them directly to Giannis's suite. Ignoring the lurch of her heart, she followed him across the vast sitting room. 'The bathroom is through there,' he said, pointing towards a door. 'There is a spare robe that you can use and I'll call room service and have someone collect your dress. Would you like some more wine, or coffee?'

'I think I've had enough coffee for one night.' She gave him a rueful smile and her stomach muscles tightened when his eyes focused intently on her mouth.

She had definitely had enough wine, Ava thought as she shot into the opulent marble-tiled bathroom and locked the door, before releasing her breath on a shaky sigh. It must be her out-of-control imagination that made her think she had seen a predatory hunger in Giannis's gaze. She wondered if he looked at every woman that way, and made them feel as though they were the most beautiful, the most desirable woman he had ever met. Probably. Giannis had a reputation as a playboy and he possessed an effortless charm that was irresistible.

But not to her. She was immune to Giannis's magnetism, she assured herself. As she stripped off her coffee-soaked dress and reached for the folded towelling robe on a shelf, she caught sight of her reflection in the mirror above the vanity unit. Her face was flushed and her eyes looked huge beneath her fringe. Usually she wore her hair up in a chignon but tonight she had left it loose and it reached halfway down her back. The layers that the hairdresser had cut into it made her hair look thick and lustrous, gleaming like spun gold beneath the bright bathroom light.

Ava stared at herself in the mirror, startled by her transformation from ordinary and unexciting to a sensual Siren. She had bought a seamless black bra to wear beneath her dress and her nipples were visible through the semi-transparent cups. The matching black thong that she had worn for practical reasons—so that she would not have a visible panty-line—was the most daring piece of lingerie she had ever owned.

She ran her hands over her smooth thighs above the lacy bands of her hold-up stockings and felt a delicious ache low in her pelvis. She felt sexy and seductive for the first time since Craig had dumped her as she pictured Giannis's reaction if he saw her in her revealing underwear.

She shook her head. It must be the effects of the wine that had lowered her inhibitions and filled her mind with erotic images. Cursing her wayward thoughts, she slipped her arms into the robe and tied the belt firmly around her waist. Of course he was not going to see her underwear. She had come to his hotel suite for one purpose only— to ask him to give her brother another chance. Taking a deep breath, Ava opened the bathroom door and prepared to throw herself on Giannis Gekas's mercy.

CHAPTER TWO

HE WAS SPRAWLED on a sofa, his long legs stretched out in front of him and his arms lying along the back of the cushions. He had removed his jacket and tie and unfastened the top few shirt buttons, to reveal a vee of olive-gold skin and a sprinkling of black chest hairs. Giannis looked indolent and yet Ava sensed that beneath his civilised veneer he was a buccaneer who lived life by his rules and ruthlessly took what he wanted. Plenty of women would want to try to tame him but she was sure that none would succeed. Giannis Gekas answered to no one, and her nerve almost deserted her.

He stood up as she entered the sitting room and walked over to take her dress from her. 'I rinsed out most of the coffee and wrung out as much water as I could,' she explained as she handed him the soggy bundle of material.

'I have been assured that your dress will be laundered and returned to you as quickly as possible,' he told her as he strode across the room and opened the door of the suite to give the dress to a member of the hotel's staff who was waiting in the corridor.

Giannis closed the door and came back to Ava. 'I ordered you some English tea and some petits fours,' he said, indicating the silver tea service on the low table in front of the sofa. 'Please, sit down.'

'Thank you.' She tore her eyes from him, her attention caught by a large canvas leaning against the wall. 'That's the Mark Derring painting from the auction.'

'I followed your advice and bid for it. You were sitting next to me,' he reminded her in a sardonic voice that made her think he was remembering how she had swapped the place name cards. 'Didn't you realise that I had offered the highest bid for the painting?'

Heat spread across her face. She could hardly admit that she had been so busy trying to hide her fierce awareness of him that she hadn't taken much notice of the auction. Giannis gave one of his lazy smiles, as if he knew how fast her heart was beating, and Ava forgot to breathe as she was trapped by the gleam in his eyes. She did not remember when he had moved closer to her, but she was conscious of how much taller than her he was when she had to tilt her head to look at his face.

He was utterly gorgeous, but it was not just his impossibly handsome features that made her feel weak and oddly vulnerable. Self-assurance shimmered from him and, combined with his simmering sensuality, it was a potent mix that made her head spin.

'Congratulations on winning the painting in the auction,' she murmured, desperate to say something and shatter the spell that his fathomless dark eyes and his far too sexy smile had cast on her. She was stupidly flattered that he had taken her advice about the artwork. Her self-confidence had been knocked by Craig's attitude when she'd admitted that she was the daughter of one of the UK's most notorious criminals. Thinking of her father reminded her of her brother, and she sank down onto the sofa while she mentally prepared what she was going to say to Giannis. It did not help her thought process when he sat down next to her.

'Help yourself to a petit four,' he said, offering her the plate of irresistible sweet delicacies.

'I shouldn't,' Ava murmured ruefully as she reached for a chocolate truffle. She bit into it and gave a blissful sigh when it melted, creamy and delicious, on her tongue. 'Chocolate is my weakness, unfortunately.'

He shrugged. 'Are you one of those women who starve themselves because the fashion industry dictates that the feminine figure should be stick-thin?'

'I think it's patently obvious that I don't starve myself,' she said drily. The belt of the towelling robe had worked loose and she flushed when she glanced down and saw that the front was gaping open, revealing the upper slopes of her breasts above her bra. She quickly pulled the lapels of the robe together.

'I am glad to hear it. Women should have curves.' Giannis looked deeply into her eyes and the heat in his gaze caused her heart to skip a beat. 'Before the regrettable incident with the coffee you looked stunning in your dress, and you have an exquisite figure, Ava,' he said softly. 'I am flattered that you wanted to sit next to me at dinner.'

Clearly, Giannis believed she had swapped the name cards because she was interested in him, but her motive had been completely different. Ava swallowed. 'I need to…' She did not finish her sentence and her breath caught in her throat when he lifted his hand and lightly brushed his thumb pad across the corner of her mouth.

'You had chocolate on your lips,' he murmured, showing her the smear of chocolate on his thumb that he had removed from her mouth. Her eyes widened when he put his thumb into his own mouth.

How could such an innocuous gesture seem so erotic? She was mesmerised as she watched his tongue flick out to lick his thumb clean. Unconsciously her own tongue darted out to moisten her lips and the feral growl that Giannis gave caused her stomach muscles to clench.

Remember why you are here, Ava ordered herself. But it was impossible to think about her brother when Giannis shifted along the sofa so that he was much too close. Her heart was thumping so hard in her chest that she was surprised it wasn't audible. It felt unreal to be in a luxurious hotel room with a devastatingly gorgeous man who was looking at her as if she was his ultimate fantasy. Somewhere in a distant recess of her brain she knew she should deliver her rehearsed speech, but her sense of unreality deepened when Giannis lifted his hand and stroked her cheek before he captured her chin between his fingers.

'What are you doing?' she gasped. It was imperative that she should seize her chance to talk to him about Sam.

'I would like to kiss you, beautiful Ava.' His voice was soft like velvet caressing her senses. 'And I think that perhaps you would like me to kiss you? Am I right? Do you want me to do this…?' He brushed his mouth over hers, tantalising her with a promise of sweeter delight to follow.

On one level Ava was appalled that she was allowing a stranger to kiss her, but she did not pull away when Giannis slid his hand beneath her hair to cup her nape and drew her towards him.

Sexual chemistry had fizzed between them from the moment they had set eyes on one another, she acknowledged. Neither of them had eaten much at dinner because they had been sending each other loaded glances. She could not fight her body's instinctive response to Giannis and with a helpless sigh she parted her lips. A tremor ran through her when he kissed her again and reality disappeared.

It was as though she had been flung to the far reaches of the universe where nothing existed but Giannis's lips moving over hers, tasting her, enticing her. His warm breath filled her mouth and she felt the intoxicating heat of his body through his white shirt when she placed her hands flat on his chest.

In a minute she would end this madness and push him away, she assured herself. She had been curious to know what it would be like to be kissed by an expert. And Giannis was certainly an expert. Ava did not have much experience of men but she recognised his mastery in the bone-shaking sensuality of his caresses.

He lifted his mouth from hers and trailed his lips over her cheek and up to her ear, exploring its delicate shape with his tongue before he gently nipped her earlobe with his teeth. A quiver ran through her and she arched her neck as he kissed his way down her throat and nuzzled the dip where her collarbone joined. Her skin felt scorched by the heat of his mouth. She wanted more— she wanted to feel his lips everywhere, tasting her and tantalising her with sensual promise.

At last he lifted his head. He was breathing hard. Ava stared at him with wide, unfocused eyes. She had never felt so aroused before, except in her dreams. Perhaps this was a dream, and if so she did not want to wake up.

'Your skin is marked where that idiot waiter spilled boiling-hot coffee down you,' Giannis murmured. She followed his gaze and saw that the front of her robe had fallen open again. There was a patch of pink skin on the upper slope of one breast.

'It's nothing.' She tried to close the robe but he brushed her hand away and deftly untied the belt before he stood up and drew her to her feet. It was as if she were trapped in a strange dreamlike state where she could not speak, and she did not protest when he pushed the robe off her shoulders and it fell to the floor.

Giannis rocked back on his heels and subjected her to a slow, intense scrutiny, starting with her stiletto-heeled shoes and moving up her stockings-clad legs and the expanse of creamy skin above her lacy stocking tops. Ava could not move, could hardly breathe as his gaze lingered on her black silk thong before he finally raised his eyes to her breasts with their pointed nipples jutting provocatively beneath the semi-transparent bra cups.

'Eísai ómorfi,' he said hoarsely.

Even if she hadn't understood the Greek words—which translated to English meant *you are beautiful*—there was no mistaking the heat in his gaze, the hunger that made his eyes glitter like polished jet. Ava knew she wasn't really beautiful. Passably attractive was a more realistic description. But Giannis had sounded as if he genuinely thought she was beautiful. The desire blazing in his eyes restored some of her pride that had been decimated by Craig's rejection.

Soon she would end this madness, she assured herself again. But for a few moments she wanted to relish the sense of feminine power that swept through her when Giannis reached for her and she saw that his hand was shaking. Europe's most sought-after playboy was *shaking* with desire for her. It was a heady feeling. A wildness came over her, a longing to just once throw off the restraints she had imposed on herself since she was seventeen and had discovered the truth about Terry McKay.

When she was younger she had never told anyone that her father was a criminal, but the strain of keeping her shameful secret had meant that she was always on her guard. Even with Craig, she had never been able to completely relax and enjoy sex. She'd assumed she had a low sex drive, but now the fire in her blood and the thunderous drumbeat of desire in her veins revealed a passionate, sensual woman who ached for fulfilment.

Giannis pulled her into his arms and crushed her against his broad chest, making her aware of how strong he was, how muscular and *male* compared to her soft female body. But she was strong too, she realised, feeling him shudder when she arched into him so that the hard points of her nipples pressed against his chest. He claimed her mouth, his lips urgent, demanding her response, and with a low moan she melted into his heat and fire. She kissed him back with a fervency that drew a harsh groan from his throat when at last he lifted his head and stared into her eyes.

'I want you,' he said in a rough voice that made her tremble deep inside. 'You drive me insane, lovely Ava. I want to see you naked in my bed. I want to touch your body and discover all your secrets, and then I want to…' He lowered his head and whispered in her ear in explicit detail all that he wanted to do to her.

Ava's stomach dipped. Somewhere back in the real world the voice of her common sense urged her to stop, *now*, before she did something she might regret later. But another voice insisted that if she let this moment, this man slip away she would regret it for ever. She did not understand what had happened to sensible Ava Sheridan, but shockingly she did not care. Only one thing was in her mind, in her blood. *Desire, desire*—it pulsed through her veins and made her forget everything but the exquisite sensations Giannis was creating when he cupped one of her breasts in his hand and stroked her nipple through the gossamer-fine bra cup.

She gave a low moan as he slipped his hand inside her bra and played with her nipple, rolling the hard peak be-

tween his fingers, causing exquisite sensation to shoot
down to that other pleasure point between her legs. '*Oh.*'
She would die if he did not touch her *there* where she
ached to feel his hands.

His soft laughter made her blush scarlet when she realised that she had spoken the words out loud. 'Come
with me.' Giannis caught hold of her hand and something—disappointment? Frustration?—tautened his features when she hesitated. 'What is it?'

She wanted to tell him that she did not have one-night
stands and she had never, ever had sex with a stranger.
She wasn't impetuous or daring. She was old before her
time, Ava thought bleakly. Just for once she wanted to
be the sexually confident woman that Giannis clearly
believed she was.

He smiled, his eyes lit with a sensual warmth that
made her insides melt. 'What's wrong?' he said softly,
lifting his hand to brush her hair back from her face.
The oddly tender gesture dispelled her doubts and the
hunger in his gaze caused a sensuous heat to pool between her thighs.

'Nothing is wrong,' she assured him in a breathy voice
she did not recognise as her own. She slid her hands over
his shirt and undid the rest of the buttons before she
pushed the material aside and skimmed her palms over
his bare chest. His skin felt like silk overlaid with wiry
black hairs that arrowed down to the waistband of his
trousers. She heard him draw a quick breath when she
stroked her fingertips along his zip.

'You're sure?'

She didn't want to step out of the fantasy and question
what she was doing. The new, bold Ava tilted her head
to one side and sent him a lingering look from beneath

the sweep of her lashes. 'What are you waiting for?' she murmured.

He laughed—a low, husky sound that caused the tiny hairs on her skin to stand on end. Every cell of her body was acutely aware of him and the promise in his glittering dark eyes sent a shiver of excitement through her.

Without saying another word, he led her by the hand into the bedroom. Ava was vaguely aware of the sophisticated décor and the lamps dimmed so that they emitted a soft golden glow. In the centre of the room was an enormous bed. Someone—presumably the chambermaid—had earlier turned back the bedspread and Ava's heart skipped a beat when she saw black silk sheets.

The four-poster bed had been designed for seduction, for passion, and it occurred to her that Giannis would surely not have intended to spend the night alone. Perhaps he regularly picked up women for sex. The slightly unsettling thought quickly faded from her mind and anticipation prickled across her skin when he shrugged off his shirt and deftly removed his shoes and socks before he unzipped his trousers and stepped out of them.

He was magnificent—lean-hipped and with a powerfully muscular chest and impressive six-pack. In the lamplight his skin gleamed like polished bronze, his chest and thighs overlaid with black hairs. Her gaze dropped lower to his tight black boxer shorts which could not conceal his arousal, and the growl he gave as she stared at him evoked a primitive need to feel him inside her.

'Take off your bra,' he ordered.

Her stomach flipped. She would have preferred him to undress her, and on some level her brain recognised that he was giving her the opportunity to change her mind. He wasn't going to force her to do anything she did not want to do. She roamed her eyes over his gorgeous body and desire rolled through her. Slowly she reached behind her back and unclipped her bra, letting the cups fall away from her breasts.

Giannis swallowed audibly. 'Beautiful.' His voice was oddly harsh, as if he was struggling to keep himself under control. He shook his head when she put her hands on the lacy tops of her hold-up stockings and prepared to roll them down her legs. 'Leave them on,' he growled. 'And your shoes.' He closed the gap between them in one stride and pulled her into his arms so that her bare breasts pressed against his naked chest. Ava felt a shudder run through him. *'Se thélo,'* he muttered.

She knew the Greek words meant *I want you* and she was left in no doubt when he circled his hips against hers and she felt the solid ridge of his arousal straining beneath his boxers. Driven beyond reason by a hunger she had never felt before, had never believed she was capable of feeling, she slipped her hand into the waistband of his boxers and curled her hand around him.

'Witch.' He pulled off his boxer shorts and kicked them away. Ava felt a momentary doubt when she saw how hugely aroused he was. But then he scooped her up and laid her down on the bed, and the feel of his hard, male, totally naked body pressing down on her blew away the last of her inhibitions. She trapped his face between her hands and tugged his mouth down to hers, arching against him when he claimed her lips in a devastating kiss.

It was wild and hot, passion swiftly spiralling out of control and shooting her beyond the stratosphere to a place she had never been before, where there was only the sensation of his warm skin pressed against hers and his seeking hands exploring her body and finding her pleasure spots with unerring precision.

'*Oh.*' She gave a thin cry when Giannis bent his head to her breast and flicked his tongue back and forth across its distended peak.

'Do you like that?' His voice was indulgent as if he knew how much she liked what he was doing to her, but Ava was too spellbound by him to worry about his arrogance. She sighed with pleasure when he drew her nipple into his mouth and sucked hard so that she almost climaxed right then. He transferred his attention to her other breast and she dug her fingers into his buttocks, feeling the awesome length of his erection pushing between her legs. There was no thought in her head to deny him, when to do so would deny her the orgasm that she could already sense building deep in her pelvis.

Somehow he untangled their limbs and shifted across the mattress. Frantically she grabbed hold of him and he laughed softly. Ignoring her hands tugging at him, he reached for his wallet on the bedside table and took out a condom. 'You *are* eager, aren't you?' he murmured. 'Here—' he put the condom into her hand '—you put it on for me.'

Ava fumbled with the foil packet, not wanting to admit that she had never opened a condom before. Craig had always prepared himself for sex, and when they had made love it had been over quickly, leaving her dissatisfied and convinced that the problem lay with her.

Finally she managed to tear the foil with her fingernail and then unrolled the condom down his length.

'*Theos*, you're going to kill me.' His chest heaved when she finally completed her task. He pushed aside her flimsy black silk thong and stroked his fingers over her silken flesh, parting her so that he could slide one finger inside her.

It felt amazing but it wasn't enough—not nearly

enough. Ava could hear her panting breaths as she lifted her hips towards his hand, needing more, needing him…
'Please…'

'I know,' he growled. She heard a ripping sound as he tore her thong, and then he simply took her with a hard, deep thrust that expelled the breath from her lungs in a shocked gasp.

He stilled and stared down at her, his shoulder muscles bunching as he supported himself on his hands. The lamplight cast shadows over his face, emphasising the angles and planes of his chiselled features. A beautiful stranger who had claimed her body. 'Did I hurt you?' The concern in his voice touched her heart.

'No…' She clutched his shoulders as she felt him start to withdraw. The shock of his penetration was receding and her internal muscles stretched so that she could take him deeper inside her, filling her, fulfilling her most secret fantasies when he began to move.

He must have sensed that he needed to slow the pace and at first he was almost gentle as he circled his hips against hers and kissed her breasts and throat, making his way up to her mouth to push his tongue between her lips while he drove deep inside her.

She arched her hips to meet each stroke, unaware of the frantic cries she made as he established a powerful rhythm. He thrust deeper, harder, taking her higher until she clawed her nails down his back, desperate to reach a place that she had never managed to reach before, except when she pleasured herself.

He laughed softly. 'Relax, and it'll happen.'

'It won't. I can't…' Ava gave a sob of frustration. There must be something wrong with her that made it impossible for her to reach an orgasm during sex.

She felt Giannis slip his hand between their joined

bodies and then he did something magical with his fingers, while he continued his rhythmic thrusts, faster, faster…

It felt so good. The way he expertly moved his hand, as if he knew exactly how to give her the utmost pleasure. It felt unbelievably good and the pressure inside her was building, building to a crescendo. Suddenly she was there, suspended for timeless seconds on the edge of ecstasy before the wave crashed over her and swept her up in a maelstrom of intense pleasure that went on and on, pulsing, pounding through her, tearing a low cry from her throat.

Even when the ripples of her orgasm started to fade, he continued to move inside her with an urgency that took her breath away. He gripped her hips and reared over her, his head thrown back so that the cords on his neck stood out. Incredibly, Ava climaxed for a second time, swift and sharp, as Giannis gave a final thrust and emitted a savage groan as he pressed his face into her neck while great shudders racked his body.

In the afterglow, a sense of peace enfolded her and she lay quite still, not wanting him to move away, not ready to face the reality of what had just happened. Gradually the thunderous beat of his heart slowed. She loved the feel of his big, strong body lying lax on top of her and of his arms around her, holding her close. Her limbs felt heavy and the lingering ripples of her orgasm triggered delicious tingles deep in her pelvis.

So *that* was what poets wrote sonnets about, she thought, smiling to herself. There wasn't something wrong with her, as Craig had suggested. Sex with Giannis had been mind-blowing and had proved that her body was capable of experiencing the most intense passion. From Giannis's reaction he had enjoyed having sex with her. She wasn't frigid. She was a responsive, sexually confident woman.

He lifted his head at last and looked down at her, his dark eyes unfathomable, making Ava realise once again that even though they had just shared the most intimate act that two people could experience, she did not know him. Oh, she'd gleaned a few facts about him on the Internet. Mainly about his business success or which model or actress he'd dated, although there was actually very little information about him. She knew nothing about the real Giannis Gekas—his family, his interests, even mundane things such as what kind of food he liked. There was an endless list of unknowns—all the tiny snippets of information that people at the beginning of a conventional relationship would find out about each other.

All she knew was that they had been drawn together by a combustible sexual chemistry, and when she became aware of him hardening once more while he was still buried deep inside her, nothing else mattered.

'You are irresistible, *omorfiá mou*,' he murmured. 'I want you again.'

Excitement coiled through her and she wrapped her legs around his back to draw him deeper inside her. He groaned. 'You would tempt a saint. But first I need to change the condom. Don't go away.' He dropped a brief but utterly sensual kiss on her mouth—a promise of further delights to follow—before he lifted himself off her and strode into the bathroom.

Ava watched him, her gaze clinging to his broad shoulders before sliding lower to the taut curves of his buttocks, and molten heat pooled between her thighs. Everything about tonight felt unreal, as if she was in the middle of an erotic dream that she did not want to end.

CHAPTER THREE

GIANNIS STEPPED OUT of the shower cubicle and blotted the moisture from his skin before he knotted a towel around his hips and walked into the bedroom. He glanced at the bed and saw that Ava was still fast asleep. Her honey-blonde hair spilled across the black silk pillows and her hand was tucked under her cheek. She looked young and unexpectedly innocent but looks were deceptive and there had been no hint of the ingénue about her last night.

The memory of her standing in front of him in stiletto heels, sheer black stockings and a minuscule pair of knickers had a predictable effect on his body, and he was tempted to whip off his towel and wake her for morning sex. But there wasn't time, and he felt no more than a fleeting regret as he turned away from the bed, striding over to the wardrobe to select a shirt to wear with his suit. While he dressed, he thought about his schedule for the day.

He had meetings in Paris in the afternoon and a social function to attend in the evening. But first he planned to drive to his house in Hertfordshire that he had recently purchased, to inspect the renovations that had been completed and pay the workmen a bonus. It would be useful to have a permanent base in the UK, but another reason he had bought Milton Grange was because the grounds included a particularly fine garden. Giannis hoped that his mother might like to visit the house in the summer, and perhaps tending to the roses would lift her spirits, which had been low lately. Although there was nothing new about that, he thought heavily.

He had spent most of his adult life trying to make his mother happy. His conscience insisted that caring for her was a small penance and could never atone for his terrible lapse of judgement that had resulted in the death of his father. He despised himself even more because he found his mother difficult. Even his sister had suggested that their *mitera*'s relentless misery was intended to make him feel guilty.

Giannis sighed as his thoughts switched from his mother to another thorn in his side. Ever since Stefanos Markou had announced that he intended to sell Markou Shipping and retire from business, Giannis had tried to persuade the old man to sell his ships to him. The Markou fleet of six small cargo ships would be an ideal addition to The Gekas Experience.

TGE already operated ten vessels offering luxurious cruises around the Mediterranean and the Caribbean. River cruising was becoming increasingly popular and Giannis wanted to expand the company and make TGE the world leader in this emerging tourist market. The Markou fleet of ships would need major refurbishments to turn them into high-end luxury river cruisers, but it was cheaper to upgrade existing ships than to commission a new fleet of vessels.

To Giannis's intense frustration, Stefanos had rejected his very generous financial offer. That was to say—Stefanos had not actually turned him down but he kept adding new conditions before he would sell. Giannis had already agreed to employ the entire Markou Shipping workforce and retrain the staff so that they could work on his cruise ships. Far more problematic was Stefanos's insistence that he wanted to sell his company to a married man.

'Markou Shipping's ethos is family first,' Stefanos had told Giannis. 'Many of the current staff are second or even third generation employees and they share the company's values of loyalty and propriety. How do you think they would feel if I sold the company to you—a notorious playboy who regards women only as pleasurable diversions? But if you were to choose a wife and settle down it would show that you believe in the high ideals which my great-grandfather, who started Markou Shipping one hundred years ago, held dear.'

Giannis had no desire to marry, but a rival potential buyer had shown interest in purchasing the Markou fleet of vessels. Norwegian businessman Anders Tromska was married and the father of two children. Stefanos approved of Tromska for being a dedicated family man who had never been involved in any kind of scandal or photographed by the paparazzi with a different blonde on his arm every week.

Giannis was prepared to increase his financial offer for the fleet of ships. But for once he had discovered that money could not solve a problem. It seemed that the only way he might persuade Stefanos to sell to him was if he magically conjured himself a wife.

He slipped his arms into his jacket and pushed the Markou problem to the back of his mind for now, turning his thoughts instead to a happier situation. His beloved *Nerissa*—a classic motor yacht which had been his father's first boat—had been repaired and restored after it had been vandalised.

Giannis had kept the boat moored at St Katharine Dock and he stayed on it whenever he visited London. He had been furious when he'd heard that a gang of youths had boarded the boat one night and held a party. A fire had somehow started in the main cabin and quickly ripped through the boat. It turned out that a cleaner who worked for the valeting company employed to maintain the boat had stolen the keys and taken his thuggish friends aboard *Nerissa*. The gang had escaped before the police arrived, apart from the cleaner, who had been arrested and charged with criminal damage.

The manager of the boat valeting company had been deeply apologetic. 'The youth who took the keys to your boat has a police record for various petty crimes. His social worker persuaded me to give him a job. To be honest he seemed like a nice lad, and his sister who accompanied him to his interview was anxious for me to give him a chance. But they say that bad blood will out in the end,' the manager had said sagely.

In Giannis's opinion, the cleaner who he held responsible for wrecking his boat deserved to be locked up in jail and the keys thrown away. *Nerissa* was special to him and he had wonderful memories of idyllic days spent on her with his father. Now that the boat had been repaired he had arranged for her to be taken back to Greece, to his home on the island of Spetses.

The sound of movement from the bed compelled Giannis to turn his head and look across the room. Ava rolled onto her back and the sheet slipped down to reveal one perfect round breast, creamy pale against the black silk sheet and adorned with a dusky pink nipple that Giannis had delighted in tormenting with his mouth the previous night.

One night with the golden-haired temptress was not enough to sate his desire for her, he acknowledged. His arousal was uncomfortably hard beneath his close-fitting trousers. He would take her phone number and call her on his next trip to London, he decided. Maybe he would instruct his PA to clear his diary for a few days so that he could fly up to Scotland with Ava. His imagination ran riot as he pictured them staying at a castle and having hot sex in front of a blazing log fire. He had heard that it often rained in the Highlands, and they would have to pass the time somehow.

But that was for the future. Right now he had a busy day ahead of him. He glanced at his watch and strode over to the bed to wake Sleeping Beauty. He had asked for his car to be brought to the front of the hotel ready for him to drive to Hertfordshire and he was keen to be on his way. But his conscience—which was frankly under-used—insisted on this occasion that he could not simply disappear and leave Ava asleep.

'Good morning.' He leaned over the bed and watched her long eyelashes flutter and settle back on her cheeks. 'It's time to get up, angel-face.' Impatience edged into his voice, and he put his hand on her shoulder to give her a gentle shake.

Long hazel-coloured lashes swept upwards. Her grey eyes were dazed with sleep before she blinked and focused on his face.

'Oh. My. God.' Her appalled expression was almost comical. 'I thought you were a dream.'

Giannis grinned. 'I aim to please. You were pretty amazing last night too.' His gaze lingered on her bare breast and she made a choked sound as she dragged the sheet up to her chin. 'But it is now morning,' he told her. 'Nine o'clock, to be precise. And incredibly tempting though you are, I have a busy schedule and you need to get dressed.'

'Oh, my God,' Ava said again. She sat up and pushed

her tangled blonde hair out of her eyes. The faint quiver of her lower lip made her seem oddly vulnerable. Giannis was surprised by the inexplicable urge that came over him to hold her in his arms and comfort her. But why did he think she needed to be comforted when he was certain she had enjoyed the passionate night they had spent together as much as he had? Just as pertinently, what qualified him to offer comfort to anyone? He destroyed things, and Ava, with her curiously innocent air, would do well to stay away from him, he reminded himself.

He was used to being instantly obeyed and he frowned when, instead of jumping out of bed, Ava slumped back against the pillows and covered her face with her hands. Giannis struggled to hide his irritation. 'You were not so shy last night,' he drawled.

'Last night was a mistake.' Her voice was muffled behind her hands. 'I must have had too much to drink.'

His jaw hardened. 'You drank a small glass of wine during dinner. Don't try to make out that you were unaware of what you were doing when you undressed in front of me, or suggest that I took advantage of you. When I asked if you were sure you wanted to have sex, you more or less begged me to take you.'

She jerked upright and dropped her hands away from her face, shaking her head so that her hair swirled around her shoulders like a curtain of gold silk. 'I did not *beg*.' There was outrage in her voice but she continued in a low tone, 'I know what I did. I was responsible for my behaviour and I'm not blaming you. But I shouldn't have slept with you. What I mean is that I should have spoken to you…asked you… Oh, this is so awkward.' Her eyes widened even more. 'Did you say that it's nine o'clock? Oh, my *God*.'

She scrambled off the bed and tugged the sheet around

her, but not before Giannis had glimpsed her naked body. At some point during the night he had removed her stockings using his teeth to tug them down her legs. He watched Ava struggle to put her bra on while she clutched the sheet to her like a security blanket. 'Don't you think it's a little late for modesty?' he said sardonically.

She picked up her torn thong from the floor and looked as though she was about to burst into tears. 'I have to go,' she said wildly. 'Sam will be going mad wondering where I am. I was supposed to have an important conversation with you last night.'

'About what?'

She bit her lip. 'It's a delicate matter.'

Giannis counted to ten beneath his breath. 'I'm in a hurry, so whatever it is you want to say—for God's sake get on with it.'

This couldn't be happening, Ava thought frantically. In a minute she would wake up from a nightmare. But in the cold light of morning she could not fool herself that having wild sex with Giannis last night had been a dream. She felt a sensation like wet cement congealing in the pit of her stomach with the knowledge that, as a result of her irresponsible behaviour, she had lost her chance to plead with Giannis to drop the charges against her brother. She felt sick with shame and guilt.

The sound of a familiar ringtone cut through the tense atmosphere and she scrabbled in her handbag to retrieve her phone. Her heart lurched when she saw that it was her brother calling.

'Sam, I've been…unavoidably delayed.' She dared not look at Giannis. 'You will have to ring for a taxi to take you to the courthouse, and I'll meet you there. You'll have to hurry—' she felt her anxiety rise '—your case is due to be heard by the magistrate in half an hour, and you mustn't be late.'

'The magistrate is ill,' Sam said when Ava paused for breath. 'I've just heard that the court cases today have been postponed.'

Ava heard relief in her brother's voice and she felt a rush of emotion. Sam hadn't said much in the weeks leading up to his court hearing, but she knew he was scared at the prospect of being sent to prison. 'Thank goodness.' She breathed out a heavy sigh. 'I don't mean it's good that the magistrate is ill, of course, but it gives us a bit more time.'

'Time to do what?' her brother said flatly. 'My case has only been delayed for a few days and it's still likely that I'll be sent to a YOI.'

Ava knew that young offender institutions tended to be grim places and she understood why Sam was scared. He might be eighteen but he would always be her kid brother. 'Not necessarily.' She tried to sound optimistic. 'I can't talk now. I'll see you at home later.'

She replaced her phone in her bag, and her eyes widened as she watched Giannis open his briefcase and throw some documents on top of a pile of bank notes. He closed the briefcase but Ava had a sudden flashback to when she had been a little girl, and had seen her father counting piles of bank notes on the kitchen table.

'Payday,' he'd told her when she had asked him about the money.

'You must be a good businessman to earn so much money, Daddy,' Ava had said trustingly. She had idolised her father.

Terry had winked at her. 'Oh, I'm an expert, honeybunch. I'm going to use this money to buy a house in Cyprus. What do you think of that?'

'Where's Cyprus?'

'It's near to Greece. The villa I'm buying is next to the beach, and it has a big swimming pool so you will be able to teach your baby brother to swim when he's older.'

'Why aren't we going to live in England any more?'

Her father had given her an odd smile. 'It's too hot for me to live here.' It had been the middle of winter at the time and Ava had felt confused by her father's reply. But years later she had learned that Terry McKay had moved his family abroad after he'd received a tip-off that he was about to be arrested on suspicion of carrying out several armed raids on jewellery shops in London.

She dragged her mind from the past as she caught sight of her reflection in the full-length mirror. She looked like a tart with her just-got-out-of-bed hair and panda eyes where her mascara had smudged. Her lips were fuller and redder than usual, and remembering how Giannis had covered her mouth with his and kissed her senseless made her feel hot all over. She could not have a serious conversation with him about her brother while she was naked and draped in a silk sheet.

As if he had read her thoughts, Giannis walked over to the wardrobe and took out her evening gown. 'Your dress has been cleaned, but I guessed you would not want to be seen leaving the hotel this morning wearing a ball gown so I ordered you something more appropriate to wear.' He handed her a bag with the name of a well-known design house emblazoned on it. 'I'll leave you to get dressed. Please hurry,' he said curtly before he strode out of the bedroom.

Ava scooted into the en suite bathroom and looked longingly at the bath, the size of a small swimming pool. She had discovered new muscles and she ached everywhere. But Giannis was no longer the charming lover of last night and he had not hidden his impatience this morning, she thought ruefully as she bundled her hair into a shower cap before taking a quick shower.

The bag he had given her contained a pair of beautifully tailored black trousers and a cream cashmere sweater. There was also an exquisite set of silk and lace underwear. Remembering her ripped thong brought a scarlet flush to her cheeks. She did not recognise the shameless temptress she had turned into last night. Giannis had revealed a side to her that she hadn't known existed.

Grimacing at the sight of her kiss-stung lips in the mirror, she brushed her hair and caught it up in a loose knot on top of her head. At least she looked respectable, although she shuddered to think how much the designer clothes must have cost. Everything fitted her perfectly, and when she slipped on the black stiletto heels she'd worn the previous evening she was pleasantly surprised by how slim and elegant she looked. Stuffing her evening gown into the bag that had held her new clothes, she walked into the sitting room.

Giannis was speaking on his phone but he finished the call when he saw her and strolled across the room. His intent appraisal caused her heart to miss a beat. 'I see that the clothes fit you.'

'How did you know my size?'

'I have had plenty of experience of the female figure,' he drawled.

Inexplicably Ava felt the acid burn of jealousy in her stomach at the idea of him making love with other women. Love had nothing to do with it, she reminded herself. Giannis was a notorious womaniser and she was simply another blonde who had shared his bed for one night. No doubt he would have forgotten her name by tomorrow.

'Obviously I'll pay for the clothes,' she said crisply. 'Can you give me your bank details so that I can transfer what I owe you, or would you prefer a cheque?'

'Forget it. I don't want any money.'

'No way will I allow you to buy me expensive designer clothes. I'll find out what they cost and send a cheque for the amount to your London office.'

His eyes narrowed. 'How do you know that I have an office in London?'

'I found out from the Internet that you own a cruise line company called The Gekas Experience. TGE UK's offices are in Bond Street.' Ava hesitated. 'I wrote to you a few weeks ago about a serious matter, but you did not reply.'

'Sheridan,' he said slowly. 'I wondered why your name on the place card at dinner last night seemed familiar.' He frowned. 'I'm afraid you will have to jog my memory.'

She took a deep breath. 'My brother, Sam McKay, used to work for a boat valeting company called Spick and Span.' Giannis's expression hardened, and she continued quickly. 'Sam had got involved with a gang of rough youths who made out that they were his friends. They coerced him into taking them aboard one of the boats that he valeted in St Katharine Dock. I don't know if the gang meant to vandalise the boat, but a fire broke out. My brother was horrified, and he stayed on board to try to put the flames out while the rest of the gang got away. He was the only one to be arrested and charged with criminal damage. But he never meant for your boat to be damaged.' Ava's voice wavered as Giannis's dark brows drew together in a slashing frown. 'It was just a silly prank that got out of hand.'

'A prank? The *Nerissa* was nearly destroyed. Do you know how many thousands of pounds of damage your brother and his friends caused?' Giannis said harshly. 'It wasn't just the financial cost of having the boat repaired. The sentimental value of everything that was lost is incalculable. My father designed every detail of *Nerissa*'s interior and he was so proud of that boat.'

'I'm sorry.' Ava was shocked by the raw emotion in Giannis's voice. She had only considered the financial implications of the fire, and it hadn't occurred to her that the boat might be special to him. It made the situation even worse. 'Sam really regrets that he allowed the gang on board. He thought that they just wanted to have a look at the boat, and he was horrified by what happened.' She bit her lip. 'My brother is scared of the gang members, which is why he refused to give their names to the police. He's young and impressionable, but honestly he's not a bad person.'

Giannis's brows rose. 'The manager of the boat valeting company told me that your brother already had a criminal record by the age of sixteen. Sam McKay clearly has a complete disregard for the law.'

He picked up his briefcase and walked over to the penthouse suite's private lift. 'I remember the letter you sent asking me to drop the charges against your brother. I did not reply because frankly I was too angry. Sam broke the law and he must face the consequences,' he said coldly.

'Wait!' Ava hurried across the room as the lift doors opened and she followed Giannis inside. She jabbed her finger on the button to keep the door open. 'Please hear me out.'

'I'm in a hurry,' he growled.

'When I read in a newspaper that you would be attending the charity fundraising dinner I decided to try to meet you. My friend works for the event's management company which organised the evening, and Becky arranged for me to sit at the same table as you. I hoped to persuade you to find it in your heart to give my brother another chance.'

'I don't have a heart.' Giannis reached out and pulled her hand away from the button and the lift doors instantly closed. 'Your methods of persuasion were impressive, I'll grant you. But it was a wasted performance, angel-face.'

Ava gave him a puzzled look. 'What do you mean?'

'Oh, come on. You obviously had sex with me because you thought I would let your brother off the hook.'

'I did *not*. I didn't plan to go to bed with you—it just… happened,' she muttered, shame coiling through her like a venomous serpent. To say that she had handled things badly would be an understatement. Last night she had behaved like the slut that Giannis clearly believed she was, but she refused to give up trying to help Sam.

The lift doors opened on the ground floor and she shot out behind Giannis when he stepped into the foyer. 'My reason for having sex with you had nothing to do with my brother,' she told him, her stiletto heels tapping out a staccato beat on the marble floor as she tried to keep pace with his long stride. Her voice seemed to echo around the vast space and she blushed when she became aware of the curious glances directed at her by other hotel guests. The terribly sophisticated receptionist standing behind the front desk arched her brows.

'Why don't you announce on national TV that we slept together?' Giannis threw her a fulminating look, his dark eyes gleaming like obsidian.

'I'm sorry.' Ava lowered her voice. 'I don't want you

to have the wrong impression of me. I don't usually sleep with men I've only just met and I don't understand why I behaved the way I did last night. I suppose it was chemistry. There was an instant attraction that neither of us could resist.'

He growled something uncomplimentary beneath his breath. 'Next you'll be telling me that we were both shot through the heart by Cupid's arrow.' Giannis halted beside a pillar. 'Last night was fun, angel-face, and maybe I'll look you up the next time I'm in town. But I'm not going to drop the charges against your hooligan brother. Even if I wanted to, I don't think it would be possible. As I understand English law, it is the Crown Prosecution who decide if the case should go to court.'

'You could instruct your lawyer to withdraw your complaint of criminal damage inflicted on your boat, and if you refuse to provide evidence to the court the case against Sam will be dropped.'

She grabbed Giannis's arm as he turned to walk away and felt his rock-hard bicep ripple beneath his jacket. 'It's true that Sam has a police record. Like I said, he was drawn into the gang culture through fear. It's not easy being a teenager in the East End,' she said huskily. 'Sam will almost certainly be given a custodial sentence and I'm scared of what will happen to him in a young offender institution. My brother is not a hardened criminal; he's just a silly kid who made a mistake.'

'Several mistakes,' Giannis said sardonically. 'Perhaps spending a few uncomfortable weeks in prison will teach him to respect the law in future.'

Giannis had not been lying when he'd stated that he did not have a heart, Ava thought bleakly. His phone rang, and she dropped her hand from his arm and moved a few steps away from him, although she was still able to overhear his conversation. A few minutes later he finished the call, and his expression was thunderous as he strode across the lobby without glancing in her direction.

She gave chase and caught up with him, positioning herself so that she was standing between him and the door of the hotel. 'I appreciate you must be annoyed that, from the sound of it, you might have lost a business deal to buy a fleet of ships. But I can't... I *won't* stand by and watch my brother be sent to prison.'

His dark brows lowered even further. 'How the hell do you know about my business deal?'

'I can speak Greek and I couldn't help but hear some of your conversation just now, concerning someone called Markou who has rejected your offer to buy his shipping company.' Ava bit her lip, and something flashed in Giannis's dark eyes that reminded her of the stark sexual hunger in his gaze when he had taken her to bed last night. 'I'm sure your business deal is important to you, but my brother is important to me,' she said huskily. 'Is there any way I can persuade you to give Sam another chance?'

He did not reply as he stepped past her and nodded to the doorman, who sprang forwards to open the door.

Ava followed Giannis out of the hotel and shivered as a gust of wind swirled around her and tugged at her chignon. Although it was early in September, autumn had already arrived with a vengeance. A thunderstorm was forecast but at the moment drizzle was falling and she could feel it soaking through her cashmere jumper. The miserable weather suited her mood of hopelessness as through a blur of tears she saw a sleek black car parked in front of the hotel.

She watched Giannis unlock the car and throw his briefcase onto the back seat. The knowledge that she had failed to save her brother from a likely prison sentence felt like a knife in Ava's heart.

'Have you never done anything in your past that you regret?' she called after him. He hesitated and swung round to face her, his dark brows snapping together.

Desperate to stop him getting into his car and driving away, Ava raced down the hotel steps but she stumbled in her high heels and gave a cry as she felt herself falling. There was nothing she could do to save herself. But then, miraculously, she felt two strong arms wrap around her as Giannis caught her and held her against his chest. In the same instant, on the periphery of her vision she saw a bright flash and wondered if it had been a lightning strike as the storm blew up.

The thought slipped away as the evocative scent of Giannis's aftershave swamped her senses. Still in a state of shock after her near fall, she rested her cheek on his shirt front and heard the erratic thud of his heart beneath her ear. She wished she could remain in his arms for ever. The crazy notion slid into her mind and refused to budge.

There was another flash of bright light. 'Who is your mystery blonde, Mr Gekas?' a voice called out.

Ava heard Giannis swear beneath his breath. 'What's happening?' she asked dazedly, lifting her head from his chest and blinking in the blinding glare of camera flashes.

When a taxi had dropped her at the hotel entrance the previous evening she had noticed the crowd of paparazzi who had gathered to take photos of the celebrity guests arriving at the party. Evidently some of them had waited all night to snap guests leaving the hotel the next morning, and they had struck gold when they had spotted Europe's most notorious playboy and a female companion.

'Hey, Mr Gekas, over here.' A photographer aimed a

long-lens camera at them. 'Can you tell us the name of your girlfriend?'

'I certainly can,' Giannis said calmly. To Ava's surprise, he did not move away from her as she had expected. Instead he kept his arm clamped firmly around her waist as he turned her to face the paparazzi. 'Gentlemen,' he drawled, 'I would like to introduce you to Miss Ava Sheridan—my fiancée.'

She couldn't have heard him correctly. Ava jerked her eyes to his face. *'What...?'* she began, but the rest of her words were obliterated as his dark head swooped down and he crushed her lips beneath his.

The kiss was a statement of pure possession. Giannis ground his mouth against hers, forcing her lips apart and demanding her response, re-igniting the flame inside her so that she was powerless to resist him.

Ava felt dizzy from a lack of oxygen when he finally lifted his head a fraction. *'What the hell?'* she choked, struggling to drag air into her lungs when he pressed her face into his shoulder.

'I need you to be my fake fiancée,' he growled, his lips hovering centimetres above hers. 'Play along with me and I'll drop all the charges against your brother.'

Her eyes widened. 'That's *blackmail.*'

His fingers bit into her upper arms as he hauled her hard up against his whipcord body. To the watching photographers they must have looked like lovers who could not keep their hands off each other. 'It's called business, baby. And you and I have just formed a partnership.'

CHAPTER FOUR

'You've got a damned nerve.'

Giannis flicked a glance at Ava, sitting stiffly beside him. It was the first time she had uttered a word since he had bundled her into his car and driven away from the hotel. But her simmering silence had spoken volumes.

Tendrils of honey-blonde hair had worked loose from her chignon to curl around her cheeks. She smelled of soap and lemony shampoo and he had no idea why he found her wholesome, natural beauty so incredibly sexy. He cursed beneath his breath. She was an unwelcome distraction but she might be the solution to his problem with Stefanos Markou.

He focused his attention on the traffic crawling around Marble Arch. 'It was damage limitation,' he drawled. 'Thanks to social media, pictures of us leaving the hotel will have gone viral within minutes. I couldn't risk my reputation. Anyone who saw the photographs of us together would have assumed that you are my latest mistress.'

Ava made a strangled sound. 'You couldn't risk *your* reputation? What about mine? Everyone will believe that I am engaged to the world's worst womaniser. I can't believe you told the photographers that I am your fiancée.' She ran a hand through her hair, evidently forgetting that she had secured it on top of her head. Her chignon started to unravel and she cursed as she pulled out the remaining pins and combed her fingers through her hair.

'You're right,' she muttered, scrolling through her phone. 'The news of our so-called engagement is all over social media. Thankfully my mother is at a yoga retreat in India where there is no Internet connection. She was seriously stressed about my brother and I persuaded her to go abroad and leave me to deal with the court case. But Sam is bound to see this nonsense and I can't imagine what he's going to say.'

'Presumably he will be grateful to you for helping him to avoid going to prison,' Giannis said drily. He sensed Ava turn her head to stare at him, and a brief glance in her direction revealed that her eyes were the icy grey of an Arctic sky.

'You can't really expect me to go through with the ridiculous charade of pretending to be your fiancée,' she snapped.

'Oh, but I can, *glykiá mou*.'

For some reason her furious snort made him want to smile. Usually he avoided highly emotional women but Ava's wildly passionate nature fascinated him. She was beautiful when she was angry and even more gorgeous when she was aroused, he brooded. Memories of her straddling him, her golden hair tumbling around her shoulders and her bare breasts, round and firm like ripe peaches, caused Giannis to shift uncomfortably in his seat.

He cleared his throat. 'I thought you wanted to keep your brother out of jail?'

'I do. But two minutes before we walked out of the hotel you had refused to help Sam. I don't understand why you have changed your mind, or why you need me to be your fake fiancée.'

'Like I said, the reason is business. More specifically, the only chance I have of doing a deal with Stefanos Markou is if I can prove to him that I am a reformed character. He has refused to sell Markou Shipping to me because he disapproves of my lifestyle and he thinks I am a playboy.'

'You *are* a playboy,' Ava interrupted.

'Not any more.' Giannis grinned at her. 'Not since I fell in love with you at first sight and decided to marry you and produce a tribe of children. Markou is an old-fashioned romantic and you, angel-face, are going to persuade him to sell his ships to me.'

Her expression became even more wintry. 'There's not a chance in hell that I'd marry you and even less chance I'd agree to have your children.'

Giannis's fingers tightened involuntarily on the steering wheel as a shaft of pain caught him unawares. He had thought he'd dealt with what had happened five years ago, but sometimes he felt an ache in his heart for the child he might have had. Caroline had told him she'd suffered a miscarriage, but in his darkest hours he wondered if she had decided not to allow her pregnancy to continue because she hadn't wanted to be associated with him after he'd admitted that he had spent a year in prison.

He forced his mind away from the past. 'Forgive me for sounding cynical, but I am a very wealthy man and most women I've ever met would happily marry for hard cash. However, I have no intention of marrying you. I simply want you to pretend that we are engaged and planning our wedding. I'm gambling that Stefanos would prefer to sell Markou Shipping to me rather than to a rival company because he knows I will have the ships refurbished in Greece and employ the local workforce. All we have to do is convince him that I have turned into a paragon of virtue thanks to the love of a good woman.'

'How are *we* going to do that?' Ava's tone dripped ice.

'I will make a formal announcement of our engagement and ensure that our relationship receives as much media coverage as possible. Stefanos has invited all the bidders who are interested in buying his company to meet him on his private Greek island in one month's time. With you by my side, an engagement ring on your finger, I am confident that he will sell Markou Shipping to me. The deal is as good as done,' he said with satisfaction.

She frowned. 'Are you saying that—supposing I was mad enough to agree to the pretence—I would have to be your fake fiancée for a whole month and go to Greece with you?'

'One month is less than the prison sentence your brother would be likely to receive,' Giannis reminded her. 'It will be necessary for you to live at my home in Greece because Stefanos is not stupid and he will only believe our relationship is genuine if we are seen together regularly. From now on, every time we are out in public we must act as if we are madly in love.'

'It would require better acting skills than I possess,' Ava muttered.

'On the contrary, I thought you were very convincing when you kissed me outside the hotel.'

She made a choked sound as if she had swallowed a wasp. 'I was in a state of shock after hearing you tell the photographers that I was your fiancée.' After a tense pause, she said, 'What will happen if Stefanos sells his company to you and then we end our fake engagement and you go back to your bachelor lifestyle that he disapproves of? Won't he be angry when he realises he was duped?'

Giannis shrugged. 'There will be nothing he can do once the sale is finalised.'

'Isn't that rather unfair?'

'Life is not always fair.' Irritation made his voice curt. He really did not need a lecture on morals from Ava. 'It was not fair that your brother wrecked my boat, but I am offering you a way to help Sam stay out of prison. Face it, angel-face, we both need each other.'

'I suppose so,' she muttered. 'But I can't give up a month of my life. What am I supposed to do about my job, for instance?'

'You told me you are between jobs since you moved from Scotland to London. What do you do, anyway? I noticed you avoided talking about your career.'

She grimaced. 'I am a victim care officer, and I try to help people who have been the victims of crime. I worked for a victim support charity in Glasgow and I have been offered a similar role with an organisation in London.'

'When will you start the new job?'

Ava seemed reluctant to answer him. 'The post starts in November.'

'So there is nothing to stop you posing as my fiancée now.'

'You are *so* arrogant. Do you always expect people to jump at your command? How do you know that I don't have a boyfriend?'

'If you do, I suggest you dump him because he clearly doesn't satisfy you in bed.' Giannis's lips twitched when Ava muttered something uncomplimentary. She was prickly and defensive and he had no idea why she fascinated him. Well, he had some idea, he acknowledged derisively as he pictured her sprawled on black silk sheets wearing only a pair of sheer stockings. He glanced at her and she quickly turned her head away, but not before he'd seen a flash of awareness in her eyes.

Last night they had been dynamite in bed and sex

with her had been the best he'd had in a long, long time. Was that why he had come up with the fake engagement plan? Giannis dismissed the idea. He'd been forced to take drastic action when the paparazzi had snapped him and Ava leaving the hotel, having clearly spent the night together. He could not risk that his playboy reputation might lose him the deal with Stefanos Markou.

His inconvenient desire for Ava would no doubt fade once he had secured Markou's fleet of ships. The only thing he cared about was fulfilling the promise he had made over his father's coffin, to provide for his mother and sister. Money and the trappings of wealth were all that he could give them to try to make up for what he had stolen from them. Yet sometimes his single-minded pursuit of success felt soulless, and sometimes he wondered what would happen if he ever opened the Pandora's Box of his emotions. It was safer to keep the lid closed.

'Did you choose to work with crime victims because your brother got into trouble with the police?' Giannis succumbed to his curiosity about Ava. She had made an unusual career choice for someone who had learned etiquette and social graces at a Swiss finishing school. At dinner last night he had noted how comfortable she was with the other wealthy guests, and he was confident she would act the role of his fiancée with grace and charm that would delight Stefanos Markou.

She shook her head. 'Sam was still in primary school when I went to university to study criminology.'

'Why criminology?'

For some reason she stiffened, but her voice was non-committal. 'I found it an interesting subject. But moving away to study and work in Scotland meant I wasn't around to spot the signs that Sam was having problems, or that my mother didn't know how to cope with him when he fell in with a rough crowd.' She sighed. 'I blame myself.'

'Why do you blame yourself for your brother's behaviour? Each of us has to take responsibility for our actions.'

Every day of the past fifteen years, Giannis had regretted that he'd drunk a glass of wine when he and his father had dined together at a *taverna*. Later, on the journey back to the family home, he had driven too fast along the coastal road from Athens and misjudged a sharp bend. Nothing could excuse his fatal error of judgement. If there was any justice in the world then he would have died that night instead of his father.

Ava insisted that her brother regretted taking a gang of thugs aboard *Nerissa* and damaging the boat. She clearly loved her brother, and Giannis felt a begrudging admiration for her determination to help Sam. He remembered how scared *he* had felt at nineteen when he had stood in a courtroom and heard the judge sentence him to a year in prison.

He had deserved his punishment and prison had been nothing compared to the lifetime of self-recrimination and contempt he had sentenced himself to. The car accident had been a terrible mistake, yet not one of his relatives had supported him. His sister had been too young to understand, but his mother would never stop blaming him, Giannis thought heavily.

He looked at Ava and she blushed and quickly turned her head to the front as if she was embarrassed that he had caught her staring at him.

'What about your father?' he asked her as he slipped the car into gear and pulled away from the traffic lights. At least the traffic was flowing better as they headed towards Camden. 'Did he try to give guidance to your brother?'

'Dad…left when Sam was eight years old.'

'Did you and your brother have any contact with him after that?'

'No.'

'It is my belief that children, especially boys, benefit from having a good relationship with their father. Although I realise my views might be regarded as old-fashioned by feminists,' Giannis said drily.

'I suppose it would depend on how good the father was,' Ava muttered.

She glanced at Giannis's hard profile and wondered what he would say if she told him that it had been difficult for her and Sam to have a relationship with their father after he had been sentenced to fifteen years in prison. Her mother had refused to allow Sam to visit Terry McKay at the maximum-security jail which housed some of the UK's most dangerous criminals. Ava had visited her father once, but she had found the experience traumatic. It had been bad enough having to suffer the indignity of being searched by a warden to make sure she was not smuggling drugs or weapons into the jail.

Seeing her father in prison had been like looking at a stranger. She had found it impossible to accept that the man she had trusted and adored had, unbeknown to his family, been a violent criminal and ruthless gangland boss. The name Terry McKay was still feared by some people in the East End of London. Perhaps if Sam had seen the grim reality of life behind bars he might not hero-worship his father as a modern-day Robin Hood character, Ava thought heavily. She was prepared to do everything in her power to prevent her brother from turning to a life of crime, and keeping him out of a young offender institution was vital. Giannis had offered her a way to give Sam another chance, but could she really be his fake fiancée?

She had assumed after they had spent the night together that she would never see him again. Memories of her wildly passionate response to his lovemaking made her want to squirm with embarrassment, but she remembered too how he had groaned when he had climaxed inside her. Did he intend that they would be lovers for the duration of their fake engagement? The little shiver of anticipation that ran through her made her despair of herself. If she had an ounce of common sense she would refuse to have anything more to do with him.

But there was Sam to consider.

Desperate to stop her thoughts from going round in circles, she searched for something to say to Giannis. 'Do you have a good relationship with your father?' If she could build up a picture of him—his family and friends, his values, she might have a better understanding of him.

He was silent for so long that she thought he was not going to answer. 'I did,' he said at last in a curt voice. 'My father is dead.'

'I'm sorry.' Evidently she had touched a raw nerve, and his forbidding expression warned her to back off. She sighed. 'This isn't going to work. We are two strangers who know nothing about each other. We'll never convince anyone that we are madly in love and planning to get married.'

To her surprise, Giannis nodded. 'We will have to spend some time getting to know each other. I can't afford any slip-ups when we meet Stefanos. Let's start with some basics. Why do you and your brother have different surnames? Have you ever been married?'

'No.' Her voice was sharper than she had intended, and she flushed when he threw her a speculative look before he turned his eyes back to the road. For some reason she found herself explaining. 'There was someone who I was sure…' She bit her lip. 'But I was wrong. He didn't love me the way I'd hoped.'

'Did you love him?'

'I thought I did.' She did not want to talk about Craig. 'After my parents divorced I took my mother's maiden name.'

Ava breathed a sigh of relief when he did not pursue the subject of her brother's surname. Giannis was Greek and it was possible that he did not associate the name McKay with an East End gangster. If he knew of the crimes her father had committed she was sure he wouldn't want her to pose as his fake fiancée and he was likely to refuse to drop the charges against Sam.

Giannis slowed the car to allow a bus to pull out. 'Where did you learn Greek? I did not think the language is routinely taught in English schools.'

'My family lived in Cyprus when I was a child, although I went to boarding school in France and then spent ten months at a finishing school in Switzerland.'

'Why did your parents choose not to live in England?'

'Um…my mother hated the English weather.' It was partly the truth, but years later Ava had learned that the real reason her father had taken his family to live abroad had been the lack of an extradition agreement between the UK and Cyprus, which had meant that Terry could not be arrested and sent back to England.

Her thoughts were distracted when a cyclist suddenly swerved in front of the car. Only Giannis's lightning reaction as he slammed on the brakes saved the cyclist from being knocked off his bike.

'That was a close call.' She looked over at Giannis and was shocked to see that he was grey beneath his tan. His skin was drawn so tight across his face that his sharp cheekbones were prominent. Beads of sweat glistened on his brow and she noticed that his hand shook when he raked his fingers through his hair.

Ahead there was an empty space by the side of the road and Ava waited until he had parked the car and switched off the engine before she murmured, 'You didn't hit the cyclist. He was riding like an idiot and it was fortunate for him that you are a good driver.'

Giannis gave an odd laugh that almost sounded as though he was in pain. 'You don't know anything about me, angel-face.'

'That's the point I've been making,' she said quietly. 'We are not going to be able to carry off a fake engagement.'

'For your brother's sake you had better hope that we do.' The stark warning in Giannis's voice increased Ava's tension, and when he got out of the car and walked round to open her door she froze when she recognised an area of London that was painfully familiar to her.

'Why have we come here? I thought you were taking me home.' It occurred to her that he had not asked where she lived, and she had been so stunned after he'd told the photographers she was his fiancée that she had let him drive her away from the hotel without asking where they were going.

'Hatton Garden is the best place to buy jewellery.'

'That doesn't explain why you have brought me here.' She was aware that Hatton Garden was known worldwide as London's jewellery quarter and the centre of the UK's diamond trade. It was also the place where her fa-

ther had masterminded and carried out his most auda-
cious robbery.

Ava remembered when she was a little girl, before the
family had moved to Cyprus, her father had often taken
her for walks to Covent Garden and St Paul's Cathedral.
They had always ended up in Hatton Garden and strolled
past the many jewellery shops with their windows full of
sparkling precious gems. She had loved those trips with
her father, unaware that Terry McKay had been assessing
which shops would be the easiest to break into.

'For our engagement to be believable you will need
to wear an engagement ring. Preferably a diamond the
size of a rock that you can flash in front of the photographers,' Giannis drawled. He glanced at his watch. 'Try
not to take too long choosing one.' He took his phone out
of his jacket pocket. 'I need to tell my pilot to have the jet
ready for us to leave earlier than I'd originally planned.'

Ava stared at him. 'You own a *jet*?'

'It's the quickest way to get around. We should be in
Paris by lunchtime. I'm going to be busy this afternoon
but I'll arrange for a personal shopper to help you choose
some suitable clothes. This evening we will be attending
a high-profile function at the Louvre that is bound to at-
tract a lot of media interest. By tomorrow morning half
the world will believe that we are in love.'

'Wait…' She stiffened when he slid his hand beneath
her elbow and tried to lead her towards a jewellery store.
Her heart plummeted when she saw the name above the
shop front.

Ten years ago her father had carried out an armed robbery at the prestigious Engerfield's jewellers and stolen
jewellery with a value of several million pounds. But
Terry McKay's luck had finally run out and he had been
caught trying to flee back to Cyprus on his boat. In court,

CCTV footage had shown him threatening a young female shop assistant with a shotgun.

Ava had been devastated to discover that her father was a ruthless gangster. Even worse, several national newspapers had published a photo of her and her mother with the suggestion that they must have been aware of Terry's criminal activities. If Julie McKay *had* harboured suspicions about her husband, she had not told her daughter. But Ava knew that her mother had worshipped Terry and been blind to his faults.

She stared at the jewellery shop. 'I can't go in there.'

Giannis frowned. 'Why not? Engerfield's is arguably the best jewellers in London.'

'What I mean is that I can't wear an engagement ring or go to Paris with you until I've seen my brother and explained that our relationship is fake.'

'You cannot tell anyone the truth in case someone leaks information to the press. I mean it,' Giannis said harshly as Ava opened her mouth to argue. 'No one must have any idea that our engagement is not real.'

'But what am I going to say to Sam?'

He shrugged. 'You'll have to invent a story that we met a few weeks ago, and after a whirlwind romance I asked you to marry me. That will explain why I dropped the charges against Sam because I did not want to prosecute my future brother-in-law.'

'I don't want to lie to my brother,' she choked. 'I hate deception.'

'Do you really want to have to admit to him that you slept with me the night we met? *That* is the truth, Ava, and I will have no qualms about telling Sam how we got into this situation.'

'*You* told the paparazzi that I am your fiancée. The situation is all your fault.' She winced when Giannis tightened his grip on her arm and escorted her through the door of the jewellers.

'Smile,' he instructed her in a low tone when a silver-haired man walked over to meet them.

Somehow Ava managed to force her lips to curve upwards, but inside she was quaking as she recognised Nigel Engerfield. Ten years ago he had been commended for his bravery after he had tried to protect his staff from the gang of armed thieves led by her father. At the time of her father's trial Ava remembered seeing the shop manager's photograph in the newspapers. Would he remember *her* from the photo of Terry McKay's family that had appeared in the press a decade ago? She was sure she did not imagine that the manager gave her a close look, but to her relief he turned his gaze from her and smiled at Giannis.

'Mr Gekas, what a pleasure to see you again. How can I help you?'

'We would like to choose an engagement ring. Wouldn't we, darling?' Giannis slid his arm around Ava's waist and his dark eyes glittered as he met her startled glance. 'This is my fiancée...'

'Miss Sheridan,' Ava said quickly, holding out her hand to Nigel Engerfield. She was scared he might remember that Terry McKay had a daughter called Ava.

'Please accept my congratulations, Mr Gekas and... Miss Sheridan.' The manager's gaze lingered on Ava. 'If you would like to follow me, I will take you to one of our private sitting rooms so that you can be comfortable while you take your time to peruse our collection of engagement rings. Is there a particular style or gemstone that you are interested in?'

'What woman doesn't love diamonds?' Giannis drawled.

Nigel Engerfield nodded and left the room, returning a

few minutes later carrying several trays of rings, and accompanied by an assistant bearing a bottle of champagne and two glasses. The champagne cork popped and the assistant handed Ava a flute of the sparkling drink. She took a cautious sip, aware that she had not eaten breakfast. Maybe Giannis had the same thought because he set his glass down on the table without drinking from it.

'Please sit down and take as much time as you like choosing your perfect ring,' the manager invited Ava, placing the trays of rings on the table in front of her.

She looked down at the glittering, sparkling rings and felt sick as she remembered how, when she was a little girl, she had loved trying on her mother's jewellery. After her father had been arrested, the police had confiscated all the jewels that Terry had stolen—including her mother's wedding ring. Everything from Ava's privileged childhood—the luxury villa in Cyprus, the exotic holidays and expensive private education—had been paid for with the proceeds of her father's criminal activities. There was nothing she could do to erase her sense of guilt, but working as a VCO was at least some sort of reparation for what her father had done.

'Do you see anything you like, darling?' Giannis's voice jolted her from the past. She looked over to where he was standing by the window. Sunlight streamed through the glass, and his dark hair gleamed like raw silk when he ran a careless hand through it. His face was all angles and planes, as beautiful as a sculpted work of art. But he was not made from cold marble. Last night his skin had felt warm beneath her fingertips when she had explored his magnificent body.

Ava could recall every detail of his honed musculature that was now hidden beneath his superbly tailored suit. Oh, yes, she saw something she liked, she silently answered his question. His eyes captured hers, and her heart missed a beat when she glimpsed a predatory gleam in his gaze.

Hastily she looked down at the glittering rings displayed against black velvet cushions. Even though the shop manager had suggested she should take her time to choose a ring, she knew that Giannis wanted her to hurry up.

Inexplicably a wave of sadness swept over her. Choosing an engagement ring was supposed to be a special occasion for couples who were in love. The young assistant who had poured the champagne had looked enviously at Giannis and clearly believed that their romance was genuine. But Ava knew she was an imposter. The web of deceit they were spinning would grow and spread as they sought to convince Stefanos Markou that Giannis had given up his womanising ways because he had fallen in love with her. But of course he never would love her. He needed her so that he could win a business deal and she needed him to save her brother from prison.

What they were doing was wrong, Ava thought miserably. How could she even trust that Giannis would keep his side of their arrangement? He was playing the role of attentive lover faultlessly, but it was just an act—although that did not stop a stupid, idiotic part of her from wishing that his tender smile was real.

'Sweetheart?' Giannis walked over to the sofa and sat down beside her. 'If you don't like any of the rings, I am sure Mr Engerfield has others that you can look at.'

She swallowed. 'I can't do this…'

The rest of her words were smothered by Giannis's mouth as he swiftly lowered his head and kissed her. 'I think you are a little overwhelmed by the occasion,' he murmured, smiling softly at her stunned expression. He looked over at the shop manager. 'Would you mind leaving us alone?'

As soon as Nigel Engerfield and his assistant had stepped out of the room, Giannis did not try to hide his impatience. 'What is the matter?' he growled to Ava. 'All you have to do is choose a diamond ring, but anyone would think you are about to undergo root canal treatment.'

'I never wear jewellery and I hate diamonds,' she muttered.

He swore. 'I thought we had an agreement, but if you've changed your mind I will find another way to persuade Stefanos Markou to sell his ships to me—and your brother will go to prison.'

Ava bit her lip. 'How do I know that you will drop the charges against my brother?'

'You have my word.'

'Your word means nothing.' She ignored the flash of anger in his eyes. 'Phone your lawyer now and instruct that you no longer want to press charges against Sam.'

Giannis glared at her. 'How do I know you won't immediately go to the press and deny that you are my fiancée?'

'You'll have to trust me.' Ava glared back at him and refused to be cowed by his black stare. In the tense silence that stretched between them she could hear the loud thud of her heart in her ears. Giannis was a man used to being in control, but if he thought she was a pushover he had a nasty surprise coming to him.

Finally he took out his phone and made a call. 'It's done,' he told her moments later. 'You heard me inform my lawyer that I have decided not to press a charge of criminal damage against Sam McKay. Now it is your turn to keep to your side of the bargain.'

Ava felt light-headed with relief that Sam would not face prosecution and prison. 'I won't let you down,' she assured Giannis huskily. She glanced at the trays and selected an ostentatious diamond solitaire ring. 'Does this have enough bling to impress the paparazzi?'

He frowned at her choice and studied the other rings. 'This one is better,' he said as he picked out a ring and slid it onto her finger.

She stared down at her hand, and her throat felt oddly constricted. 'Really?' she tried to ignore the emotions swirling inside her as she said sarcastically, 'Don't you think a pink heart is romantic overload?'

'It's a pink sapphire. You said you dislike diamonds, although there are a few small diamonds surrounding the heart. But the ring is pretty and elegant and it suits your small hand.'

The ring was a perfect fit on her finger and, despite Ava's insistence that she did not like jewellery, she instantly fell in love with the pink sapphire's simplicity and delicate beauty. Once again she felt a tug on her heart. Didn't every woman secretly yearn for love and marriage, for the man of her dreams to place a beautiful ring on her finger and tell her that he loved her?

Giannis was hardly her fairy tale prince, she reminded herself. If they had not been spotted by the paparazzi leaving the hotel together, she would have been just another of his one-night stands. She stood up abruptly and moved away from him. 'I don't care which ring I have. It's simply to fool people into thinking that we are engaged and I'll only have to wear it for a month.'

He followed her over to the door but, before she could open it, he caught hold of her shoulder and spun her round to face him. His brows lowered when he saw her mutinous expression. 'For the next month I will expect you to behave like you are my adoring fiancée, not a stroppy adolescent, which is your current attitude,' he said tersely.

'Let go of me.' Her eyes darkened with temper when he backed her up against the door. He was too close, and her senses leapt as she breathed in his exotic aftershave. 'What are you doing?'

'Giving you some acting lessons,' he growled and, before she had time to react, he covered her mouth with his and kissed the fight out of her.

He kissed her until she was breathless, until she melted against him and slid her arms up the front of his shirt. The scrape of his rough jaw against her skin sent a shudder of longing through Ava. It shamed her to admit it, but Giannis only had to touch her and he decimated her power of logical thought. She pressed herself closer to his big, hard body, a low moan rising in her throat when he flicked his tongue inside her mouth.

And then it was over as, with humiliating ease, he broke the kiss and lifted his hands to unwind her arms from around his neck. Only the slight unsteadiness of his breath indicated that he was not as unaffected by the kiss as he wanted her to think.

His voice was coolly amused as he drawled, 'You are an A-star student, *glykiá mou*. You almost had *me* convinced that you are in love with me.'

'Hell,' Ava told him succinctly, 'will freeze over first.'

CHAPTER FIVE

PARIS IN EARLY autumn was made for lovers. The September sky was a crisp, bright blue and the leaves on the trees were beginning to change colour and drifted to the ground like red and gold confetti.

Staring out of the window of a chauffeur-driven limousine on his way back to his hotel from a business meeting, Giannis watched couples holding hands or strolling arm in arm next to the Seine. What it was to be in love, he thought cynically. Five years ago he had fallen hard for Caroline when he'd met her during a business trip to her home state of California. *Theos*, he had believed that she loved him. But the truth was she had loved his money and had hoped he would pay for her father's political campaign to become the next US President.

Caroline's pregnancy had been a mistake but, as long as they were married, a baby, especially if it was a boy, might help her father's campaign, she'd told Giannis. Images of widower Brice Herbert cuddling his grandchild would appeal to the electorate.

However, having a son-in-law who had served a prison sentence would have been a disaster for Brice Herbert's political ambition. Caroline had reacted with horror when Giannis had revealed the dark secret of his past. He'd sensed that she had been relieved when she'd lost the baby. Motherhood had not been on her agenda when there was a chance she could be America's First Lady. It was probably a blessing in disguise, she'd said, and it meant that there was no reason for them to marry. But he could never believe that the loss of his child was a blessing. It had felt as if his heart had been ripped out, and confirmed his belief that he did not deserve to be happy.

The limousine swept past the Arc de Triomphe while Giannis adeptly blocked out thoughts of his past and focused on the present. Specifically on the woman who was going to help him prove to Stefanos Markou that he had given up his playboy lifestyle. He should have predicted that Ava would argue when he had given her his credit card and sent her shopping, he brooded.

'I packed some things when you drove me home to collect my passport. There is nothing wrong with my clothes,' she'd told him in a stiff voice that made him want to shake her.

'I am a wealthy man and when we are out together in public, people will expect my fiancée to be dressed in haute couture,' he had explained patiently. 'Fleur Laurent is a personal shopper and she will take you to the designer boutiques on the Champs-élysées.'

Most women in Giannis's experience would have been delighted at the chance to spend his money, but not Ava. She was irritating, incomprehensible and—he searched for another suitable adjective that best summed up his feelings for her. *Ungrateful.* She did not seem to appreciate that he was doing her a huge favour by dropping the criminal damage charge against her brother.

Giannis frowned as he remembered meeting Sam McKay briefly when he'd driven Ava home before they had flown to Paris. He had been surprised when she'd directed him to pull up outside a shabby terraced house. It was odd that her family had moved from Cyprus to a run-down area of East London. Perhaps there had been a change in her parents' financial circumstances, he'd mused.

He had insisted on accompanying Ava into the house to maintain the pretence of their romance. He wasn't going to risk her brother selling a story to the press that their engagement was fake. But, instead of a swaggering teenager, he'd discovered that Sam was a lanky, nervous-looking youth who had stammered his thanks to Giannis for dropping the criminal charges against him. Sam had admitted that he'd been stupid and regretted the mistakes he had made.

Giannis understood what it was like to regret past actions and, to his surprise, he'd found himself feeling glad that he had given Ava's brother a chance to turn his life around. While Ava had gone upstairs to look for her passport, Sam had shyly congratulated him on becoming engaged to his sister and had voiced his opinion that Ava deserved to be happy after her previous boyfriend had broken her heart.

The limousine drew up outside the hotel and Giannis glanced at his watch. His meeting had overrun but there was just enough time for him to shower and change before the evening's function at the Louvre started. He hoped Ava would be ready on time. *Theos*, he hoped she hadn't run out on him.

He was aware of a sinking sensation in his stomach as the possibility occurred to him. He acknowledged that he had struggled to concentrate during his business meeting because he had been anticipating spending the evening with Ava. If he hadn't known himself better he might have been concerned by his fascination with her.

But experience had taught him that desire was a transitory emotion.

'I wouldn't have thought that you would be interested in a fashion show,' she had remarked when he'd told her about the evening's event.

'The show is for new designers to demonstrate their talent. I sponsor a young Greek designer called Kris Antoniadis. You may not have heard of him, but I predict that in a few years he will be highly regarded in the fashion world. At least I certainly hope so because I am Kris's main financial sponsor and I have invested a lot of money in him.'

'Is money the only thing you are interested in?' she'd asked him in a snippy tone which gave the impression she thought that making money was immoral.

He had looked her up and down and allowed his eyes linger on the firm swell of her breasts beneath her cashmere sweater. 'It's not the *only* thing that interests me,' he'd murmured, and she'd blushed.

There was no sign of her in their hotel suite, but Giannis heard the sound of a hairdryer from the en suite bathroom. Stripping off his jacket and tie as he went, he strode into the separate shower room and then headed to the dressing room to change into a tuxedo.

He returned to the sitting room just as Ava emerged from the bedroom, and Giannis felt a sudden tightness in his chest. His brain acknowledged that the personal shopper had fulfilled the brief he'd given her to find an evening gown that was both elegant and sexy. But as he stared at Ava he was conscious of the way another area of his anatomy reacted as his blood rushed to his groin.

'You look stunning,' he told her, and to his own ears his voice sounded huskier than usual as his customary sangfroid deserted him.

'Thank you. So do you.' Soft colour stained her cheeks. Giannis was surprised by how easily she blushed. It gave her an air of vulnerability that he chose to ignore.

'The personal shopper said I should wear a statement dress tonight—whatever a statement dress is. But I don't think you will approve when I tell you how many noughts were on the price tag,' she said ruefully.

'Whatever it cost it was worth it.' Giannis could not tear his eyes off her. The dress was made of midnight-blue velvet, strapless and fitting tightly to her hips before the skirt flared out in a mermaid style down to the floor. Around her neck she wore a matching blue velvet choker with a diamanté decoration. Her hair was caught up at the sides with silver clasps and rippled down her back in silky waves.

He had a mental image of her lying on the bed wearing only the velvet choker, her creamy skin and luscious curves displayed for his delectation. Desire ran hot and urgent through his veins and he was tempted to turn his vision into reality.

Perhaps Ava could read his mind. 'I don't know why you booked a hotel suite with only one bedroom. The deal was for me to be your *fake* fiancée.' She walked past him and picked up the phone. 'I'm going to call reception and ask for a room of my own.'

Giannis crossed the room in two strides and snatched the receiver out of her hand. 'If you do that, how long do you think it will take for a member of the hotel's staff to reveal on social media that we don't share a bed? We are supposed to be madly in love,' he reminded her.

'Did you assume I would be your convenient mistress for the next month? You've got a damned nerve,' she snapped.

He considered proving to her that it had been a reasonable assumption to make. Sexual chemistry simmered between them and all it would take was one kiss, one touch, to cause a nuclear explosion. He watched her tongue dart out to moisten her lower lip and the beast inside him roared.

Somehow Giannis brought his raging hormones under control. What was important was that their 'romance' gained as much public exposure as possible so that Stefanos Markou believed he was a reformed character preparing to devote himself to marriage and family—the ideals that Stefanos believed in.

Throughout the day Giannis had asked himself why he was going to the lengths of pretending to be engaged, simply to tip a business opportunity in his favour. But the truth was that he needed Markou Shipping's fleet of ships to enable him to expand his cruise line company into the river-cruising market. The ships could be refitted during the winter and be ready to take passengers early next summer, which would put TGE ahead of its main competitors.

'We can sort out sleeping arrangements later,' he told Ava. 'The car is waiting to take us to the Louvre. Are you ready for our first performance, *agápi mou*?'

'I am not your love.'

'You are when we are out in public.' He took hold of her arm and frowned when she flinched away from him. 'You'll have to do better than that if we are going to convince anyone that our relationship is genuine.' Impatience flared in him at her mutinous expression. 'We made a deal and I have carried out my side of it,' he reminded her. 'You told me that I would have to trust you, and I did. But perhaps I was a fool to believe your word?'

'I am completely trustworthy,' she said in a fierce voice. 'I will pretend to be your fiancée. But why would anyone believe that you—a handsome billionaire play-boy who has dated some of the world's most beautiful women—have fallen in love with an ordinary, nothing special woman like me?' She worried her bottom lip with her teeth. 'What are we going to say if anyone asks how we met?'

He shrugged. 'We'll tell them the truth. We met at a dinner party and there was an immediate attraction be-tween us. And, by the way, there is nothing ordinary about the way you look in that dress,' he growled, his eyes fixed on her pert derrière encased in tight blue vel-vet when she turned around to check her appearance in the mirror.

'Sexual attraction is not the same thing as falling in love,' she muttered.

She was nervous, Giannis realised with a jolt of sur-prise. If he had been asked to describe Ava he would have said that she was determined and strong—he guessed she'd have to be in her job working with crime victims. But the faint tremor of her mouth revealed an unexpected vulnerability that he could not simply dismiss. For their fake engagement to be successful, he realised that he would have to win her confidence and earn her trust.

He lifted his hand to brush a stray tendril of hair off her face. 'But mutual attraction is how all relationships begin, isn't it?' he said softly. 'You meet someone and *wham*. At first there is a purely physical response, an alchemy which sparks desire. From those roots love might begin to grow and flourish.' His jaw hardened as he thought of Caroline. 'But it is just as likely to wither and die.'

'Are you speaking from experience?' Ava's gentle tone pulled Giannis's mind from the past and he stiffened when he saw something that looked worryingly like compassion in her grey eyes. If she knew the truth about him he was sure that her sympathy would fade as quickly as Caroline had fallen out of love with him.

For a fraction of a second he felt a crazy impulse to admit to Ava that sometimes when he saw a child of about four years old he felt an ache in his heart for the child he might have had. If Caroline hadn't… *No.* He would not think of what she might have done. There was no point in torturing himself with the idea that Caroline had ended her inconvenient pregnancy after he had told her he'd been to prison. The possibility that his crass irresponsibility when he was nineteen had ultimately resulted in the loss of two lives was unbearable.

Ignoring Ava's question, he walked across the room and opened the door. 'We need to go,' he told her curtly, and to his relief she preceded him out of the suite without saying another word.

Ava applauded the models as they sashayed down the runway in the magnificent Sculpture Hall of the Musée du Louvre. The venue of the fashion show was breathtaking, and the clothes worn by the impossibly slender models ranged from exquisite to frankly extraordinary. The collection by the Greek designer Kris Antoniadis brought delighted murmurs from the audience, and the fashion journalist sitting in the front row next to Ava endorsed Giannis's prediction that Kris, as he was simply known, was the next big thing in the fashion world.

'Of course Kris could not have got this far in his career without a wealthy sponsor,' Diane Duberry, fashion editor of a women's magazine, explained to Ava. 'Giannis Gekas is regarded as a great philanthropist for his support of the Greek people during the country's recent problems. He set up a charity which awards bursaries to young entrepreneurs trying to establish businesses in Greece. But I don't know why I am telling you about Giannis when you must know everything about him.'

Diane looked at Giannis's hand resting possessively on Ava's knee, and then at the pink sapphire ring on Ava's finger, and speculation gleamed in her eyes. 'You succeeded where legions of other women have failed and tamed the tiger. Where did the two of you meet?'

'Um…we were seated next to each other at a dinner party.' Ava felt herself flush guiltily even though technically it was the truth.

'Lucky you.' Diane winked at her. 'Who needs a dessert from the sweet trolley when a gorgeous Greek hunk is on the menu?'

Ava was saved from having to think of a reply when the compère of the fashion show came onto the stage and announced that the Young Designer award had been won by the Greek designer, Kris Antoniadis. Kris then appeared on the runway accompanied by models wearing dresses from his bridal collection.

Giannis stood up and drew Ava to her feet. 'Showtime,' he murmured in her ear. 'Just smile and follow my lead.'

Without giving her a chance to protest, he slid his arm around her waist and whisked her up the steps and onto the runway, just as Kris was explaining to the audience how grateful he was to Giannis Gekas for supporting his career. There was more applause and brilliant flashes of light from camera flashes when Giannis stepped forwards, tugging Ava with him.

'I cannot think of a better place to announce my engagement to my beautiful fiancée than in Paris, the world's most romantic city,' he told the audience. With a flourish he lifted Ava's hand up to his mouth and pressed his lips to the pink sapphire heart on her finger.

He was a brilliant actor, she thought caustically. Her skin burned where his lips had brushed and she wanted to snatch her hand back and denounce their engagement as a lie. The idea of deceiving people went against her personal moral code of honesty and integrity. But she must abide by her promise to be Giannis's fake fiancée because he had honoured his word and halted criminal proceedings against her brother.

And so she obediently showed her engagement ring to the press photographers and looked adoringly into Giannis's eyes for the cameras.

At the after-show party she remained by his side, smiling up at him as if she was besotted with him. For his part he kept his arm around her while they strolled around the room, stopping frequently so that he could introduce her to people he knew.

Waiters threaded through the crowded room carrying trays of canapés and drinks. Ava sipped champagne and felt the bubbles explode on her tongue. Her senses seemed sharper, and she was intensely aware of Giannis's hand resting on her waist and the brush of his thigh against hers. He was holding a flute of champagne but she noted that he never drank from it.

'Do you ever drink alcohol?' she asked him curiously. 'You didn't have any wine at the fundraising dinner, and I noticed that you are not drinking tonight.'

'How very perceptive of you, *glykiá mou*.' He spoke lightly, but Ava felt him stiffen. 'I avoid drinking alcohol because I like to keep a clear head.'

Something told her there was more to him being teetotal than he had admitted. But, before she could pursue the subject, he took her glass out of her fingers and gave it and his own glass to a passing waiter. Catching hold of her hand, he led her onto the dance floor and swept her into his arms.

Her head swam, not from the effects of the few sips of champagne she'd had, but from the intoxicating heat of Giannis's body pressed up against hers and the divine fragrance of his aftershave mixed with his own unique male scent. He was a good dancer and moved with a natural rhythm as he steered them around the dance floor, hip to hip, her breasts crushed against the hard wall of his chest. He slid one hand down to the base of her spine and spread his fingers over her bottom. Her breath caught in her throat when she felt the solid ridge of his arousal through their clothes.

Ava closed her eyes and reminded herself that Giannis's attentiveness was an act to promote the deception that they were engaged. But there was nothing pretend about the sexual chemistry that sizzled between them. She had never been more aware of a man, or of her own femininity, in her life. Her traitorous mind pictured the big bed in the hotel suite they were sharing. Of course she had no intention of also sharing the bed with him, she assured herself. She had agreed to be his fake fiancée in public only.

But, to keep up the pretence, when the disco music changed to a romantic ballad and Giannis pulled her closer, she slid her hands up to his shoulders. And when he bent his head and brushed his mouth over hers, she parted her lips and kissed him with a fervour that drew a low groan from him.

'We have to get out of here,' he said hoarsely.

Her legs felt unsteady when he abruptly dropped his arms away from her. 'Come,' he growled, clamping his arm around her waist and practically lifting her off her feet as he hurried them out of the museum. The car was waiting for them and, once he had bundled her onto the back seat and closed the privacy screen between them and the driver, he lifted her onto his lap, thrust one hand into her hair and dragged her mouth beneath his.

His kiss was hot and urgent, a ravishment of her senses, as passion exploded between them. Ava sensed a wildness in Giannis that made her shake with need. She remembered Diane Duberry, the fashion journalist at the show, had congratulated her for having tamed the tiger. But the truth was that Giannis would never allow any woman to control him.

Her head was spinning when he finally tore his mouth from hers to allow them to drag oxygen into their lungs. His chest heaved, and when she placed her hand over his heart she felt its thudding, erratic beat. The car sped smoothly through the dark Paris streets and Ava succumbed to the master sorcerer's magic. Giannis trailed his lips down her throat and over one naked shoulder. She did not realise he had unzipped her dress until he tugged the bodice down and cradled her breasts in his big hands.

Her sensible head reminded her that it was shockingly decadent to be half naked in the back of a car and her wanton behaviour was not what she expected of herself. But her thoughts scattered when Giannis bent his head and his warm breath teased one nipple before he closed his mouth around the rosy peak and sucked, hard. Ava could not repress a moan of pleasure, and when he transferred his attention to her other nipple she ran her fingers through his silky dark hair and prayed that he would never stop what he was doing to her.

'I have no intention of stopping, *glykiá mou*,' he said in an amused voice. Colour flared on her face as she realised that she had spoken her plea aloud. But when he returned his mouth to her breasts she tipped her head back and gasped as lightning bolts of sensation shot down to her molten core between her thighs.

Giannis yanked up her long flared skirt and skimmed his hand over one stocking-clad leg, but the dress was designed to fit tightly over her hips and he could not go any further. He swore. 'I hope the other clothes you bought are more accessible.'

Ava shared his frustration but while she was wondering if she could possibly wriggle out of her dress the car came to a halt and Giannis shifted her off his knees. 'We've arrived at the hotel,' he said coolly, straightening his tie and running a hand through his hair. 'You had better tidy yourself up.'

His words catapulted her back to reality and she frantically pulled the top of her dress into place. 'Will you zip me up?'

He refastened her dress seconds before the driver opened the rear door. Giannis stepped onto the pavement and offered Ava his hand. She blinked in the glare of camera flashes going off around them. Photographers were gathered outside the entrance to the hotel and she felt mortified as she imagined how dishevelled she must look as she emerged from the car.

'Here, have this.' Giannis slipped off his jacket and draped it around her shoulders. Glancing down, Ava saw that she had failed to pull the top of her dress up high enough, and her breasts were in danger of spilling out. Hot-faced, she huddled into his jacket as he escorted her into the hotel.

They entered the lift and Ava's reflection in the mirrored walls confirmed the worst. 'I look like a harlot,' she choked, running her finger over her swollen mouth. 'The photographers must have guessed we were making out on the back seat of the car. If the pictures they took just now appear in tomorrow's newspapers, everyone will think that we can't keep our hands off each other.'

Giannis was leaning against the lift wall, one ankle crossed over the other and his hands shoved into his trouser pockets. His bow tie was dangling loose and Ava flushed as she remembered how she had frenziedly torn off his tie and undone several of his shirt buttons. He looked calm and unruffled, the exact opposite of how she felt.

'The point of tonight was to advertise the news of our engagement to the press.' He dropped his gaze to where her breasts were partially exposed above the top of her dress. 'Thanks to your wardrobe malfunction we certainly got maximum exposure,' he drawled.

He sounded amused, and Ava felt sick as she realised what a fool she was. 'I suppose you knew that the paparazzi would be at our hotel,' she said stiffly. 'Is that why you made love to me in the car?'

'Actually I didn't know. But I should have guessed that they would find out which hotel we are staying at.' His eyes narrowed on her flushed face. 'I'm sorry if the photographers upset you.'

'I'm sorry that I ever agreed to be your fake fiancée.' The lift stopped at the top floor and she preceded Giannis along the corridor, despising herself for her fierce awareness of him even now, after he had humiliated her.

'But you are not sorry that your brother has avoided a prison sentence,' he said drily as he opened the door of their suite and ushered her inside. He caught hold of her arm and spun her round to face him. 'I kissed you because you have driven me insane all evening and I couldn't help myself. I have never wanted any woman as badly as I want you.'

With an effort Ava resisted the lure of his husky, accented voice that almost fooled her into believing he meant it. 'You can stop acting now that there is no audience to deceive. We're alone, in case you hadn't noticed.'

His dark eyes gleamed. 'I am very aware of that fact, *glykiá mou.*'

CHAPTER SIX

SOMETHING IN GIANNIS'S voice sent a shiver of apprehension—if she was honest it was *anticipation*—across Ava's skin. She did not fear him. It was her inability to resist his charisma that made her fearful, she admitted. She broke free from him and marched into the suite's only bedroom, intending to lock herself in. But he was right behind her and his soft laughter followed her as she fled into the en suite bathroom.

Splashing cold water onto her face cooled her heated skin, and she removed the silver clips that were hanging from her tangled hair. But she could not disguise her reddened mouth or the hectic glitter in her eyes. She felt undone, out of control, and it scared the hell out of her. If she was going to survive the next month pretending to be Giannis's fiancée, she would have to make it clear that she would not allow him to manipulate her.

Taking a deep breath, she returned to the bedroom but the sight of him in bed, leaning against the pillows, made her want to retreat back to the bathroom. His arms were folded behind his head and his chest was bare. Her heart lurched at the thought that he might be naked beneath the sheet that was draped dangerously low over his hips. She was fascinated by the fuzz of black hairs that arrowed over his flat stomach and disappeared beneath the sheet. Her eyes were drawn to the obvious bulge of his arousal beneath the fine cotton.

'Feel free to stare,' he drawled.

Blushing hotly, she jerked her eyes back to his face and his expression of arrogant amusement infuriated her. 'When you said we would discuss the sleeping arrangements, I assumed that *you* would spend the night on the sofa,' she snapped.

'The replica eighteenth-century chaise longue looks beautiful but it is extremely uncomfortable.' He picked up the big bolster cushions that he'd piled up behind his shoulders and laid them down the centre of the bed. 'It's a big bed and I won't encroach on your half—unless you invite me to.' He grinned at her outraged expression. 'I must say that I am encouraged by your choice of nightwear.'

It was only then that she noticed the confection of black silk and lace arranged on the pillow next to Giannis. She remembered the personal shopper had picked out several items of sexy lingerie, but Ava hadn't explained that her engagement to Giannis was fake and she would not need them. She guessed that the hotel chambermaid who had unpacked her clothes must have laid out the nightgown. Although gown was an exaggeration, she thought darkly as she snatched the tiny garment off the pillow and stalked into the dressing room.

The clothes she had brought with her from London were still in her suitcase. She found her grey flannel pyjamas and changed into them before she hung the velvet evening dress in the wardrobe. That was the last time she would dare to wear a strapless dress, she vowed, wincing as she remembered how her breasts had almost been exposed to the photographers until Giannis had covered her with his jacket.

She had been grateful for his protective gesture. And

he'd insisted that he had not expected the paparazzi to be outside the hotel. Ava bit her lip. Perhaps she was a fool but she believed him. After all, he had kept his side of their deal and halted the criminal case against her brother.

She grimaced as she looked at herself in the mirror. Her passion-killer pyjamas had been designed for comfort and when Giannis saw them she was sure he would have no trouble keeping to his side of the bed. Which was what she wanted—wasn't it?

She pictured him the previous night at the hotel in London, his sleek, honed body poised above her before he'd slowly lowered himself onto her as he'd entered her with one hard thrust. Why not enjoy what he was offering for the next month? whispered a voice of temptation. Sex without strings and no possibility of her getting hurt because—unlike in a normal relationship—she had no expectations that a brief affair with Giannis might lead to something more meaningful. Their engagement was a deception but he had been totally honest with her. Maybe it was time to be honest with herself and admit that she wanted him.

Before she could chicken out, she pulled off her pyjamas and slipped on the black negligee. It was practically see-through, dotted with a few strategically placed lace flowers, and it was the sexiest item of clothing she had ever worn. She walked into the bedroom and the feral sound Giannis made as he stared at her tugged deep in her pelvis.

'I hope you realise that the likelihood of me remaining on my side of the bolsters is zero. You look incredible, *omorfiá mou*.'

There was no doubt that his appreciation was genuine. His arousal was unmissable, jutting beneath the sheet, but more surprising was the flush of dark colour on his cheekbones. Ava's self-confidence rose with every step she took across the room towards him. The light from the bedside lamp sparked off the pink sapphire on her finger as she looked down at the engagement ring, watching its iridescent gleam.

'You can keep the ring after our engagement ends,' Giannis told her.

'No!' She shook her head. 'I am giving you a month of my life but you haven't bought me. I will wear your ring and pretend to be your fiancée in public. But when we are alone—' she pulled off the ring and put it down on the bedside table '—whatever I do, however I behave, is my choice.'

His eyes narrowed as she untied the ribbon at the front of her negligée so that the two sides fell open, exposing her firm breasts and betrayingly hard nipples. 'And what do you choose to do?' he said thickly.

'This.' She whipped the sheet away to reveal his naked, aroused body and climbed on top of him so that she was straddling his hips. 'And this,' she murmured as she leaned forwards and covered his mouth with hers.

For a heart-stopping second he did not respond and she wondered if she had misunderstood, that he didn't want her. But then his arms came around her like iron bands and held her so tightly that she could not escape. He opened his mouth to the fierce demands of her kiss and kissed her back with a barely leashed hunger that made her heart race.

'So you want to take charge, do you?' he murmured as she traced her lips over the prickly black stubble on his jaw. His indulgent tone set an alarm bell off in her head. Clearly, Giannis believed that he was the one in control, and he was simply allowing her to take the dominant role while it suited him.

'You had better believe it,' she told him sweetly. Still astride him, she sat upright and ran her hands over his chest. Her smile was pure innocence as she bent her head and closed her mouth around one male nipple, scraping her teeth over the hard nub.

'Theos...' His body jerked beneath her and he swore when she moved her mouth across to his other nipple and bit him, hard. 'You little vixen.' He tried to grab her hair but she shook it back over her shoulders and moved down his body, pressing hot kisses over his stomach and following the line of dark hairs down lower. Very lightly, she ran her fingertips up and down his shaft and he tensed.

'Not this time, angel,' he muttered. 'I want you too badly.'

She flicked her tongue along the swollen length of him and gave a husky laugh of feminine triumph when he groaned. 'I'm in charge and don't you forget it,' Ava told him. 'I'm not your puppet, so don't think you can control me.'

'You are so fierce.' He laughed but there was something in his voice that sounded like respect. And when he moved suddenly and rolled her beneath him he stared into her eyes for what seemed like eternity, as if he wanted to read her mind. 'You fascinate me. No other woman has done that before,' he admitted.

He slipped his hand between her legs and discovered that she was as turned-on as he was. Keeping his eyes locked with hers, he eased his fingers inside her until she moaned. 'Who is in charge now, angel?' he teased softly. But Ava no longer cared if she won or lost the power struggle. She reached down between their bodies and curled her hand around him, making him groan. Maybe they were both winners, she thought. 'You are ready for me, Ava *mou*.' He swiftly donned a condom before he moved over her and entered her with a slow, deep thrust that delighted her body and touched her soul. With a flash of insight that shook her, she acknowledged that she would always be ready for him. She guessed that Giannis had made a slip of his tongue when he'd called her *my* Ava.

They flew to Greece the next day, and in the evening attended a party held at reputedly Athens' most chic rooftop bar where the cosmopolitan clientele included several international celebrities. The paparazzi swarmed in the street outside the venue and there was a flurry of flashlights as Giannis Gekas and his English fiancée posed for the cameras.

From the rooftop bar the views of the sunset over the city were amazing. But Giannis only had eyes for Ava. She looked stunning in a scarlet cocktail dress that showed off her gorgeous curves, and he was impatient for the party to finish so that he could take her back to his penthouse apartment and reacquaint himself with her delectable body. Their sexual chemistry was hotter than anything he'd experienced with his previous mistresses.

He smiled to himself as he imagined Ava's reaction if he was ever foolish enough to refer to her as his mistress. No doubt she would reply with a scathing comment designed to put him in his place. He enjoyed her fiery nature, and never more so than when they had sex and she became a wildcat with sharp claws. He bore the marks from where she had raked her fingernails down his back when they'd reached a climax together last night. Afterwards, she had reminded him of a contented kitten, warm and soft as she snuggled up to him and flicked her tongue over her lips like a satisfied cat after drinking a bowl of cream.

Giannis had intended to ease his arm from beneath her and move her across to the other side of the bed. But he'd felt reluctant to disturb her and he must have fallen asleep because when he'd next opened his eyes his head had been pillowed on Ava's breasts, and he'd been so aroused that he ached. He had kissed her awake and ignored her protests that had quickly become moans of pleasure when he'd nudged her legs apart with his shoulders and pressed his mouth against her feminine core to feast on her sweetness.

With an effort Giannis dragged his mind from his erotic memories when he realised that he had not been listening to the conversation going on around him. The group of guests he was standing with were looking at him, clearly waiting for him to say something. He glanced at Ava for help.

'I was just explaining that we haven't set a date for our wedding yet,' she said drily. 'We are not in a rush.'

'On the contrary, *agápi mou*, I am impatient to make you my wife as soon as possible.' He slipped his arm around her waist and smiled with his customary effortless charm at the other guests. 'I hope you will forgive me for selfishly wanting to have my beautiful bride-to-be to myself,' he murmured before he led Ava away.

'Why did you say that we will get married soon?' she demanded while he escorted her out of the crowded bar. Once they were outside and walking to where he had parked the car, she pulled away from him. 'There was no need to overdo the devoted fiancé act. All that staring into my eyes as if I was the only woman in the world was unnecessary.'

He grinned at her uptight expression. 'I need to convince Stefanos Markou that our engagement is genuine and I am serious about settling down. The woman in the blue dress who we were talking to is a journalist with a popular gossip magazine. No doubt the next edition will include several pages devoted to discussing our imminent wedding.'

Ava bit her lip. 'More deception,' she muttered. 'One lie always leads to another. I realise it's just a game to you, but when our fake engagement ends I will face public humiliation as the woman who nearly married Giannis Gekas.'

'It will cost my company in the region of one hundred million pounds to buy Markou's fleet of ships. An investment of that size is hardly a game,' Giannis told her curtly. 'Once I've secured the deal with Stefanos I will give a press statement explaining that you broke off our engagement because you fell out of love with me.'

It wouldn't be the first time it had happened, he brooded. His jaw clenched as he thought of Caroline. At least he'd discovered before he'd made an utter fool of himself that Caroline had been more in love with his money than with him.

Giannis sensed that Ava sent him a few curious glances during the journey back to his apartment block. He parked in the underground car park and when they rode the lift up to the top floor he could not take his eyes off her. She was a temptress in her scarlet dress and vertiginous heels and he had been in a state of semi-arousal all evening as he'd imagined her slender legs wrapped around his back.

His desire for her showed no sign of lessening—yet. But he had no doubt that it would fade and he'd grow bored of her. His mistresses never held his interest for long. Perhaps if he sought some sort of counselling, a psychologist would suggest that his guilt over his father's death was the reason he avoided close relationships. But Giannis had no intention of allowing anyone access to his soul.

After ushering Ava into the penthouse, he crossed the huge open-plan living room and opened the doors leading to his private roof garden. 'Would you like a drink?' he asked her.

'Just fruit juice, please.'

He headed for the kitchen, and returned to find her out on the terrace, standing by the pool. The water appeared black beneath the night sky and reflected the silver stars. 'Is that how you keep in such great physical shape?' she murmured, indicating the pool.

His heart lurched at her compliment. *Theos*, she made him feel like a teenager with all the uncertainty and confusion brought on by surging hormones, he acknowledged with savage self-derision. 'I complete fifty lengths every morning. But I prefer to swim in the sea when I am at my house on Spetses.'

Ava sipped her fruit juice and glanced at the bottle of beer in his hand. 'You don't need to keep a clear head tonight?' She obviously remembered the reason he had given her for why he hadn't drunk champagne at the fashion show in Paris.

'It's non-alcoholic beer,' he admitted.

'Why are you afraid of not being in control?'

Rattled by her perception, his eyes narrowed. 'I'll ask you the same question.'

'Touché.' She smiled ruefully. 'I don't like surprises.'

'Not even nice ones?'

'I've never had a nice surprise.' She looked at the city skyline. 'The Acropolis looks wonderful lit up at night. Have you always lived in Athens?'

Giannis could not understand why he felt frustrated by her determination to turn the conversation away from herself. In his experience women were only too happy to talk about themselves, but Ava, he was beginning to realise, was not like any other woman.

He shrugged. 'I grew up just along the coast at Faliron and I am proud to call myself an Athenian.'

'Perhaps I could do some sightseeing while you are at work? I know you have arranged for us to attend various social functions in the evenings so that we are seen together, but you have a business to run during the day.'

'I'll show you around the city. One of the perks of owning my own company is that I can delegate.' As Giannis spoke he wondered what the hell had got into him. He'd never delegated in his life and his work schedule was by his own admittance brutal. Driven by his need to succeed, he regularly worked fourteen-hour days and he couldn't remember the last time he'd spent more than a couple of hours away from his computer or phone.

The more time he spent with Ava, the quicker his inexplicable fascination with her would lead to familiarity and, by definition, boredom, he assured himself. He put down his drink and walked towards her, noting with satisfaction how her eyes widened and her tongue flicked over her lips, issuing an unconscious invitation that he had every intention of accepting.

'There is an even better view of the Acropolis from the bedroom,' he said softly.

She hesitated for a few seconds and when she put her hand in his and let him lead her through the apartment to the master suite he was aware of the hard thud of his heart beneath his ribs. He stood behind her and turned her to face the floor-to-ceiling windows which overlooked Greece's most iconic citadel, situated atop a vast outcrop of rock. 'There.'

'It's so beautiful,' she said in an awed voice. 'What

an incredible view. You can just lie in bed and stare at a piece of ancient history.'

'Mmm…' He nuzzled her neck and slid his arms around her to test the weight of her breasts in his hands. 'I can think of rather more energetic things I'd like to do in bed, *agápi mou.*'

She pulled the pink sapphire ring from her finger and dropped it onto the bedside table. 'I'm not your love now that we are alone,' she reminded him.

'But you are my lover.' He unzipped her dress and when it fell to the floor she stepped out of it before she turned and wound her arms around his neck.

'Yes,' she whispered against his mouth. 'For one month I will be your lover.'

As he scooped her up and laid her down on the bed, Giannis knew he should be relieved that Ava understood the rules. But perversely he felt irritated. Perhaps it was because her words had sounded like a challenge that provoked him to murmur, 'You might want our affair to last longer than a month.'

'I won't.' She watched him undress and reached behind her shoulders to unclip her bra, letting it fall away from her breasts. 'But you might fall in love with me.'

'Impossible,' he promised her. 'I already told you I don't have a heart.' He pushed her back against the mattress and covered her body with his, watching her eyes widen when he pushed between her thighs.

'However, I do have this, *glykiá mou,*' he murmured before he possessed her with one fierce thrust followed by another and another, taking them higher until they arrived at the pinnacle and tumbled over the edge together.

Afterwards, he shifted across the bed and tucked his hands behind his head, determined to emphasise to Ava that sex was all he was prepared to offer. Too many people mistook lust for love, Giannis brooded. He'd made that mistake himself once, when he had fallen for Caroline. But he had learned his lesson and moved on.

After busy, bustling Athens, Ava discovered that life on the beautiful island of Spetses moved at a much slower pace. Thankfully.

She frowned as the thought slipped into her mind. She should be glad that she was halfway through her fake engagement to Giannis. So why did she wish that time would slow down?

She hadn't expected to *like* him, she thought ruefully. They had stayed at his apartment in the city for two weeks, ostensibly so that they could be seen together at high society events. The shock news that Greece's most eligible bachelor had chosen a bride had sparked fevered media interest, leading Ava to remark drily that Stefanos Markou could not have missed reports about their romance, unless he had been visiting remote indigenous tribes in the Amazon rainforest.

But for the most part they'd managed to evade the paparazzi when Giannis had kept his word and showed her Athens. Not just the tourist attractions, although of course they did visit the Acropolis and the nearby Acropolis Museum, as well as the Byzantine Museum.

They climbed the steep winding path to the top of Lycabettus Hill and sat at the top to watch the sunset over the city. He took her to the pretty neighbourhood of Plaka and they strolled hand in hand along the narrow streets lined with pastel-coloured houses where cerise-pink bougainvillea tumbled from window boxes. And he took her to dinner at little *tavernas* tucked away in side streets off the tourist track, where they ate authentic Greek food and Giannis entertained her with stories of the places he had visited around the world and the people he had met. He was an interesting and amusing companion and Ava found herself falling ever deeper under his spell.

Spetses was a twenty-minute helicopter flight from Athens, although most people did not have a helipad in their garden like Giannis, and visitors to the island made use of the red and white water taxis. The island was picturesque, with whitewashed houses and cobbled streets around the harbour. Cars were banned in the town centre and the sight of horse-drawn carriages rattling along gave the impression that Spetses belonged to a bygone era. That feeling was reflected in Villa Delphine, Giannis's stunning neo-classical mansion, with its exquisite arches and gracious colonnades. The exterior walls were painted pale yellow, and green shutters at the windows gave the house an elegant yet homely charm.

Ava was relieved that Villa Delphine looked nothing like the extravagant but tasteless house in Cyprus where she had lived for part of her childhood, until her father had been arrested and she had discovered the truth about him. Every happy memory from the first seventeen years of her life now seemed grubby, contaminated by her father's criminality. But at least Sam had been given another chance, and she was hopeful that he would keep out of trouble from now on.

She returned her phone to her bag and watched Giannis walk up the beach towards her. He had been swimming in the sea and water droplets glistened on his olive-gold skin and black chest hairs. His swim-shorts sat low on his hips and Ava's mouth ran dry as she studied his impressive six-pack. Heat flared inside her when he hunkered down in front of her and dropped a tantalisingly brief kiss on her mouth.

'Did you get hold of your brother?'

'I've just finished speaking to him. He is helping out on my aunt and uncle's farm in Cumbria and he says it hasn't stopped raining since he arrived. I didn't tell him that it's twenty-five degrees in Greece. I'm just relieved he's away from the East End and its association with—' She broke off abruptly.

'Association with what?'

'Oh…historically the area of London around Whitechapel was well-known for being a rough place,' she prevaricated. Desperate to avoid the questions that she sensed Giannis wanted to ask, she placed her hands on either side of his face and pulled his mouth down to hers. He allowed her to control the kiss and, as always, passion swiftly flared. But when Ava tried to tug him down beside her, he lifted his lips from hers with an ease that caused her heart to give a twinge.

'Unfortunately there is not time for you to distract me with sex,' he said in a dry tone that made her blush guiltily. 'My mother is joining us for lunch.'

She packed her sun cream and the novel she had been reading into her bag and stood up. 'I thought your mother was in New York?' Giannis had told her that his mother, Filia, and his younger sister, Irini, shared the house next door to Villa Delphine. Irini was an art historian, currently working at a museum in Florence.

'Mitera has flown back from the US early to meet you,' he said as he followed her along the path which led from the private beach up to the house.

Ava halted and swung round to look at him. 'You *have* explained to your mother that I am not really your fiancée—haven't you? We can't lie to her,' she muttered when he remained silent. 'It's not fair. She might be excited that you are going to get married and perhaps give her grandchildren.'

'My mother is an inveterate gossip,' he said curtly. 'If I told her the truth about us, she would be on the phone within minutes to tell a friend, who would tell another friend, and the story that you are my fake fiancée would be leaked to the press within hours.'

He lifted his hand and traced his finger over her lips. 'Don't pout, *glykiá mou,* or it will look as though we have had a lover's tiff,' he teased. His earlier curtness had been replaced by his potent charm and he pulled her into his arms and kissed her until she melted against him. But had his kiss been to distract her? Ava asked herself as she ran upstairs to shower and change out of her bikini before his mother arrived.

When she walked into the salon some half an hour later, wearing an elegant pale blue shift dress from a Paris design house, she heard voices from the terrace speaking in Greek. The woman dressed entirely in black was evidently Giannis's mother. Ava took a deep breath and was about to step outside and introduce herself, but she hesitated as Filia Gekas's voice drifted through the open French doors.

'Have you been honest with this woman who you have decided to marry, Giannis? Have you told Ava *everything* about you?'

CHAPTER SEVEN

SECRETS AND LIES. They lurked in every corner of the dining room, taunting Ava while she forced herself to eat her lunch and attempted to make conversation with Giannis's mother. It was an uphill task, for Filia was a discontented woman whose only pleasure in life, it seemed, was criticising her son.

Ava had no idea what the other woman had meant, or what Giannis was supposed to have told her. Perhaps it was something that would only be relevant if he truly intended to marry her—which, of course, he did not. She was trapped in a deception that would only end once he had secured his business deal with Stefanos Markou.

She glanced at him across the table and found he was watching her broodingly as if he was trying to fathom her out. Ava guiltily acknowledged that she had her own secrets. But why should she tell Giannis that her father was serving a prison sentence for armed robbery? In a few weeks' time there might be a brief media frenzy when it was announced that the engagement between Greece's golden boy and his English fiancée was over, but the paparazzi would quickly forget about her, as, no doubt, would Giannis.

She pulled her mind back to the conversation between Giannis and his mother. 'I don't know why you paid a fortune for a holiday to the Maldives,' Filia said sharply. 'You know I dislike long-haul flights.'

'It is hardly any longer than the flight time to New York,' Giannis pointed out mildly. 'I bid for the trip at a charity auction because I hoped you would enjoy a spa break in an exotic location.'

His mother sniffed and turned to Ava. 'I was surprised when Giannis told me that the two of you are engaged to be married. He has never mentioned you before.'

Ava felt heat spread over her cheeks. 'It was a whirlwind courtship,' she murmured.

Filia gave her a speculative look. 'My son is a very wealthy man. Can I ask why you agreed to marry him?'

'Mitera!' Giannis frowned at his mother but she was unabashed.

'It is a reasonable question to ask.' She turned her sharp black eyes back to Ava. 'Well?'

Ava said the only thing she could say. 'I…love him.' Her voice sounded strangely husky and she did not dare look across the table at Giannis. One lie always led to another lie, she thought bleakly. But she must have sounded convincing because his mother gave her a searching look and then nodded.

'Good,' Filia said. 'Love and trust are vital to a successful marriage.'

Ava gave a quiet sigh of relief when Giannis came to her rescue and asked his mother about her trip to New York. Evidently it had been a disaster, for which she blamed him. The five-star hotel where he had arranged for her to stay had, according to Filia, been atrocious. 'Rude staff, and the bed had a lumpy mattress.'

'I am sorry you were disappointed,' he told his mother with commendable patience. Ava glanced at him, telling herself that if he looked amused by her lie about being in love with him she would empty the water jug over his head, and never mind what conclusion his mother might draw.

He met her gaze across the table and the gleam in his dark eyes made her tremble as a shocking realisation dawned on her. It couldn't be true, she assured herself frantically. But the erratic thud of her heart betrayed her. Had she managed to sound convincing to his mother because she was actually falling in love with Giannis?

The helicopter swooped low over the sea and Ava felt her stomach drop. She did not realise that her swift intake of breath had been audible, but Giannis looked up from his laptop. He was seated opposite her in the helicopter's luxurious cabin and leaned forwards to take her hand in his warm grasp.

'Don't worry,' he said reassuringly. 'Vasilis is a good pilot. We will be landing in a few minutes. Stefanos's private island, Gaia, is below us now.'

She nodded and turned her head to look out of the window at the pine tree covered island, edged by golden beaches and set in an azure sea. It was easier to let Giannis think she was nervous of flying in the helicopter. She certainly could not tell him of her terrifying suspicion, which might explain the nauseous feeling she'd experienced for the past few days.

She'd put her queasiness down to some prawns she'd eaten at a restaurant a few evenings before. But while she had packed her suitcase this morning she'd found the packet of tampons she had brought to Spetses with her in the expectation that she would need them.

Her period was only a couple of days late, Ava tried to reassure herself. But a doom-laden voice in her head reminded her that she was never late. Her mind argued that Giannis had used a condom every time they'd had sex. Even when he'd followed her into the shower cubicle and stood behind her so that she had felt his arousal press against her bottom, he had been prepared. She could not be pregnant. Probably her churning stomach and uncomfortably sensitive breasts were signs that her period was about to start.

She sighed. Her mood swings were another indication that she was worrying unnecessarily. When the helicopter had taken off from Spetses she had been thankful that her oversized sunglasses hid her tears. Ava knew she was unlikely to ever return to the island. Giannis had said that they would go to his apartment in Athens after meeting Stefanos Markou and he would arrange for his private jet to fly her back to London.

Apart from the awkward lunch with Giannis's mother, the past two weeks that they had spent at Villa Delphine had been like a wonderful dream where each perfect day rolled into the next, and every night Giannis had made love to her and their wildfire passion blazed out of control. But since Ava had woken early that morning, feeling horribly sick, and crept silently into the bathroom so as not to wake him, her insides had been knotted with dread.

The helicopter landed and Giannis climbed out and offered Ava his hand to assist her down the steps. 'You are still pale,' he said, frowning as he studied her.

'I'm nervous,' she admitted. 'Your hope of buying Markou Shipping is the reason we have spent the last month pretending to be engaged, but what if Stefanos guesses that I am your fake fiancée?'

'Why should he? People tend to believe what they see. That is why conmen are sometimes able to persuade elderly ladies to hand over their life savings.'

Her father had been the cleverest conman of all, Ava

thought bitterly. He had fooled his own wife and children with his affable charm. Suddenly she could not wait for the deception she was playing with Giannis to be over. But then her relationship with him would finish—unless her suspicion, and a pregnancy test when she had a chance to buy one, proved positive. The knot of dread in her stomach tightened.

As they walked across the lawn towards a sprawling villa, Giannis slid his arm around her waist and urged her forwards to meet the grey-haired man waiting for them on the terrace. Stefanos Markou shook Giannis's hand before he turned to Ava.

'I admit I was surprised when Giannis announced his decision to marry. But now that I have met you, Ava, I understand why he is in a hurry to make you his wife.' Stefanos smiled. 'My wife read in a magazine that you are planning a Christmas wedding.'

'Christmas is more than two months away and I don't think I can wait that long,' Giannis murmured. Ava's heart gave a familiar flip when he looked down at her with a tender expression in his eyes that her common sense told her was not real. He was a brilliant actor, she reminded herself, but her mouth curved of its own accord into an unconsciously wistful smile.

Stefanos laughed. 'The other bidders who want to buy Markou Shipping are already here. So, let us get down to business, Giannis, while Ava talks of wedding dresses with my wife and daughters.'

He led them into the villa and introduced Ava to his wife, Maria, and his three daughters, who between them had seven children of their own—all girls. Stefanos sighed. 'It seems that I am not destined to have a grandson to pass Markou Shipping on to. Unfortunately my only nephew is a hopeless businessman and so I made the decision to sell the company and retire.'

The small island of Gaia was a picturesque paradise. Stefanos's wife and daughters were friendly and welcoming, but Ava felt a fraud for having to pretend to be excited about her supposed forthcoming wedding. The little grandchildren were a delight, but when she held the youngest baby of just six weeks old she found herself imagining what it would be like to cradle her own baby in her arms. She tried to quell her sense of panic, and inexplicably she felt an ache in her heart as she pictured a baby with Giannis's dark hair and eyes.

Eventually she made the excuse of a headache and slipped away to walk on the beach. When she turned back towards the villa, she saw Giannis striding along the sand to meet her.

'Well?' she asked him anxiously.

A wide grin spread across his face and he looked heartbreakingly handsome. He put his hands on either side of her waist and swung her round in the air. 'It's done,' he told her in a triumphant voice. 'I persuaded Stefanos to sell his company to me. I had to increase my financial offer, but the main reason he agreed was because he is convinced that when you and I marry I will settle down to family life and embrace the values that Stefanos believes are important. Work can start immediately to refit and upgrade the Markou fleet of ships to turn them into luxury cruisers.'

'And I can go home,' Ava said quietly.

Giannis set her back on her feet, but he kept his arms around her and a faint frown creased between his brows. 'It will take a few days for the paperwork to be finalised and signed. Stefanos is giving a party tonight for all the Markou Shipping employees and he will announce that

I am buying the company. It will be an opportunity for me to reassure the workforce that they will continue to be employed by TGE. Stefanos has invited us to spend the night on Gaia and the helicopter will pick us up and take us to Athens in the morning.'

The breeze blew Ava's long hair across her face and Giannis caught the golden strands in his hand and tucked them behind her ear. His dark eyes gleamed with something indefinable that nevertheless made her heart beat too fast. 'I cannot see a reason why you should rush back to England, can you, *glykiá mou*?' he murmured.

She *should* remind him that they had made a deal, and now that she had kept her side of it there was no reason for her to stay in Greece with him. Was he saying that he did not want her to leave? What would he say if she *was* pregnant? Would he still want her and their child? Her thoughts swirled around inside her head. She caught her lower lip between her teeth, and the feral growl he made evoked a wild heat inside her so that when he claimed her mouth and kissed her as if he could never have enough of her she gave up fighting herself and simply melted in his fire.

That evening, the guests were ferried from the mainland to Gaia by boat. As the sun set, the usually peaceful island was packed with several hundred partygoers enjoying Stefanos's generous hospitality. A bar and barbecue had been set up on the beach and a famous DJ had flown in from New York to take charge of the music.

Ava had convinced herself that her niggling stomach ache was a sign that her period was about to start, and with Giannis in an upbeat mood she decided to have fun at the party and live for the moment. He was flatteringly attentive and hardly left her side all evening.

She told herself that he was continuing to act the role of adoring fiancé until his business deal with Stefanos had been signed. But the way he held her close while they danced and threaded his fingers through her hair was utterly beguiling.

'Don't go away,' he murmured midway through the evening. He claimed her mouth in a lingering kiss, as if he was reluctant to leave her, before he went to join Stefanos on the stage at one end of the ballroom. There was loud applause from Markou Shipping's employees when Giannis explained that everyone would keep their jobs and be offered training opportunities at TGE.

'Gullible idiots.' A voice close to Ava sounded cynical. She looked over at the man who had spoken and he caught her curious glance. 'You don't believe that Gekas will keep his word, do you? He has promised to retain Markou's workforce simply to persuade the old fool to sell the company to him. But Gekas isn't interested in saving Greek jobs. All he wants is the ships and in a few months he will sack the workers.'

The man laughed at Ava's startled expression. 'Giannis Gekas fools everyone with his charming manner, including you, it seems. You obviously haven't heard the rumours that Mr Nice Guy has a nasty side.'

It must have been the cool breeze drifting in through the window that made the hairs on the back of Ava's neck stand on end. 'What do you mean?'

'Rumours have circulated for some time that Gekas has links with an organised crime syndicate and that he uses TGE to hide his money-laundering activities.'

'If there was any substance to those rumours, surely the authorities would have investigated Giannis?' Ava said sharply. 'And Stefanos would not have sold Markou Shipping to someone he suspected of being a criminal.'

'It's like I said. Old Markou is a fool who has been taken in by Gekas's apparent saintliness. Setting up a charity to help young Greeks establish new businesses was a clever move.' The man shrugged. 'As for the police, it's likely that some of them are being bribed, or they are too scared of what will happen to them and their families if they start to investigate Gekas's business methods. The Greek mafia are not a bunch of Boy Scouts; they are ruthless mobsters.'

Ava's mouth was dry and she could feel her heart hammering beneath her ribs. 'Do you have any proof to back up your allegations, Mr...?' She paused, hoping the man would introduce himself.

'Of course nothing can be proved. Gekas is too clever for that. And I'm not telling you my name because I don't want to end up at the bottom of the sea with a bullet through my brain.'

Nothing the man had said could be true, Ava tried to reassure herself. But what did she *actually* know about Giannis? whispered a voice in her head. She stared at the man. 'You have no right to make such awful, unsubstantiated accusations against Giannis. Why should I believe you?'

'How do you think that Gekas became a billionaire by his mid-thirties? The luxury cruise market was badly hit by the economic meltdown in Greece and other parts of Europe, yet TGE makes huge profits.'

The man laughed unpleasantly. 'Racketeering is a more likely source of Gekas's fortune. Some years ago a journalist tried to investigate him but your fiancé has powerful friends in high places and I assume the journalist was bribed to keep his nose out of Gekas's private life.'

With another sneering laugh the man walked away and disappeared from Ava's view in the crowded ballroom. The dancing had started again and she saw Giannis walk down the steps at the side of the stage. None of what she had heard about him could be true. *Could it?* He had captivated her with his legendary charm but was she, along with all the other people at the party, including Stefanos Markou, a gullible fool who had been taken in by Giannis's charisma?

She had seen it happen before. Everyone who had met her father had fallen for his cockney good humour, but at his trial Terry McKay had been exposed as a ruthless gangland boss who had used bribery and intimidation to evade the law. She had no proof that the accusations made by a stranger against Giannis were true, Ava reminded herself.

A memory pushed into her mind, of the morning in the hotel in London after they had spent the night together. He had opened his briefcase and she'd been shocked to see that it contained piles of bank notes. At the time she had thought it odd that he carried so much cash around but she'd been focused on trying to persuade Giannis to drop the charges against her brother. However, the incident had reminded her of how her father had kept large quantities of bank notes hidden in odd places in the house in Cyprus.

Then there was what she had overheard Giannis's mother say. *'Have you told Ava everything about you?'* What had Filia meant? What secret about himself had Giannis kept from her? And why did his mother disapprove of her only son?

The throbbing music was pounding in Ava's ears and she felt hot and then cold, and horribly sick. The flashing disco ball hanging from the ceiling was spinning round and round, making her dizzy, and she was afraid she was going to faint.

'Ava.' Suddenly Giannis was standing in front of her, his chiselled features softening as he studied her. 'What's the matter, *glykiá mou*?'

His voice was husky with concern, and Ava despised herself for wishing that she could ignore the rumours she had heard about him. But why would the party guest have made up lies about Giannis?

'Migraine,' she muttered. 'I get them occasionally and the bright disco lights are making it worse. If you don't mind I'd like to go to bed and hopefully sleep it off.'

'I'll take you back to our room and stay with you,' he said instantly.

'No, you should remain at the party and celebrate winning your business deal.'

Giannis swore softly. 'The deal isn't important.'

'How can you say that, when it was the reason we have pretended to be engaged?'

His smile made Ava's heart skip a beat, despite everything she had heard about him. 'Our relationship may have started out as a pretence but I think we both realise that the spark between us shows no sign of fading,' he murmured. He frowned when she swayed on her feet. 'But we won't discuss it now. You need to take some painkillers.'

She needed to be alone with her chaotic thoughts, and she was relieved when she saw Stefanos beckon to Giannis from across the room. 'I think you are needed. I'll be fine,' she assured him, and hurried out of the ballroom before he could argue.

Later that night, when Giannis quietly entered the bedroom and slid into bed beside her, Ava squeezed her eyes shut and pretended to be asleep. And the next morning when she rushed to the bathroom to be sick he was sympathetic, believing that a migraine was the cause of her nausea. His tender concern during the helicopter flight back to Athens added to her confusion. It seemed impossible that he could be involved with the criminal underworld.

Her father had given the appearance of being a loving family man and she had adored him, Ava remembered bleakly. She had been devastated when details of Terry McKay's violent crimes were revealed during his trial. For seventeen years her father had hidden his secret life from her. In the one month that she and Giannis had pretended to be engaged she'd learned virtually nothing about him, except that he was a good actor.

A car was waiting to drive them from Athens airport to the city centre. On the way, she persuaded Giannis to drop her off at a pharmacy, making the excuse that she needed to buy some stronger painkillers for her headache.

'I wish I didn't need to go to the office but I have an important meeting.' He pressed his lips to her forehead. 'Take the migraine tablets and go to bed,' he bade her gently.

One lie always led to more lies, Ava thought miserably when she bought a pregnancy test and hurried back to the penthouse apartment. Her hands shook as she followed the instructions on the test. She still clung to the hope that her late period and bouts of sickness were symptoms of a stomach upset.

The minutes went by agonisingly slowly while she paced around the bathroom. Finally it was time to check the result. Taking a deep breath, she looked at the test and grabbed the edge of the vanity unit as her legs turned to jelly. Her disbelief as she stared at the positive result swiftly turned to terror.

She was expecting Giannis's baby. But who—and more importantly *what*—was Giannis Gekas? Was he the charismatic lover who she had begun to fall in love with? Or was he a criminal who hid his illegal activities behind the façade of a successful businessman and philanthropist?

Feeling numb from the two huge shocks she had received in the space of twenty-four hours, Ava placed a trembling hand on her stomach. It seemed incredible that a new life was developing inside her and she felt an overwhelming sense of protectiveness for her baby. She would have been worried about telling Giannis of her pregnancy *before* she had heard the rumours about him. This was the man, after all, who had insisted that he did not have a heart.

Now the prospect filled her with dread. Supposing he was a man like her father—a criminal and a liar? A cold hand squeezed her heart. What if her ex, Craig, was right and there *was* a criminal gene that her baby might inherit from *both* parents? Ava was the absolute opposite of her father, and she had spent her adult life subconsciously trying to atone for his crimes in her job supporting victims of crime. She would bring her child up to be honest and law-abiding, but would Giannis share her ideals?

She sank down onto the edge of the bath and covered her face with her hands. Even if she could bring herself to ask him outright if he was a criminal, he was bound to deny it. She did not know if she could trust him—and for that reason she dared not tell him that she was having his baby.

Giannis let himself into the apartment and walked noiselessly down the passageway towards the bedroom. He had a ton of work to do following his successful bid to buy Markou Shipping, but he'd been unable to concentrate during his meeting with TGE's board because he had

been worried about Ava. She had looked pale and fragile when he'd left her at the pharmacy and he felt guilty
that he had not taken care of her. His conscience pricked
that he should have brought her home and stayed with
her while he sent his housekeeper out to buy medication
for Ava's migraine.

He did not understand what had happened to him over
the past month. His plan that Ava should pose as his
fake fiancée had seemed simple enough. But they had
become lovers and, more surprisingly, friends. He had
even taken her to Spetses, although he'd never invited
any of his previous mistresses to Villa Delphine, which
he regarded as his private sanctuary. He'd told himself
that the trip to the island was to promote the pretence that
they were engaged but, instead of staying for a weekend
as he'd intended, they had spent two weeks there. He had
even found himself resenting the few hours each day that
he'd had to get on with some work because he'd wanted
to spend time with Ava, at the pool or the beach or—his
preferred option—in bed.

She was beautiful, intelligent, sometimes fierce, often
funny and always sexy. It was little things, Giannis
mused. Like the way she ate a fresh peach for breakfast
every morning with evident enjoyment, licking the juice
from her lips with her tongue. Or how she migrated over
to his side of the bed in the middle of the night so that
when he woke in the morning she was curled up against
his chest, warm and soft and infinitely desirable.

Theos, he was behaving like a hormone-fuelled teenager, Giannis thought impatiently as he felt the aching
hardness of his arousal. He opened the bedroom door
quietly, not wanting to disturb Ava if she was asleep. But
the bed was empty. He recognised the suitcase standing
on the floor as the one she had brought with her from

London. A passport was lying on top of it. The wardrobe doors were open and he could see hanging inside were the dresses that the personal shopper in Paris had helped Ava choose.

Something was not right and he felt a sinking sensation in his stomach as Ava walked out of the bathroom and froze when she saw him. She carefully avoided his gaze and Giannis's eyes narrowed. He leaned nonchalantly against the door frame and kept his tone deliberately bland. 'Are you going somewhere, *glykiá mou*?'

'There is no need for you to refer to me as your sweetheart now that you have secured your deal with Stefanos.' She finally glanced at him and he wondered why she was nervous. 'I managed to book a seat on a flight to London leaving this afternoon.'

Icy fingers curled around his heart. 'You need to get back to the UK in a hurry? How is your headache, by the way?' he said drily.

A pink stain swept along her cheekbones. 'It's much better, thank you.' She caught her bottom lip between her teeth and Giannis fought the urge to walk over to her and cover her mouth with his. 'I thought that now you have persuaded Stefanos to sell his company to you, there is no point in me staying in Greece. I really want to go back and focus on my career.'

Anger flickered inside him and he wanted to tell her that there was every bloody point. They were good together—in bed and out of it. Not that he had any intention of admitting how much he enjoyed her company. This inconvenient attraction he felt for her—he refused to call it an obsession—*would* fade. He just could not say exactly when.

'I thought we decided at Stefanos's party that there was no reason for you to return to the UK immediately.'

'*You* decided. You didn't ask me what I wanted.' She glared at him. 'It sounds familiar, doesn't it?'

What the hell had happened to have brought about a dramatic change in Ava's attitude? Giannis searched his mind for clues that might explain why she was speaking to him in a cool voice that echoed the wintry expression in her grey eyes. Before they had gone to meet Stefanos she had responded to him with an eagerness that made his heart pound. But he noticed how she stiffened when he walked towards her.

She had acted oddly, almost secretively, when she'd shot out of the car and hurried into the pharmacy earlier, he remembered. Maybe her edginess was because it was a certain time in her monthly cycle. Relieved that he had found a likely explanation, he relaxed and murmured, 'I have a suggestion. You are not due to begin your new job in London for nearly another month. Why not stay in Greece until then? And when you return to England we could still meet up. I visit London fairly regularly for business, and I could rent an apartment for us.'

'Are you asking me to be your mistress?'

Giannis hid his irritation. Had she been hoping for more? For him to suggest that they make their fake engagement real, perhaps? Women were all the same, always wanting more than he was prepared to give. With a jolt of surprise he realised that he was not completely opposed to the idea of having a conventional relationship with Ava.

He shrugged. 'Mistress, lover—what does it matter?' He stretched out his hand to stroke her hair and his jaw hardened when she shrank from him. They could play games all day, he thought grimly. He had a sudden sense that he was standing on the edge of a precipice and his gut clenched with something like fear as he prepared to leap into the unknown. 'What matters is that I don't want this…us…to end—yet. I need to know what you want, Ava.'

He thought she hesitated, but maybe he imagined it. She picked up her suitcase and said in a fierce voice that stung Giannis as hard if she had slapped him, 'I want to go home.'

CHAPTER EIGHT

A BLAST OF bitingly cold January air followed Giannis through the door when he strode into TGE UK's plush office building in Bond Street. He disliked winter and London seemed particularly gloomy now that the party season was over. Even the festive lights along Oxford Street had lost some of their sparkle.

He had spent a miserable Christmas with his mother, swamped by guilt, as he was every year, because he knew he was the cause of her unhappiness. For New Year he had stayed at an exclusive ski resort in Aspen. But as the clock had struck midnight he'd made an excuse to the sultry brunette who had hung on his arm all evening and returned to his hotel room alone.

Maybe he was coming down with the flu virus that was going around, he brooded. He was rarely ill, but it might explain his loss of appetite, inability to sleep and a worrying indifference to work, friends and sex. Especially sex.

When Ava had handed him the pink sapphire heart ring before she'd walked out of his apartment in Athens without a backward glance, Giannis had assumed that he would have no trouble forgetting her. He'd thought he had been successful when he'd danced at the New Year's Eve party with the brunette whose name eluded him. But when Dana?—Donna?—had offered to perform a private striptease for him he had thought of Ava's long honey-blonde hair spilling over her breasts, her cool grey eyes and her fiery passion and he had finally admitted to himself that he missed her.

There were a few unopened letters on his desk and he frowned as he flicked through them. His secretary at the UK office had been rushed into hospital with appendicitis shortly before Christmas. The temp who had replaced Phyllis should have opened his private mail and forwarded anything of importance to him. It was obvious that some of the envelopes contained Christmas cards, but as it was now the second week in January he was tempted to throw them in the bin. Exhaling heavily, he opened a card, glanced at the picture of an improbably red-breasted robin and turned it over to read the note inside.

The handwriting was difficult to decipher and he was surprised to see the name 'Sam McKay' scrawled at the bottom of the card. Giannis remembered that Ava had said her brother had struggled at school because he was dyslexic.

Dear Mr Gekas
I wanted to say thanks for letting me off about the
damage done to your boat. It was desent of you.
Sorry about you and Ava not getting married. Its a
shame it didnt work out and about the baby.
Happy christmas
Sam McKay

Baby! Giannis reread the note twice more and tried to make sense of it. Whose baby? He looked at the date stamp on the card's envelope and swore when he saw that Sam had posted it on the fifteenth of December—more than three weeks ago.

He could hear his heartbeat thudding in his ears as a shocking idea formed in his brain. Could Ava be pregnant with *his* baby? If so, then why hadn't she told him? The blood in his veins turned to ice. What the hell had Sam meant in his badly written note when he'd said that it was a shame about the baby? Had Ava suffered a miscarriage? Or had she…?

Giannis swallowed the bile that rose up in his throat. The memory of when Caroline had told him that she was no longer pregnant still haunted him. He had felt as if his heart had been ripped out, but Caroline had regarded her pregnancy as an inconvenience.

He stared at Sam's unsatisfactory note and sucked in a sharp breath when he thought back to the day three months ago at the apartment in Athens when Ava had acted so strangely. Had she known that she was pregnant but had decided that a baby would not fit in with her career?

Theos, he was terrified that history was repeating itself. First Caroline, and now Ava. Something cold and hard settled in the pit of his stomach. He had lost one child, but if Ava was expecting his baby he would move heaven and earth to have a second chance at fatherhood.

Giannis picked up the phone on the desk and noticed that his hand was shaking as he put a call through to his secretary's office. The temp answered immediately. 'Cancel all my meetings,' he told her brusquely. 'I'll be out for the rest of the day.'

There was a 'sold' sign outside the terraced house in East London where, four months ago, Giannis had taken Ava to collect her passport before they had flown to Paris. If she had already moved away he would find her, he vowed grimly as he walked up the front path and hammered his fist on the door. If she was pregnant and hoped to keep his child from him, she would discover that there was nowhere on earth she could hide.

The front door opened and Ava's eyes widened when she saw him. She quickly tried to close the door but Giannis put his foot out to prevent her.

'What do you want?' she demanded, but beneath her sharp tone he sensed her fear. Of him? He ignored the peculiar pang his heart gave and used his shoulder to push the door wider open so that he could step into the narrow hallway.

'I want the truth.' He handed her the Christmas card he'd received from her brother. Looking puzzled, she read the note inside the card and flushed.

'I haven't explained to Sam that I pretended to be your fiancée so you would drop the charges against him,' she said stiffly. 'I suppose he thinks I'm upset that our engagement is over—which I'm not, of course.'

'Only one part of your brother's note interests me,' Giannis told her coldly. 'Is the baby that Sam refers to *my* baby?' He watched the colour drain from Ava's face and felt dangerously out of control.

'I don't have to tell you anything. And you have no right to force your way into my house.' She backed up along the hallway as he walked towards her.

'Were you pregnant when you left Athens?'

Instead of replying, she spun round and ran into the sitting room. Giannis was right behind her and he found that he had to squeeze past numerous boxes. Evidently the contents of the house had been packed up ready to be loaded onto a removals van. He came out in a cold sweat, thinking that if he had not read Sam's note for another few days he would have been too late to confront Ava.

'Answer me, damn it,' he said harshly.

Ava was cornered in the cramped room and she grabbed a heavy-based frying pan from one of the packing boxes. 'Stay away from me,' she said fiercely, waving the frying pan in the air. 'I'll defend myself if I have to.'

Giannis forced himself to control his temper when he heard real fear in her voice. 'I'm not going to harm you,' he growled. 'All I want is your honesty. I have a right to know if you had conceived my child.'

After several tense seconds she slowly lowered her arm and dropped the frying pan back into the box. Her teeth gnawed on her bottom lip. 'All right…*yes*. I had just found out that I was pregnant when I flew back to London.'

Giannis stared at her slender figure in dark jeans and a loose white sweater. Her honey-gold hair was tied in a ponytail and her peaches-and-cream skin glowed with health. She looked even more beautiful than he remembered. But she did not look pregnant. Surely there would be some sign by now? When his PA in Greece had been expecting, her stomach had seemed to grow bigger daily.

He shoved his hands into his coat pockets and clenched his fingers so tightly that his nails bit into his palms. 'You said that you *were* pregnant,' he said stiltedly, fighting to hold back the volcanic mass of his emotions from spewing out. 'Does it mean that either by accident or design there is no longer a baby?'

Now she stared back at him and her eyes were as dark as storm clouds. 'Accident or design? I don't think I understand.'

'Your brother said in the Christmas card that it was a shame about the baby. And before you left Athens you told me you wanted to focus on your career. Did you terminate the pregnancy?'

She reeled backwards and knocked over a box of

Christmas decorations, sending gaudy baubles rolling across the carpet. '*No*, I did not.'

Giannis snatched a breath. He needed her to spell it out for him. 'So you are carrying my child?'

'Yes.' Her voice was a whisper of sound, as if she was reluctant to confirm the news that blew him away. 'Sam thought it was a shame that we had broken up when I am expecting your baby,' she muttered.

Euphoria swept through Giannis but it was swiftly replaced with anger. 'Why the hell did you try to keep it a secret from me? I had a right to know that I am to be a father.'

'Don't take that moral tone with me. You have no rights to this baby, Giannis.' Colour flared on Ava's pale cheeks and her eyes flashed with temper. 'I know what you are. I've heard the rumour that you are involved with the Greek mafia.'

'*What?*' Shock ricocheted through Giannis. He wondered if Ava was joking, even if the joke was in very poor taste. But as they faced each other across the room full of packing boxes and spilt shiny baubles he realised that she was serious.

'No doubt you will deny it. But I didn't tell you about my pregnancy because I won't take the risk of my baby having a criminal for a father.' She crossed her arms defensively in front of her and glared at him.

He kept his hands in his pockets in case he was tempted to shake some sense into her. Not that he would ever lay a finger on a woman in anger, and certainly not the mother of his child. Giannis's heart lurched as the astounding reality sank in that Ava was expecting his baby.

Five years ago he had lost his unborn child, but by a miracle he had been given another chance to be a father. A chance perhaps of redemption. He wanted to be a good father, as his own father had been, and he would love his child as deeply as his father had loved him. Emotions that he had buried for the last fifteen years threatened to overwhelm him. But he had to deal with Ava's shocking accusation and somehow defuse the volatile situation.

'Of course I deny that I belong to a criminal organisation because it's not true. Who told you the rumour about me?'

'I'm not prepared to say.'

'It must have been at Stefanos's party.' Giannis knew he had guessed correctly when Ava dropped her gaze. He remembered that her attitude towards him had changed when they had spent the night on Gaia. She had left the party early, saying she had a headache. When she had been sick the next morning she had blamed it on a migraine, but she must have known then that she was pregnant.

Fury swirled, black and bitter, inside him at the realisation that Ava had tried to hide his child from him because she had believed an unfounded rumour. A memory flashed into his mind.

'I saw you talking to Petros Spyriou at the party while I was with Stefanos. Did he tell you the ridiculous story that I am a criminal?'

'I don't know the name of the man who spoke to me.'

'So you believed the words of a stranger without question and without giving me a chance to refute his slanderous allegations?' When she bit her lip but said nothing, Giannis continued, 'We had been lovers for a month before we went to Gaia, yet what we shared clearly meant nothing to you.'

'What did we share, Giannis, other than sex and lies? You blackmailed me to be your fake fiancée so that you could trick Stefanos to sell his company to you.' Her voice faltered. 'When I heard a rumour that you use TGE as a cover for your criminal activities I didn't know what to believe.'

'So you ran away,' he said scathingly. The savage satisfaction he felt when colour flared on her face did not lessen his unexpected sense of betrayal, of hurt, *damn it*, that she had so little faith in him.

When they had stayed on Spetses he had spent more time with her than he'd done with any other woman. Even when he had dated Caroline for nearly a year, their relationship had amounted to meeting for dinner a couple of times a week and occasional weekends together when their work schedules had aligned.

'Petros Spyriou is Stefanos's nephew,' he told Ava. 'Petros believes that his uncle should have put him in charge of Markou Shipping instead of selling the company to me. He is jealous of me, which is why he made up disgusting lies about me.' Giannis gave a grim laugh. 'Petros succeeded in scaring you away but he'll find himself in court facing charges of slander and defamation of character.'

'He said that a few years ago a journalist tried to investigate you but was dissuaded from publishing information that he'd discovered about you.'

Inside his coat pockets, Giannis curled his hands into fists and wished that Stefanos's weasel of a nephew was standing in front of him. His criminal record had been expunged ten years after he'd served his prison sentence, which was standard procedure in Greek law. But somehow a journalist had found out about it and demanded money to keep quiet. Giannis had been loath to give in to blackmail, but coming soon after he'd broken up with Caroline, and the loss of his first child, his emotions had been raw and he'd been desperate to keep the details of his father's death out of the media spotlight.

He had no idea how Stefanos's nephew had found out about the journalist, and he guessed that Petros did not know what information the journalist had discovered. But the suggestion that there were secrets Giannis wanted to keep hidden must have been useful to Petros when he'd told Ava lies about him being involved with the Greek mafia. The story was so crazy it was laughable—yet Ava had believed Petros and as a result she had hidden her pregnancy, Giannis thought bitterly.

His jaw clenched as he remembered that while they had lived together at Villa Delphine he had been tempted to confess to Ava that he had been responsible for his father's untimely death. Thank God he had not bared his soul to her. He certainly would not tell her the truth now. He could imagine her horrified reaction and he dared not risk her disappearing again with his baby.

'Everything Petros told you was pure fabrication.' He shrugged. 'Believe me, or don't believe me. I don't give a damn. But you won't keep my child from me. If you attempt to, I will seek custody and I will win because I have money and power and you have neither.'

'No court ruling would allow a baby to be separated from its mother,' Ava snapped, but she had paled.

Giannis flicked his eyes over her, his emotions once more under control. 'Are you willing to take the risk?'

His black gaze was so cold. Ava gave a shiver. It seemed impossible that Giannis's eyes had ever gleamed with warmth and laughter. Or that they had once been friends as well as lovers. But their wild passion had resulted in the baby that was growing bigger in her belly every day. Giannis's child. It was strange how emotive those two words were, and even stranger that when she had seen him standing on the doorstep her body had quivered in response to his potent masculinity.

She must be the weakest woman in the world, she thought bleakly. He had barged his way into her home and threatened to try to take her baby from her, yet her heart ached as she roamed her eyes over his silky hair and the sculpted perfection of his features. She had thought about him constantly for the last three months but, standing in the chaotic sitting room, he was taller than she remembered and his shoulders were so broad beneath the black wool coat he wore.

He was like a dark avenging angel, but was his anger justified? Had she been too ready to believe the rumour that he was a criminal because of her father's criminality? Ava wondered. Supposing Stefanos's jealous nephew *had* lied? If she hadn't had that devastating conversation with Petros, she would have told Giannis as soon as she'd done the test that she was pregnant, and perhaps he would not be looking down his nose at her as if she were something unpleasant that he had scraped off the bottom of his shoe.

A loud knock on the front door broke the tense silence in the sitting room. She glanced towards the window and saw a lorry parked outside the house. 'We'll have to continue this conversation another time,' she told Giannis. 'The removals firm are here to take my mother's furniture into storage now that she has sold the house.'

He frowned. 'I thought this house belonged to you, and you had sold it because you planned to move away so that I couldn't find you.'

'I lived here with my family before we moved to Cyprus. My father had registered the deeds of the house in my mother's name. After my dad...' she hesitated '...after my parents divorced, Mum, Sam and I came back to live here, although I went away to university. My mother and her new partner have bought a bed and breakfast business in the Peak District.'

'So where will you live? I assume you will need to stay in the East End to be near to your work. At least while you are able to continue working until the baby is born,' Giannis said, the groove between his brows deepening.

She looked away from him. 'I was made redundant from my job when the victim support charity I worked for couldn't continue to fund my role. I've arranged to rent a room in a friend's house, but I'm thinking of moving back to Scotland where property is cheaper and I will be nearer to Sam and Mum.'

She would need help from her family after she became a single mother, Ava thought as she hurried down the hallway to open the front door. The removals team trooped in and it quickly became clear that she and Giannis were in the way, when the men started to carry furniture and boxes out to the van.

'You had better go,' she told him. 'My friend Becky, who I am going to stay with, offered to come over later to collect my things as I don't have a car.'

'I'll put whatever you want to take with you in my car and drive you to her house.' Giannis's crisp tone brooked no argument. 'Which boxes are yours?'

She pointed to two packing boxes by the window and when his brows rose she said defensively, 'I don't like clutter, or see the point in having too many clothes.'

'Is that why you left the dresses that I'd bought for you during our engagement back at the apartment in Athens?'

'I left the clothes and the engagement ring behind because you did not buy me, Giannis.' The idea that he had paid for the designer dresses and the beautiful pink sapphire ring with money he might have made illegally was repugnant to Ava, and a painful reminder of her privileged childhood which she'd later discovered had been funded by her father's crimes.

Giannis's eyes narrowed but he said nothing as he picked up one of the boxes which contained her worldly possessions. But when Ava bent down to pick up the second box he said sharply, 'Put it down. You should not be lifting heavy things in your condition.'

'Who do you think packed all the boxes and lugged them down the stairs?' she said drily. 'Mum is busy getting her new house ready and I have spent weeks clearing this place, ready for the new owners to move in.'

'From now on you will not do any strenuous activity that could harm my baby,' Giannis growled. His accent was suddenly thicker and he sounded very Greek and *very* possessive. Ava supposed she should feel furious that he was being so bossy, but her stupid heart softened at his concern for his child. Since she'd left Athens she had debated endlessly with herself about whether she should tell him she was pregnant. One reason for not doing so was that she had assumed he would be angry at having fatherhood foisted on him. She was surprised by his determination to be involved with the baby.

She had already given the house keys to the estate agent and when she walked down the front path for the last time Ava realised that she was severing the final link with her father. Number fifty-one Arthur Close was where Terry McKay had plotted his armed robberies and controlled his turf. He had been a ruthless gangland boss, but to Ava he had been a fun person who had built her a treehouse in the garden. She had been utterly taken in by her father's charming manner but finding out the truth about him had left her deeply untrusting.

After the bitterly cold wind whipping down Arthur

Close, the interior of Giannis's car was a warm and lux-urious haven. Ava sank deep into the leather upholstery and gave him the postcode of Becky's house.

'Put your seat belt on,' he reminded her. But, be-fore she could reach for it, he leaned across her and she breathed in the spicy scent of his aftershave. He smelled divine, and for a moment his face was close to hers and she hated herself for wanting to press her lips to the dark stubble that shaded his jaw.

He secured her seat belt and she released a shaky breath when he moved away from her and put the car into gear. Did her body respond to Giannis because it in-stinctively recognised that he was the father of her child? How could she still desire him when she did not know if she could trust him? she wondered despairingly. The sight of his tanned hands on the steering wheel evoked memories of how he had pleasured her with his wickedly inventive fingers. *Stop it,* she told herself, and closed her eyes so that she was not tempted to look at him.

He switched the radio onto a station playing easy lis-tening music, and the smooth motion of the car had a soporific effect on Ava. She'd been lucky that she'd had few pregnancy symptoms and the sickness she had ex-perienced in the first weeks had gone. But the bone-deep tiredness she felt these days was quite normal, the mid-wife had told her at her check-up. It was nature's way of making her rest so that the baby could grow.

When she opened her eyes she wondered for a mo-ment where she was, before she remembered that Giannis had offered to take her across town to Becky's house. So why were they driving along the motorway? The clock on the dashboard showed that she had been asleep for nearly an hour.

She jerked her gaze to Giannis. 'This isn't the way to

Fulham. Where are you taking me?' Panic flared and she unconsciously placed her hand on her stomach to protect the fragile new life inside her.

'We are going to my house in St Albans. We'll be there in about ten minutes.' He glanced at her. 'We need to talk.'

'I don't want to talk to you.' She reached for the door handle and Giannis swore.

'It's locked. Are you really crazy enough to want to throw yourself out of the car travelling at seventy miles an hour?'

His words brought her to her senses. 'I have nothing to say to you. You…threatened to take my baby from me.' Her voice shook and she sensed that he sent her another glance.

'I was angry,' he said roughly.

'That doesn't make it okay to speak to me the way you did.'

'I know.' He exhaled heavily. 'I don't want to fight with you, Ava. But I want what is best for the baby, and I do not believe that being brought up in a bedsit and being dumped in a nursery for hours every day while you go to work is anywhere near the best start in life that we can give to our child.' He paused for a heartbeat and said quietly, 'Do you?'

Unable to think of an answer, she turned her head to look out of the window so that he would not see the tears that had filled her eyes when he'd said *our child*. For the first time since she had stared in disbelief at the positive sign on the pregnancy test, she felt that she wasn't alone. It made her realise how scared she had been at the prospect of having a baby on her own, with no one to share the worry and responsibility with. Her mother was busy with her new life and partner, and her brother thankfully seemed to be sorting himself and enjoyed working on their

aunt and uncle's farm. There was no one she could rely
on apart from Giannis. But, despite his assurance that he
wasn't a criminal, she did not know if she believed him.

They left the motorway and drove through a small village before Giannis turned the car through some wrought
iron gates which bore a sign saying 'Milton Grange'. At
the end of the winding driveway stood a charming Geor-
gian house built on four storeys, with mullioned windows
and ivy growing over the walls.

Snow had been falling lightly for the last half an hour
and the bay trees in front of the house were dusted with
white frosting. But, although the snow looked pretty, Ava
was glad to step into the warm hallway where they were
greeted by Giannis's housekeeper.

'The fire is lit in the drawing room and lunch will be
in half an hour,' the woman, whom Giannis introduced
as Joan, said when she had taken their coats.

'What a beautiful house,' Ava murmured as she looked
around the comfortably furnished drawing room, deco-
rated in soft neutral shades so that the effect was calm-
ing and homely.

'I bought it as an investment,' Giannis told her. 'But
it's too big, especially as I do not live here permanently. I
arranged for a charity which provides help to parents and
families of disabled children to use the top two floors as
a respite centre. Builders reconfigured the upper floors
and in effect turned one large house into two separate
properties.'

Ava sat down in an armchair close to the fire and fur-
thest away from the sofa where Giannis took a seat. He
gave her a sardonic look but said evenly, 'Would you like
tea or coffee?' A tray on the low table in front of him held
a cafetière and a teapot.

'Tea, please. I should only drink decaffeinated coffee,

but actually I've gone off coffee completely since I've been pregnant. Just the smell of it made me sick at first.'

He frowned. 'Do you suffer very badly with morning sickness? It can't be good for the baby if you are unable to keep food down. Are you eating well?'

'I'm fine now, and I'm eating too well.' She gave a rueful sigh. 'If I'm not careful I'll be the size of a house.'

'You look beautiful,' he said gruffly. Ava swallowed as her eyes met his and she felt a familiar tug deep in her pelvis. He was *so* handsome and she suddenly wished that the situation between them was different, and instead of offering her a cup of tea he would whisk her upstairs and make long, slow and very satisfying love to her.

'How far along is your pregnancy?'

'I'm eighteen weeks. At twenty weeks I am due to have another ultrasound scan to check the baby's development and I'll be able to find out the sex.' She bit her lip. 'It's possible that I conceived the first time we slept together in London.'

'As I recall, neither of us slept much that night,' he drawled in that arrogant way of his which Ava found infuriating.

'But now we must deal with the consequences of our actions,' she said flatly.

He took a sip of his coffee and said abruptly, 'I would like to come to your scan appointment. Do you want to find out the baby's sex?'

'I think I do. I suppose you hope it's a boy.' If the baby was a girl, perhaps Giannis would lose interest in his child. Her hand shook slightly as she placed the delicate bone china teacup and saucer down on the table.

'I will be equally happy to have a daughter or a son. All that matters is that the child is born safe and well.'

His words echoed Ava's own feelings and her emotions threatened to overwhelm her. She was too warm sitting by the fire, but she did not want to move nearer to Giannis. Instead she pulled off her jumper and only then remembered that the strap-top she was wearing beneath it was too small. The material was stretched over her breasts, which had grown two bra sizes bigger. She hoped he would assume that the flush she could feel spreading across her face was due to the warmth of the fire and not because she'd glimpsed a raw hunger in his eyes that evoked a molten heat inside her. She tensed when he stood up and strolled over to where she was sitting.

'You said that you are currently without a job, so how were you planning to manage financially?'

'My old job in Glasgow is still available. Working as a VCO is not a popular or well-paid career,' she said ruefully. 'I will be entitled to maternity pay for a few months after the baby is born, but then I'll have to go back to work to support both of us.'

'I want to be involved with my child,' Giannis told her in a determined voice. 'And of course I will provide financial support for you and the baby.'

'I don't want your money,' she said stubbornly. She could not bear for him to think that she had trapped him with her pregnancy because he was wealthy.

'What you want and what I want is not important. The only thing that matters is that we do the right thing for our child, who was unplanned but not unwanted—am I right that we at least agree on that?' he said softly.

His voice was like rough velvet and Ava nodded, not trusting herself to speak when she felt so vulnerable. 'What do you suggest then?' she asked helplessly.

He hesitated for a heartbeat. 'I think we should get married.'

CHAPTER NINE

For a few seconds Ava could not breathe, and there was an odd rushing sensation in her ears. Giannis had not said that he *wanted* to marry her, she noted. And why would he? All he wanted was the baby she carried, and she was simply a necessary part of the equation.

'You're crazy,' she said flatly. 'It wouldn't work.'

He pulled up a footstool and sat down in front of her, so close that it would be easy to stretch out her hand and touch the silken darkness of his hair—easy and yet impossible.

'What is the alternative?' he asked levelly. 'Even if we came to an amicable agreement about shared custody, a child needs stability, which I can provide in Greece at Villa Delphine. I could buy a house for you in England and we could send our child back and forth between us like a ping-pong ball—Christmas with you, first birthday with me, and so on. But that wouldn't make me happy, I don't think it would make you happy and I'm certain it would not be a happy childhood for our son or daughter.'

Ava couldn't argue with his logic. Everything Giannis said made sense. But her emotions weren't logical or sensible; they were all over the place. She tensed when he took hold of her hand and rubbed his thumb lightly over the pulse thudding in her wrist.

'Like it or not, you and the baby are my responsibility and I want to take care of both of you.' He met her gaze and the gleam in his dark eyes sent a quiver of reaction through her. 'Our relationship worked very well for the month that we pretended to be engaged,' he murmured.

It would be too easy to be seduced by his charisma and fall under his spell, but if she was going to survive him she had to be strong and in control. 'We did not have a relationship—we had sex,' she reminded him tartly.

The word hung in the air between them, taunting Ava with memories of their wild passion and Giannis's body claiming hers with powerful thrusts.

'Don't knock it, *glykiá mou*,' he drawled. 'You enjoyed it as much as I did.'

Hot-faced with embarrassment, she dropped her gaze from his amused expression and wondered what he was thinking. Her pregnancy was not really showing yet, but she was conscious of her thickening waistline which meant that she had to leave the button on her jeans undone. Before Giannis had met her, he had slept with some of the world's most beautiful women—and she doubted his bed had been empty for the past months that they had been apart.

'So, do you expect it to be a proper marriage?' she said stiffly.

His eyes narrowed. 'I do not expect anything, certainly not intimacy, unless you decide it is what you want.'

She should feel relieved by Giannis's assurance that he would not put pressure on her to consummate their marriage, but Ava felt even more confused. He was a red-blooded male and celibacy would not be a natural state for him. But perhaps he intended to find pleasure elsewhere. For her own protection she needed to ignore the chemistry between them while she was still unsure if she could believe his insistence that he was not a criminal.

Giannis stood up and offered her his hand to help her to her feet. 'What is your answer?'

She ignored his hand. 'I need time to consider my options.' Her tone was as cool as his. They could have been discussing a business deal instead of a decision which would affect the rest of their lives. But her pregnancy had already had a fundamental effect, and it occurred to her that, whether or not she accepted his proposal, they would be linked for ever by the child they had created between them.

'Do not consider them for too long,' he said as he ushered her out of the drawing room and across the hall to the dining room. 'I intend for us to be married well before the baby is born.' The implacable note in Giannis's voice warned Ava that the only option he would accept was her agreement to become his wife.

'The gel will feel cold, I'm afraid,' the sonographer said cheerfully before she squirted a dollop of thick, clear lubricant onto Ava's stomach.

Ava tried to suck her tummy in as the sonographer smeared the gel over her bump. She was intensely conscious of Giannis sitting beside the hospital bed where she was lying for the ultrasound scan. Her top was tucked up under her breasts and her trousers were pushed down low on her hips, leaving her stomach bare. From her angle, looking down her body, her stomach seemed huge, which was hardly surprising after she had spent the past couple of weeks enjoying Giannis's housekeeper's wonderful cooking, she thought ruefully.

'I understand you need to eat for two,' Joan had said cheerfully when Giannis announced that he and Ava would be getting married as soon as it could be arranged. The wedding could not take place until twenty-eight days after they had given notice at the local register office.

The bright lights in the scanning room made the pink sapphire ring on Ava's finger sparkle. This time her engagement was real, and her heart lurched at the thought that very soon she would be Giannis's wife.

She had accepted his proposal the day after he had asked her to marry him—following a sleepless night when she'd faced the stark choice of having to believe him or Stefanos Markou's nephew. On a practical level she knew that Giannis was determined to be a father to his baby and she concluded that she would be in a better position to safeguard herself and her child if she was married to him.

'You can choose a different ring if you would prefer not to wear this one,' he'd said when he had returned the pink sapphire heart to her.

Ava had slid the ring onto her finger and told herself that she hadn't missed it being there for the past few months. 'It seems fitting to keep the ring that you gave me while I was your fake fiancée, seeing as our marriage will be one of convenience,' she'd said stubbornly, determined he would not know how much she had missed him.

His eyes had gleamed dangerously but he'd said evenly, 'Whatever you wish, *glykiá mou.*'

What she had wished was for him to pull her into his arms and kiss her senseless so that she could pretend they were lovers back on Spetses—before rumours, doubts and her pregnancy had driven a wedge between them. But Giannis had walked out of the room and she'd felt too vulnerable to go after him and make the first move to try to break the stalemate in their relationship.

She pulled her mind back to the present as the sonographer moved the probe over her stomach. 'If you look on the screen, here is Baby's heart—you can see it beating. And this here is one of Baby's hands…and just here is the other hand…' The sonographer pointed to the grey image on the screen. 'You can make out Baby's face quite clearly.'

Ava caught her breath as she stared at her baby's tiny features. She felt Giannis squeeze her fingers. She'd already had a scan at twelve weeks, to accurately date her pregnancy, but this was his first experience of seeing his child and she wondered how he felt now that the baby was a tangible reality rather than something they had spoken about.

The sonographer spent several minutes studying the baby's vital organs and taking measurements. 'Everything looks absolutely as it should do,' she said at last. 'I understand that you have decided to find out the baby's sex.'

'Yes,' they both replied at the same time.

The sonographer smiled. 'You are going to have a little boy. Congratulations.'

Ava tore her eyes from the image of her son—*her son*! Blinking back tears of pride and joy, she glanced at Giannis. Her heart turned over when she saw a tear slide down his cheek as he stared intently at the screen. He dashed his hand over his face and when he turned to her he showed no sign of the fierce emotion she had witnessed although, when she looked closely, his eyes were suspiciously bright.

'Now we know what colour to paint the nursery,' he murmured.

She nodded, unable to speak past the lump that had formed in her throat. Whatever happened between them, she knew now, without doubt, that Giannis would love his son and would never be parted from him. Which meant that somehow they would have to make their unconventional marriage work.

Another thought slid insidiously into her mind as she remembered her ex's scathing comments when she had admitted to him that her father was the infamous East End gangster, Terry McKay. Craig had decided against marrying her for fear that their children might grow up to be criminals like their grandfather.

Of course there was not a 'criminal' gene, Ava tried to reassure herself. But she couldn't forget what Stefanos's nephew had told her about Giannis being involved in organised crime. If the rumour about him was true, and if there was such a thing as a 'criminal' gene, what would the future hold for the baby?

In the car on the way back to Milton Grange neither of them spoke much. Ava's thoughts were going round and round in her head and she did not have the energy to try to breach the emotional distance that existed between her and Giannis. His playboy reputation when she had first met him had made her believe that he was not capable of feeling strong emotions, but that was patently not true, she realised as she remembered the tears on his face when he had seen the scan images of his baby son.

When they arrived at the house he went straight to his study, citing an important business phone call that he needed to make. The cold, grey weather at the end of January did not encourage Ava to go out for a walk, and instead she made use of the heated swimming pool in the conservatory.

She hadn't got round to buying a maternity swimsuit, and the bikini that she'd bought from a boutique on Spetses barely fitted over her fuller breasts. But no one was going to see her, and the midwife had said that swimming was a good form of exercise during pregnancy. The water was warm and she swam several laps before she climbed out of the pool and wrung her dripping-wet hair between her hands. A sudden blast of cold air rushed into the conservatory as the door opened, and her heart gave a jolt when Giannis strode in wearing a towelling robe.

'You said you would be working all afternoon,' she muttered, feeling heat spread over her face as he stared at her ridiculously small bikini that revealed much more of her body than she was comfortable with. She was tempted to run across to the lounger where she had left her towel, but she couldn't risk slipping on the wet tiles.

'I was bored of working and decided to come and swim with you.' He shrugged off his robe and Ava roamed her gaze hungrily over his muscular chest covered in black hairs that arrowed down his taut abdomen and disappeared beneath the waistband of his swim-shorts.

'Well, I've got out of the pool now.' Her flush deepened when she realised the inanity of her statement.

'I can see that,' he mocked her softly. But as he walked towards her his smile faded and his dark eyes glittered with a feral hunger that confused her.

'Stop staring at me.' She tried to cover the gentle swell of her stomach with her hands but could do nothing to disguise the fact that her breasts were almost spilling out of her bikini top. She felt exposed, knowing she looked fat, and sure that Giannis must be comparing her to all the gorgeous women who had shared his bed in the past.

He halted in front of her and she noticed a nerve jump in his cheek. 'How can I take my eyes from you when you take my breath away?' he said thickly.

Ava bit her lip. 'I was slim the last time you saw me in a bikini.' She had nearly said naked, but memories of when they had lain together, skin on skin, their limbs entwined and their bodies joined would only add fuel to the fire burning inside her.

'You look incredible.' Dark colour winged along his cheekbones. 'Can you feel the baby move?'

'I've felt flutters rather than kicks at this stage but the midwife said that the baby's movements will become stronger as he grows bigger.'

Giannis was focused on her bump. 'May I touch you?'

She gave a hesitant nod. It was his baby too, and she could not deny him the chance to be involved in her pregnancy. But when he placed his hand on her stomach and stretched his fingers wide over its swell she trembled and hoped he had no idea of the molten heat that pooled between her thighs.

'There, did you feel that?' She caught hold of his hand and moved it slightly lower on her stomach just as a fluttering sensation inside her happened again.

He drew an audible breath. *'Theos,'* he said in an oddly gruff voice. 'Between us we have created a miracle, *glykiá mou.'*

Standing this close to him was creating havoc with her emotions. She needed to move away from him and break the spell that he always cast on her. But it was too late, and she watched helplessly as his dark head descended.

'Giannis,' she whispered, but it was a plea rather than a protest and the fierce gleam in his eyes told her that he knew it. His breath warmed her lips before he covered her mouth with his and kissed her the way she had longed for him to kiss her, the way she had dreamed about him kissing her every night since she had left Greece.

She couldn't resist him. It did not even occur to her to try. He was the father of her unborn child, the man she was going to marry, and she wanted him to make love to her. Even the knowledge that *love* played no part in their relationship did not matter at that moment, as desire swept like wildfire through her veins. She had been starved of him and she pressed her body up against his, closing her eyes as she sank into the sensual pleasure of his kiss.

His hand was still resting on her stomach, and she held her breath when he moved lower and ran his fingers over the strip of bare skin above the waistband of her bikini bottoms. She willed him to slip his fingers beneath the stretchy material and touch her where she ached to be touched. She wanted him to push his fingers inside her, and incredibly she felt the first ripples of an orgasm start to build deep in her pelvis before he had even caressed her intimately.

Tension of a different kind ran through her as she faced up to where this was leading. How could she give herself to Giannis when she had doubts about him? In many ways, it had been easier to have sex with him while she had pretended to be his fiancée because she'd assumed that their relationship would end at the same time as their fake engagement. But now she was going to be Giannis's wife—if not for ever then certainly until their child was old enough to be able to cope with them separating. If she made love with Giannis she would reveal her vulnerability that she was desperate to hide from him.

But then suddenly it was over as he wrenched his mouth from hers. She swayed on her feet when he abruptly snatched his arm from around her waist. He swore as he swung away from her and dived into the water.

Ava watched him swim to the far end of the pool and wondered if he had somehow been aware of her doubts. A more likely explanation for his rejection was that he found her pregnant shape a turn-off. Giannis had been attentive because she was carrying his child, but he'd made it clear that he did not want her.

At least she knew where she stood with him, Ava told herself as she dragged her towel around her unsatisfied body to hide the shaming hard peaks of her nipples. He was marrying her to claim his baby. And she had agreed to be his wife because she feared that he would seek custody of their son—not immediately perhaps, but she couldn't bear to live with the threat hanging over her.

Why the hell had he come on to Ava like a clumsy adolescent on a first date? Giannis asked himself furiously as he powered through the water. He heard the conservatory door bang, signalling her departure, but he kept on swimming lap after lap, punishing himself for his loss of control.

Since he had seen the grainy scan images of his child he'd felt as if he were on an emotional rollercoaster. Ava's pregnancy had seemed unreal until the moment the sonographer had pointed out on the screen the baby's tiny heart beating strongly. In that instant he'd realised that nothing—not money or possessions or power—were important compared to his son.

Back at the house he'd paced restlessly around his study, unable to concentrate on a financial report he was supposed to be reading. Work had always been his favourite mistress, the area of his life where he knew he excelled, but—just as when he had taken Ava to Spetses—he had wanted to be with her instead of sitting at his desk.

Walking into the pool house and seeing her in a tiny bikini had blown him away. Pregnancy had turned her into a goddess and he had been transfixed by her generous curves—her breasts like ripe peaches and the lush swell of her belly where his child lay. He'd wanted to touch her and feel a connection with his baby, and when he'd felt the faint movements of a fragile new life a sense of awed wonder had brought a lump to his throat. Something utterly primal had stirred in his chest. His child. His woman. He would die to protect both of them, he acknowledged.

Had he kissed Ava to stake his claim? With savage self-derision he admitted that he'd felt a basic need to pull her down onto a lounger and possess her in the most fundamental way. Desire had drummed an insistent beat in his blood and in his loins. He had forgotten that she did not trust him—although he should not be surprised by her wariness after he had threatened to take her child, he thought grimly.

He had kissed her for the simple reason that he could not resist her, but when he'd felt her stiffen in rejection he knew he had no one to blame but himself. When he'd persuaded her—or pressurised her, his conscience pricked—to marry him, he had promised himself that he would be patient and wait for her to come to him. Instead he'd behaved like a jerk, and in truth he was shocked that she had got under his skin to the degree that she dominated his thoughts and disturbed his dreams.

It would not happen again, Giannis vowed as he climbed out of the pool. He would control his desire for Ava because too much was at stake. He had discovered that he wanted more from her than sex. He wanted everything—her soft smile and infectious laughter, her cool, incisive intelligence and her fiery passion. And he wanted his child. Even if he failed to win all that he hoped for, he *would* have his son.

By the middle of February a thaw had turned the winter wonderland of snow and ice to grey slush, just in time for the wedding which was to take place in the private chapel in the grounds of Milton Grange. Not that Ava cared about the weather when her marriage to Giannis would be as fake as their engagement five months earlier had been.

Since the incident by the pool they had maintained an emotional and physical distance from each other. The closest contact they'd had was when their hands had accidentally brushed as they'd passed each other on the landing, on the way to their separate bedrooms.

She was thankful that the wedding would be a small affair. It had been arranged at short notice, and both her mother and Giannis's mother were on holiday in the warmer climes of the southern hemisphere and could not attend. Her best friend Becky was coming, and Sam had promised to be there. Ava was looking forward to seeing him—although if her brother had not been partly responsible for damaging Giannis's boat she would not now be pregnant and about to marry a man who had become so remote that sometimes she wondered if the close bond she had felt between them on Spetses had been in her imagination.

But the problem was not only Giannis, she acknowledged. Her trust issues meant that she found it difficult to lower her guard. And now her father was once more in the forefront of her mind.

It had started with an email she'd received from an author who was writing a book about East End gangs and had discovered that Ava was Terry McKay's daughter. The author wanted to ask her about her childhood growing up with her notorious gangster father.

She sent a message back saying that she never discussed her father. But Ava knew she could not stop the book being published. People were fascinated by crime, and even though she had changed her name to Sheridan there was always a chance that she would be revealed as Terry McKay's daughter.

It would be unfair for Giannis to find out about her father in a newspaper article or book review, her conscience nagged. She ought to tell him the truth about her background before she married him. Especially as she had come to believe that Stefanos's nephew had lied about Giannis having links to a criminal organisation.

But she could not forget Craig's suggestion that her children might take after her criminal father, and she was fearful of Giannis's reaction. Would he reject her and his son? Maybe she should just keep quiet and hope that he never discovered her real identity. Tormented by indecision, she withdrew into herself—which did not go unnoticed by Giannis.

'You're very pale, and you have barely spoken a word all day,' he commented during dinner on the evening before their wedding. He frowned. 'Do you feel unwell? The baby…'

'I feel fine, and I've felt the baby kicking and I'm sure he is fine too,' she was quick to reassure him. She knew that Giannis's obsessive concern about her health was because he cared about his child. But how would he feel if he was to learn that his son's genes came from a very murky pool? She pushed her food around her plate, her appetite non-existent. 'It's just pre-wedding nerves.'

He gave her a brooding look from across the table. 'There is no reason for you to feel nervous. I have told you that I will not make demands on you,' he said tersely.

If only he would! Ava wished he would whip off the tablecloth, plates and all, and make hot, urgent love to her on the polished mahogany dining table. Sex would at least be some sort of communication between them, rather than the current state of simmering tension and words unspoken.

There had been times over the past weeks when she had caught Giannis looking at her with a hungry gleam in his dark eyes that made her think he still desired her. But then she remembered how he had wrenched his mouth from hers that day by the pool, and her pride would not risk another humiliating rejection if she made the first move.

She went to bed early, giving the excuse that she was tired, and ignored his sardonic expression as he glanced at the clock which showed that it was eight o'clock. Surprisingly she fell asleep, but woke with a start from a dream where she was standing in the church with Giannis and someone in the congregation halted the wedding and denounced her as a gangster's daughter. The look of disgust on Giannis's face stayed in her mind after she had opened her eyes and her stomach gave a sickening lurch as she jumped out of bed and, without stopping to pull on her robe, ran down the hall to his room.

'Ava.' Giannis was sitting up in bed, leaning against the pillows. The black-rimmed reading glasses he wore only added to his rampant sex appeal and in the soft light from the bedside lamp his bare chest gleamed like bronze, covered with whorls of dark hairs. He dropped the documents that he had been studying onto the sheet and sat bolt upright, concern stamped on his handsome face. 'What's wrong?'

'I can't marry you,' she blurted out.

CHAPTER TEN

GIANNIS'S BREATH WHISTLED between his teeth. It was not the first time that Ava had made him feel as if he had been punched in his gut. Her accusation that he was involved in criminal activities had made him furious and her lack of faith in him had hurt more than he cared to admit. Did she still believe Petros's lies, or was there another problem? He racked his brain for something he might have done which had caused her to want to call off the wedding.

'I have done my best to reassure you I do not expect anything from our marriage that you are not willing to give,' he said curtly.

The way she bit her lower lip had a predictable effect on his body and he was grateful that the sheet concealed his uncomfortably hard arousal. She looked mouth-wateringly sexy in a peach-coloured silk negligee that showed off the creamy upper slopes of her breasts—so round and firm, separated by the deep vee of her cleavage where he longed to press his face. He forced himself to concentrate when she spoke.

'I am well aware that you find me sexually unattractive,' she snapped, but her voice shook a little and Giannis had the crazy idea that she sounded hurt. 'That isn't the issue.'

'What is the issue?' He was too tempted to pull her down onto the bed and clear up the misunderstanding about his sexual feelings for her to give a damn about an 'issue'. But Ava was clearly distraught and he resolved to be patient. 'Come, *glykiá mou*,' he murmured. 'Tell me what is troubling you.'

She stopped pacing up and down the room and swung round to face him. 'I haven't been honest with you.'

For one heart-stopping second Giannis wondered if the child she carried was his. She had told him it was likely that she'd conceived the first time they'd had sex, but could she have already been pregnant when he'd met her? If that was so, why would she have hidden her pregnancy from him after she'd left Greece? his mind pointed out.

'When you asked if I wanted to invite my father to the wedding, I told you that I am not in contact with him,' Ava said in a low tone. 'What I failed to say is that my father is serving a fifteen-year prison sentence for armed robbery.'

Giannis released his breath slowly as the tension seeped from him. He felt guilty that he had doubted her. Of course the baby was his. But it occurred to him that there would be no harm in following his lawyer's advice and arranging for a paternity test when the baby was born.

'Do you mean you do not want to get married without your father being present?' It was the only reason he could think of that might explain why she was so upset.

'I mean that I am the daughter of Terry McKay, who once had the dubious honour of being Britain's most wanted criminal.' She buried her face in her hands and gave a sob. 'I'm so ashamed. My father carried out a string of jewellery raids in Hatton Garden and he was involved in drug smuggling and extortion. We—my mum,

Sam and I—knew nothing about his secret life as a criminal until he was arrested and sent to prison.'

Giannis slid out from beneath the sheet and quickly donned a pair of sweatpants before he walked over to Ava and gently pulled her hands down from her face. The sight of tears on her cheeks tugged on his heart. 'Why do you feel ashamed? You were not responsible for your father's behaviour,' he said softly.

'I loved my dad and trusted him. I had no idea that he was a ruthless gangland boss.' She gave another sob. 'The man I thought I knew had fooled me all my life. I find it hard to trust people,' she admitted. 'I was desperate to prevent my brother from turning to a life of crime.'

'I can understand why you were so anxious to save Sam from being sent to a young offenders' institution. And why you believed Petros's lies about me,' Giannis said slowly. He drew Ava into his arms and his heart gave a jolt when she did not resist and sank against him while he lifted his hand and smoothed her hair back from her face. Oddly, he felt as though a weight had been lifted from him now that he knew why she had listened to Stefanos's nephew.

'I'm sorry,' she said huskily. 'I should have known that you are a million times a better man than Petros tried to convince me when he said you were involved in criminal activities.'

A better man? Giannis rested his chin on the top of her head so that he did not have to look into her eyes. What would Ava say if he told her that he had killed his father? Not deliberately—but his stupidity and arrogance when he was nineteen had led to him making a terrible mistake that he would regret for the rest of his life. His conscience insisted that he *should* tell her what he had done. But then she might refuse to marry him or allow him to see his child. His jaw hardened. It was a risk he was not prepared to take.

'I was afraid to tell you about my dad because of how it might make you feel for the baby.'

Puzzled by her words, he eased away from her a fraction and stared at her unhappy face.

'My ex-boyfriend decided not to marry me in case our children inherited a criminality gene. What if our child—?' She broke off, choked by tears.

'Your ex was clearly an idiot.' Giannis drew her close once more. 'Children learn from their environment and our son will have the security of being loved and nurtured by his parents. The things we teach him when he is a child will shape the man he'll grow up to be.'

'I suppose you're right,' she said shakily. Giannis felt her body relax against him as he stroked his hand down the length of her silky golden hair. Hearing that her father was a criminal explained a lot of things and he admired her determination to protect her brother.

He could not pinpoint the exact moment that his desire to comfort her turned to desire of a very different kind. Perhaps she picked up the subtle signals his body sent out—the uneven rise and fall of his chest as his breathing quickened and the hard thud of his heart.

He looked into her eyes and saw her pupils dilate. She licked her tongue over her lips in an unconscious invitation and the ache in his gut became unbearable.

'I know you want me,' he said thickly, and watched a flush of heat spread down from her face to her throat and across her breasts. 'Why did you reject me when we were in the pool house?'

'It was *you* who rejected me. You dived into the swimming pool because you couldn't bear to be near me.'

'You froze when I put my hands on you, and I assumed that you did not like me touching you.'

Ava's blush deepened. 'I liked it too much. But I wasn't sure if I could trust you.' She hesitated and said huskily, 'I'm sorry I listened to Petros.'

'So, do you like it when I touch you here?' Giannis murmured as he slid his hand over the swell of her stomach. He felt a fierce pride knowing that his baby was nestled inside her. He moved his hand lower and heard her give a soft gasp when he lifted up the hem of her negligee and stroked his fingers lightly over the silky panel of her panties between her legs.

'Don't tease me,' she whispered. 'My body has changed from when we first met. I don't want pity sex.'

He made a sound somewhere between a laugh and a groan as he pulled off his sweatpants and pressed the hard length of his arousal against her stomach. 'Does this feel like pity sex, *glykiá mou*?'

His hands shook when he tugged her nightgown over her head and cupped her bounteous breasts in his palms. 'It's true that your body has changed with pregnancy and you are even more beautiful. Have you any idea how gorgeous you are with your erotic curves that I want to explore with my hands and lips? Do you know how it makes me feel when I look at your body, so ripe and full with my child? I feel like I am the king of the world,' he told her rawly. 'And I want to make love to you more than I have ever wanted anything in my life.'

'Then stop talking and make love to me,' she demanded, her fierce voice making him smile before he claimed her mouth and kissed her as if the world was about to end and this was the last time he would taste her sweet lips. He was so hungry. Never in his life had he felt such an overwhelming need for a woman. But

Ava was not any other woman—she was *his*, insisted a primal beast inside him, and the possessiveness he felt was shockingly new.

Despite their mutual impatience, Giannis was determined to take the time to savour every delicious dip and curve of Ava's body. Her breasts, he discovered, were incredibly sensitive, so that when he stroked his hands over the creamy globes and flicked his tongue across one dusky pink nipple and then the other she gave a thin cry that evoked an answering growl deep in his throat.

He lifted her and laid her on the bed, but when she tried to pull him down on top of her he evaded her hands and moved down her body, hooking her legs over his shoulders before he lowered his mouth to her slick feminine heat.

The taste of her almost sent him over the edge, but he ruthlessly controlled his own desire and devoted himself to his self-appointed task of pleasuring her. And he was rewarded when she arched her hips and dug her fingers into his shoulders. Her honey-gold hair was spread across the pillows and Giannis had never seen a more beautiful sight than Ava's rose-flushed face in the throes of her climax.

Only then, when she was still shuddering, did he spread her legs wide and position himself above her, entering her with exquisite care until he was buried deep within her velvet softness.

'I won't break,' she whispered in his ear, as if she guessed that he was afraid to let go of his iron self-control. She moved with him, matching his rhythm as they climbed to the peak together, and when he shattered, she shattered around him. And beneath his ribs the ice surrounding Giannis's heart cracked a little.

* * *

The following day, pale sunshine burst through the clouds and danced over the carpet of snowdrops in the church-yard when Ava posed on the chapel steps with Giannis for the wedding photographer. On her finger was the simple gold band he had put there, and next to it the pink sapphire heart ring that had been his unexpected choice when she'd been his fake fiancée, a lifetime ago, it seemed.

And in a way it was a lifetime. Her name was no longer Sheridan, or McKay. She was Ava Gekas, Giannis's wife, and in a scarily few months she would be a mother.

'Your bump barely shows,' Becky—whom Ava had chosen to be her maid of honour—whispered when the two of them had entered the private chapel where the other guests were assembled and Giannis was waiting for her at the altar. The ivory silk coat-dress Ava had chosen instead of a full-length bridal gown was cleverly cut to disguise her pregnancy, and her bouquet of palest pink roses, white baby's breath and trailing ivy made a pretty focal point.

Giannis was devastatingly handsome in a charcoal-grey suit that emphasised his lean, honed physique. Ava found she was trembling when she stood beside him, ready for the ceremony to begin.

'Are you cold, *glykiá mou*?' he murmured as he took her unsteady hand in his firm grasp. 'I'll warm you later.' The wicked glint in his eyes brought soft colour to her pale cheeks. He might not love her, but their wild passion the previous night was proof that he desired her and gave her hope that they could make something of their marriage. For their child's sake they would have to, Ava mused, and decided that the burst of winter sunshine was a good omen.

The wedding reception was held at a hotel in the village, and afterwards a car drove them to the airfield where Giannis's private jet was waiting to fly them to Greece.

'We will come back after the baby is born,' he said when the plane took off and Ava gave a wistful sigh. 'If you would prefer to live at Milton Grange, I can move my work base to England.'

She stared at him in surprise. 'Would you really do that? I thought you wanted our son to grow up in Greece.'

'We'll make a safe and secure home for him wherever we live, but I want you to be happy, *glykiá mou.*'

Hope unfurled like a fragile bud inside Ava. She had been worried that Giannis might want everything his way, but it sounded as if he was willing to make compromises. She smiled at him. 'I'll be happy living at Villa Delphine. Spetses is a beautiful place to bring up a child, and thankfully it's warmer than England,' she said ruefully. 'I'm looking forward to swimming in the sea.'

He laughed. 'You won't be able to do that for another few months. The sea temperature doesn't warm up until about June.'

'When the baby is due.' She felt butterflies in her stomach at the prospect of giving birth. 'It will be good to take the baby swimming when he is a few months old.'

'And I'll teach him how to sail when he is old enough. I was five when my father first took me sailing, and I loved the excitement of skimming over the waves in Patera's yacht.'

Giannis rarely mentioned his father. Ava looked at him curiously. 'Did your interest in boating have anything to do with your decision to run a cruise line company?'

He nodded. 'My father ran a business giving chartered cruises around the Greek islands. The *Nerissa* was his first motor yacht. There was a lot of competition from other charter operators but, instead of getting into a price war, Patera's idea was to offer a high standard of luxury on the boats, aimed at attracting wealthy clients.' A shadow crossed his face. 'After my father died, I continued to offer exclusivity rather than cheap cruises. The Gekas Experience was my father's brainchild and I was determined to make it successful in his honour.'

'You must miss him,' she said softly.

'I think about him every day. He was a wonderful man and a kind and patient father, as I hope I will be to our son.' Giannis hesitated and Ava sensed that he was about to say something else, but he turned his head and looked out of the window and she felt his barriers go up.

The idea that he was hiding something from her was not an auspicious start to their marriage. But when they arrived on Spetses just as the sun was setting, Giannis insisted on carrying her over the threshold of Villa Delphine as if she were a proper bride and their marriage a true romance, as his staff who were waiting in the entrance hall to greet them clearly believed.

'I have a surprise for you,' he said as he took her hand and led her upstairs. He opened the door on the landing next to the master bedroom. 'What do you think?'

Ava looked around the room that had been turned into a nursery, with pale blue walls and a frieze of farmyard animals. There was a white-painted cot that at the moment was filled with a collection of soft toys, but soon it was where their baby would sleep.

'We can change anything that you don't like,' Giannis said when she remained silent.

She swallowed the lump in her throat. 'It's beautiful and I don't want to change a thing.'

'I asked the builders to create a connecting door into our room,' he explained.

'Our room' had a nice sound, Ava thought as she followed him through the new doorway into the bedroom and went unresistingly into his arms when he drew her towards him.

'I love the nursery.' *I love you.* She kept the words in her heart. Giannis did not love her and that made her feel vulnerable. She felt guilty that she had not trusted him at the beginning of her pregnancy, and it was understandable that it might take him a while to forgive her. But last night had proved that he desired her, and it was a start. She wound her arms around his neck, smiling at his impatient curse when he discovered the dozens of tiny buttons that fastened her dress.

'Patience is a virtue,' she reminded him sweetly, and he punished her by ravishing her mouth with his before he trailed his lips down her throat and tormented her nipples with his tongue until she pleaded for mercy. 'I want you,' she told him when they were both naked and he pulled her down onto the bed.

He grinned as he lounged back against the pillows like an indolent Sultan and beckoned her by crooking his finger. 'Then take me,' he invited. And she did, with a fierce passion that made him groan when she took him deep inside her and made love to him with her body, her heart and her soul.

Afterwards, when he held her in his arms and stroked her hair, Ava pressed her lips against his shoulder and silently whispered the secret in her heart. Give it time, she told herself when he kissed the tip of her nose and settled her against him.

'Go to sleep, *glykiá mou.* You've had a tiring day,' he murmured. They were not the words she longed for him to say, but she thought that he cared for her a little. For the first time since she had learned the truth about her father when she was seventeen, Ava finally relaxed her guard and allowed hope and happiness to fill her heart.

Springtime in Greece arrived earlier than in the UK and the countryside on Spetses was a riot of colourful red poppies and white rock roses with their bright orange centres. Pink daisies bobbed their heads in the breeze and the scents of chamomile and thyme filled the air.

Ava loved the island and quickly grew to think of it as her home. It helped that she spoke Greek, and she chatted with the locals in the market and the little cafés where she stopped for coffee when she went shopping in the pretty town around the old harbour. Some days Giannis travelled to his office in Athens by helicopter, but more often he worked in his study and joined her for lunch on the terrace.

He introduced her to his friends who lived on the island and Ava was surprised that some of them were married couples with children. She had been worried that he would miss his playboy lifestyle and she was heartened that he seemed comfortable and relaxed when they met up with other families.

The weeks slipped by and it seemed that every day the sun shone in the azure sky. The only black cloud to darken Ava's sunny mood was Giannis's mother. Filia had been away, staying with relatives in Rhodes, but when she returned to Spetses Giannis invited her to dinner at Villa Delphine.

Her sharp gaze flew to Ava's baby bump. 'I wondered why the wedding was arranged so quickly,' she said with a sniff. 'Giannis did not do me the courtesy of telling me that I am to be a grandmother.'

Ava shot him a startled glance. It was strange that he hadn't announced her pregnancy to his mother. During dinner she was aware of an undercurrent of tension that her attempts at conversation could not disguise. 'Did you enjoy your trip?' she asked Filia in a desperate bid to break the strained silence between mother and son.

Filia shrugged. 'Loneliness travels with me wherever I go,' she said as her black eyes rested on Giannis. Ava was glad when the uncomfortable evening came to an end. Filia gathered up her shawl and purse. 'I hope you will act more responsibly when *you* are a father than you did with your own father,' she told Giannis.

'Do not doubt it. I will take the greatest care of my son,' he replied curtly.

Later, Ava found him standing outside on the terrace. The night was dark, the moon obscured by clouds, but it emerged briefly and cast a cold gleam over Giannis's hard profile. He looked remote and austere and she did not know how to reach him.

'Your mother is an unhappy woman,' she observed quietly.

He stiffened when she placed her hand over his on the balustrade. His reaction felt like a very definite rejection that stirred up her old feelings of vulnerability. 'I was the cause of her unhappiness,' he said in a clipped voice, but he did not offer any further explanation and Ava was too uncertain of their tenuous relationship to ask him what he meant.

'I'm going to bed,' she murmured. 'Are you coming too?' When they made love she felt closer to him, emotionally as well as physically, and maybe she would find out what was on his mind.

'I have some paperwork to read through and I'll be up in a while.' He brushed his lips over hers but lifted his head without giving her a chance to respond, leaving her longing for him to kiss her properly. 'Don't wait up for me.'

Giannis watched Ava walk back inside the house and swore beneath his breath as he pictured her hurt expression. He knew he should go after her, scoop her into his arms and carry her up to their bedroom, as he knew she had wanted him to do. Of course he wanted to make love to her. Sex wasn't the problem. She was in the third trimester of her pregnancy and he found her curvaceous figure intensely desirable. Their hunger for one another was as urgent as it had always been—although she did not have quite so much energy and often fell asleep in his arms before he'd even withdrawn from her body.

He felt an odd sensation as if his heart was being crushed in a vice when he thought of her curled up beside him, her face flushed from passion and her honey-gold hair spread across the pillows. He loved to stroke his hands over the swell of her stomach where his son was nestled inside her. Sometimes when the baby moved, Giannis could actually see the outline of a tiny hand or foot. It would not be long now before the baby was here, but his excitement was mixed with trepidation. What did he know about fatherhood and caring for a baby? What if he made a mistake and harmed his son, as he had made a tragic mistake years ago?

Tonight, his mother's reference to what he had done had reminded him of the fragility of life. As if he needed reminding, he thought grimly. He could never forget the consequences of his irresponsibility when he was nineteen, or forgive himself, as quite clearly his mother was unable to do. Now, as he awaited the birth of his baby, he missed his father more than ever. It tore at his heart to know that his son would not meet his grandfather, and would never know the affection and kindness that his *patera* had showered on Giannis. But he would love his own son as deeply as his father had loved him, he vowed.

He gripped the balustrade rail and stared across the beach at the black sea, dappled with silver moonlight. His father had loved the sea, and Giannis felt closest to him on Spetses. That was why he wanted his son to grow up on the island, and thankfully Ava seemed happy living at Villa Delphine. But would she be happy to live in Greece with him if he admitted that he had caused his father's death and been sent to prison for driving after he'd drunk alcohol, which the coroner had suggested had been a likely reason for the fatal car crash?

She might decide that he was not fit to be a father and take his son back to England. The memory of Caroline's reaction to his confession five years earlier haunted him. He could not risk losing his baby, and with a sudden flash of insight he realised that he did not want to lose Ava. He had married her so that he could claim his child, but over the past months since their wedding she had slipped beneath his guard.

His jaw clenched. If he wasn't careful he would find himself falling in love with Ava, which had never been part of his plan. He had been in love with Caroline—at least he'd be certain at the time that he loved her, and her rejection had hurt. But the loss of his first child had hurt him far more. A voice inside him whispered that what he had felt for Caroline had been insignificant compared to the riot of feeling that swept through him when he thought of his wife.

Theos, what a mess. Giannis strode across the terrace and entered the house. He hesitated at the foot of the stairs before he turned and walked resolutely into his study, acknowledging self-derisively that work offered a safety net and a hiding place from his complicated emotions.

But when he switched on his laptop and read the email that pinged into his inbox from the journalist who had tried to blackmail him five years ago he felt a hard knot of fear in the pit of his stomach, knowing that he could never escape from his past.

CHAPTER ELEVEN

AVA HAD NO idea what time Giannis had come to bed the previous night. With only six weeks to go until her due date, she often felt a bone-deep tiredness and, despite her efforts to remain awake and talk to him, she had fallen asleep. In the morning she had seen an indent on the pillow next to her where his head had lain, and when she'd gone downstairs he was already working in his study.

But at least his black mood seemed to have lifted and he greeted her with a smile when she reminded him that she had a routine check-up with the midwife. In a couple more weeks they would move into the apartment in Athens so that she would be near to the private maternity hospital where the baby would be born.

'I'll come to your appointment with you,' he offered. 'But it's too far for you to walk into town. Thomas can take us in the horse and carriage.' His phone rang, and his smile faded and was replaced with a disturbingly harsh expression when he glanced at the screen. 'I'm sorry, *glykiá mou*, I need to take the call. What time is your appointment?'

'In half an hour, but I want to do some shopping first. Thomas will take me to the town, and I'll see you later.'

Cars were not allowed in Spetses Town, and Ava enjoyed the novelty of travelling in an open-topped carriage, shaded from the hot sun by a parasol and listening to the sound of the horse's hooves clipping along the road. She gave a soft sigh of contentment. Her life at Villa Delphine was idyllic and Giannis's tenderness towards her lately made her feel cherished in a way she had never felt before. For some reason he had a difficult relationship with his mother, hence his tense mood last night. But Ava was focused on becoming a mother herself and pregnancy cocooned her from the real world.

At the clinic, the midwife listened to the baby's heartbeat and was satisfied that all was well. 'I'll give you your medical notes so that you can take them to the maternity hospital on the mainland when you go into labour,' the midwife explained as she handed Ava a folder.

Out of idle curiosity Ava skimmed through her notes. She spoke Greek fluently but she was not so good at reading the language, and she assumed she must have misunderstood the last sentence on the page.

'Does it say that a blood sample will be taken from the baby when he is born?' Her confusion grew when the midwife nodded. 'Is it standard procedure in Greece?'

'Only when a paternity test has been requested by the parents,' the midwife told her.

Ava's heart juddered to a standstill. She certainly had not requested a test to prove the baby's paternity. But Giannis must have done so—which meant he must have doubts that the child she was carrying was his.

Somehow she managed to walk calmly out of the clinic and smiled at Thomas when he helped her into the carriage. But she felt numb with shock. Since she'd married Giannis, she had believed that all the misunderstandings between them had been resolved and they did not have secrets. But all this time he had suspected her

of trying to foist another man's child on him. She felt
sick. So hurt that there was a physical pain in her chest.

When she arrived back at the villa and heard the helicopter's engine—an indication that Giannis was about to
leave the island—anger surged like scalding lava through
her veins. She almost collided with him in the entrance
hall as she ran into the house, and he was on his way out.

He looked tense and distracted, and he frowned when
she thrust the folder containing her medical notes at him.
'I need to talk to you.'

Concern flashed in his eyes. 'Is there a problem with
the baby?'

'The baby is fine. The problem is *you*.' As she spoke,
Ava asked herself why Giannis would be so anxious
about the baby's welfare if he really believed it wasn't
his child.

'Why did you ask for a paternity test to be carried out
when our son is born?' she demanded. 'Don't try to deny
it,' she said furiously when his eyes narrowed. 'The request
for a blood test is written in my notes. Do you think that
when I left you after we had been to Stefanos Markou's
party, I immediately hooked up with some other guy?'

'No,' he said tersely. 'But at the time I asked for the
paternity test I thought it was possible that you had already been pregnant before we slept together in London.'

She shook her head. 'How could you doubt my integrity like that?'

'Like you doubted me when you believed a jealous
man's lies about me being a criminal?' he shot back. He
raked his hand through his hair, and Ava noted that he
avoided making eye contact with her. 'Look, something
important has come up and I have to go to Athens.'

'You're *leaving*? Am I not important enough for you
to want to stay and discuss a major issue with our rela-

tionship? Clearly I'm not,' she said dully when he picked up his briefcase and strode across the hall.

He paused in the doorway and turned to look at her. 'I realise that we need to talk, and we will as soon as I have dealt with a…problem at the office.' His voice sounded oddly strained. 'To tell you the truth I had forgotten about the paternity test. And it could not have been carried out without your consent.'

'The truth is that you don't care about me and I was stupid to hope that you would ever fall in love with me, as I…' She broke off and stared at his granite-hard features.

'As you…what?'

'It doesn't matter,' she said wearily. 'You're in too much of a hurry to talk to me, remember?'

Giannis looked as though he was about to speak, but he shook his head. 'Something arrived for you while you were out. Look in the bedroom,' he told her before he walked out of the villa.

A few minutes later, Ava heard the helicopter take off while she was climbing the stairs up to the second floor. She pushed open the door of the master bedroom and stopped dead, the tears that she had held back until then filling her eyes. On her dressing table was the biggest bouquet of red roses she had ever seen. At least three dozen perfect scarlet blooms arranged in a crystal vase and exuding a heavenly fragrance that filled the room. Propped up against the vase was a card and she recognised Giannis's bold handwriting.

For my beautiful wife. You are everything I could ever want or hope for. Giannis

There was no mention of love, but surely the roses were a statement that he felt something for her? Ava's fingers trembled as she touched the velvety rose petals. She sank down onto the edge of the bed and gave a shaky sigh. If the roses had been delivered before she had gone to her antenatal appointment and discovered that Giannis had asked for a paternity test on their baby she would have taken his romantic gesture as a sign that he loved her and she would have told him how she felt about him.

Now that she had calmed down, she could understand why he had requested the test. They had been strangers when they had slept together for the first time. Not only had she believed Stefanos's nephew's lies about Giannis, but she had kept it secret that her father was a criminal. They had both hidden things from each other, but if their marriage was going to work—and the roses were an indication that Giannis wanted her to be his wife—then they must be honest about their feelings.

He had promised that they would talk when he returned home. But the prospect of waiting for him at the villa did not appeal to Ava, and she picked up the phone and asked Thomas to take her to Athens on the speedboat that Giannis kept moored at Villa Delphine's private jetty.

By the time she reached TGE's offices in the city it was lunchtime and most of the staff were away from their desks. Giannis's PA, Sofia, greeted Ava with a smile. 'He's still in a meeting. I'm just off to lunch but I'll let him know that you are here.'

'No, don't disturb him,' Ava said quickly. 'I'll wait until he has finished.' It would give her a chance to prepare what she wanted to say to him. How hard could it be to say the three little words *I love you*?

But as the minutes ticked by while she waited in his secretary's office, she felt increasingly nervous. Maybe he had given her the red roses simply because he knew that she liked flowers, and wishful thinking had made her read more into his gift?

From inside Giannis's office, Ava could hear voices. She stiffened when one voice suddenly became louder and distinctly aggressive. 'I'm warning you, Gekas. Give me one million pounds or I'll go public with the story that you spent a year in prison for killing your father when you were drunk. I can't imagine that TGE's shareholders will be so keen to support Greece's golden boy when they hear that you are an ex-convict,' the voice sneered.

'And I'm warning you that I will not tolerate your blackmail attempt,' Giannis snarled. His eyes narrowed on the lowlife journalist who had called him that morning and demanded to see him. Demetrios Kofidis was the reason he'd had to leave Ava and come to Athens, and he was impatient to deal with the scumbag so that he could hurry back to Spetses and reassure his wife that he trusted her implicitly.

He cursed himself for ever thinking of having a paternity test when he knew in his heart that the baby was his. It was a pity he had not listened to his heart, he thought grimly. He could only hope that he hadn't left it too late to tell Ava in words what he had tried to say with the roses.

'You paid me to keep quiet about your past five years ago,' the journalist said. 'Pay up again, Gekas, or I'll sell the story to every tabloid in Europe and beyond.'

Giannis pushed back his chair and stood up. 'You think you're clever, Kofidis, but I recorded our conversation and before you arrived I alerted the police about you. If you publish anything about me you will be arrested for attempted blackmail quicker than you can blink. Now get out of my sight.'

He kept his gaze fixed on the journalist when he heard

the faint click of the office door opening. 'I told you that I don't want to be disturbed, Sofia.'

'Giannis.' Ava's voice was a whisper, but it sliced through Giannis's heart like a knife as he jerked his eyes across the room and saw her standing in the doorway. One hand rested protectively on the burgeoning swell of her stomach. Her honey-blonde hair was loose, tumbling around her shoulders, and she was so beautiful that his breath became trapped in his throat.

'What are you doing here, *glykiá mou*?' he began, trying to sound normal, trying to hide the fear that churned in his gut as he wondered how much she had heard of his conversation with the journalist. 'Sweetheart…'

'You went to prison, and you didn't tell me.'

'I can explain. It was an accident… I drove my father home from a restaurant and…'

'You didn't tell me,' she repeated slowly. 'I thought there were no more secrets between us, but all this time you held something back from me—because you don't trust me.'

'I *do* trust you.' Giannis crashed his hip bone against the corner of the desk in his hurry to reach Ava, but as he strode across the room she stepped back into the outer office.

'There have been too many secrets and lies between us—and that is the biggest lie of all,' she choked, before she spun round and ran over to the door.

'Ava, wait.' Giannis cursed as he followed her into the lobby. His offices were on the ground floor and the lobby was bustling with staff returning from their lunch break. He apologised when he knocked into someone. Ahead of him Ava had reached the front entrance. The glass doors slid open and she walked out. Moments later he followed her outside.

'Ava.'

She was hurrying down the flight of concrete steps in front of the building and glanced over her shoulder at him. In that instant she stumbled, and Giannis watched in horror as she lost her footing and fell down the remaining steps. It seemed to happen in slow motion and, just as when he had taken a bend in the road too fast sixteen years earlier, he felt shock, disbelief and a sense of terror that made him gag.

He was still at the top of the steps and there was nothing he could do to save Ava. She gave a startled cry and landed on the pavement with a sickening thud. And then she was silent. Motionless.

Giannis heard a rushing noise in his ears and a voice shouting, *'No! No!'* Much later he realised that it had been his voice shouting, pleading. *No!* He couldn't lose Ava and his baby.

He raced down the steps and dropped onto his knees beside her, carefully rolling her onto her back. Her eyes were closed and her face was deathly pale. A purple bruise was already darkening on her brow.

'Ava *mou*, wake up.' He felt for her pulse and detected a faint beat. Glancing up, he saw a crowd of people had gathered. 'Call an ambulance,' he shouted. 'Quickly.'

Someone must have already done so, and he heard the wail of a siren. But Ava did not open her eyes, and when Giannis looked down her body he saw blood seeping through her dress.

His heart stopped. *Theos*, if she lost the baby she would never forgive him and he would never forgive himself. If he lost both of them... A constriction in his throat prevented him from swallowing. He brushed his hand over his wet eyes. He could not contemplate his life without Ava. It would be a joyless, pointless existence, and nothing more than he deserved, he thought bleakly.

From then on everything became a blur when the ambulance arrived and the paramedics took charge and carefully lifted Ava onto a stretcher. As the ambulance raced to the hospital her eyelids fluttered on her cheeks, but she slipped in and out of consciousness and her dress was soaked with blood.

'My wife *will* be all right, won't she?' Giannis asked hoarsely.

'We will soon be at the hospital,' the paramedic replied evasively. 'The doctors will do everything they can to save her life and the child's.'

The last time Giannis had cried had been at his father's funeral, but his throat burned and his eyes ached with tears as he lifted Ava's cold, limp hand to his lips. 'Don't leave me, *agápi mou*,' he begged. 'I should have told you about my father, and I wish I had told you that I love you, my angel. I'm sorry that I didn't, and I promise I will tell you how much you mean to me every day for the rest of our lives, if only you will stay with me.'

He thought he might have imagined that he felt her fingers move in his hand. And he needed every ounce of hope when they arrived at the hospital and Ava was rushed into Theatre. 'A condition called placental abruption occurred as a result of your wife's fall,' the doctor explained to Giannis. 'It means that the placenta has become detached from the wall of the uterus and she has lost a lot of blood. The baby must be delivered as soon as possible to save the lives of both the child and the mother.'

For the second time in his life he had maybe left it too late to say what was in his heart, Giannis thought when a nurse showed him into a waiting room. Pain ripped through him as he remembered how he had stood at his father's graveside and wished he had told his *patera* how much he loved and respected him, and how one day he hoped to be as good a father to his own child.

Now his baby's and Ava's lives were in the balance. They were both so precious to him but he was unable to help them. All he could do was pace up and down the waiting room and pray.

Ava opened her eyes, and for the first time in three days her head did not feel as if a pneumatic drill was driving into her skull. In fact the concussion she'd suffered after falling down the steps had been unimportant compared to nearly losing her baby. Of course she had no memory of the emergency Caesarean section she'd undergone or, sadly, of the moment her son had been born.

When she'd come round from the anaesthetic Giannis had told her that, despite the baby's abrupt entry into the world six weeks early, he weighed a healthy five pounds. They had settled on the name Andreas during her pregnancy and, although she had still felt woozy when she had been taken in a wheelchair to the special care baby unit, she had been able to hold her tiny dark haired son in her arms and she'd wept tears of joy and relief that he was safe and well.

Now, seventy-two hours after the shocking events that had preceded the baby's early arrival, she looked across the room and her heart skipped a beat when she saw Giannis sitting in a chair, cradling Andreas against his shoulder. The tender look on his face as he held the baby was something Ava would never forget, and the unguarded expression in Giannis's eyes as he looked over at her filled her with hope and longing.

'You're still here,' she murmured. 'I thought you might

go back to the apartment for a few hours. The nurses will look after Andreas in the nursery now that he has been moved from the special care ward.'

'I'm not going anywhere until the two of you are ready to be discharged from hospital.' His gentle smile stole Ava's breath. 'How are you feeling?'

'Much better.' She'd had a blood transfusion, stitches and she was pumped full of drugs to fight infection and relieve pain, but her son was worth everything she'd been through. She sat up carefully and held out her arms to take the baby. 'He's so perfect,' she said softly. Her heart ached with love as she studied Andreas's silky-soft black hair and his eyes that were as dark as his daddy's eyes.

'He is a miracle. You both are.' Giannis's voice thickened. '*Theos*, when I saw you fall down those steps and I feared I had lost both of you…' His jaw clenched. 'I didn't know what I would do without you,' he said rawly.

It was the first time that either of them had mentioned what had happened, and the deep grooves on either side of Giannis's mouth were an indication of what he must have felt, believing he might lose the baby he had been so desperate for. Ava handed Andreas to him. 'He's fallen asleep. Will you put him in the crib?'

She rested her head against the pillows and thought how gorgeous Giannis looked in faded jeans and a casual cream cotton shirt. She was glad that a nurse had helped her into the shower earlier and she had managed to wash her hair.

He came back and sat down on the chair next to her bed. Suddenly she felt stupidly shy and afraid, and a whole host of other emotions that made her pleat the sheet between her fingers rather than meet his gaze. 'What happened to your father?' she asked in a low tone.

Giannis exhaled slowly. 'I was nineteen and had just

set up TGE with my father. We'd gone to a restaurant for dinner and during the meal I drank a glass of wine. I certainly did not feel drunk, but even a small amount of alcohol can impair your judgement. Driving home, I took a steep bend in the road too fast and the car over-turned. I escaped with a few cuts and bruises, but my father sustained serious injuries.'

His eyes darkened with pain. 'I held him in my arms while we waited for the ambulance, and he made it to the hospital but died soon afterwards. I have never touched alcohol since that night, even though I've often wished that I could numb my grief and guilt.'

'Why didn't you tell me?' Ava could not disguise her hurt. 'It wasn't overhearing what you had done that upset me, but realising that you had kept such a huge secret from me. I trusted you when I told you about my father being a criminal, but you only ever shut me out, Giannis.'

'I was afraid to admit what I had done,' he said heavily. 'A few years ago I fell in love.'

Jealousy stabbed Ava through her heart. 'What happened?'

'Caroline fell pregnant. Her father was an American senator who was campaigning in the Presidential elections, and when I admitted that I had served a prison sentence Caroline refused to marry me because—in her words—having an ex-convict as a son-in-law might have damaged her father's political ambitions. She told me she had suffered a miscarriage, but I'm fairly certain that she chose not to go ahead with the pregnancy. I overheard her on the phone telling a friend that she had dealt with the pregnancy problem,' he answered Ava's unspoken question.

'So when you found out that I had conceived your baby, you were worried that I might do the same as your ex-girlfriend?'

He grimaced. 'I was determined to have my child, and I treated you unforgivably when I forced you to marry me.'

She stared at his handsome face and her heart turned over when she saw that his eyelashes were wet. This was a different Giannis—a broken Giannis, she thought painfully. His vulnerability hurt her more than anything else. 'You didn't force me,' she said huskily. 'I chose to marry you, knowing that you had asked me to be your wife because you wanted your son.'

'No, Ava *mou*. That was not the reason I proposed marriage.'

She dared not believe the expression in his eyes, the softening of his hard features as he stared at her intently. 'I need to tell you something,' she said shakily. 'I heard the things you said in the ambulance. At least, I think I heard you, but maybe I dreamed it...' She broke off and bit her lip, aware of her heart thudding in her chest. 'Why did you ask me to marry you?'

'I love you.'

The three little words hovered in the air, but were they a tantalising dream? Ava wondered. Did she have the courage to give her absolute trust to Giannis?

'Don't!' Her voice shook and tears trembled on her eyelashes. 'Don't say it if you don't mean it.'

'But I do mean it, *agápi mou,*' he said gently. 'I love you with all my heart and soul.' Suddenly his restraint left him and he leapt to his feet, sending his chair clattering onto the floor. He sat on the edge of the bed and captured her hands in his.

'I adore you, Ava. I never knew I could feel like this, to love so utterly and completely that I cannot contemplate my life without you.' He stroked her hair back from her face with a trembling hand. 'When you left Athens I couldn't understand why I was so miserable until my head accepted what my heart had been telling me. I missed you, and I decided to ask you if we could start again. But then I read the Christmas card from your brother and discovered you were pregnant with my child.'

'And you were angry,' Ava said quietly.

'I was scared. I don't deserve you or our son.' He swallowed convulsively. 'I destroyed my family with my reckless behaviour, and I'm terrified that I might somehow hurt you and Andreas. *Theos...*' His face twisted in pain. 'It is my fault that you fell down those damned steps and you and the baby could have died. I should have been honest with you about what happened to my father. And of course I don't want a paternity test. I know Andreas is mine. But I've made so many mistakes and I have to let you and my son go. If you want to take Andreas to live in England I won't stop you. All I ask is that you allow me to be part of his life.'

Ava listened to the torrent of emotion that spilled from Giannis. It was as if a dam had burst and his feelings— his love for her—poured out, healing her hurt and filling her with joy.

'Oh, Giannis. Darling Giannis.' She wrapped her arms around his neck and clung to him. 'The only way you could ever hurt me is if you stop loving me. The only place I want to be is with you, because I love you so much.'

'Really?' The uncertainty in his voice tore Ava's heart. She put her hands on either side of his face. 'You have to learn to forgive yourself and believe me when I say that you deserve to be happy and loved by me and your son and the family that we will create together.'

'Ava,' he groaned as he pulled her into his heat and fire and held her so close that she felt the thunderous beat of his heart. '*S'agapó, kardiá mou*. I love you, my heart. My sweet love.'

He kissed her then—wondrously, as if she was everything he had ever wanted or would ever need. And she kissed him with all the love in her heart and her tears of happiness mingled with his as he threaded his fingers through her hair and gently eased her back against the pillows.

'We will never have secrets,' Giannis murmured between kisses.

Ava smiled. '*Did* I hear you say in the ambulance that you would tell me every day how much you love me, or did I dream it?'

'It was no dream, *kardiá mou*. It was a promise that I intend to keep for ever.'

EPILOGUE

THEY TOOK ANDREAS to Spetses when he was four weeks old. Despite his traumatic birth he was a strong and healthy baby with a good set of lungs, his father noted ruefully at two o'clock one morning. Ava recovered remarkably quickly and was delighted to be able to fit into her jeans two months after her son's birth. Her confidence in Giannis's love grew stronger with every day, and the first time they made love again was deeply emotional as they showed with their bodies their adoration for each other.

Life could not be better, Ava thought one afternoon as she pushed Andreas in his pram around the garden of Villa Delphine. Giannis had reluctantly gone to his office in Athens, but he'd called her a while ago to say that he was on his way home. 'Your *patera* will be here soon,' she said to Andreas and when he gave her a gummy smile she told him that both the Gekas males in her life had stolen her heart.

Her spirits dipped when she saw Giannis's mother walking across the lawn. Filia's waspish expression softened as she looked in the pram. 'My grandson grows bigger every time I see him,' she commented, and Ava felt guilty that she did not invite her mother-in-law to Villa Delphine as often as she should. The visits were always strained and she knew that Giannis found his mother difficult.

'Where is my son?' Filia demanded. 'Giannis promised weeks ago that he would arrange for his private jet to fly me to Italy so I can visit my daughter, but I still have not heard when the trip will be. I suppose he has forgotten about me.'

'Giannis has been busy at work lately, and he spends as much time as he can with Andreas, but I'm sure he hasn't forgotten about your trip,' Ava explained.

'No doubt he expects me to take a commercial flight. He is so wealthy, but he gives me nothing.'

Ava nearly choked. She knew that Giannis had bought his mother the beautiful house she lived in on Spetses, and he paid for her living expenses and her numerous holidays. 'I don't think you are being fair to him,' she murmured.

Filia snorted. 'It isn't fair that I have spent the last fifteen years a widow, thanks to Giannis.' She gave Ava a sharp look. 'I suppose he has told you that he was responsible for his father's death?'

Giannis froze with his hand on the gate which led into the garden. He knew that the tall hedge screened him from Ava and his mother, who were standing some way across the lawn. But he could see them and he could hear their voices.

'Giannis told me what happened sixteen years ago.' Ava's voice was as cool and clear as a mountain stream. 'I know that he loved his father very much, and his grief has been made worse by his feelings of guilt. It breaks my heart to know that he can't forgive himself,' she said softly.

Hidden behind the hedge, Giannis brushed a hand over his wet eyes.

'Why do you defend him?' he heard his mother ask.

'Because he made a terrible mistake that I know he has regretted every day since the accident. It was an accident with devastating consequences, but it was an *accident*. I know that the man I love is a good and honourable man.'

'So you do love him?' Filia said with a snort. 'You did not marry him because he is rich?'

'I married Giannis because I love him with all my heart, and I'd love him if he didn't have a penny to his name.' Ava's fierce voice carried across the garden. 'What happened in the past was tragic, but it is also a tragedy that you have not forgiven your own son.' She put her hands on her hips. 'Your constant criticism of Giannis has to stop, or I am afraid that you will no longer be welcome at Villa Delphine to visit Andreas.'

His wife was a warrior, Giannis thought, shaken to his core by Ava's defence of him. She was amazing. He opened the gate and strode across the garden. His footsteps were noiseless on the soft grass, but his mother was facing him and she immediately appealed to him.

'I hope you will not allow your wife to threaten to withhold my grandson from me? Say something to her, Giannis.'

'There are many things I want to say to Ava. But I will speak to her alone. Leave us, please,' he told his mother curtly. She opened her mouth to argue but, after looking at his expression, she clearly thought better of it and without another word she turned and walked out of the garden.

'I'm sorry if I upset your mother,' Ava said ruefully. 'But I meant what I said. I won't let her upset you. What are you doing?' she asked as Giannis pushed the pram across the garden and into the summer house.

'The bedroom is too far away for what I have in mind,' he murmured as he pulled her into his arms.

Her eyes widened when he pressed his aching arousal against her pelvis. 'Mmm—what exactly do you have in mind?'

'I want to make love to you, darling heart,' Giannis said thickly. 'But first I need to tell you how much I love you, and thank you for loving me and for giving me our gorgeous son.' He tugged the straps of her sundress down and roamed his hands over her body.

'You are so beautiful, so perfect. Mine, for eternity.' He threw the cushions from the garden furniture onto the floor and laid her down before covering her body with his. And there he made love to her with fierce passion and a tenderness that made Ava realise that dreams could come true.

'Eternity sounds perfect,' she agreed.

* * * * *

COMING SOON!

We really hope you enjoyed reading this book. If you're looking for more romance, be sure to head to the shops when new books are available on

Thursday
9th August

To see which titles are coming soon, please visit
millsandboon.co.uk

MILLS & BOON

Coming next month

THE HEIR THE PRINCE SECURES
Jennie Lucas

He eyed the baby in the stroller, who looked back at him with dark eyes exactly like his own. He said simply, 'I need you and Esme with me.'

'In London?'

Leaning forward, he whispered, 'Everywhere.'

She felt the warmth of his breath against her skin, and her heartbeat quickened. For so long, Tess would have done anything to hear Stefano speak those words.

But she'd suffered too much shock and grief today. He couldn't tempt her to forget so easily how badly he'd treated her. She pulled away.

'Why would I come with you?'

Stefano's eyes widened. She saw she'd surprised him.

Giving her a crooked grin, he said, 'I can think of a few reasons.'

'If you want to spend time with Esme, I will be happy to arrange that. But if you think I'll give up my family and friends and home—' she lifted her chin '—and come with you to Europe as some kind of paid nanny—'

'No. Not my nanny.' Stefano's thumb lightly traced her tender lower lip. 'I have something else in mind.'

Unwilling desire shot down her body, making her nipples taut as tension coiled low in her belly. Her pride was screaming for her to push him away but it was difficult to hear her pride over the rising pleas of her body.

'I—I won't be your mistress, either,' she stammered, shivering, searching his gaze.

'No.' With a smile that made his dark eyes gleam, Stefano shook his head. 'Not my mistress.'

'Then…then what?' Tess stammered, feeling foolish for even suggesting a handsome billionaire prince like Stefano would want a regular girl like her as his mistress. Her cheeks were hot. 'You don't want me as your nanny, not as your mistress, so—what? You just want me to come to London as someone who watches your baby for free?' Her voice shook. 'Some kind of…p-poor relation?'

'No.' Taking her in his arms, Stefano said quietly, 'Tess. Look at me.'

Although she didn't want to obey, she could not resist. She opened her eyes, and the intensity of his glittering eyes scared her.

'I don't want you to be my mistress, Tess. I don't want you to be my nanny.' His dark eyes burned through her. 'I want you to be my wife.'

Continue reading
THE HEIR THE PRINCE SECURES
Jennie Lucas

Available next month
www.millsandboon.co.uk

LET'S TALK
Romance

For exclusive extracts, competitions
and special offers, find us online:

Or get in touch on 0844 844 1351*

For all the latest titles coming soon, visit
millsandboon.co.uk/nextmonth

*Calls cost 7p per minute plus your phone company's price per minute access charge